SOLDIERS OF FORTUNE

broadview editions
series editor: L.W. Conolly

SOLDIERS OF FORTUNE

Richard Harding Davis

edited by Brady Harrison

broadview editions

Library and Archives Canada Cataloguing in Publication

Davis, Richard Harding, 1864–1916.

Soldiers of Fortune / Richard Harding Davis ; edited by Brady Harrison.

(Broadview editions)
Includes bibliographical references.
ISBN 1-55111-679-0

1. Americans—South America—Fiction. 2. South America—Fiction.
I. Harrison, Brady, 1963- II. Title. III. Series.

PS1522.S6 2006   813'.52   C2006-900631-8

Broadview Editions

The Broadview Editions series represents the ever-changing canon of literature in English by bringing together texts long regarded as classics with valuable lesser-known works.

Advisory editor for this volume: Jennie Rubio

Broadview Press is an independent, international publishing house, incorporated in 1985. Broadview believes in shared ownership, both with its employees and with the general public; since the year 2000 Broadview shares have traded publicly on the Toronto Venture Exchange under the symbol BDP. We welcome comments and suggestions regarding any aspect of our publications—please feel free to contact us at the addresses below or at broadview@broadviewpress.com.

North America
Post Office Box 1243, Peterborough, Ontario, Canada K9J 7H5
3576 California Road, Post Office Box 1015, Orchard Park, NY, USA 14127
Tel: (705) 743-8990; Fax: (705) 743-8353;
email: customerservice@broadviewpress.com; www.broadviewpress.com

UK, Ireland, and continental Europe
NBN International, Estover Road, Plymouth PL6 7PY UK
Tel: 44 (0) 1752 202300   Fax: 44 (0) 1752 202330
email: enquiries@nbninternational.com

Australia and New Zealand
UNIREPS, University of New South Wales
Sydney, NSW, 2052 Australia
Tel: 61 2 9664 0999; Fax: 61 2 9664 5420
email: info.press@unsw.edu.au

Broadview Press gratefully acknowledges the financial support of the Government of Canada through the Book Publishing Industry Development Program for our publishing activities.

Typesetting and assembly: True to Type Inc., Mississauga, Canada.

The author of the book and the publisher have made every attempt to locate authors of copyrighted material or their heirs and assigns, and would be grateful for information that would allow them to correct any errors or omissions in a subsequent edition of the work.

PRINTED IN CANADA

Contents

Acknowledgements • 7
Introduction • 9
Richard Harding Davis: A Brief Chronology • 33
A Note on the Text • 37

Soldiers of Fortune • 39

Appendix A: Images of Davis
  1. Davis as he looked when he first came to New York
     in 1890 • 225
  2. The Three Gringos • 226
  3. Davis in his Spanish-American War kit • 227
  4. Davis and Theodore Roosevelt at the beginning of
     the Spanish-American War • 228

Appendix B: How Others Saw Davis
  1. Booth Tarkington, "Richard Harding Davis" (1916) • 229
  2. From Theodore Roosevelt, letter to James Brander
     Matthews (6 December 1892) • 230
  3. From Theodore Roosevelt, letter to James Brander
     Matthews (30 January 1894) • 231
  4. From Stephen Crane, letter to Nellie Crouse (26 January
     1896) • 231
  5. From Frank Norris, "Van Bubbles' Story" (1897) • 231
  6. Theodore Roosevelt, "Davis and the Rough Riders"
     (1916) • 232

Appendix C: Reviews of *Soldiers of Fortune*
  1. *New York Times* (5 June 1897) • 235
  2. *The Critic* (5 June 1897) • 236
  3. *The Atlantic Monthly* (December 1897) • 237
  4. *The Nation* (20 January 1898) • 239

Appendix D: Social Darwinism, Survival of the Richest, and
Other Notions of Anglo-American Superiority
  1. From Herbert Spencer, *Social Statics* (1897) • 241
  2. From Charles Darwin, *The Descent of Man* (1874) • 243
  3. From Rebecca Harding Davis, "Life in the Iron-Mills"
     (1861) • 244
  4. From Andrew Carnegie, *The Gospel of Wealth* (1900) • 245
  5. From Theodore Roosevelt, "The Expansion of the White
     Races" (18 January 1909) • 248

Appendix E: Davis and Others on American Masculinity
1. From Richard Harding Davis, *Captain Macklin* (1902) • 251
2. From Richard Harding Davis, "William Walker, The King of the Filibusters" (1906) • 251
3. From Theodore Roosevelt, "The Strenuous Life" (10 April 1899) • 252
4. From William James, "Letter on Governor Roosevelt's Oration" (15 April 1899) • 255

Appendix F: Davis and Others on American Imperialism
1. From John L. O'Sullivan, "Annexation" (July 1845) • 257
2. From José Martí, "Cuba and the United States" (1889) • 258
3. From Richard Harding Davis, *Three Gringos in Venezuela and Central America* (1896) • 260
4. From Mark Twain, "To the Person Sitting in Darkness" (1901) • 261
5. From Theodore Roosevelt, "The Administration of the Island Possessions" (22 August 1902) • 262

Select Bibliography • 265

Acknowledgements

A number of people and institutions have given generously of their time, energy, and expertise to this project, and I am very grateful for their assistance. In particular, my thanks go to Jill Bergman for taking apart—and then helping me to put back together—my contributions to this book, and to John Glendening for taking the time to discuss the work of Charles Darwin and Herbert Spencer with me. One could not ask for better colleagues. I also owe many thanks, as always, to Sue Samson and the staff at the Mansfield Library at the University of Montana. Without their assistance, this project would not have been possible. My deepest appreciation, as well, to the University of Montana for providing funds to hire a first-rate research assistant, Laura Gronewald, to help with the preparation of the manuscript. The support of Chris Knight, Chair of the Department of English, and Jerry Fetz, Dean of the College of Arts and Sciences, has been invaluable. Finally, this project could not have been realized without the thoughtful support, critiques, and guidance of Julia Gaunce, Leonard Conolly, the readers of the original proposal, and the staff at Broadview.

I would like to thank the following individuals and organizations for permission to re-print passages from copyrighted materials:

Excerpt from the letters of Stephen Crane. (Reprinted by permission of the publisher from *Stephen Crane: Letters*, edited by R.W. Stallman and Lillian Gilkes, New York: New York UP, 1960.)

Excerpt from José Martí's "Cuba and the United States." (Reprinted by permission of the publisher from *Our America: Writings on Latin America and the Struggle for Cuban Independence*, ed. Philip S. Foner, trans. Elinor Randall; additional trans. Juan de Onís and Roslyn Held Foner. New York: Monthly Review Press, 1977.)

Excerpts from the letters of Theodore Roosevelt. (Reprinted by permission of the publisher from *The Letters of Theodore Roosevelt*, *Volume I*, ed. Elting E. Morison. Cambridge, MA: Harvard UP, 1951.)

Introduction

In January 1897, Richard Harding Davis, in the company of Frederic Remington and in the employ of the New York *Journal*, arrived in Cuba to cover the island's struggle for independence from Spain.[1] As Davis—engaged in his first venture as a war correspondent—tells us, before he landed at the "Pearl of the Antilles," he had been opposed to the United States' intervention in the war. What he learned when he began to explore the island, however, forced him to change his mind. The Spanish colonialists not only waged war against the Cubans, but also showed little regard for American lives or property. Angry at the policies of what he considered a second-rate European power, in his 1897 collection of articles from the *Journal*, the reporter calls on the nation to follow through on the principle of hemispheric authority first articulated in the Monroe Doctrine:[2]

We have been too considerate, too fearful that as a younger nation, we should appear to disregard the laws laid down by older nations. We have tolerated what no European power would have tolerated; we have been patient with men who have put back the hand of time for centuries, who lie to our representatives daily, who butcher innocent people, who gamble with the lives of their own soldiers in order to gain a few more

---

1 Already well-known as a journalist and sketch artist, Remington (1861–1909) would become increasingly famous as a painter and sculptor. He specialized in canvases and bronzes of vivid scenes from the old West, and he wrote and illustrated a number of books, including *Pony Tracks* (1895), *Crooked Trails* (1898), and *The Way of an Indian* (1906). The New York *Journal*, owned by William Randolph Hearst (1863–1951), practiced what became known as "yellow journalism," or a style of reportage that relied on sensationalism over facts and that sought to titillate rather than to inform readers.

2 First articulated by President James Monroe (1758–1831) in his 2 December 1823 address to the United States Congress, the doctrine asserted that European powers could no longer seek colonial territories in the Americas and that the US was the rightful power in the New World. Although Monroe, at the time, did not have the power to enforce his doctrine, later administrations have relied on its principles to justify US interventions in the Caribbean and Central and South America.

stars and an extra stripe, who send American property to the air in flames and murder American prisoners.[1]

Although Davis expresses concern for the travails of the Cubans, he focuses even more on Spain's disregard for American interests and power. The Spanish, he makes clear, have gone too far, have exerted their influence in the Caribbean for long enough. The US he insists, should respond with force, should push the tired colonial power out of the New World (and beyond), should take its rightful place on the world stage alongside the great powers.

Already celebrated as a reporter and writer of short stories, Davis was a man to whom others would listen. As Christopher P. Wilson argues, war correspondents enjoyed considerable social and political influence in the era, and were often "mythologized as masculine, globe-trotting vagabonds":

> As a "soldier of fortune"—[Julian] Ralph called the corre-spondent a "knight of the pen" from our "free and enlightened land"—the reporter's worldly experience ostensibly baptized him as an American representative. Thus, when he pro-nounced on "civilized" conduct or drew the line between genuine revolution and merely lawless "banditry," he spoke *both* to American audiences and his own "foreign" inter-viewees themselves.[2]

Taking advantage of his cultural capital, Davis told his American readers what many of them wanted to hear about American power and responsibilities, and he added his voice to those of men like President William McKinley and Assistant Secretary of the Navy Theodore Roosevelt who were already beginning to envision a more bellicose and expansionist America. A champion of masculinity and imperial values, Davis was perhaps the most important writer of the American fin de siècle to herald the soon-to-be abundantly realized American *imperium*, and his pro-nouncements in *Cuba in War Time*, *Three Gringos in Venezuela and Central America* (1896), and other travelogues and newspaper

---

1 Richard Harding Davis, *Cuba in War Time* (New York: R.H. Russell, 1897), 129.

2 Christopher P. Wilson, "Plotting the Border: John Reed, Pancho Villa, and Insurgent Mexico" in *Cultures of United States Imperialism*, ed. Amy Kaplan and Donald Pease (Durham: Duke UP, 1993), 343. Julian Ralph, like Davis, was a celebrated war correspondent.

articles did their small part to fan the already smoldering fires of American imperial desire.

If Davis called for a more truculent foreign policy in his non-fiction, he also dramatized his beliefs in his most celebrated novel, *Soldiers of Fortune* (1897). A hugely popular and com-mercially successful adventure tale, *Soldiers* was the third best-selling novel of the year behind Henryk Sienkiewicz's *Quo Vadis*, a tale of early Christians, and James Lane Allen's *The Choir Invisible*, a historical romance, and like Harriet Beecher Stowe's *Uncle Tom's Cabin* (1852) and William J. Lederer and Eugene Burdick's *The Ugly American* (1958), Davis' romance must be counted as one of those rare works of fiction that powerfully impacts the political culture of its day.[1] Like Stowe and Lederer and Burdick, Davis wanted to win hearts and minds, wanted to reach into his readers and stir their imperial passions and fan-tasies. He wanted both to entertain his audience and to assure them that the US could rule an overseas military and economic empire (and look good doing it). Davis wanted to arouse his readership, and he did just that; as Davis biographer Arthur Lubow contends, the swashbuckling story of Robert Clay and the US-owned mine he runs in Olancho, an imaginary South American nation, was so popular and "so widely read that, in some unquantifiable way, it doubtless helped prime the national psyche for the collective adventure in Cuba."[2] Remarkably, the book you now have in hand helped push the nation toward war with Spain and thereby did its part in the creation of the turn-of-the-century spectacular American empire. The US had already achieved a more circumspect hemispheric hegemony, but as Mark Twain would say, the wrapping and pretty bows soon fell from the (imperial) package following victory in Cuba

---

1 Although most readers are doubtlessly familiar with *Uncle Tom's Cabin*, *The Ugly American* probably does not have a very wide audience today. A huge best-seller when it was first published, the novel was widely cir-culated and discussed in Washington; many politicians shared Lederer and Burdick's alarm over the rise of communism in Asia. The hastily written polemic called for a far more aggressive US foreign policy, and the novel did its part to agitate already brewing Cold War fears of global communism. In some small measure, *The Ugly American* did its part to push the US along the road to war in Vietnam.

2 Arthur Lubow, *The Reporter Who Would be King* (New York: Charles Scribner's Sons, 1992), 124.

and the Philippines.[1] *Soldiers*, currently enjoying a resurgence of critical interest, was one of the most important books of its time; it remains one of the most important novels in the canon of American imperial literature.

Richard Harding Davis: Life, Works, and Critical Reception

An overview of Davis' life and works poses some serious challenges to brevity: he had several careers, wrote scores of articles, travelogues, stories, novels, and plays, ventured abroad a great deal, and knew, socialized, and sometimes worked alongside some of the best known and celebrated journalists, writers, painters, actors, adventurers, and political figures of his day. He crossed paths with such literary luminaries as Jacob Riis, Stephen Crane, Jack London, and Rudyard Kipling, enjoyed the company of artists Charles Dana Gibson and John Singer Sargent, dined with stage and film stars Ethel Barrymore and John Barrymore, and reported on the exploits and campaigns of such soldiers and politicians as General Leonard Wood, Theodore Roosevelt, and Winston Churchill.[2] Davis seems to have known just about

---

1 For more on Twain (1835–1910), his views on the US colonial war in the Philippines following the Spanish-American War, and the politics of the Anti-Imperialist League, see Appendix F.

2 Jacob Riis (1849–1914) American journalist and photographer, most remembered for his account of life in the immigrant slums of New York, *How the Other Half Lives* (1890); Stephen Crane (1871–1900), American author of *The Red Badge of Courage* (1895) and other novels and stories; Jack London (1876–1919), American writer and social critic best known for *The Call of the Wild* (1903) and other tales of adventure; Rudyard Kipling (1865–1936), British author and Nobel laureate best known for his works set in India during the Raj, including *The Jungle Book* (1894) and *Kim* (1901); John Singer Sargent (1856–1925), American painter celebrated for his portraits of the socially prominent; Ethel Barrymore (1879–1959), American actor and winner of an Oscar in 1944 for her performance in *None But the Lonely Heart*; John Barrymore (1882–1942), American actor and younger brother of Ethel, most remembered for his performances of Hamlet; General Leonard Wood (1860–1927), American solider, co-founder of the Rough Riders, and later Governor General of the Philippines; Theodore Roosevelt (1858–1919), 26th President of the United States; Winston Churchill (1874–1965), British Prime Minister, author of numerous works, including the six volume history, *The Second World War* (1948–53), and winner of the Nobel Prize for literature.

everyone who was anyone at the turn of the century, and he was incredibly active, moving from one article, story, or book to another, from one adventure or war to another, from one remote outpost or world capital to another. He was always on the lookout for the next opportunity, assignment, or paycheck (he went through money as quickly as he earned it), and if we cannot here record all his literary and geographical to-ings and fro-ings, we can hit the highlights of his remarkably restless and productive life.[1]

Davis' father, L. (Lemuel) Clarke Davis (1835–1904), was born in Sandusky, Ohio, but Clarke's father relocated the Davises to Philadelphia following the death of his wife. An intellectual, courtly young man, Clarke studied law and was admitted to the Pennsylvania bar, but found himself more and more drawn to the life of a journalist. While still practicing law, he began to edit two legal publications, *Law Reports* and the *Legal Intelligencer*, and he eventually left the law to become a full-time journalist. Over the course of his career, he rose to the top of his profession, becoming editor of the Philadelphia *Public Ledger*. His interest in writing and literature clearly had a significant impact on his son's desire to become a journalist, and while Richard learned a great deal from his father, he had an especially close relationship with his mother, Rebecca Harding Davis (1831–1910), and she had a far deeper influence on his writing life.

In 1861, the *Atlantic Monthly* published "Life in the Iron-Mills," a novella by Rebecca Blaine Harding, a then unknown young writer who had been born in Washington, Pennsylvania, and whose family had moved to Wheeling, in what was then the state of Virginia, when she was five. A powerful work of literary realism and naturalism, the story presented the harsh living con-

---

Charles Dana Gibson (1867–1944) was one of the most popular American artists of the early twentieth century and of particular interest to us as the illustrator of many of Davis' works. His pen-and-ink drawings appeared in *Life*, *Scribner's*, *Harper's*, and other leading magazines, and he is most remembered for his glamorous representations of young, upper class women. For Gibson, the ideal American woman was tall, slim-wasted, swan-necked, and stately, and was often accompanied by a dashing young man, modeled after Davis. Gibson's original illustrations for *Soldiers of Fortune* are included in this edition.

1 For a much more detailed look at Davis' life, see Lubow's excellent biography, *The Reporter Who Would Be King* (1992) and *The Adventures and Letters of Richard Harding Davis* (New York: Charles Scribner's Sons, 1917), compiled and edited by Davis' brother, Charles Belmont Davis.

ditions and short, brutal lives of immigrant industrial workers in an iron and cotton town modeled after Wheeling. The story not only impressed such Olympians as Ralph Waldo Emerson and Nathaniel Hawthorne—both of whom invited its author to visit them in Boston—but also prompted Clarke to write a letter of appreciation.[1] To his surprise, when he received a reply, he learned that the author of such a dark and powerful story was a woman—the tale had been unsigned in the *Atlantic*—and they soon began a correspondence. The letter writing grew into visits back and forth, and they married on 5 March 1861. Rebecca not only established herself as an important and productive writer—in addition to scores of essays and articles for popular publications, she wrote many short stories and numerous novels, including *Margaret Howth* (1862), *Waiting for the Verdict* (1868), and *John Andross* (1874)—but also became the most important literary figure in her son's life. Although Richard could never equal the power of his mother's best work, she was his closest mentor and ally, and he often sought her out to discuss ideas for projects or to receive her comments on outlines and drafts.[2] More importantly for our consideration of *Soldiers* (and as we shall see), his mother had such an impact on him that he rewrote her finest novella, "Life in the Iron-Mills," into his best-selling, swashbuckling tale of imperial derring-do: in an odd Oedipal twist, he seems to have wanted to show that he could outdo his mother.

Richard was born on 18 April 1864, in Philadelphia, Pennsylvania, followed by two siblings, Charles Belmont Davis (1866–1926) and Nora Davis (1872–1958). As a boy, Davis enjoyed sports, particularly baseball and football, and often wrote and staged rambling, action-filled melodramas with his brother, Charles, and other children from their neighborhood in Philadelphia. Imaginative and energetic, he nevertheless did poorly at school. As Charles writes, "My brother went to the

---

1 Ralph Waldo Emerson (1803–82), American philosopher and poet, best known for *Nature* (1836), "Self-Reliance" (1841), and other essays and addresses. Nathaniel Hawthorne (1804–64), American author of *The Scarlet Letter* (1850) and numerous other celebrated novels and stories.

2 Many critics feel that Rebecca squandered her considerable talents in order to satisfy the demands of the marketplace. Although Richard rarely aspired to write "literature," Rebecca emerged in her first publication as a serious author; nevertheless, financial demands—and Clarke's suspect literary tastes—pushed her toward popular material that would sell.

Episcopal Academy and his weekly report never failed to fill the whole house with an impenetrable gloom and ever-increasing fears as to the possibilities of his future. At school and at college Richard was, to say the least, an indifferent student."[1] He managed to survive the early years, but matters became increasingly dire as he approached college. After withdrawing from the Episcopal Academy (a preparatory school), two years short of graduation, Richard received private tutoring from Rebecca's brother, Wilse Harding, a physics professor at Lehigh University, and then tried his luck at the Swarthmore College Preparatory School. After failing there, he tried another school before enrolling at Lehigh in 1882. A poor fit for a primarily engineering school—he went about the campus and Bethlehem dressed as an English gentlemen, complete with a faux English accent—he found temporary havens on the intercollegiate football team and at the *Burr*, a student monthly, before the faculty requested he withdraw at the end of his junior year due to his abysmal grades. Bitter about failing to earn his degree, he tried one last time at Johns Hopkins, where he excelled at cricket but little else. Davis at last gave up on a formal education, but before looking for employment, took a trip to Santiago, Cuba, with William W. Thurston, an old friend and president of the Bethlehem Iron Company. Thurston was in Cuba to oversee a mining operation, and the sojourn proved critical to Davis' career: it supplied him with the raw materials and settings for *Soldiers*. Upon his return, he took up his father's profession and began his ascent, with a few bumps along the way, of the literary and social worlds of fin de siècle America.

With his father's assistance, Davis secured a position as a cub reporter at the Philadelphia *Record* in 1886. Still dressing like a dandy, and still slipshod in his work, he was fired from the paper for failing to complete an assignment on time; the shock of being fired seems finally to have provoked Davis into taking life a little more seriously, and he soon found employment at the Philadelphia *Press*. For three years, he learned his trade at the *Press*, working diligently on every task no matter how dull. He did, however, have a few choice assignments, including interviewing Walt Whitman at his home in Camden, reporting on the Johnstown flood, and, more importantly for his career, covering crime in Philadelphia's impoverished,

---

1 Davis, *Adventures and Letters*, 2.

immigrant neighborhoods.[1] Adopting a costume appropriate to seedy dives, he managed to infiltrate a gang of thieves operating out of Sweeney's saloon in the spring of 1887. Davis' articles about the criminal demimonde made his reputation in Philadelphia. Ambitious, he took the next logical step in his career, and moved to New York in 1889. He soon secured a post at the New York *Evening Sun* for thirty dollars a week, reporting on crime and the courts. He followed the police on raids in the Bowery, New York's then-infamous slum area, and covered one of the most sensational sex crimes of the era, William Kemmler's hatchet-murder of his lover, a married woman. The story got even better: Kemmler was the first New Yorker sentenced to die in the electric chair on April 6, 1890.

While still at the paper, Davis returned to the sort of fiction he had been writing for the *Burr*, and penned his first story about a fashionable clubman named Cortlandt Van Bibber. His tales of Van Bibber's comic misadventures, complete with ironic asides and colorful portraits of New Yorkers of all classes, established Davis' literary credentials, and his intertwining careers of reporter and writer began their meteoric rise. Like many of his fellow journalists, Davis believed that being a reporter was the perfect training ground for aspiring writers, and he began to author stories and newspaper columns about slum dwellers even as he continued to dash off Van Bibber stories. He also began writing a story about a street-smart, quick-thinking, and slang-talking young press boy named Gallegher. The appearance of "Gallegher" in the August 1890 issue of *Scribners's Magazine* made Davis, as Lubow remarks, "Byronically famous overnight," and he was soon publishing stories in many of the leading periodicals of the day.[2] Never one to focus, he also turned to writing travel pieces and adventure tales, and at the end of 1890 quit his job as a reporter at the *Evening Sun* to become the managing editor at *Harper's Weekly*.

The next five years were a remarkably productive time for Davis. His first book, *Gallegher and Other Stories* appeared in 1891, and sold quickly; one year later, *Van Bibber and Others* sold

---

1 Walt Whitman (1819–92), American poet and essayist. As a young reporter for the Brooklyn *Eagle*, Whitman wrote several bellicose editorials calling for US intervention in Mexico in the years leading up to the Mexican-American War. The Johnstown, Pennsylvania, flood occurred on 31 May 1889.

2 Lubow, *Reporter*, 68.

out its first run in two days. He then set off on a trip to Texas and Colorado that formed the basis of his first full-length travelogue, *The West from a Car Window* (1892). Once back in New York, he hastily prepared for a trip to London with the hopes of establishing himself in English society, just as he had begun to do in fashionable Gotham circles; this trip resulted in numerous articles collected as *Our English Cousins* (1894). Several more adventures abroad resulted in two further travelogues, *The Rulers of the Mediterranean* (1894) and *About Paris* (1895), a collection of stories with American protagonists set in foreign locales, *The Exiles* (1894), and a frothy novel, *The Princess Aline* (1895), in the mode of Anthony Hope's *The Prisoner of Zenda* (1894).[1] With nine titles to his credit in only five years, Davis then really got to work and embarked on the most important adventures and books of his career.

In January 1895, in the company of Somers Somerset, a twenty-year old British heir to the dukedom of Beaufort, and Lloyd Griscom, the twenty-two year old son of a Philadelphia shipping magnate (and later American ambassador to Brazil and Italy), he set sail from New Orleans for an extended tour of Central America and Venezuela. Davis, already at work on a romance set in a mythical South American country modeled after the Cuba he had experienced years earlier, hoped that the journey would provide him with further settings and details for his novel, and the trio (accompanied by Somerset's gaunt valet) traveled together for three months. The adventure not only yielded a detailed travelogue, *Three Gringos in Venezuela and Central America*, but also influenced Davis' political convictions. From what he saw in Honduras, the isthmians clearly did not understand the workings of democracy or commerce, and they most certainly needed a more powerful nation to guide them:[2] "The Central American citizen is no more fit for a republican form of government than he is for an arctic exploration, and what

---

1 Anthony Hope, pen name of Sir Anthony Hope Hawkins (1863–1933), English novelist and playwright. A swashbuckling tale of mistaken identities and schemes against the crown, *The Prisoner of Zenda* tracks the adventures of Rudolf Rassendyll, an Englishman, in "Ruritania." Rassendyll finds himself embroiled in a plot to oust the royal family, and he rallies to defend the king and his betrothed, Princess Flavia.

2 Geographically, Central America is an isthmus, or a narrow strip of land connecting two larger territories; hence, anyone who lives in Central America may be referred to as an "isthmian."

he needs is to have a protectorate established over him, either by the United States or by another power; it does not matter which, so long as it leaves the Nicaragua Canal in our hands."[1] To say the least, Davis emerged from the journey with a raft of imperial attitudes and assumptions about the desirability and rightness of US interventionism, and he brought these forward—in resplendent fashion—to his next book, *Soldiers of Fortune*.

After his return from Latin America in the spring of 1895, Davis resumed work on *Soldiers* while summering in Marion, Massachusetts. As Lubow recounts, the novelist wrote his most bellicose romance under the most pleasing circumstances:

> He developed a comfortable routine. After breakfasting at the Hotel Sippican, he would work for two hours, and then walk the elm-shaded streets to pick up the mail and join the Clarks [a wealthy family from Chicago that, like Davis' family, would summer in Marion] for a swim. Following lunch, he would work until four, when Cecil [Clark] would arrive to take him driving until suppertime. He would read after supper and then pay a final call on the Clarks before bedtime.[2]

Living an idyllic life of a successful man of letters, and beginning his courtship of Cecil Clark, Davis was at the top of his game. A skilled, even slick, writer, he offered his audience plenty of action, a dashing leading man, a beautiful young heroine, scores of corrupt Latin American foes, stashes of gold, a coup, and a dramatic climax. Readers responded, we can speculate, not only to the requisite ingredients of the romance, but to the tale's stirring portrayal of American know-how, economic prowess, and imperial swagger. Clay, the dashing hero, dashes confidently into the fray, and *Soldiers* proved so popular that in addition to being a bestseller, it was adapted for the stage in 1902 (where it flourished both critically and commercially) and for the screen in 1914 (where it flopped).[3]

Never one to rest—and never one to allow an opportunity to pass him by—Davis, after trips to Moscow and Budapest, trav-

1 Richard Harding Davis, *Three Gringos in Venezuela and Central America* (New York: Harper and Brothers, 1896), 146.

2 Lubow, *Reporter*, 126.

3 According to Fairfax Downey, "a computation made in 1932 showed more than 521,000 copies [of *Soldiers*] sold." See Downey's *Richard Harding Davis: His Day* (New York: Charles Scribner's Sons, 1933), 129.

eled to Cuba to cover the rebels' struggle for independence from Spain. This journey, as noted earlier, not only led to a series of articles collected as *Cuba in War Time*, but also positioned Davis as an "expert" on the island. Once hostilities broke out between the US and Spain in 1898, he was a natural to return to report on the war, and he soon attached himself to Roosevelt and his Rough Riders.[1] Davis knew a good story-in-the-making when he saw one and he celebrated "the Colonel" and his men in a series of colorful articles in the London *Times* and New York *Herald*. His coverage of Roosevelt perhaps marks the high water mark of his career as a journalist and of his impact on public opinion: he did his part in writing the legend of Teddy Roosevelt.[2] His dispatches helped to make Roosevelt a hero; in small measure, he helped pave the Rough Rider's road to the White House. And, in his usual two-for-one way, Davis also turned his articles into two books about the war, *A Year from a Reporter's Notebook* (1898) and *The Cuban and Porto Rican Campaigns* (1898). To say the least, the Spanish-American War was good to Davis, but it also marked the beginning of his fall from literary and public prominence. He would never again be so important a player; he would never again achieve the same levels of critical and popular success as a writer. His personal life would also never be quite the same again

In 1899, after several years of courtship, Davis married Cecil Clark. In his mid-thirties, he was many years her senior, and he had grown accustomed to a bachelor life of travel and

---

1   The "Rough Riders" was the popular nickname of the First United States Volunteer Cavalry, the regiment that Roosevelt helped to raise and then led in Cuba. Colorful alliteration was the theme of the day: "Roosevelt's Rough Riders" were also known as "Teddy's Terrors."

2   The war also provided Davis with the opportunity to do some fighting of his own. In a moment of martial exuberance, he scooped up a rifle from a wounded American soldier and joined the fight. As he wrote to his family in July 1898, the Rough Riders "were caught in a clear case of ambush":

> I got excited and took a carbine and charged to the sugar house, which was what is called the key to the position. If the men had been regulars I would have sat in the rear as B— did, but I knew every other one of them, had played football, and all that sort of thing, with them, so I thought as an American I ought to help. The officers were falling all over the shop, and after it was all over Roosevelt made me a long speech before some of the men, and offered me a captaincy in the regiment any time I wanted it. (Davis, *Adventures and Letters*, 254–55)

professional zig-zagging. An intelligent, artistic, and independent young woman, Cecil originally turned down Davis' proposal, but she relented and became his companion on many of his subsequent adventures: she traveled with him to South Africa in January 1900, in order that he could report on the Boer War; she also traveled with him to Europe, Japan, Russia, and the Congo as he covered still other wars and conflicts. They never had any children together, and although they purchased Crossroads Farm at Mount Kisco, New York—the sort of rural retreat and gentlemen's estate that Davis had been dreaming about for years—they were perhaps too much in motion to settle into any sort of domestic routine. Eventually, Cecil and Davis began to drift apart, and they divorced in 1912. The failure of their marriage always bothered Davis, and he seems to have missed Cecil even as they moved on with their lives: she to her studies and painting and he to his writing and further adventures.

During his years with Cecil, Davis, ever the hard-worker, produced no fewer than four books of journalism and travel writing, three collections of short stories or novellas, three novels, and several plays. Of all of these, *Captain Macklin* (1902) may be his best, most mature and searching work. A narrative of empire, like *Soldiers*, the novel recounts the life of Royal Macklin, a young American soldier who becomes caught up in a revolution and filibustering war in Honduras. Far more critical of US political and economic interference in the affairs of weaker nations than *Soldiers*, *Macklin*, perhaps predictably, neither sold well nor received positive reviews. Although Davis hoped that the novel would establish his reputation as a serious artist, its failure drove him, as he wrote to a friend in 1906, back to writing popular fluff: "Macklin I always thought was the best thing I ever did, and it was the one over which I took the most time and care. Its failure was what as Maggie Cline used to say, 'drove me into this business' of play writing."[1]

In 1912, less than a month after his divorce from Cecil had been finalized, Davis married Bessie McCoy (born Elizabeth Genevieve McEvoy), an actress twenty-four years his junior. He had been smitten with her when he first saw her on the stage in the 1908 musical, *The Three Twins*. He returned to see

---

1 Davis, *Adventures and Letters*, 317.

the play many times, and finally secured an introduction. Bessie was cool toward Davis—he was already married *and* old enough to be her father—but she eventually began to reciprocate his affections. After their wedding, they settled into Crossroads, and Davis once more poured his energies into work, penning numerous short stories and plays (he wrote twenty-five in his lifetime). He also traveled once more to Cuba in 1914 to be on the set for the film adaptation of *Soldiers of Fortune*. When World War I broke out, he traveled to Europe to work, yet again, as a war correspondent. After his return from France, and to his great delight, his only child was born on 4 January 1915. Davis and Bessie had been wishing for a girl, and they named her Hope after the heroine of *Soldiers of Fortune*. Sadly, he did not get to see his daughter grow up: Davis died of a massive heart attack on 11 April 1916, a week shy of his fifty-second birthday.

Lauded in his day, Davis' popular renown as a writer and adventurer has faded over time, and the advent of the Moderns and their aesthetics of experimentation, complexity, and alienation certainly made much of his canon appear decidedly old-fashioned and distinctly minor. Although *Soldiers* has been in and out of print ever since its initial publication, much of his work—at least since Scribners published the twelve-volume "Crossroads Edition" of his stories and novels in 1916—has not often been republished. Nevertheless, if his star has faded somewhat, he has consistently been a subject of historical, biographical, and critical interest. His brother's *Adventures and Letters of Richard Harding Davis* (1917), for example, remains a gold mine of information about Davis' life, exploits, and opinions. Prior to Arthur Lubow's extraordinary *The Reporter Who Would Be King* (1992), two other biographies explored the author's life: Fairfax Downey's engaging (if somewhat baggy) *Richard Harding Davis: His Day* (1933) and Gerald Langford's excellent critical study, *The Richard Harding Davis Years* (1961). Davis also figures prominently in Charles H. Brown's fine history, *The Correspondents' War: Journalists in the Spanish-American War* (1967). More recently, John Seelye has authored a superb study of Davis's fiction and, especially, non-fiction, *War Games: Richard Harding Davis and the New Imperialism* (2003). I also offer extended readings of *Soldiers* and *Macklin* in my *Agent of Empire: William Walker and the Imperial Self in American Literature* (2004), a study of the literary after-life of one of

Davis' heroes.[1] In addition, Davis has been the subject of a number of excellent scholarly articles and biographical essays.[2] If his work has enjoyed a steady, albeit modest interest since his death, his critical reputation has enjoyed a renaissance in recent years as scholars and readers have become increasingly concerned with the history, literatures, and cultures of United States imperialism. Any consideration of the literary canon of the American empire must include a consideration of Davis' life and works.

Reading *Soldiers of Fortune*

When Davis sat down to write *Soldiers*, we can, with some confidence, say that he wanted to write a popular novel. Always on the look-out for a payday, and a shrewd reader of the literary tastes *and* political passions of the *fin de siècle*, he offers not only a rousing treatment of the familiar pleasures of the romance genre, but also a heady portrait of imperial masculinity; he not only wants to entertain his readers with a brisk plot, bold characters, and an exotic setting, but he also wants to tap into and stir the expansionist and jingoistic currents then swirling through Washington and the nation. Yet even as Davis mixes the pleasures of the romance with the pleasures of imperial fantasy, a more personal, less obvious motive also gives shape to the novel: just as he wants to please his readers, he also wants—whether consciously or unconsciously, we cannot say—to outdo his mother: *Soldiers* can be read as a rewrite of Rebecca's "Life in the Iron-Mills."

To begin, we need to situate Davis and *Soldiers* in their historical moment: the setting, plot, and characters arise, with considerable literary license, from the history of US economic and military interventionism abroad in the years leading up to the Spanish-American War. Although we do not have the space here to exhume the long and involute history of the American

---

1 William Walker (1824–60), American filibuster, or soldier of fortune, who raised a private army and conquered Nicaragua (1856–57) until being forced out of the isthmus by the combined forces of Central America. Walker has been the subject of a number of poems, plays, stories, novels, and films; he is a clear inspiration for Davis' *Soldiers* and *Macklin* and the explicit subject of "William Walker, The King of the Filibusters" in Richard Harding Davis, *Real Soldiers of Fortune* (New York: Charles Scribner's Sons, 1906).

2 See the Select Bibliography for further critical and historical studies of Davis and his work.

empire—there's an "American empire"?—we can nevertheless briefly recount a few instances, from among the staggering number of US overseas interventions in the half-century before the war in Cuba, of the nation's growing influence in the Caribbean basin and beyond. In the 1850s, the era of Manifest Destiny, Americans began to turn their energies toward developing an overseas economic and political dominion.[1] Early in the decade, for example, the US supplied military forces to defend US firms during their construction of a railroad across Panama; in 1852, American forces landed in Buenos Aires, Argentina, to safeguard US-owned commercial enterprises. In 1853, Commodore Matthew Calbraith Perry sailed for Tokyo Bay with a squadron of four ships to "open" Japanese ports to American trade. In the same decade, American forces were also sent to China, the Fiji Islands, Uruguay, and Turkey to protect, in what has become the standard parlance, "American lives and property."

Over the next ten years, the US also undertook missions to Mexico, Nicaragua, and Formosa. In 1871, the nation sent attack ships to Korea in retaliation for the Korean attack on an American ship, the *General Sherman*; in 1874, US forces were sent to Hawaii to preserve order and to protect American economic interests. In the 1880s, American troops were deployed to Egypt, Panama, Guatemala, and elsewhere; in the same years, American firms built railroads and established fruit plantations throughout Central America (with a particular concentration in Honduras, the first "banana republic") and also took over Mexico's mining and oil industries. This list of military and economic interventions could go on and on, but we can safely say that Davis took his setting and plot not only from his 1886 journey to Cuba, but also from the sustained pattern of US economic interventions— supported by US military force—around the world: an American hero, when threatened, must protect American lives and property in a sweltering, treacherous hinterland.

If Davis wanted to dramatize what was going on abroad in the years leading up to the Spanish-American War, he more importantly wanted to stir the imperial desires simmering throughout

---

1 Manifest Destiny: the belief popular in the 1840s and 1850s that US territorial expansion—both continental and extra-continental—was both inevitable and a matter of the will of God. The agents of manifest destiny pushed for war against Mexico and the annexation of Texas, California, and the Oregon territory. For more on Manifest Destiny, see Appendix F.

the nation. Many Americans—including Davis, Roosevelt, and countless others—believed that the US, due to its ever-growing population and economic means, was poised on the verge of greatness, had always been destined to take its place alongside the great powers. The dreams and desires of Manifest Destiny were still very much alive, and the country now possessed the power to realize the old ambitions. The jingos, or those who clamored for a far more truculent foreign policy, for the construction of an overseas economic and military empire, wanted the US to follow through on the Monroe Doctrine; by the late 1890s, Cuba had become the focus of these energies. As we saw in *Cuba in War Time*, Spain's continued presence in the New World angered Davis, and he and his fellow reporters did their best to inflame public passions. As Charles A. Dana, editor of the New York *Sun* wrote after a US steamer, *Alliança*, claimed to have been chased and fired upon by a Spanish ship on 8 March 1895, "The next Spanish gunboat that molests an American vessel ought to be pursued and blown out of the water."[1] The struggle for Cuban independence and the list of Spanish atrocities and insults were daily fodder for the press, and Davis, in *Soldiers*, sought to play upon the same passions, to do what he could with a novel to inflame his reader's imperial fantasies. He wanted his country-men to step forward, to be bold, to lead the leaders, and his romance offers a vivid portrait of how he believed Americans should act in the world. By the time *Soldiers* hit the stands in 1897, readers did not have to work very hard to see "Olancho" as a sort of Cuba.

In keeping with the tenor of the times, Davis offers a particular vision of American imperialism: he exalts imperial masculinity. Jingos like Davis and Roosevelt believed, as Kristin L. Hoganson writes, that "military endeavors built manhood": "Convinced that strife helped constitute manhood, Roosevelt advocated strenuosity as a guiding principle for all endeavors. But some endeavors, he felt, were inherently more strenuous than others. Most strenuous of all was war, and close behind lay empire."[2] Davis, ever sensitive to the mood of his era, offers Clay as the embodiment of American imperial masculinity: young, dashing,

---

1 Quoted in Charles H. Brown, *The Correspondents' War: Journalists in the Spanish-American War* (New York: Charles Scribner's Sons, 1967), 3.
2 Kristin L. Hoganson, *Fighting for American Manhood* (New Haven: Yale UP, 1998), 144. For more on Roosevelt's views on masculinity and "the strenuous life," see Appendices E and F.

daring, he steps forward to protect the mine, even if that means seizing power in Olancho. Men such as Davis and Roosevelt feared that young American men would grow soft, would fall into timidity and sloth if they were not challenged on the field of battle or the plains of empire. To their minds, the generation that had fought the Civil War had made the nation great, and with its passing, the next generations must also prove themselves, must test their manhood in combat and take their part in running world affairs. Davis skillfully plays upon the jingos' fantasies of masculine triumph: where the Reagan era had Rambo as its paragon of rejuvenated, hypermasculine American power, and where the Bush II era has the (good) Terminator as its symbol of paternal muscle, the *fin de siècle* had Robert Clay as its daydream of imperial vigor. When provoked, Clay rises to the occasion. He fires a pistol, swings a sword, defends the mine, falls in love (with a rather young woman)—all this, and yet he barely breaks a sweat.

A canny reader of the public's bellicose mood and a shrewd navigator of popular literary tastes, Davis takes up one of the oldest and most tried-and-true of literary genres as the vehicle for his fantasy of imperial ascendancy: the romance.[1] A form dating back at least to classical Greece, the prose romance usually features a growing love interest—with all sorts of complications, separations, and misunderstandings—between the hero and heroine who, after many perilous adventures and daring escapes, stand together and enjoy the usual sort of happy ending: an engagement or marriage. The tales of King Arthur and his knights remain perhaps the most famous of all romances in English, and they often feature quests, battles with magical creatures, courtly manners and speech, and foreground the ideals of loyalty, courage, and honor. *Soldiers* belongs to this long tradition of adventures stories set in exotic locales, but instead of dragons or black knights, Clay faces corrupt Latin American generals; instead of winning the hand of a princess or a queen, he falls for Hope Langham, the daughter of the mine's American owner; instead of fealty to the king, Clay owes his allegiance to the mine and US economic interests; instead of descents into realms of

---

1 I have argued elsewhere that *Soldiers* should be read as an exemplum of the "mercenary" romance, or tales that feature young Americans caught up in coups and revolutions abroad. For more on this sub-genre of the romance, and its importance in the literatures of American imperialism, see *Agent of Empire*.

magic or the supernatural, Davis takes his readers into the dangerous, yet exciting outposts of the nascent *imperium*. As the enduring popularity of the romance suggests, the genre offers ready pleasures to readers: we are elevated from the mundane and quotidian; we get to participate in great action and adventures; we imagine ourselves as bold heroes or beautiful heroines (Davis' primary readers in his day were young women); we triumph over great odds; our limbs intact, and feeling pretty good about ourselves, we walk away happy.[1]

A close reading of *Soldiers* shows Davis to be a master of the romance genre; it also shows him to be engaged in an odd Oedipal struggle with his mother for literary ascendancy. Close to his mother, and constantly seeking her input on his work, he transforms her tale of poverty and suffering into a swashbuckling tale of the riches and economic promise of the New World. In "Life in the Iron-Mills," Rebecca offers a story about the harsh life of Hugh Wolfe, an iron-mill worker who sculpts powerful statues from *korl*, a waste product of the smelting process, only to destroy them in fits of anger over his condition. Hugh and his cousin, Deb, endure incredible hardships; they work unending shifts, eat rotten food, sleep in a crowded tenement, and then return to mills to suffer more for the profit of the lucky few like Kirby, the mill-owner's son. The painful routine breaks their bodies and spirits and the novella offers one of the darkest portraits of America in the nineteenth century; the New World has not turned out to be the new Eden, but rather a dystopic wasteland of pain and degradation.

Davis, like his mother, centers his novel on iron as an emblem of economic power, but rather than offering a critique of the excesses and failings of American capital, he celebrates American ingenuity, risk-taking, and commercial acumen. In sharp contrast to his mother, Davis wants to reclaim the dream of the Americas as lands of opportunity and riches, wants to laud the hard work, skill, and daring of US entrepreneurs. Unlike Rebecca, he does

---

1 Some of the popular romances of our time: the *Star Wars* or *Indiana Jones* movies, the million or more rewrites of the grail quest (including such phenomenal bestsellers as *The Da Vinci Code* and refreshing spoofs such as *Monty Python and the Holy Grail*), and even such high-brow fare as Thomas Pynchon's *Gravity's Rainbow* (1973) or Don DeLillo's *The Names* (1982) or *Mao II* (1991). For more on Pynchon and DeLillo as romancers, see John McClure's *Late Imperial Romance* (New York: Verso, 1994).

not worry about human suffering or the ceaseless toil of the underclasses; he stands clearly on the side of capital, and scarcely makes mention of the workers, other than to assure his readers that Clay runs an efficient and safe mine. Davis upends and rewrites his mother's novella in order to extol the US' growing economic and military might, and we can see this in detail after detail.

Where Rebecca, for example, offers Kirby as a heartless capitalist, Davis offers Langham as a relatively fair-minded businessman who does what he can to improve the lives of his workers. In "Life," as Kirby and his two guests, Dr. May and Mitchell, take a tour of the mill, they come across one of Hugh's sculptures and engage in a conversation about who is responsible for the putrid lives of the workers. Each, in turn, absolves themselves of any responsibility for the uplift or upkeep of Hugh and the others, and Kirby, the voice of social Darwinism, speaks for capital: "*Ce n'est pas mon affaire*. I have no fancy for nursing infant geniuses. I suppose there are some stray gleams of mind and soul among these wretches. The Lord will take care of his own; or else they can work out their own salvation."[1] Kirby rejects any suggestion that industry needs to do more for the welfare of labor, and he makes his position perfectly clear: "If I had the making of men [...] these men who do the lowest part of the world's work should be machines,—nothing more,—hands. It would be kindness. God help them!" Rebecca portrays capitalism as a dehumanizing mode of production and she has little regard for men like Kirby.[2]

In contrast, Langham seems much less vicious and somewhat more concerned with the plight of the worker. He supplies "zinchuts" and maintains a small clinic "for the fever-stricken and the casualties." Davis admits that the mine can be a dangerous place, but Clay has mastered all the latest and safest procedures and takes great care in instructing his men on how to do their jobs. He understands the technology, and runs an efficient and highly profitable enterprise. Where Kirby loathes the workers and sees them as subhuman brutes, Langham does at least a little to keep them happy and healthy. Where Rebecca presents a scathing dissection of greed, Davis offers a much more benign take on industrialization; big business, he suggests, is not a destroyer of body

---

1 Rebecca Harding Davis, *Life in the Iron-Mills and Other Stories*, ed. Tillie Olsen (New York: Feminist Press, 1985), 34.
2 For a fuller excerpt from this key passage in "Life in the Iron-Mills," see Appendix D3.

and soul, but rather a means to social and political development. He answers his mother's charge that capitalism has broken the promise of the New World; the Americas, he insists, have only just begun to yield their bounty.

While we could also point to other ways in which Davis rewrites "Life"—we could, for example, compare Deb's unrequited love for Hugh to Hope's interest in Clay—perhaps the most striking revision can be seen in the representations of the two male protagonists: where Rebecca feminizes Hugh, Davis portrays Clay as an exemplum of imperial masculinity. Unlike Clay, Hugh possesses neither strength nor good looks, and, ground down by hard labor, poverty, and squalor, his has become an object of derision among his fellow workers. He looks, the other men think, like a woman: "Physically, Nature had promised the man but little. He had already lost the strength and instinct vigor of a man, his muscles were thin, his nerves weak, his face (a meek, woman's face) haggard, yellow with consumption. In the mill he was known as one of the girl-men: 'Molly Wolfe' was his *sobriquet*."[1] Hugh struggles to survive, struggles to express his life through a crude, yet moving art; he represents loss, a gifted young man destroyed by the rapacity of others. Clay, on the other hand, represents American power. He has everything: a superb physique, abundant energy, charisma, sure knowledge of how one advances in the world, and the will to succeed. Clay has been a cowboy, an adventurer in Africa, and he now runs a vast American mine. He embodies American vigor; most importantly, he represents the ease with which Davis believes the US will rise to hemispheric and even global dominance. He is everything Hugh is not, and, once more, Davis rejects his mother's pessimistic vision.

Davis rewrites his mother's work in order to foreground his own political and imperial views, but he also revises her novella in order to claim his place as a writer not only in the family but in the wider world. In his famous study, *The Anxiety of Influence* (1973), Harold Bloom argues that poets revise and distort the work of earlier poets.[2] The "belated" poet, faced with the achievement of his precursors, experiences a range of emotions, including envy and fear of the earlier writer's dominance, and responds

---

1 Davis, *Life*, 23–24.
2 For more on Bloom's theories, see *The Anxiety of Influence: A Theory of Poetry*, 2nd ed. (New York: Oxford UP, 1997).

in his own writing by distorting the work of the earlier writer beyond conscious recognition. The later poet, in Bloom's view, enters into a kind of Oedipal relationship with his literary forebears, and although Bloom focuses largely on the male tradition in poetry, we can recast his model as a means to understand Davis' reworking of "Life." Faced with the accomplishments and reputation of his mother, Davis tried to emerge from Rebecca's shadow by reformulating her best work into what he hoped was his best work. He must, in this case, displace his mother—and not his father—to assume pre-eminence in a family of writers. Rather than seeking to replace his father in his mother's affections, as Sigmund Freud would have it in the Oedipal complex, Davis sought to replace his mother in the reading public's affections.

Such a psychoanalytical reading of *Soldiers* does not, however, negate our reading of the romance as a novel of its day and as a fantasy of imperial ascendancy. Although we could speculate further on the possible connections between a man's desire to outdo a woman on the battlefield of letters and a potentially kindred desire to outdo other men on the battlefields of empire, and although we could dive much more deeply into particular scenes and features of the romance (there is so much more to be said about Davis and *Soldiers*), we must nevertheless leave these and other interpretative and critical matters for the classroom and individual readers. Before you, then, you have one of the most popular novels of the 1890s by one of the most popular writers of the *fin de siècle*. Davis may have fallen somewhat off the literary map of America, but his work may well resonate with our era; at the very least, *Soldiers* remains one of the most important works of US overseas adventurism and empire-building.

Soldiers of Fortune in Context: A Note on the Appendices

As readers will soon discern, the appendices serve to situate Davis' life and work in their literary, historical, and cultural contexts. Appendices A and B offers us views of Davis: A, "Images of Davis," provides us with photographs of his famous visage and adventurous life; B, "How Others Saw Davis," contains a number of different contemporary takes on Davis and his writings. Not all of his peers, as the excerpts suggest, admired the journalist-author, and some go so far as to mock his fiction and fondness for combat- or safari-type outfits. Appendix C, "Reviews of *Soldiers of Fortune*," presents contemporary judgments on *Soldiers*, and while some turn-of-the-century readers found much to admire in the novel—particularly its depictions of American masculinity and imperial daring—others found Clay's career rather suspect and argued that Davis' achievement in the romance did not elevate him to the highest ranks of American letters. Few of his contemporaries (or later readers) would place him in the company of such literary giants as Edith Wharton, Henry James, or Theodore Dreiser; at the same time, he was one of the top adventure writers of his day, somewhere down the slopes of Olympus from Stephen Crane and Jack London.

As Edward Caudill writes in *Darwinian Myths: The Legends and Misuses of a Theory* (1997), "the Spanish-American War took place after Herbert Spencer's philosophy of social Darwinism had crested in popularity": "Social Darwinism was convenient but unnecessary as a justification for war. People and publications blended economics, nationalism, and race to suit numerous perspectives, sometimes adding heavy doses of Darwin, at other times little or none."[1] Appendix D, "Social Darwinism, Survival of the Richest, and Other Notions of Anglo-American Superiority," situates *Soldiers* within this fluctuating cultural context. Although Davis was not himself a social Darwinist, he certainly shared notions of the racial and economic superiority of what Roosevelt and others referred to as "the white races." Many of Spencer and Charles Darwin's ideas about natural selection and the survival of the fittest were circulating in American culture in the late nineteenth century, and while the selections from Spencer, Darwin, Rebecca Harding Davis, and Andrew Carnegie suggest the scope of the infiltration of these ideas into literary, social, political, and economic thinking, the excerpts from Davis and Roosevelt show that, along with concepts of social Darwinism, good old-fashioned racism, sundry prejudices, and Manifest Destiny's belief in the Providential mission of the US were alive and well at the *fin de siècle*. Concepts of social Darwinism churn in the heady background to the American imperial project, and *Soldiers* betrays traces of these rather ruthless views of human nature and "civilization."

If the demons of social Darwinism lurk in the background, issues of imperial masculinity stand very much in the foreground of Davis' life and writings. *Soldiers* exemplifies his faith in American manhood, and Appendix E, "Davis and Others on American

---

1   Edward Caudill, *Darwinian Myths: The Legends and Misuses of a Theory* (Knoxville: U of Tennessee P, 1997), 79.

Masculinity," collects a range of largely celebratory views of imperial adventurers, both in fiction and in the real world. The appendix includes, among others, an excerpt from Roosevelt's urtext of American imperial masculinity, "The Strenuous Life" (1899): this essay must be counted as one of the most important works in the canon of the American empire, and Roosevelt lets his readers know, in no uncertain terms, what it means to be a real man, a man capable of serving not only his community, but his nation and the greater world. Not everyone, however, shared Roosevelt and Davis' hardy views of masculinity: the section closes with a contemporary's stinging portrait of Roosevelt as a serious case of arrested-development.

Appendix F, "Davis and Others on American Imperialism," provides arguably the most important contexts for reading *Soldiers* and offers starkly competing takes on the desirability and ethics of seeking an extra-continental *imperium*. On one side, we have the advocates of expansionism and imperialism: John L. O'Sullivan, the author of the phrase, "Manifest Destiny," Roosevelt, and Davis. On the other, we have the staunch opponents of empire: José Martí, a Cuban writer and patriot, and Mark Twain, one of the most critical anti-imperial voices in the nation. While Martí proceeds cautiously in his defense of Cuban independence from both Spain *and* the US, Twain attacks with a Swift-like fury, decrying the policies of McKinley and Roosevelt. The arguments set forth both for and against interventionism perhaps make this the most relevant section to our own times. Whatever the case, they offer compelling perspectives on the problems associated with a democracy seeking new lands and new realms of economic, military, and political influence abroad.

Richard Harding Davis: A Brief Chronology

1864   18 April: Richard Harding Davis born, Philadelphia, Pennsylvania, to L. (Lemuel) Clarke Davis (b. 23 September 1835, Sandusky, Ohio) and Rebecca Blaine Harding Davis (b. 24 June 1831, Washington, Pennsylvania).

1864–70   Davis family lives first with Clarke's recently widowed sister, Carrie Cooper, and then rents homes in North Philadelphia.

1866   24 January: Charles Belmont Davis (d. 1926), Richard's brother, born.

1870   Davis family purchases a home at 230 South Twenty-first Street, his parents' home until their deaths. Family summers in a small cottage, dubbed "Vagabond's Rest," on the Manasquan River, near Point Pleasant, New Jersey.

1872   16 October: Nora Davis (d. 1958), Richard's sister, born.

1882   Enrolls at Lehigh University.

1885   Flunks out of Lehigh.

1886   Enrolls, briefly, at Johns Hopkins University. Drops out and travels to Cuba with William W. Thurston, president of the Bethlehem Steel Company.

1886–89   Works as a cub reporter for the *Record*, but is fired for sub-standard work. Soon lands a position at another Philadelphia newspaper, the *Press*: interviews Walt Whitman and covers the Johnstown flood. Also writes letter of admiration to Robert Louis Stevenson. In 1888, begins writing a weekly gossip column, "The Lime Light Man," for the Philadelphia *Stage*.

1889   Moves to New York; begins work at the New York *Evening Sun*.

1890   Becomes managing editor of *Harper's Weekly*. Publishes "Gallegher" in *Scribner's*.

1891   Publishes *Gallegher and Other Stories* and *Stories for Boys*.

1892   *Van Bibber and Others* (stories) and *The West from a Car Window* (travelogue, with illustrations by Frederic Remington).

1892–93 Travels in Europe; extended stays in London and Paris, and cruises the Mediterranean.

1893   Under pressure from the magazine's owners, agrees to step-down from his position as managing editor of *Harper's*; becomes, nominally, an "associate editor."

1894   *Our English Cousins* (travelogue), *The Rulers of the Mediterranean* (travelogue), and *The Exiles* (stories).

1895   *About Paris* (travelogue) and *The Princess Aline* (among the top-ten best-selling American novels of the year). Travels in Latin America (January–March).

1896   *Three Gringos in Venezuela and Central America* (travelogue) and *Cinderella and Other Stories*.

1896–97 Travels to Moscow to report on the Coronation of Czar Nicholas II, to Budapest for the Millennial Celebration, to Cuba to cover the island's struggle for independence from Spain, to Washington for President William McKinley's inauguration, to Greece as a war correspondent on the Greco-Turkish War, and finally to London to report on Queen Victoria's diamond jubilee.

1897   *Soldiers of Fortune*, his most popular work, and *Cuba in War Time* (journalism).

1898   Travels to Cuba to cover the Spanish-American War. *The King's Jackal* (novella), *A Year from a Reporter's Notebook* (journalism), *The Cuban and Porto Rican Campaigns* (journalism).

1899   4 May: marries Cecil Clarke (1877–1955) in Marion, Massachusetts. *The Lion and the Unicorn* (stories).

1900   Travels, with Cecil, to South Africa to report on the Boer War. *With Both Armies in South Africa* (articles on the war).

1902   Purchases "Crossroads Farm," Mount Kisco, Westchester County, New York. *Ransom's Folly* (novellas) and

Captain Macklin (novel). *Soldiers of Fortune*, adapted for the stage by Augustus Thomas, opens at the Savoy Theatre in New York and enjoys considerable commercial and critical success. Travels, with Cecil, to Spain and England and visits Rudyard Kipling.

1903   *The Bar Sinister* (stories).

1904   14 December: Clarke Davis, aged 69, dies. *Ransom's Folly* (play) and *The Dictator* (farce). Sails, with Cecil, to Japan to cover the Russo–Japanese War. Also travels to China.

1906   *Miss Civilization* (play) and *Real Soldiers of Fortune* (essays). Travels to Cuba.

1907   Travels, with Cecil, to the Congo to report on atrocities. *The Scarlet Car* (stories) and *The Congo and the Coasts of Africa* (travel essays; thought by some critics to be his worst book). Further travels to Cuba and London.

1908   *Vera the Medium* (novel).

1909   *The White Mice* (novel).

1910   29 September: Rebecca Harding Davis, aged 79, dies. *Notes of a War Correspondent* (journalism).

1912   18 June: divorces Cecil.

1912   8 July: marries Bessie McCoy (Elizabeth Genevieve McEvoy; 1887–1931) in Greenwich, Connecticut.

1914   Travels to Cuba for the filming of *Soldiers of Fortune*. With Augustus Thomas once more at the helm as screenwriter and director, the feature film nevertheless receives poor reviews and flops at the box office. Travels to Mexico, hoping for violence to break out between the US and its southern neighbor. As his brother notes, he was "greatly disappointed" that there was no war. Sails for England to report on World War I. *With the Allies* (journalism).

1915   4 January, birth of Hope Davis (1915–76), to Richard and Bessie. She is named after the heroine of *Soldiers of Fortune*. Travels in Europe.

1916   *With the French in France and Salonika* (journalism).

1916   11 April: dies, aged 51, at Crossroads Farm. Cremated and the ashes interred in a grave next to his parents in Leverington Cemetery, Philadelphia. Scribner's begins to publish the "Crossroads Edition" of Davis' novels and stories.

A Note on the Text

This edition follows the standard practice of using the "Crossroads Edition" (1917) as its copy-text. Although Davis was frustrated by the sometimes sloppy copyediting and presentation of some of his works, he died before he could oversee the production of a standard edition of his fiction or collected works. Nevertheless, the "Publisher's Note" to the twelve-volume Crossroads collection of his novels and stories assures us that "this edition has been prepared in pursuance of a plan long contemplated, and on lines discussed and arranged with Mr. Davis a year or so ago. It has now been completed with what is believed to be a full knowledge of his wishes."[1] In accordance with the "Crossroads Edition," this edition also includes Charles Dana Gibson's original illustrations for *Soldiers of Fortune*.

---

1   "Publishers' Note," in Richard Harding Davis, *Van Bibber and Others*, Crossroads Edition (New York: Charles Scribner's Sons, 1918), vii.

Soldiers of Fortune

To Irene and Dana Gibson[1]

---

1 Davis dedicated *Soldiers of Fortune* to his longtime friends, Irene Lang-
   horne Gibson and Charles Dana Gibson. A striking beauty, Irene, for
   many of her peers, seemed to be the living embodiment of the "Gibson
   Girl," or the feminine ideal depicted in many of her husband's most
   famous illustrations.

"It is so good of you to come early," said Mrs. Porter, as Alice Langham entered the drawing-room. "I want to ask a favor of you. I'm sure you won't mind. I would ask one of the *débutantes*, except that they're always so cross if one puts them next to men they don't know and who can't help them, and so I thought I'd just ask you, you're so good-natured. You don't mind, do you?"[1]

"I mind being called good-natured," said Miss Langham, smiling. "Mind what, Mrs. Porter?" she asked.

"He is a friend of George's," Mrs. Porter explained, vaguely. "He's a cowboy. It seems he was very civil to George when he was out there shooting in New Mexico, or Old Mexico, I don't remember which. He took George to his hut and gave him things to shoot, and all that, and now he is in New York with a letter of introduction. It's just like George. He may be a most impossible sort of man, but, as I said to Mr. Porter, the people I've asked can't complain, because I don't know anything more about him than they do. He called to-day when I was out and left his card and George's letter of introduction, and as a man had failed me for to-night, I just thought I would kill two birds with one stone, and ask him to fill his place, and he's here. And, oh, yes," Mrs. Porter added, "I'm going to put him next to you, do you mind?"

"Unless he wears leather leggings and long spurs I shall mind very much," said Miss Langham.

"Well, that's very nice of you," purred Mrs. Porter, as she moved away. "He may not be so bad, after all; and I'll put Reginald King on your other side, shall I?" she asked, pausing and glancing back.

The look on Miss Langham's face, which had been one of amusement, changed consciously, and she smiled with polite acquiescence.

"As you please, Mrs. Porter," she answered. She raised her eyebrows slightly. "I am, as the politicians say, 'in the hands of my friends.'"

"Entirely too much in the hands of my friends," she repeated, as she turned away. This was the twelfth time during that same winter that she and Mr. King had been placed next to one another at dinner, and it had passed beyond the point when she

---

1 Debutant, an upper-class young woman making her formal "debut" before society; in fin de siècle New York society, the term suggested that the young woman was now eligible for—and actively seeking—marriage.

could say that it did not matter what people thought as long as she and he understood. It had now reached that stage when she was not quite sure that she understood either him or herself. They had known each other for a very long time; too long, she sometimes thought, for them ever to grow to know each other any better. But there was always the chance that he had another side, one that had not disclosed itself, and which she could not discover in the strict social environment in which they both lived. And she was the surer of this because she had once seen him when he did not know that she was near, and he had been so different that it had puzzled her and made her wonder if she knew the real Reggie King at all.

It was at a dance at a studio, and some French pantomimists gave a little play. When it was over, King sat in the corner talking to one of the Frenchwomen, and while he waited on her he was laughing at her and at her efforts to speak English. He was telling her how to say certain phrases, and not telling her correctly, and she suspected this and was accusing him of it, and they were rhapsodizing and exclaiming over certain delightful places and dishes of which they both knew in Paris with the enthusiasm of two children. Miss Langham saw him off his guard for the first time, and instead of a somewhat bored and clever man of the world, he appeared as sincere and interested as a boy.

When he joined her, later, the same evening, he was as entertaining as usual, and as polite and attentive as he had been to the Frenchwoman, but he was not greatly interested, and his laugh was modulated and not spontaneous. She had wondered that night, and frequently since then, if, in the event of his asking her to marry him, which was possible, and of her accepting him, which was also possible, whether she would find him, in the closer knowledge of married life, as keen and light-hearted with her as he had been with the French dancer. If he would but treat her more like a comrade and equal, and less like a prime minister conferring with his queen! She wanted something more intimate than the deference that he showed her, and she did not like his taking it as an accepted fact that she was as worldly-wise as himself, even though it were true.

She was a woman and wanted to be loved, in spite of the fact that she had been loved by many men—at least it was so supposed—and had rejected them.

Each had offered her position, or had wanted her because she was fitted to match his own great state, or because he was ambitious, or because she was rich. The man who could love her as she once believed men could love, and who could give her something else besides approval of her beauty and her mind, had not disclosed himself. She had begun to think that he never would, that he did not exist, that he was an imagination of the playhouse and the novel. The men whom she knew were careful to show her that they appreciated how distinguished was her position, and how inaccessible she was to them. They seemed to think that by so humbling themselves and by emphasizing her position they pleased her best, when it was what she wanted them to forget. Each of them would draw away backward, bowing and protesting that he was unworthy to raise his eyes to such a prize, but that, if she would only stoop to him, how happy his life would be! Sometimes they meant it sincerely; sometimes they were gentlemanly adventurers of title, from whom it was a business proposition; and in either case she turned restlessly away and asked herself how long it would be before the man would come who would pick her up on his saddle and gallop off with her, with his arm around her waist and his horse's hoofs clattering beneath them, and echoing the tumult in their hearts.

She had known too many great people in the world to feel impressed with her own position at home in America; but she sometimes compared herself to the Queen in "In a Balcony," and repeated to herself, with mock seriousness:

And you the marble statue all the time
They praise and point at as preferred to life,
Yet leave for the first breathing woman's cheek,
First dancer's, gypsy's or street balladine's![1]

And if it were true, she asked herself, that the man she had imagined was only an ideal and an illusion, was not King the best of the others, the unideal and ever-present others? Every one else seemed to think so. The society they knew put them constantly together and approved. Her people approved. Her own mind approved, and, as her heart was not apparently ever to be considered, who could say that it did not approve as well? He was certainly a very charming fellow, a manly, clever companion, and one who bore about him the evidences of distinction and thorough breeding. As far as family went, the Kings were as old as a

---

1 "In a Balcony" (1855), a verse drama by English poet, Robert Browning (1812–89).

young country could expect, and Reggie King was, moreover, in spite of his wealth, a man of action and ability. His yacht journeyed from continent to continent, and not merely up the Sound to Newport, and he was as well known and welcome to the consuls along the coasts of Africa and South America as he was at Cowes or Nice.[1] His books of voyages were recognized by geographical societies and other serious bodies, who had given him permission to put long disarrangements of the alphabet after his name. She liked him because she had grown to be at home with him, because it was good to know that there was some one who would not misunderstand her, and who, should she so indulge herself, would not take advantage of any appeal she might make to his sympathy, who would always be sure to do the tactful thing and the courteous thing, and who, while he might never do a great thing, could not do an unkind one.

Miss Langham had entered the Porters' drawing-room after the greater number of the guests had arrived, and she turned from her hostess to listen to an old gentleman with a passion for golf, a passion in which he had for a long time been endeavoring to interest her. She answered him and his enthusiasm in kind, and with as much apparent interest as she would have shown in a matter of state. It was her principle to be all things to all men, whether they were great artists, great diplomats, or great bores. If a man had been pleading with her to leave the conservatory and run away with him, and another had come up innocently and announced that it was his dance, she would have said, "Oh, is it?" with as much apparent delight as though his coming had been the one bright hope in her life.

She was growing enthusiastic over the delights of golf, and unconsciously making a very beautiful picture of herself in her interest and forced vivacity, when she became conscious for the first time of a strange young man who was standing alone before the fireplace looking at her, and frankly listening to all the nonsense she was talking. She guessed that he had been listening for some time, and she also saw, before he turned his eyes quickly away, that he was distinctly amused. Miss Langham stopped gesticulating and lowered her voice, but continued to keep her eyes

---

1   Yacht-owning New Yorkers could sail east on Long Island Sound, an estuary connecting numerous rivers with the Atlantic Ocean, and land again at any number of coastal towns, including posh Newport, Rhode Island. Cowes, a harbor town on the Isle of Wight, off the coast of England; Nice, a harbor town on the French Riviera.

on the face of the stranger, whose own eyes were wandering around the room, to give her, so she guessed, the idea that he had not been listening, but that she had caught him at it in the moment he had first looked at her. He was a tall, broad-shouldered youth, with a handsome face, tanned and dyed, either by the sun or by exposure to the wind, to a deep ruddy brown, which contrasted strangely with his yellow hair and mustache and with the pallor of the other faces about him. He was a stranger apparently to every one present, and his bearing suggested, in consequence, that ease of manner which comes to a person who is not only sure of himself, but who has no knowledge of the claims and pretensions to social distinction of those about him. His most attractive feature was his eyes, which seemed to observe all that was going on, not only what was on the surface, but beneath the surface, and that not rudely or covertly but with the frank, quick look of the trained observer. Miss Langham found it an interesting face to watch, and she did not look away from it. She was acquainted with every one else in the room, and hence she knew this must be the cowboy of whom Mrs. Porter had spoken, and she wondered how any one who had lived the rough life of the West could still retain the look, when in formal clothes, of one who was in the habit of doing informal things in them.

Mrs. Porter presented her cowboy simply as "Mr. Clay, of whom I spoke to you," with a significant raising of the eyebrows, and the cowboy made way for King, who took Miss Langham in. He looked frankly pleased, however, when he found himself next to her again, but did not take advantage of it throughout the first part of the dinner, during which time he talked to the young married woman on his right, and Miss Langham and King continued where they had left off at their last meeting. They knew each other well enough to joke of the way in which they were thrown into each other's society, and, as she said, they tried to make the best of it. But while she spoke, Miss Langham was continually conscious of the presence of her neighbor, who piqued her interest and her curiosity in different ways. He seemed to be at his ease, and yet from the manner in which he glanced up and down the table and listened to snatches of talk on either side of him he had the appearance of one to whom it was all new and who was seeing it for the first time.

There was a jolly group at one end of the long table, and they wished to emphasize the fact by laughing a little more hysterically at their remarks than the humor of those witticisms seemed to justify. A daughter-in-law of Mrs. Porter was their leader in this, and at one point she stopped in the middle of a story and, waving her hand at the double row of faces turned in her direction, which had been attracted by the loudness of her voice, cried gayly: "Don't listen. This is for private circulation. It is not a *jeune-fille* story."[1] The *débutantes* at the table continued talking again in steady, even tones, as though they had not heard the remark or the first of the story, and the men next to them appeared equally unconscious. But the cowboy, Miss Langham noted out of the corner of her eye, after a look of polite surprise, beamed with amusement and continued to stare up and down the table as though he had discovered a new trait in a peculiar and interesting animal. For some reason, she could not tell why, she felt annoyed with herself and with her friends, and resented the attitude which the newcomer assumed toward them.

"Mrs. Porter tells me that you know her son George?" she said. He did not answer her at once, but bowed his head in assent, with a look of interrogation, as though, so it seemed to her, he had expected her, when she did speak, to say something less conventional.

"Yes," he replied, after a pause, "he joined us at Ayutla. It was the terminus of the Jalisco[2] and Mexican Railroad then. He came out over the road and went in from there with an outfit after mountain lions. I believe he had very good sport."

"That is a very wonderful road, I am told," said King, bending forward and introducing himself into the conversation with a nod of the head toward Clay; "quite a remarkable feat of engineering."

"It will open up the country, I believe," assented the other, indifferently.

"I know something of it," continued King, "because I met the men who were putting it through at Pariqua, when we touched there in the yacht. They shipped most of their plant to that port, and we saw a good deal of them. They were a very jolly lot, and they gave me a most interesting account of their work and its difficulties."

Clay was looking at the other closely, as though he was trying to find something back of what he was saying, but as his glance seemed only to embarrass King he smiled freely again in assent, and gave him his full attention.

"There are no men to-day, Miss Langham," King exclaimed,

---

1 A story unsuitable for "jeune-fille," or young women.
2 A state on central Mexico's Pacific coast; Ayutla is a town in Jalisco.

suddenly, turning toward her, "to my mind, who lead as picturesque lives as do civil engineers. And there are no men whose work is as little appreciated."

"Really?" said Miss Langham, encouragingly.

"Now those men I met," continued King, settling himself with his side to the table, "were all young fellows of thirty or thereabouts, but they were leading the lives of pioneers and martyrs—at least that's what I'd call it. They were marching through an almost unknown part of Mexico, fighting Nature at every step and carrying civilization with them. They were doing better work than soldiers, because soldiers destroy things, and these chaps were creating, and making the way straight. They had no banners either, nor brass bands. They fought mountains and rivers, and they were attacked on every side by fever and the lack of food and severe exposure. They had to sit down around a camp-fire at night and calculate whether they were to tunnel a mountain, or turn the bed of a river or bridge it. And they knew all the time that whatever they decided to do out there in the wilderness meant thousands of dollars to the stockholders somewhere up in God's country, who would some day hold them to account for them. They dragged their chains through miles and miles of jungle, and over flat alkali beds and cactus, and they reared bridges across roaring cañons.[1] We know nothing about them and we care less. When their work is done we ride over the road in an observation-car and look down thousands and thousands of feet into the depths they have bridged, and we never give them a thought. They are the bravest soldiers of the present day, and they are the least recognized. I have forgotten their names, and you never heard them. But it seems to me the civil engineer, for all that, is the chief civilizer of our century."

Miss Langham was looking ahead of her with her eyes half-closed, as though she were going over in her mind the situation King had described.

"I never thought of that," she said. "It sounds very fine. As you say, the reward is so inglorious. But that is what makes it fine."

The cowboy was looking down at the table and pulling at a flower in the centre-piece. He had ceased to smile. Miss

---

1 Alkali beds, or flats, are dried-out desert lakes, notable for high concentrations of precipitated dry and glistening salts. Perhaps the most famous alkali bed in the US is the Bonneville Salt Flats, in northwestern Utah, the site of many automobile and jet-car land-speed records.

Langham turned on him somewhat sharply, resenting his silence, and said, with a slight challenge in her voice:

"Do you agree, Mr. Clay," she asked, "or do you prefer the chocolate-cream soldiers, in red coats and gold lace?"

"Oh, I don't know," the young man answered, with some slight hesitation. "It's a trade for each of them. The engineer's work is all the more absorbing, I imagine, when the difficulties are greatest. He has the fun of overcoming them."

"You see nothing in it then," she asked, "but a source of amusement?"

"Oh, yes, a good deal more," he replied. "A livelihood, for one thing. I—I have been an engineer all my life. I built that road Mr. King is talking about."

★★★★★

An hour later, when Mrs. Porter made the move to go, Miss Langham rose with a protesting sigh. "I am so sorry," she said; "it has been most interesting. I never met two men who had visited so many inaccessible places and come out whole. You have quite inspired Mr. King—he was never so amusing. But I should like to hear the end of that adventure; won't you tell it to me in the other room?" Clay bowed. "If I haven't thought of something more interesting in the meantime," he said.

"What I can't understand," said King, as he moved up into Miss Langham's place, "is how you had time to learn so much of the rest of the world. You don't act like a man who had spent his life in the brush."

"How do you mean?" asked Clay, smiling—"that I don't use the wrong forks?"

"No," laughed King, "but you told us that this was your first visit East, and yet you're talking about England and Vienna and Voisin's.[1] How is it you've been there, while you have never been in New York?"

"Well, that's partly due to accident and partly to design," Clay answered. "You see I've worked for English and German and French companies, as well as for those in the States, and I go abroad to make reports and to receive instructions. And then I'm what you call a self-made man; that is, I've never been to college. I've always had to educate myself, and whenever I did get a

---

1 A fashionable Parisian restaurant.

holiday it seemed to me that I ought to put it to the best advantage, and to spend it where civilization was the furthest advanced—advanced, at least, in years. When I settle down and become an expert, and demand large sums for just looking at the work other fellows have done, then I hope to live in New York, but until then I go where the art galleries are biggest and where they have got the science of enjoying themselves down to the very finest point. I have enough rough work eight months of the year to make me appreciate that. So whenever I get a few months to myself I take the Royal Mail to London, and from there to Paris or Vienna. I think I like Vienna the best. The directors are generally important people in their own cities, and they ask one about, and so, though I hope I am a good American, it happens that I've more friends on the Continent than in the United States."

"And how does this strike you?" asked King, with a movement of his shoulder toward the men about the dismantled table.

"Oh, I don't know," laughed Clay. "You've lived abroad yourself; how does it strike you?"

Clay was the first man to enter the drawing-room. He walked directly away from the others and over to Miss Langham, and, taking her fan out of her hands as though to assure himself of some hold upon her, seated himself with his back to every one else.

"You have come to finish that story?" she said, smiling.

Miss Langham was a careful young person, and would not have encouraged a man she knew even as well as she knew King, to talk to her through dinner, and after it as well. She fully recognized that because she was conspicuous certain innocent pleasures were denied her which other girls could enjoy without attracting attention or comment. But Clay interested her beyond her usual self, and the look in his eyes was a tribute which she had no wish to put away from her.

"I've thought of something more interesting to talk about," said Clay. "I'm going to talk about you. You see I've known you a long time."

"Since eight o'clock?" asked Miss Langham.

"Oh, no, since your coming out, four years ago."

"It's not polite to remember so far back," she said. "Were you one of those who assisted at that important function? There were so many there I don't remember."

"No, I only read about it. I remember it very well; I had ridden over twelve miles for the mail that day, and I stopped half-way back to the ranch and camped out in the shade of a rock and read all the papers and magazines through at one sitting, until the sun went down and I couldn't see the print. One of the papers had an account of your coming out in it, and a picture of you, and I wrote East to the photographer for the original. It knocked about the West for three months and then reached me at Laredo, on the border between Texas and Mexico, and I have had it with me ever since."

Miss Langham looked at Clay for a moment in silent dismay and with a perplexed smile.

"Where is it now?" she asked at last.

"In my trunk at the hotel."

"Oh!" she said, slowly. She was still in doubt as to how to treat this act of unconventionality. "Not in your watch?" she said, to cover up the pause. "That would have been more in keeping with the rest of the story."

The young man smiled grimly, and pulling out his watch pried back the lid and turned it to her so that she could see a photograph inside. The face in the watch was that of a young girl in the dress of a fashion of several years ago. It was a lovely, frank face, looking out of the picture into the world kindly and questioningly, and without fear.

"Was I once like that?" she said, lightly. "Well, go on."

"Well," he said, with a little sigh of relief, "I became greatly interested in Miss Alice Langham, and in her comings out and goings in, and in her gowns. Thanks to our having a press in the States that makes a specialty of personalities, I was able to follow you pretty closely, for, wherever I go, I have my papers sent after me. I can get along without a compass or a medicine-chest, but I can't do without the newspapers and the magazines. There was a time when I thought you were going to marry that Austrian chap, and I didn't approve of that. I knew things about him in Vienna. And then I read of your engagement to others—well—several others; some of them I thought worthy and others not. Once I even thought of writing you about it, and once I saw you in Paris. You were passing on a coach. The man with me told me it was you, and I wanted to follow the coach in a fiacre;[1]—but he said he knew at what hotel you were stopping, and so I let you go, but you were not at that hotel, or at any other—at least, I couldn't find you."

"What would you have done—?" asked Miss Langham. "Never mind," she interrupted, "go on."

---

1 A small coach for hire.

"Well, that's all," said Clay, smiling. "That's all, at least, that concerns you. That is the romance of this poor young man."

"But not the only one," she said, for the sake of saying something.

"Perhaps not," answered Clay, "but the only one that counts. I always knew I was going to meet you some day. And now I have met you."

"Well, and now that you have met me," said Miss Langham, looking at him in some amusement, "are you sorry?"

"No—" said Clay, but so slowly and with such consideration that Miss Langham laughed and held her head a little higher. "Not sorry to meet you, but to meet you in such surroundings."

"What fault do you find with my surroundings?"

"Well, these people," answered Clay, "they are so foolish, so futile. You shouldn't be here. There must be something else better than this. You can't make me believe that you choose it. In Europe you could have a salon, or you could influence statesmen. There surely must be something here for you to turn to as well. Something better than golf-sticks and salted almonds."

"What do you know of me?" said Miss Langham, steadily. "Only what you have read of me in impertinent paragraphs. How do you know I am fitted for anything else but just this? You never spoke with me before to-night."

"That has nothing to do with it," said Clay, quickly. "Time is made for ordinary people. When people who amount to anything meet they don't have to waste months in finding each other out. It is only the doubtful ones who have to be tested again and again. When I was a kid in the diamond mines in Kimberley,[1] I have seen the experts pick out a perfect diamond from the heap at the first glance, and without a moment's hesitation. It was the cheap stones they spent most of the afternoon over. Suppose I *have* only seen you to-night for the first time; suppose I shall not see you again, which is quite likely, for I sail to-morrow for South America—what of that? I am just as sure of what you are as though I had known you for years."

Miss Langham looked at him for a moment in silence. Her beauty was so great that she could take her time to speak. She was not afraid of losing any one's attention.

"And have you come out of the West, knowing me so well, just to tell me that I am wasting myself?" she said. "Is that all?"

---

1 A major diamond center in Cape province, South Africa.

"That is all," answered Clay. "You know the things I would like to tell you," he added, looking at her closely.

"I think I like to be told the other things best," she said, "they are the easier to believe."

"You have to believe whatever I tell you," said Clay, smiling. The girl pressed her hands together in her lap, and looked at him curiously. The people about them were moving and making their farewells, and they brought her back to the present with a start.

"I'm sorry you're going away," she said. "It has been so odd. You come suddenly up out of the wilderness, and set me to thinking, and try to trouble me with questions about myself, and then steal away again without stopping to help me to settle them. Is it fair?" She rose and put out her hand, and he took it and held it for a moment, while they stood looking at one another.

"I am coming back," he said, "and I will find that you have settled them for yourself."

"Good-by," she said, in so low a tone that the people standing near them could not hear. "You haven't asked me for it, you know, but—I think I shall let you keep that picture."

"Thank you," said Clay, smiling, "I meant to."

"You can keep it," she continued, turning back, "because it is not my picture. It is a picture of a girl who ceased to exist four years ago, and whom you have never met. Good-night."

★★★★★

Mr. Langham and Hope, his younger daughter, had been to the theatre. The performance had been one which delighted Miss Hope, and which satisfied her father because he loved to hear her laugh. Mr. Langham was the slave of his own good fortune. By instinct and education he was a man of leisure and culture, but the wealth he had inherited was like an unruly child that needed his constant watching, and in keeping it well in hand he had become a man of business, with time for nothing else.

Alice Langham, on her return from Mrs. Porter's dinner, found him in his study engaged with a game of solitaire, while Hope was kneeling on a chair beside him with her elbows on the table. Mr. Langham had been troubled with insomnia of late, and so it often happened that when Alice returned from a ball she would find him sitting with a novel, or his game of solitaire, and Hope, who had crept down-stairs from her bed, dozing in front of the open fire and keeping him silent company. The father and the younger daughter were very close to one another, and had grown especially so since his wife had died and his son and heir had gone to college. This fourth member of the family was a great bond of sympathy and interest between them, and his triumphs and escapades at Yale were the chief subjects of their conversation. It was told by the directors of a great Western railroad, who had come to New York to discuss an important question with Mr. Langham, that they had been ushered down-stairs one night into his basement, where they had found the President of the Board and his daughter Hope working out a game of football on the billiard-table. They had chalked it off into what corresponded to five-yard lines, and they were hurling twenty-two chessmen across it in "flying wedges," and practising the several tricks which young Langham had intrusted to his sister under an oath of secrecy. The sight filled the directors with the horrible fear that business troubles had turned the President's mind, but after they had sat for half an hour perched on the high chairs around the table, while Hope excitedly explained the game to them, they decided that he was wiser than they knew, and each left the house regretting he had no son worthy enough to bring "that young girl" into the Far West.

"You are home early," said Mr. Langham, as Alice stood above him pulling at her gloves. "I thought you said you were going on to some dance."

"I was tired," his daughter answered.

"Well, when I'm out," commented Hope, "I won't come home at eleven o'clock. Alice always was a quitter."

"A what?" asked the older sister.

"Tell us what you had for dinner," said Hope. "I know it isn't nice to ask," she added, hastily, "but I always like to know."

"I don't remember," Miss Langham answered, smiling at her father, "except that he was very much sunburned and had most perplexing eyes."

"Oh, of course," assented Hope, "I suppose you mean by that that you talked with some man all through dinner. Well, I think there is a time for everything."

"Father," interrupted Miss Langham, "do you know many engineers—I mean do you come in contact with them through the railroads and mines you have an interest in? I am rather curious about them," she said, lightly. "They seem to be a most picturesque lot of young men."

"Engineers? Of course," said Mr. Langham, vaguely, with the ten of spades held doubtfully in air. "Sometimes we have to depend upon them altogether. We decide from what the engineering experts tell us whether we will invest in a thing or not."

"I don't think I mean the big men of the profession," said his daughter, doubtfully. "I mean those who do the rough work. The men who dig the mines and lay out the railroads. Do you know any of them?"

"Some of them," said Mr. Langham, leaning back and shuffling the cards for a new game. "Why?"

"Did you ever hear of a Mr. Robert Clay?"

Mr. Langham smiled as he placed the cards one above the other in even rows. "Very often," he said. "He sails to-morrow to open up the largest iron deposits in South America. He goes for the Valencia Mining Company. Valencia is the capital of Olancho, one of those little republics down there."

"Do you—are you interested in that company?" asked Miss Langham, seating herself before the fire and holding out her hands toward it. "Does Mr. Clay know that you are?"

"Yes—I am interested in it," Mr. Langham replied, studying the cards before him, "but I don't think Clay knows it—nobody knows it yet, except the president and the other officers." He lifted a card and put it down again in some indecision. "It's generally supposed to be operated by a company, but all the stock is owned by one man. As a matter of fact, my dear children," exclaimed Mr. Langham, as he placed a deuce of clubs upon a deuce of spades with a smile of content, "the Valencia Mining Company is your beloved father."

"Oh!" said Miss Langham, as she looked steadily into the fire.

Hope tapped her lips gently with the back of her hand to hide the fact that she was sleepy, and nudged her father's elbow. "You shouldn't have put the deuce there," she said, "you should have used it to build with on the ace."

II

A year before Mrs. Porter's dinner a tramp steamer on her way to the capital of Brazil had steered so close to the shores of Olancho that her solitary passenger could look into the caverns the waves had tunnelled in the limestone cliffs along the coast. The solitary passenger was Robert Clay, and he made a guess that the white palisades which fringed the base of the mountains along the shore had been forced up above the level of the sea many years before by some volcanic action. Olancho, as many people know, is situated on the northeastern coast of South America, and its shores are washed by the main equatorial current. From the deck of a passing vessel you can obtain but little idea of Olancho or of the abundance and tropical beauty which lies hidden away behind the rampart of mountains on her shore. You can see only their desolate dark-green front, and the white caves at their base, into which the waves rush with an echoing roar and in and out of which fly continually thousands of frightened bats.

The mining engineer on the rail of the tramp steamer observed this peculiar formation of the coast with listless interest, until he noted, when the vessel stood some thirty miles north of the harbor of Valencia, that the limestone formation had disappeared and that the waves now beat against the base of the mountains themselves. There were five of these mountains which jutted out into the ocean, and they suggested roughly the five knuckles of a giant hand clenched and lying flat upon the surface of the water. They extended for seven miles, and then the caverns in the palisades began again and continued on down the coast to the great cliffs that guard the harbor of Olancho's capital.

"The waves tunnelled their way easily enough until they ran up against those five mountains," mused the engineer, "and then they had to fall back." He walked to the captain's cabin and asked to look at a map of the coast-line. "I believe I won't go to Rio," he said later in the day; "I think I will drop off here at Valencia."

So he left the tramp steamer at that place and disappeared into the interior with an ox-cart and a couple of pack-mules, and returned to write a lengthy letter from the Consul's office to a Mr. Langham in the United States, knowing he was largely interested in mines and in mining. "There are five mountains filled with ore," Clay wrote, "which should be extracted by open-faced workings. I saw great masses of red hematite[1] lying exposed on the side of the mountain, only waiting a pick and shovel, and at one place there were five thousand tons in plain sight. I should call the stuff first-class Bessemer ore,[2] running about sixty-three per cent metallic iron. The people know it is there, but have no knowledge of its value, and are too lazy to ever work it themselves. As to transportation, it would only be necessary to run a freight railroad twenty miles along the sea-coast to the harbor of

---

1 A reddish mineral, the chief ore of iron.
2 A high-grade ore named after Henry Bessemer (1813–98), a British inventor particularly remembered for his method of making steel.

Valencia and dump your ore from your own pier into your own vessels. It would not, I think, be possible to ship direct from the mines themselves, even though, as I say, the ore runs right down into the water, because there is no place at which it would be safe for a large vessel to touch. I will look into the political side of it and see what sort of a concession I can get for you. I should think ten per cent of the output would satisfy them, and they would, of course, admit machinery and plant free of duty."

Six months after this communication had arrived in New York City, the Valencia Mining Company was formally incorporated, and a man named Van Antwerp, with two hundred workmen and a half-dozen assistants, was sent South to lay out the freight railroad, to erect the dumping-pier, and to strip the five mountains of their forests and underbrush. It was not a task for a holiday, but a stern, difficult, and perplexing problem, and Van Antwerp was not quite the man to solve it. He was stubborn, self-confident, and indifferent by turns. He did not depend upon his lieutenants, but jealously guarded his own opinions from the least question or discussion, and at every step he antagonized the easy-going people among whom he had come to work. He had no patience with their habits of procrastination, and he was continually offending their lazy good nature and their pride. He treated the rich planters, who owned the land between the mines and the harbor over which the freight railroad must run, with as little consideration as he showed the regiment of soldiers which the Government had farmed out to the company to serve as laborers in the mines. Six months after Van Antwerp had taken charge at Valencia, Clay, who had finished the railroad in Mexico of which King had spoken, was asked by telegraph to undertake the work of getting the ore out of the mountains he had discovered and shipping it North. He accepted the offer and was given the title of General Manager and Resident Director, and an enormous salary, and was also given to understand that the rough work of preparation had been accomplished, and that the more important service of picking up the five mountains and putting them in fragments into tramp steamers would continue under his direction. He had a letter of recall for Van Antwerp, and a letter of introduction to the Minister of Mines and Agriculture. Further than that he knew nothing of the work before him, but he concluded, from the fact that he had been paid the almost prohibitive sum he had asked for his services, that it must be important, or that he had reached that place in his career when he could stop actual work and live easily, as an expert, on the work of others.

Clay rolled along the coast from Valencia to the mines in a paddle-wheeled steamer that had served its usefulness on the Mississippi, and which had been rotting at the levees in New Orleans when Van Antwerp had chartered it to carry tools and machinery to the mines and to serve as a private launch for himself. It was a choice either of this steamer and landing in a small boat, or riding along the line of the unfinished railroad on horseback. Either route consumed six valuable hours, and Clay, who was anxious to see his new field of action, beat impatiently upon the rail of the rolling tub as it wallowed in the sea.

He spent the first three days after his arrival at the mines in the mountains, climbing them on foot and skirting their base on horseback, and sleeping where night overtook him. Van Antwerp did not accompany him on his tour of inspection through the mines, but delegated that duty to an engineer named MacWilliams, and to Weimer, the United States Consul at Valencia, who had served the company in many ways and who was in its closest confidence.

For three days the men toiled heavily over fallen trunks and trees, slippery with the moss of centuries, or slid backward on the rolling stones in the waterways, or clung to their ponies' backs to dodge the hanging creepers. At times for hours together they walked in single file, bent nearly double, and seeing nothing before them but the shining backs and shoulders of the negroes who hacked out the way for them to go.[1] And again they would come suddenly upon a precipice, and drink in the soft cool breath of the ocean, and look down thousands of feet upon the impenetrable green under which they had been crawling, out to where it met the sparkling surface of the Caribbean Sea. It was three days of unceasing activity while the sun shone, and of anxious questionings around the camp-fire when the darkness fell and when there were no sounds on the mountain-side but that of falling water in a distant ravine or the calls of the night-birds.

On the morning of the fourth day Clay and his attendants returned to camp and rode to where the men had just begun to blast away the sloping surface of the mountain.

As Clay passed between the zinc sheds and palm huts of the

---

1   A large percentage of slaves brought from Africa were sold throughout South America as early as the sixteenth century. Throughout the 1840s and 1850s, a number of Latin American nations abolished slavery; Brazil became the last nation in the New World to abolish slavery in 1888.

soldier-workmen, they came running out to meet him, and one, who seemed to be a leader, touched his bridle, and with his straw sombrero in his hand begged for a word with el Señor the Director.

The news of Clay's return had reached the opening, and the throb of the dummy-engines and the roar of the blasting ceased as the assistant-engineers came down the valley to greet the new manager. They found him seated on his horse gazing ahead of him, and listening to the story of the soldier, whose fingers, as he spoke, trembled in the air with all the grace and passion of his Southern nature, while back of him his companions stood humbly, in a silent chorus, with eager, supplicating eyes. Clay answered the man's speech curtly, with a few short words, in the Spanish patois in which he had been addressed, and then turned and smiled grimly upon the expectant group of engineers. He kept them waiting for some short space, while he looked them over carefully, as though he had never seen them before.

"Well, gentlemen," he said, "I'm glad to have you here all together. I am only sorry you didn't come in time to hear what this fellow has had to say. I don't as a rule listen that long to complaints, but he told me what I have seen for myself and what has been told me by others. I have been here three days now, and I assure you, gentlemen, that my easiest course would be to pack up my things and go home on the next steamer. I was sent down here to take charge of a mine in active operation, and I find—what? I find that in six months you have done almost nothing, and that the little you have condescended to do has been done so badly that it will have to be done over again; that you have not only wasted a half-year of time—and I can't tell how much money—but that you have succeeded in antagonizing all the people on whose good-will we are absolutely dependent; you have allowed your machinery to rust in the rain, and your workmen to rot with sickness. You have not only done nothing, but you haven't a blue print to show me what you meant to do. I have never in my life come across laziness and mismanagement and incompetency upon such a magnificent and reckless scale. You have not built the pier, you have not opened the freight road, you have not taken out an ounce of ore. You know more of Valencia than you know of these mines; you know it from the Alameda to the Canal. You can tell me what night the band plays in the Plaza, but you can't give me the elevation of one of these hills. You have spent your days on the pavements in front of cafés, and your nights in dance-halls, and you have been drawing salaries every month. I've more respect for these half-breeds that you've allowed to starve in this fever-bed than I have for you.[1] You have treated them worse than they'd treat a dog, and if any of them die, it's on your heads. You have put them in a fever-camp which you have not even taken the trouble to drain. Your commissariat is rotten, and you have let them drink all the rum they wanted. There is not one of you——"

The group of silent men broke, and one of them stepped forward and shook his forefinger at Clay.

"No man can talk to me like that," he said, warningly, "and think I'll work under him. I resign here and now."

"You what—" cried Clay, "you resign?"

He whirled his horse round with a dig of his spur and faced them.

"How dare you talk of resigning? I'll pack the whole lot of you back to New York on the first steamer, if I want to, and I'll give you such characters that you'll be glad to get a job carrying a transit.[2] You're in no position to talk of resigning yet—not one of you. Yes," he added, interrupting himself, "one of you is MacWilliams, the man who had charge of the railroad. It's no fault of his that the road's not working. I understand that he couldn't get the right of way from the people who owned the land, but I have seen what he has done, and his plans, and I apologize to him—to MacWilliams. As for the rest of you, I'll give you a month's trial. It will be a month before the next steamer could get here anyway, and I'll give you that long to redeem yourselves. At the end of that time we will have another talk, but you are here now only on your good behavior and on my sufferance. Good-morning."

As Clay had boasted, he was not the man to throw up his position because he found the part he had to play was not that of leading man, but rather one of general utility, and although it had been several years since it had been part of his duties to oversee

---

1 The racist epithet, "half-breed," refers to people of mixed racial origins. In this case, a mix of Indian and European or Indian and African, or a mix of all. In the racist hierarchy of the era, to be of "pure" Spanish or Portuguese ancestry put one at the top of the social scale. Indians and blacks were at the bottom of not only the social, but the economic and political scales as well. Here, Clay participates in the racist discourses of his era.

2 An instrument used by surveyors for measuring horizontal and vertical angles; an unpleasant and heavy piece of equipment to tote around jungles and over mountains.

the setting up of machinery and the policing of a mining camp, he threw himself as earnestly into the work before him as though to show his subordinates that it did not matter who did the work, so long as it was done. The men at first were sulky, resentful, and suspicious, but they could not long resist the fact that Clay was doing the work of five men and five different kinds of work, not only without grumbling, but apparently with the keenest pleasure.

He conciliated the rich coffee-planters who owned the land which he wanted for the freight road by calls of the most formal state and dinners of much less formality, for he saw that the iron mine had its social as well as its political side. And, with this fact in mind, he opened the railroad with great ceremony, and much music and feasting, and the first piece of ore taken out of the mine was presented to the wife of the Minister of the Interior in a cluster of diamonds, which made the wives of the other members of the Cabinet regret that their husbands had not chosen that portfolio. Six months followed of hard, unremitting work, during which time the great pier grew out into the bay from MacWilliams's railroad, and the face of the first mountain was scarred and torn of its green, and left in mangled nakedness, while the ringing of hammers and picks, and the racking blasts of dynamite, and the warning whistles of the dummy-engines drove away the accumulated silence of centuries.[1]

It had been a long, uphill fight, and Clay had enjoyed it mightily. Two unexpected events had contributed to help it. One was the arrival in Valencia of young Teddy Langham, who came ostensibly to learn the profession of which Clay was so conspicuous an example, and in reality to watch over his father's interests. He was put at Clay's elbow, and Clay made him learn in spite of himself, for he ruled him and MacWilliams, of both of whom he was very fond, as though, so they complained, they were the laziest and the most rebellious members of his entire staff. The second event of importance was the announcement made one day by young Langham that his father's physician had ordered rest in a mild climate, and that he and his daughters were coming in a month to spend the winter in Valencia, and to see how the son and heir had developed as a man of business.

The idea of Mr. Langham's coming to visit Olancho to inspect his new possessions was not a surprise to Clay. It had

---

1 A "dummy engine," or "steam dummy," was a steam engine enclosed in a wooden structure to resemble a railroad passenger car. They were popular in the US from the 1830s until the end of the Civil War.

occurred to him as possible before, especially after the son had come to join them there. The place was interesting and beautiful enough in itself to justify a visit, and it was only a ten days' voyage from New York. But he had never considered the chance of Miss Langham's coming, and when that was now not only possible but a certainty, he dreamed of little else. He lived as earnestly and toiled as indefatigably as before, but the place was utterly transformed for him. He saw it now as she would see it when she came, even while at the same time his own eyes retained their point of view. It was as though he had lengthened the focus of a glass, and looked beyond at what was beautiful and picturesque instead of what was near at hand and practicable. He found himself smiling with anticipation of her pleasure in the orchids hanging from the dead trees, high above the opening of the mine, and in the parrots hurling themselves like gayly colored missiles among the vines; and he considered the harbor at night with its colored lamps floating on the black water as a scene set for her eyes. He planned the dinners that he would give in her honor on the balcony of the great restaurant in the Plaza on those nights when the band played, and the señoritas circled in long lines between admiring rows of officers and caballeros. And he imagined how, when the ore-boats had been filled and his work had slackened, he would be free to ride with her along the rough mountain roads, between magnificent pillars of royal palms, or to venture forth in excursions down the bay, to explore the caves and to lunch on board the rolling paddle-wheel steamer, which he would have repainted and gilded for her coming.[1] He pictured himself acting as her guide over the great mines, answering her simple questions about the strange machinery, and the crew of workmen, and the local government by which he ruled two thousand men. It was not on account of any personal pride in the mines that he wanted her to see them, it was not because he had discovered and planned and opened them that he wished to show them to her, but as a curious spectacle that he hoped would give her a moment's interest.

But his keenest pleasure was when young Langham suggested that they should build a house for his people on the edge of the hill that jutted out over the harbor and the great ore pier. If this were done, Langham urged, it would be possible for him to see

---

1 A boat propelled by a steam-powered paddle-wheel; the sort of boat often associated with Mark Twain and his many adventures and stories about life on the Mississippi River.

much more of his family than he would be able to do were they installed in the city, five miles away.

"We can still live in the office at this end of the railroad," the boy said, "and then we shall have them within call at night when we get back from work; but if they are in Valencia, it will take the greater part of the evening going there and all of the night getting back, for I can't pass that club under three hours. It will keep us out of temptation."

"Yes, exactly," said Clay, with a guilty smile; "it will keep us out of temptation."

So they cleared away the underbrush, and put a double force of men to work on what was to be the most beautiful and comfortable bungalow on the edge of the harbor. It had blue and green and white tiles on the floors, and walls of bamboo, and a red roof of curved tiles to let in the air, and dragons' heads for water-spouts, and verandas as broad as the house itself. There was an open court in the middle hung with balconies looking down upon a splashing fountain, and to decorate this *patio* they levied upon people for miles around for tropical plants and colored mats and awnings. They cut down the trees that hid the view of the long harbor leading from the sea into Valencia, and planted a rampart of other trees to hide the iron-ore pier, and they sodded the raw spots where the men had been building, until the place was as completely transformed as though a fairy had waved her wand above it.

It was to be a great surprise, and they were all—Clay, MacWilliams, and Langham—as keenly interested in it as though each were preparing it for his honeymoon. They would be walking together in Valencia when one would say, "We ought to have that for the house," and without question they would march into the shop together and order whatever they fancied to be sent out to the house of the president of the mines on the hill. They stocked it with wine and linens, and hired a volante and six horses, and fitted out the driver with a new pair of boots that reached above his knees, and a silver jacket and a sombrero that was so heavy with braid that it flashed like a halo about his head in the sunlight, and he was ordered not to wear it until the ladies came, under penalty of arrest. It delighted Clay to find that it was only the beautiful things and the fine things of his daily routine that suggested her to him, as though she could not be associated in his mind with anything less worthy, and he kept saying to himself, "She will like this view from the end of the terrace," and "This will be her favorite walk," or "She will swing her hammock here," and "I know she will not fancy the rug that Weimer chose."

While this fairy palace was growing the three men lived as roughly as before in the wooden hut at the terminus of the freight road, three hundred yards below the house and hidden from it by an impenetrable rampart of brush and Spanish bayonet.[1] There was a rough road leading from it to the city, five miles away, which they had extended still farther up the hill to the Palms, which was the name Langham had selected for his father's house. And when it was finally finished they continued to live under the corrugated-zinc roof of their office-building, and locking up the Palms, left it in charge of a gardener and a watchman until the coming of its rightful owners.

It had been a viciously hot, close day, and even now the air came in sickening waves, like a blast from the engine-room of a steamer, and the heat lightning played round the mountains over the harbor and showed the empty wharves, and the black outlines of the steamers, and the white front of the Custom-House, and the long half-circle of twinkling lamps along the quay. MacWilliams and Langham sat panting on the lower steps of the office-porch considering whether they were too lazy to clean themselves and be rowed over to the city, where, as it was Sunday night, was promised much entertainment. They had been for the last hour trying to make up their minds as to this, and appealing to Clay to stop work and decide for them. But he sat inside at a table, figuring and writing under the green shade of a student's lamp and made no answer. The walls of Clay's office were of unplaned boards, bristling with splinters, and hung with blue prints and outline maps of the mine. A gaudily colored portrait of Madame la Presidenta, the noble and beautiful woman whom Alvarez, the President of Olancho, had lately married in Spain, was pinned to the wall above the table.[2] This table, with its green oil-cloth top, and the lamp, about which winged insects beat noisily, and an earthen water-jar—from which the water dripped

---

1 Spanish bayonet, a short-trunked yucca, with rigid, spine-tipped leaves and clusters of white flowers, found in the southern US and throughout tropical Latin America.

2 That President Alvarez marries a Spanish noblewoman (in this case, a countess), confirms his high social (and economic and political) standing in Olancho; he is such an important and impressive man, Davis implies, that he can attract Spanish royalty and need not "settle" for an Olanchoan.

as regularly as the ticking of a clock—were the only articles of furniture in the office. On a shelf at one side of the door lay the men's machetes, a belt of cartridges, and a revolver in a holster.

Clay rose from the table and stood in the light of the open door, stretching himself gingerly, for his joints were sore and stiff with fording streams and climbing the surfaces of rocks. The red ore and yellow mud of the mines were plastered over his boots and riding-breeches, where he had stood knee-deep in the water, and his shirt stuck to him like a wet bathing-suit, showing his ribs when he breathed and the curves of his broad chest. A ring of burning paper and hot ashes fell from his cigarette to his breast and burnt a hole through the cotton shirt, and he let it lie there and watched it burn with a grim smile.

"I wanted to see," he explained, catching the look of listless curiosity in MacWilliams's eye, "whether there was anything hotter than my blood. It's racing around like boiling water in a pot."

"Listen," said Langham, holding up his hand. "There goes the call for prayers in the convent, and now it's too late to go to town. I am glad, rather. I'm too tired to keep awake, and besides, they don't know how to amuse themselves in a civilized way—at least not in my way. I wish I could just drop in at home about now; don't you, MacWilliams? Just about this time up in God's country all the people are at the theatre, or they've just finished dinner and are sitting around sipping cool green mint, trickling through little lumps of ice. What I'd like—" he stopped and shut one eye and gazed, with his head on one side, at the unimaginative MacWilliams—"what I'd like to do now," he continued, thoughtfully, "would be to sit in the front row at a comic opera, *on the aisle.* The prima donna must be very, very beautiful, and sing most of her songs at me, and there must be three comedians, all good, and a chorus entirely composed of girls. I never could see why they have men in the chorus, anyway. No one ever looks at them. Now that's where I'd like to be. What would you like, MacWilliams?"

MacWilliams was a type with which Clay was intimately familiar, but to the college-bred Langham he was a revelation and a joy. He came from some little town in the West, and had learned what he knew of engineering at the transit's mouth, after he had first served his apprenticeship by cutting sage-brush and driving stakes. His life had been spent in Mexico and Central America, and he spoke of the home he had not seen in ten years with the aggressive loyalty of the confirmed wanderer, and he was known to prefer and to import canned corn and canned tomatoes in preference to eating the wonderful fruits of the country, because the former came from the States and tasted to him of home. He had crowded into his young life experiences that would have shattered the nerves of any other man with a more sensitive conscience and a less happy sense of humor; but these same experiences had only served to make him shrewd and self-confident and at his ease when the occasion or difficulty came.

He pulled meditatively on his pipe and considered Langham's question deeply, while Clay and the younger boy sat with their arms upon their knees and waited for his decision in thoughtful silence.

"I'd like to go to the theatre, too," said MacWilliams, with an air as though to show that he also was possessed of artistic tastes. "I'd like to see a comical chap I saw once in '80—oh, long ago—before I joined the P.Q. & M. He *was* funny. His name was Owens; that was his name, John E. Owens——"

"Oh, for heaven's sake, MacWilliams," protested Langham, in dismay; "he's been dead for five years."

"Has he?" said MacWilliams thoughtfully. "Well—" he concluded, unabashed, "I can't help that, he's the one I'd like to see best."

"You can have another wish, Mac, you know," urged Langham, "can't he, Clay?"

Clay nodded gravely, and MacWilliams frowned again in thought. "No," he said after an effort, "Owens, John E. Owens; that's the one I want to see."

"Well, now I want another wish, too," said Langham. "I move we can each have two wishes. I wish——"

"Wait until I've had mine," said Clay. "You've had one turn. I want to be in a place I know in Vienna. It's not hot like this, but cool and fresh. It's an open, out-of-door concert garden, with hundreds of colored lights and trees, and there's always a breeze coming through. And Eduard Strauss,[1] the son, you know, leads the orchestra there, and they play nothing but waltzes, and he stands in front of them, and begins by raising himself on his toes,

---

1 Eduard Strauss (1835–1916), Viennese conductor, son of musician and conductor Johann Strauss (1804–49), and brother to Johann Strauss (1825–99) and Josef Strauss (1827–70), both musicians and conductors. Johann Strauss the younger, perhaps the most celebrated member of the family, wrote such famous waltzes and operettas as "The Blue Danube" (1867) and *Die Fledermaus* (1874).

and then he lifts his shoulders gently—and then sinks back again and raises his baton as though he were drawing the music out after it, and the whole place seems to rock and move. It's like being picked up and carried on the deck of a yacht over great waves; and all around you are the beautiful Viennese women and those tall Austrian officers in their long, blue coats and flat hats and silver swords. And there are cool drinks—" continued Clay, with his eyes fixed on the coming storm—"all sorts of cool drinks—in high, thin glasses, full of ice, all the ice you want——"

"Oh, drop it, will you?" cried Langham, with a shrug of his damp shoulders. "I can't stand it. I'm parching."

"Wait a minute," interrupted MacWilliams, leaning forward and looking into the night. "Some one's coming." There was a sound down the road of hoofs and the rattle of the land-crabs as they scrambled off into the bushes, and two men on horseback came suddenly out of the darkness and drew rein in the light from the open door. The first was General Mendoza, the leader of the Opposition in the Senate, and the other, his orderly. The General dropped his Panama hat to his knee and bowed in the saddle three times.

"Good evening, your Excellency," said Clay, rising. "Tell that peon to get my coat, will you?" he added, turning to Langham. Langham clapped his hands, and the clanging of a guitar ceased, and their servant and cook came out from the back of the hut and held the General's horse while he dismounted. "Wait until I get you a chair," said Clay. "You'll find those steps rather bad for white duck."[1]

"I am fortunate in finding you at home," said the officer, smiling and showing his white teeth. "The telephone is not working. I tried at the club, but I could not call you."

"It's the storm, I suppose," Clay answered, as he struggled into his jacket. "Let me offer you something to drink." He entered the house, and returned with several bottles on a tray and a bundle of cigars. The Spanish-American poured himself out a glass of water, mixing it with Jamaica rum, and said, smiling again, "It is a saying of your countrymen that when a man first comes to Olancho he puts a little rum into his water, and that when he is here some time he puts a little water in his rum."

"Yes," laughed Clay. "I'm afraid that's true."

There was a pause while the men sipped at their glasses, and looked at the horses and the orderly. The clanging of the guitar

---

1 A heavily woven cotton or linen fabric, often made into white trousers.

began again from the kitchen. "You have a very beautiful view here of the harbor, yes," said Mendoza. He seemed to enjoy the pause after his ride, and to be in no haste to begin on the object of his errand. MacWilliams and Langham eyed each other covertly, and Clay examined the end of his cigar, and they all waited.

"And how are the mines progressing, eh?" asked the officer, genially. "You find much good iron in them, they tell me."

"Yes, we are doing very well," Clay assented; "it was difficult at first, but now that things are in working order, we are getting out about ten thousand tons a month. We hope to increase that soon to twenty thousand when the new openings are developed and our shipping facilities are in better shape."

"So much!" exclaimed the General, pleasantly. "Of which the Government of my country is to get its share of ten per cent—one thousand tons! It is munificent!" He laughed and shook his head slyly at Clay, who smiled in dissent.

"But you see, sir," said Clay, "you cannot blame us. The mines have always been there, before this Government came in, before the Spaniards were here, before there was any Government at all, but there was not the capital to open them up, I suppose, or—and it needed a certain energy to begin the attack. Your people let the chance go, and, as it turned out, I think they were very wise in doing so. They get ten per cent of the output. That's ten per cent on nothing, for the mines really didn't exist, as far as you were concerned, until we came, did they? They were just so much waste land, and they would have remained so. And look at the price we paid down before we cut a tree. Three millions of dollars; that's a good deal of money. It will be some time before we realize anything on that investment."

Mendoza shook his head and shrugged his shoulders. "I will be frank with you," he said, with the air of one to whom dissimulation is difficult. "I come here to-night on an unpleasant errand, but it is with me a matter of duty, and I am a soldier, to whom duty is the foremost ever. I have come to tell you, Mr. Clay, that we, the Opposition, are not satisfied with the manner in which the Government has disposed of these great iron deposits. When I say not satisfied, my dear friend, I speak most moderately. I should say that we are surprised and indignant, and we are determined the wrong it has done our country shall be righted. I have the honor to have been chosen to speak for our party on this most important question, and on next Tuesday, sir," the General stood up and bowed, as though he were before a great assembly, "I will rise in the Senate and move a vote of want of confidence in the Government for the manner in which it has given away the richest possessions in the storehouse of my country, giving it not only to aliens, but for a pittance, for a share which is not a share, but a bribe, to blind the eyes of the people. It has been a shameful bargain, and I cannot say who is to blame; I accuse no one. But I suspect, and I will demand an investigation; I will demand that the value not of one-tenth, but of one-half of all the iron that your company takes out of Olancho shall be paid into the treasury of the State. And I come to you to-night, as the Resident Director, to inform you beforehand of my intention. I do not wish to take you unprepared. I do not blame your people; they are business men, they know how to make good bargains, they get what they best can. That is the rule of trade, but they have gone too far, and I advise you to communicate with your people in New York and learn what they are prepared to offer now—now that they have to deal with men who do not consider their own interests but the interests of their country."

Mendoza made a sweeping bow and seated himself, frowning dramatically, with folded arms. His voice still hung in the air, for he had spoken as earnestly as though he imagined himself already standing in the hall of the Senate championing the cause of the people.

MacWilliams looked up at Clay from where he sat on the steps below him, but Clay did not notice him, and there was no sound, except the quick sputtering of the nicotine in Langham's pipe, at which he pulled quickly, and which was the only outward sign the boy gave of his interest. Clay shifted one muddy boot over the other and leaned back with his hands stuck in his belt.

"Why didn't you speak of this sooner?" he asked.

"Ah, yes, that is fair," said the General, quickly. "I know that it is late, and I regret it, and I see that we cause you inconvenience; but how could I speak sooner when I was ignorant of what was going on? I have been away with my troops. I am a soldier first, a politician after. During the last year I have been engaged in guarding the frontier. No news comes to a General in the field moving from camp to camp and always in the saddle; but I may venture to hope, sir, that news has come to you of me?"

Clay pressed his lips together and bowed his head.

"We have heard of your victories, General, yes," he said; "and on your return you say you found things had not been going to your liking?"

"That is it," assented the other, eagerly. "I find that indignation reigns on every side. I find my friends complaining of the railroad which you run across their land. I find that fifteen hundred soldiers are turned into laborers, with picks and spades, working by the side of negroes and your Irish; they have not been paid their wages, and they have been fed worse than though they were on the march; sickness and——"

Clay moved impatiently and dropped his boot heavily on the porch.

"That was true at first," he interrupted, "but it is not so now. I should be glad, General, to take you over the men's quarters at any time. As for their not having been paid, they were never paid by their own Government before they came to us and for the same reason, because the petty officers kept back the money, just as they have always done. But the men are paid now. However, this is not of the most importance. Who is it that complains of the terms of our concession?"

"Every one!" exclaimed Mendoza, throwing out his arms, "and they ask, moreover, this: they ask why, if this mine is so rich, why was not the stock offered here to us in this country? Why was it not put on the market, that any one might buy? We have rich men in Olancho, why should not they benefit first of all others by the wealth of their own lands? But no! we are not asked to buy. All the stock is taken in New York, no one benefits but the State, and it receives only ten per cent. It is monstrous!"

"I see," said Clay, gravely. "That had not occurred to me before. They feel they have been slighted. I see." He paused for a moment as if in serious consideration. "Well," he added, "that might be arranged."

He turned and jerked his head toward the open door. "If you boys mean to go to town to-night, you'd better be moving," he said. The two men rose together and bowed silently to their guest.

"I should like if Mr. Langham would remain a moment with us," said Mendoza, politely. "I understand that it is his father who controls the stock of the company. If we discuss any arrangement it might be well if he were here."

Clay was sitting with his chin on his breast, and he did not look up, nor did the young man turn to him for any prompting. "I'm not down here as my father's son," he said, "I am an employee of Mr. Clay's. He represents the company. Good night, sir."

"You think, then," said Clay, "that if your friends were given an opportunity to subscribe to the stock they would feel less resentful toward us? They would think it was fairer to all?"

"I know it," said Mendoza; "why should the stock go out of the country when those living here are able to buy it?"

"Exactly," said Clay, "of course. Can you tell me this, General? Are the gentlemen who want to buy stock in the mine the same men who are in the Senate? The men who are objecting to the terms of our concession?"

"With a few exceptions they are the same men."

Clay looked out over the harbor at the lights of the town, and the General twirled his hat around his knee and gazed with appreciation at the stars above him.

"Because if they are," Clay continued, "and they succeed in getting our share cut down from ninety per cent to fifty per cent, they must see that the stock would be worth just forty per cent less than it is now."

"That is true," assented the other. "I have thought of that, and if the Senators in Opposition were given a chance to subscribe, I am sure they would see that it is better wisdom to drop their objections to the concession, and as stockholders allow you to keep ninety per cent of the output. And, again," continued Mendoza, "it is really better for the country that the money should go to its people than that it should be stored up in the vaults of the treasury, when there is always the danger that the President will seize it; or, if not this one, the next one."

"I should think—that is—it seems to me," said Clay, with careful consideration, "that your Excellency might be able to render us great help in this matter yourself. We need a friend among the Opposition. In fact—I see where you could assist us in many ways, where your services would be strictly in the line of your public duty and yet benefit us very much. Of course I cannot speak authoritatively without first consulting Mr. Langham; but I should think he would allow you personally to purchase as large a block of the stock as you could wish, either to keep yourself or to resell and distribute among those of your friends in Opposition where it would do the most good."

Clay looked over inquiringly to where Mendoza sat in the light of the open door, and the General smiled faintly, and emitted a pleased little sigh of relief. "Indeed," continued Clay, "I should think Mr. Langham might even save you the formality of purchasing the stock outright by sending you its money equivalent. I beg your pardon," he asked, interrupting himself, "does your orderly understand English?"

"He does not," the General assured him, eagerly, dragging his chair a little closer.

"Suppose now that Mr. Langham were to put fifty or let us say sixty thousand dollars to your account in the Valencia Bank, do you think this vote of want of confidence in the Government on the question of our concession would still be moved?"

"I am sure it would not," exclaimed the leader of the Opposition, nodding his head violently.

"Sixty thousand dollars," repeated Clay, slowly, "for yourself; and do you think, General, that were you paid that sum you would be able to call off your friends, or would they make a demand for stock also?"

"Have no anxiety at all, they do just what I say," returned Mendoza in an eager whisper. "If I say 'It is all right, I am satisfied with what the Government has done in my absence,' it is enough. And I will say it, I give you the word of a soldier, I will say it. I will not move a vote of want of confidence on Tuesday. You need go no further than myself. I am glad that I am powerful enough to serve you, and if you doubt me"—he struck his heart and bowed with a deprecatory smile—"you need not pay in the money in exchange for the stock all at the same time. You can pay ten thousand this year, and next year ten thousand more and so on, and so feel confident that I shall have the interests of the mine always in my heart. Who knows what may not happen in a year? I may be able to serve you even more. Who knows how long the present Government will last? But I give you my word of honor, no matter whether I be in Opposition or at the head of the Government, if I receive every six months the retaining fee of which you speak, I will be your representative. And my friends can do nothing. I despise them. *I* am the Opposition. You have done well, my dear sir, to consider me alone."

Clay turned in his chair and looked back of him through the office to the room beyond.

"Boys," he called, "you can come out now."

He rose and pushed his chair away and beckoned to the orderly who sat in the saddle holding the General's horse. Langham and MacWilliams came out and stood in the open door, and Mendoza rose and looked at Clay.

"You can go now," Clay said to him, quietly. "And you can rise in the Senate on Tuesday and move your vote of want of confidence and object to our concession, and when you have resumed your seat the Secretary of Mines will rise in his turn and tell the Senate how you stole out here in the night and tried to blackmail me, and begged me to bribe you to be silent, and that you offered to throw over your friends and to take all that we would give you and keep it yourself. That will make you popular with your friends, and will show the Government just what sort of a leader it has working against it."

Clay took a step forward and shook his finger in the officer's face. "Try to break that concession; try it. It was made by one Government to a body of honest, decent business men, with a Government of their own back of them, and if you interfere with our conceded rights to work those mines, I'll have a man-of-war down here with white paint on her hull, and she'll blow you and your little republic back up there into the mountains. Now you can go."

Mendoza had straightened with surprise when Clay first began to speak, and had then bent forward slightly as though he meant to interrupt him. His eyebrows were lowered in a straight line, and his lips moved quickly.

"You poor—" he began, contemptuously. "Bah," he exclaimed, "you're a fool; I should have sent a servant to talk with you. You are a child—but you are an insolent child," he cried, suddenly, his anger breaking out, "and I shall punish you. You dare to call me names! You shall fight me, you shall fight me to-morrow. You have insulted an officer, and you shall meet me at once, to-morrow."

"If I meet you to-morrow," Clay replied, "I will thrash you for your impertinence. The only reason I don't do it now is because you are on my doorstep. You had better not meet me to-morrow, or at any other time. And I have no leisure to fight duels with anybody." "You are a coward," returned the other, quietly, "and I tell you so before my servant."

Clay gave a short laugh and turned to MacWilliams in the doorway.

"Hand me my gun, MacWilliams," he said, "it's on the shelf to the right."

MacWilliams stood still and shook his head. "Oh, let him alone," he said. "You've got him where you want him."

"Give me the gun, I tell you," repeated Clay. "I'm not going to hurt him, I'm only going to show him how I can shoot."

MacWilliams moved grudgingly across the porch and brought back the revolver and handed it to Clay. "Look out now," he said, "it's loaded."

At Clay's words the General had retreated hastily to his horse's head and had begun unbuckling the strap of his holster, and the orderly reached back into the boot for his carbine. Clay told him in Spanish to throw up his hands, and the man, with a frightened look at his officer, did as the revolver suggested. Then Clay motioned with his empty hand for the other to desist. "Don't do that," he said, "I'm not going to hurt you; I'm only going to frighten you a little."

He turned and looked at the student lamp inside, where it stood on the table in full view. Then he raised his revolver. He did not apparently hold it away from him by the butt, as other men do, but let it lie in the palm of his hand, into which it seemed to fit like the hand of a friend. His first shot broke the top of the glass chimney, the second shattered the green globe around it, the third put out the light, and the next drove the lamp crashing to the floor. There was a wild yell of terror from the back of the house, and the noise of a guitar falling down a flight of steps. "I have probably killed a very good cook," said Clay, "as I should as certainly kill you, if I were to meet you. Langham," he continued, "go tell that cook to come back."

The General sprang into his saddle, and the altitude it gave him seemed to bring back some of the jauntiness he had lost.

"That was very pretty," he said; "you have been a cowboy, so they tell me. It is quite evident by your manners. No matter, if we do not meet to-morrow it will be because I have more serious work to do. Two months from to-day there will be a new Government in Olancho and a new President, and the mines will have a new director. I have tried to be your friend, Mr. Clay. See how you like me for an enemy. Good night, gentlemen."

"Good night," said MacWilliams, unmoved. "Please ask your man to close the gate after you."

When the sound of the hoofs had died away the men still stood in an uncomfortable silence, with Clay twirling the revolver around his middle finger. "I'm sorry I had to make a gallery play of that sort," he said. "But it was the only way to make that sort of man understand."

Langham sighed and shook his head ruefully.

"Well," he said, "I thought all the trouble was over, but it looks to me as though it had just begun. So far as I can see they're going to give the governor a run for his money yet."

Clay turned to MacWilliams.

"How many of Mendoza's soldiers have we in the mines, Mac?" he asked.

"About fifteen hundred," MacWilliams answered. "But you ought to hear the way they talk of him."

"They do, eh?" said Clay, with a smile of satisfaction. "That's good. 'Six hundred slaves who hate their masters.' What do they say about me?"

"Oh, they think you're all right. They know you got them their pay and all that. They'd do a lot for you."

"Would they fight for me?" asked Clay.

MacWilliams looked up and laughed uneasily. "I don't know," he said. "Why, old man? What do you mean to do?"

"Oh, I don't know," Clay answered. "I was just wondering whether I should like to be President of Olancho."

III

The Langhams were to arrive on Friday, and during the week before that day Clay went about with a long slip of paper in his pocket which he would consult earnestly in corners, and upon which he would note down the things that they had left undone. At night he would sit staring at it and turning it over in much concern, and would beg Langham to tell him what he could have meant when he wrote "see Weimer," or "clean brasses," or "S.Q.M." "Why should I see Weimer?" he would exclaim, "and which brasses, and what does S.Q.M. stand for, for heaven's sake?"

They held a full-dress rehearsal in the bungalow to improve its state of preparation, and drilled the servants and talked English to them, so that they would know what was wanted when the young ladies came. It was an interesting exercise, and had the three young men been less serious in their anxiety to welcome the coming guests they would have found themselves very amusing— as when Langham would lean over the balcony in the court and shout back into the kitchen, in what was supposed to be an imitation of his sister's manner, "Bring my coffee and rolls—and don't take all day about it either," while Clay and MacWilliams stood anxiously below to head off the servants when they carried in a can of hot water instead of bringing the horses round to the door, as they had been told to do.

"Of course it's a bit rough and all that," Clay would say, "but they have only to tell us what they want changed and we can have it ready for them in an hour."

"Oh, my sisters are all right," Langham would reassure him; "they'll think it's fine. It will be like camping-out to them, or a picnic. They'll understand."

But to make sure, and to "test his girders," as Clay put it, they gave a dinner, and after that a breakfast. The President came to the first, with his wife, the Countess Manuelata, Madame la Presidenta, and Captain Stuart, late of the Gordon Highlanders, and now in command of the household troops at the Government House and of the body-guard of the President.[1] He was a friend of Clay's and popular with every one present, except for the fact that he occupied this position, instead of serving his own Government in his own army. Some people said he had been crossed in love, others, less sentimental, that he had forged a check or mixed up the mess accounts of his company. But Clay and MacWilliams said it concerned no one why he was there, and then emphasized the remark by picking a quarrel with a man who had given an unpleasant reason for it. Stuart, so far as they were concerned, could do no wrong.

The dinner went off very well, and the President consented to dine with them in a week, on the invitation of young Langham, to meet his father.

"Miss Langham is very beautiful, they tell me," Madame Alvarez said to Clay. "I heard of her one winter in Rome; she was presented there and much admired."

"Yes, I believe she is considered very beautiful," Clay said. "I have only just met her, but she has travelled a great deal and knows every one who is of interest, and I think you will like her very much."

"I mean to like her," said the woman. "There are very few of the native ladies who have seen much of the world beyond a trip to Paris, where they live in their hotels and at the dressmaker's while their husbands enjoy themselves; and sometimes I am rather heart-sick for my home and my own people. I was overjoyed when I heard Miss Langham was to be with us this winter. But you must not keep her out here to yourselves. It is too far and too selfish. She must spend some time with me at the Government House."

---

1 The Gordon Highlanders, two Scottish regiments ultimately combined into one unit, were originally raised in 1787, and served with distinction in Holland, Egypt, and India, and elsewhere in the British empire. The Highlanders also battled Napoleon's forces in Portugal and Spain, and fought against the French at Waterloo in 1815. The history of the Gordon Highlanders effectively ended in 1994 when the unit was absorbed into a new Scottish regiment named, simply, "The Highlanders." Although Davis refers to Stuart as "English," his family would doubtlessly trace its ancestry back to Scotland.

"Yes," said Clay, "I am afraid of that. I am afraid the young ladies will find it rather lonely out here."

"Ah, no," exclaimed the woman, quickly. "You have made it beautiful, and it is only a half-hour's ride, except when it rains," she added, laughing, "and then it is almost as easy to row as to ride."

"I will have the road repaired," interrupted the President. "It is my wish, Mr. Clay, that you will command me in every way; I am most desirous to make the visit of Mr. Langham agreeable to him, he is doing so much for us."

The breakfast was given later in the week, and only men were present. They were the rich planters and bankers of Valencia, generals in the army, and members of the Cabinet, and officers from the tiny war-ship in the harbor. The breeze from the bay touched them through the open doors, the food and wine cheered them, and the eager courtesy and hospitality of the three Americans pleased and flattered them. They were of a people who better appreciate the amenities of life than its sacrifices.

The breakfast lasted far into the afternoon, and, inspired by the success of the banquet, Clay quite unexpectedly found himself on his feet with his hand on his heart, thanking the guests for the good-will and assistance which they had given him in his work. "I have tramped down your coffee-plants, and cut away your forests, and disturbed your sleep with my engines, and you have not complained," he said, in his best Spanish; "and we will show that we are not ungrateful."

Then Weimer, the Consul, spoke, and told them that in his Annual Consular Report, which he had just forwarded to the State Department, he had related how ready the Government of Olancho had been to assist the American company. "And I hope," he concluded, "that you will allow me, gentlemen, to propose the health of President Alvarez and the members of his Cabinet."

The men rose to their feet, one by one, filling their glasses and laughing and saying, "Viva el Gobernador," until they were all standing. Then, as they looked at one another and saw only the faces of friends, some one of them cried, suddenly, "To President Alvarez, Dictator of Olancho!"[1]

The cry was drowned in a yell of exultation, and men sprang cheering to their chairs waving their napkins above their heads,

---

1 In the company of friends, Alvarez's supporters reveal that Olancho may not be quite as democratic as they otherwise pretend.

and those who wore swords drew them and flashed them in the air, and the quiet, lazy good nature of the breakfast was turned into an uproarious scene of wild excitement. Clay pushed back his chair from the head of the table with an anxious look at the servants gathered about the open door, and Weimer clutched frantically at Langham's elbow and whispered, "What did I say? For heaven's sake, how did it begin?"

The outburst ceased as suddenly as it had started, and old General Rojas, the Vice-President, called out, "What is said is said, but it must not be repeated."

Stuart waited until after the rest had gone, and Clay led him out to the end of the veranda. "Now will you kindly tell me what that was?" Clay asked. "It didn't sound like champagne."

"No," said the other, "I thought you knew. Alvarez means to proclaim himself Dictator, if he can, before the spring elections."

"And are you going to help him?"

"Of course," said the Englishman, simply.

"Well, that's all right," said Clay, "but there's no use shouting the fact all over the shop like that—and they shouldn't drag me into it."

Stuart laughed easily and shook his head. "It won't be long before you'll be in it yourself," he said.

Clay awoke early Friday morning to hear the shutters beating viciously against the side of the house, and the wind rushing through the palms, and the rain beating in splashes on the zinc roof. It did not come soothingly and in a steady downpour, but brokenly, like the rush of waves sweeping over a rough beach. He turned on the pillow and shut his eyes again with the same impotent and rebellious sense of disappointment that he used to feel when he had wakened as a boy and found it storming on his holiday, and he tried to sleep once more in the hope that when he again awoke the sun would be shining in his eyes; but the storm only slackened and did not cease, and the rain continued to fall with dreary, relentless persistence. The men climbed the muddy road to the Palms, and viewed in silence the wreck which the night had brought to their plants and garden paths. Rivulets of muddy water had cut gutters over the lawn and poured out from under the veranda, and plants and palms lay bent and broken, with their broad leaves bedraggled and coated with mud. The harbor and the encircling mountains showed dimly through a curtain of warm, sticky rain. To something that Langham said of making the best of it, MacWilliams replied, gloomily, that he would not be at all surprised if the ladies refused to leave the ship and demanded to be taken home immediately. "I am sorry," Clay said, simply; "I wanted them to like it."

The men walked back to the office in grim silence, and took turns in watching with a glass the arms of the semaphore, three miles below, at the narrow opening of the bay.[1] Clay smiled nervously at himself, with a sudden sinking at the heart, and with a hot blush of pleasure, as he thought of how often he had looked at its great arms out-lined like a mast against the sky, and thanked it in advance for telling him that she was near. In the harbor below, the vessels lay with bare yards and empty decks, the wharves were deserted, and only an occasional small boat moved across the beaten surface of the bay.

But at twelve o'clock MacWilliams lowered the glass quickly, with a little gasp of excitement, rubbed its moist lens on the inside of his coat and turned it again toward a limp strip of bunting that was crawling slowly up the halyards of the semaphore. A second dripping rag answered it from the semaphore in front of the Custom-House, and MacWilliams laughed nervously and shut the glass.

"It's red," he said; "they've come."

They had planned to wear white duck suits, and go out in a launch with a flag flying, and they had made MacWilliams purchase a red cummerbund and a pith helmet; but they tumbled into the launch now, wet and bedraggled as they were, and raced Weimer in his boat, with the American flag clinging to the pole, to the side of the big steamer as she drew slowly into the bay. Other rowboats and launches and lighters began to push out from the wharves, men appeared under the sagging awnings of the bare houses along the river front, and the custom and health officers in shining oilskins and puffing damp cigars clambered over the side.

"I see them," cried Langham, jumping up and rocking the boat in his excitement. "There they are in the bow. That's Hope waving. Hope! hullo, Hope!" he shouted, "hullo!" Clay recognized her standing between the younger sister and her father, with the rain beating on all of them, and waving her hand to Langham. The men took off their hats, and as they pulled up alongside she bowed to Clay and nodded brightly. They sent

---

1 Semaphore, an apparatus used for visual signaling by adjusting the positions of one or more moveable arms. Semaphore also describes the technique of holding a flag in either hand and adjusting the arm positions to signal messages.

Langham up the gangway first, and waited until he had made his greetings to his family alone.

"We have had a terrible trip, Mr. Clay," Miss Langham said to him, beginning, as people will, with the last few days, as though they were of the greatest importance; "and we could see nothing of you at the mines at all as we passed—only a wet flag, and a lot of very friendly workmen, who cheered and fired off pans of dynamite."

"They did, did they?" said Clay, with a satisfied nod. "That's all right, then. That was a royal salute in your honor. Kirkland had that to do. He's the foreman of A opening. I am awfully sorry about this rain—it spoils everything."

"I hope it hasn't spoiled our breakfast," said Mr. Langham. "We haven't eaten anything this morning, because we wanted a change of diet, and the captain told us we should be on shore before now."

"We have some carriages for you at the wharf, and we will drive you right out to the Palms," said young Langham. "It's shorter by water, but there's a hill that the girls couldn't climb to-day. That's the house we built for you, Governor, with the flag-pole, up there on the hill; and there's your ugly old pier; and that's where we live, in the little shack above it, with the tin roof; and that opening to the right is the terminus of the railroad MacWilliams built. Where's MacWilliams? Here, Mac, I want you to know my father. This is MacWilliams, sir, of whom I wrote you."

There was some delay about the baggage, and in getting the party together in the boats that Langham and the Consul had brought; and after they had stood for some time on the wet dock, hungry and damp, it was rather aggravating to find that the carriages which Langham had ordered to be at one pier had gone to another. So the new arrivals sat rather silently under the shed of the levee on a row of cotton-bales, while Clay and MacWilliams raced off after the carriages.

"I wish we didn't have to keep the hood down," young Langham said, anxiously, as they at last proceeded heavily up the muddy streets; "it makes it so hot, and you can't see anything. Not that it's worth seeing in all this mud and muck, but it's great when the sun shines. We had planned it all so differently."

He was alone with his family now in one carriage, and the other men and the servants were before them in two others. It seemed an interminable ride to them all—to the strangers and to the men who were anxious that they should be pleased. They left the city at last, and toiled along the limestone road to the Palms, rocking from side to side and sinking in ruts filled with rushing water. When they opened the flap of the hood the rain beat in on them, and when they closed it they stewed in a damp, warm atmosphere of wet leather and horse-hair.

"This is worse than a Turkish bath," said Hope, faintly. "Don't you live anywhere, Ted?"

"Oh, it's not far now," said the younger brother, dismally; but even as he spoke the carriage lurched forward and plunged to one side and came to a halt, and they could hear the streams rushing past the wheels like the water at the bow of a boat. A wet, black face appeared at the opening of the hood, and a man spoke despondently in Spanish.

"He says we're stuck in the mud," explained Langham. He looked at them so beseechingly and so pitifully, with the perspiration streaming down his face, and his clothes damp and bedraggled, that Hope leaned back and laughed, and his father patted him on the knee. "It can't be any worse," he said, cheerfully; "it must mend now. It is not your fault, Ted, that we're starving and lost in the mud."

Langham looked out to find Clay and MacWilliams knee-deep in the running water, with their shoulders against the muddy wheels, and the driver lashing at the horses and dragging at their bridles. He sprang out to their assistance, and Hope, shaking off her sister's detaining hands, jumped out after him, laughing. She splashed up the hill to the horses' heads, motioning to the driver to release his hold on their bridles.

"That is not the way to treat a horse," she said. "Let me have them. Are you men all ready down there?" she called. Each of the three men glued a shoulder to a wheel, and clenched his teeth and nodded. "All right, then," Hope called back. She took hold of the huge Mexican bits close to the mouth, where the pressure was not so cruel, and then, coaxing and tugging by turns, and slipping as often as the horses themselves, she drew them out of the mud, and with the help of the men back of the carriage pulled it clear until it stood free again at the top of the hill. Then she released her hold on the bridles and looked down, in dismay, at her frock and hands, and then up at the three men. They appeared so utterly miserable and forlorn in their muddy garments, and with their faces washed with the rain and perspiration, that the girl gave way suddenly to an uncontrollable shriek of delight. The men stared blankly at her for a moment, and then inquiringly at one another, and as the humor of the situation struck them they burst into an echoing shout of laughter which rose above the noise of the wind and rain, and before which the disappointments and trials of the morning were swept away. Before they reached the Palms the sun was out and shining with fierce brilliancy, reflecting its rays on every damp leaf, and drinking up each glistening pool of water.

MacWilliams and Clay left the Langhams alone together, and returned to the office, where they assured each other again and again that there was no doubt, from what each had heard different members of the family say, that they were greatly pleased with all that had been prepared for them.

"They think it's fine!" said young Langham, who had run down the hill to tell them about it. "I tell you, they are pleased. I took them all over the house, and they just exclaimed every minute. Of course," he said, dispassionately, "I thought they'd like it, but I had no idea it would please them as much as it has. My Governor is so delighted with the place that he's sitting out there on the veranda now, rocking himself up and down and taking long breaths of sea air, just as though he owned the whole coast-line."

Langham dined with his people that night, Clay and MacWilliams having promised to follow him up the hill later. It was a night of much moment to them all, and the two men ate their dinner in silence, each considering what the coming of the strangers might mean to him.

As he was leaving the room MacWilliams stopped and hovered uncertainly in the doorway.

"Are you going to get yourself into a dress-suit to-night?" he asked. Clay said that he thought he would; he wanted to feel quite clean once more.

"Well, all right, then," the other returned, reluctantly. "I'll do it for this once, if you mean to, but you needn't think I'm going to make a practise of it, for I'm not. I haven't worn a dress-suit," he continued, as though explaining his principles in the matter, "since your spread when we opened the railroad—that's six months ago; and the time before that I wore one at MacGolderick's funeral. MacGolderick blew himself up at Puerto Truxillo, shooting rocks for the breakwater. We never found all of him, but we gave what we could get together as fine a funeral as those natives ever saw. The boys, they wanted to make him look respectable, so they asked me to lend them my dress-suit, but I told them I meant to wear it myself. That's how I came to wear a dress-suit at a funeral. It was either me or MacGolderick."

"MacWilliams," said Clay, as he stuck the toe of one boot into the heel of the other, "if I had your imagination I'd give up rail-roading and take to writing war clouds for the newspapers."

"Do you mean you don't believe that story?" MacWilliams demanded sternly.

"I do," said Clay, "I mean I don't."

"Well, let it go," returned MacWilliams, gloomily; "but there's been funerals for less than that, let me tell you."

A half-hour later MacWilliams appeared in the door and stood gazing attentively at Clay arranging his tie before a hand-glass, and then at himself in his unusual apparel.

"No wonder you voted to dress up," he exclaimed, finally, in a tone of personal injury. "That's not a dress-suit you've got on anyway. It hasn't any tails. And I hope for your sake, Mr. Clay," he continued, his voice rising in plaintive indignation, "that you are not going to play that scarf on us for a vest. And you haven't got a high collar on, either. That's only a rough blue print of a dress-suit. Why, you look just as comfortable as though you were going to enjoy yourself—and you look cool, too."

"Well, why not?" laughed Clay.

"Well, but look at me!" cried the other. "Do I look cool? Do I look happy or comfortable? No, I don't. I look just about the way I feel, like a fool undertaker. I'm going to take this thing right off. You and Ted Langham can wear your silk scarfs and bobtail coats, if you like, but if they don't want me in white duck they don't get me."

When they reached the Palms, Clay asked Miss Langham if she did not want to see his view. "And perhaps, if you appreciate it properly, I will make you a present of it," he said, as he walked before her down the length of the veranda.

"It would be very selfish to keep it all to my self," she said.

"Couldn't we share it?" They had left the others seated facing the bay, with MacWilliams and young Langham on the broad steps of the veranda, and the younger sister and her father sitting in long bamboo steamer-chairs above them.

Clay and Miss Langham were quite alone. From the high cliff on which the Palms stood they could look down the narrow inlet that joined the ocean and see the moonlight turning the water into a rippling ladder of light and gilding the dark green leaves of the palms near them with a border of silver. Directly below them lay the waters of the bay, reflecting the red and green lights of the ships at anchor, and beyond them again were the yellow lights of the town, rising one above the other as the city crept up the hill.

And back of all were the mountains, grim and mysterious, with white clouds sleeping in their huge valleys, like masses of fog.

Except for the ceaseless murmur of the insect life about them the night was absolutely still—so still that the striking of the ships' bells in the harbor came to them sharply across the surface of the water, and they could hear from time to time the splash of some great fish and the steady creaking of an oar in a rowlock that grew fainter and fainter as it grew further away, until it was drowned in the distance. Miss Langham was for a long time silent. She stood with her hands clasped behind her, gazing from side to side into the moonlight, and had apparently forgotten that Clay was present.

"Well," he said at last, "I think you appreciate it properly. I was afraid you would exclaim about it, and say it was fine, or charming, or something."

Miss Langham turned to him and smiled slightly. "And you told me once that you knew me so very well," she said.

Clay chose to forget much that he had said on that night when he had first met her. He knew that he had been bold then, and had dared to be so because he did not think he would see her again; but, now that he was to meet her every day through several months, it seemed better to him that they should grow to know each other as they really were, simply and sincerely, and without forcing the situation in any way.

So he replied, "I don't know you so well now. You must remember I haven't seen you for a year."

"Yes, but you hadn't seen me for twenty-two years then," she answered. "I don't think you have changed much," she went on. "I expected to find you gray with cares. Ted wrote us about the way you work all day at the mines and sit up all night over calculations and plans and reports. But you don't show it. When are you going to take us over the mines? To-morrow? I am very anxious to see them, but I suppose father will want to inspect them first. Hope knows all about them, I believe; she knows their names, and how much you have taken out, and how much you have put in, too, and what MacWilliams's railroad cost, and who got the contract for the ore pier. Ted told us in his letters, and she used to work it out on the map in father's study. She is a most energetic child; I think sometimes she should have been a boy. I wish I could be the help to any one that she is to my father and to me. Whenever I am blue or down she makes fun of me, and——"

"Why should you ever be blue?" asked Clay, abruptly.

"There is no real reason, I suppose," the girl answered, smiling, "except that life is so very easy for me that I have to invent some woes. I should be better for a few reverses." And then she went on in a lower voice, and turning her head away, "In our family there is no woman older than I am to whom I can go with questions that trouble me. Hope is like a boy, as I said, and plays with Ted, and my father is very busy with his affairs, and since my mother died I have been very much alone. A man cannot understand. And I cannot understand why I should be speaking to you about myself and my troubles, except—" she added, a little wistfully, "that you once said you were interested in me, even if it was as long as a year ago. And because I want you to be very kind to me, as you have been to Ted, and I hope that we are going to be very good friends."

She was so beautiful, standing in the shadow with the moonlight about her and with her hand held out to him, that Clay felt as though the scene were hardly real. He took her hand in his and held it for a moment. His pleasure in the sweet friendliness of her manner and in her beauty was so great that it kept him silent.

"Friends!" he laughed under his breath. "I don't think there is much danger of our not being friends. The danger lies," he went on, smiling, "in my not being able to stop there."

Miss Langham made no sign that she had heard him, but turned and walked out into the moonlight and down the porch to where the others were sitting.

Young Langham had ordered a native orchestra of guitars and reed instruments from the town to serenade his people, and they were standing in front of the house in the moonlight as Miss Langham and Clay came forward. They played the shrill, eerie music of their country with a passion and feeling that filled out the strange tropical scene around them; but Clay heard them only as an accompaniment to his own thoughts and as a part of the beautiful night and the tall, beautiful girl who had dominated it. He watched her from the shadow as she sat leaning easily forward and looking into the night. The moonlight fell full upon her, and though she did not once look at him or turn her head in his direction, he felt as though she must be conscious of his presence, as though there were already an understanding between them which she herself had established. She had asked him to be her friend. That was only a pretty speech, perhaps; but she had spoken of herself, and had hinted at her perplexities and her loneliness, and he argued that while it was no compliment to be asked to share another's pleasure, it must mean something when one was allowed to learn a little of another's troubles.

And while his mind was flattered and aroused by this promise of confidence between them, he was rejoicing in the rare quality of her beauty, and in the thought that she was to be near him, and near him here, of all places. It seemed a very wonderful thing to Clay—something that could only have happened in a novel or a play. For while the man and the hour frequently appeared together, he had found that the one woman in the world and the place and the man was a much more difficult combination to bring into effect. No one, he assured himself thankfully, could have designed a more lovely setting for his love-story, if it was to be a love-story, and he hoped it was, than this into which she had come of her own free will. It was a land of romance and adventure, of guitars and latticed windows, of warm brilliant days and gorgeous silent nights, under purple heavens and white stars. And he was to have her all to himself, with no one near to interrupt, no other friends, even, and no possible rival. She was not guarded now by a complex social system, with its responsibilities. He was the most lucky of men. Others had only seen her in her drawing-room or in an opera-box, but he was free to ford mountain streams at her side, or ride with her under arches of the great palms, or to play a guitar boldly beneath her window. He was free to come and go at any hour; not only free to do so, but the very nature of his duties made it necessary that they should be thrown constantly together.

The music of the violins moved him and touched him deeply, and stirred depths at which he had not guessed. It made him humble and deeply grateful, and he felt how mean and unworthy he was of such great happiness. He had never loved any woman as he felt that he could love this woman, as he hoped that he was to love her. For he was not so far blinded by her beauty and by what he guessed her character to be as to imagine that he really knew her. He only knew what he hoped she was, what he believed the soul must be that looked out of those kind, beautiful eyes and that found utterance in that wonderful voice which could control him and move him by a word.

He felt, as he looked at the group before him, how lonely his own life had been, how hard he had worked for so little—for what other men found ready at hand when they were born into the world.

He felt almost a touch of self-pity at his own imperfectness;

and the power of his will and his confidence in himself, of which he was so proud, seemed misplaced and little. And then he wondered if he had not neglected chances; but in answer to this his injured self-love rose to rebut the idea that he had wasted any portion of his time, and he assured himself that he had done the work that he had cut out for himself to do as best he could; no one but himself knew with what courage and spirit. And so he sat combating with himself, hoping one moment that she would prove what he believed her to be, and the next, scandalized at his temerity in daring to think of her at all.

The spell lifted as the music ceased, and Clay brought himself back to the moment and looked about him as though he were waking from a dream and had expected to see the scene disappear and the figures near him fade into the moonlight.

Young Langham had taken a guitar from one of the musicians and pressed it upon MacWilliams, with imperative directions to sing such and such songs, of which, in their isolation, they had grown to think most highly; and MacWilliams was protesting in much embarrassment.

MacWilliams had a tenor voice which he maltreated in the most villainous manner by singing directly through his nose. He had a taste for sentimental songs, in which "kiss" rhymed with "bliss," and in which "the people cry" was always sure to be followed with "as she goes by, that's pretty Katie Moody," or "Rosie McIntyre." He had gathered his songs at the side of camp-fires, and in canteens at the first section-house of a new railroad, and his original collection of ballads had had but few additions in several years. MacWilliams at first was shy, which was quite a new development, until he made them promise to laugh if they wanted to laugh, explaining that he would not mind that so much as he would the idea that he thought he was serious.

The song of which he was especially fond was one called "He never cares to wander from his own fireside," which was especially appropriate in coming from a man who had visited almost every spot in the three Americas, except his home, in ten years. MacWilliams always ended the evening's entertainment with this chorus, no matter how many times it had been sung previously, and seemed to regard it with much the same veneration that the true Briton feels for his national anthem.

The words of the chorus were:

He never cares to wander from his own fireside,
He never cares to wander or to roam.

With his babies on his knee,
He's as happy as can be,
For there's no place like Home, Sweet Home.[1]

MacWilliams loved accidentals, and what he called "barber-shop chords." He used a beautiful accidental at the word "be," of which he was very fond, and he used to hang on that note for a long time, so that those in the extreme rear of the hall, as he was wont to explain, should get the full benefit of it. And it was his custom to emphasize "for" in the last line by speaking instead of singing it, and then coming to a full stop before dashing on again with the excellent truth that "there is NO place like Home, Sweet Home."

The men at the mines used to laugh at him and his song at first, but they saw that it was not to be so laughed away, and that he regarded it with some peculiar sentiment. So they suffered him to sing it in peace.

MacWilliams went through his repertoire to the unconcealed amusement of young Langham and Hope. When he had finished he asked Hope if she knew a comic song of which he had only heard by reputation. One of the men at the mines had gained a certain celebrity by claiming to have heard it in the States, but as he gave a completely new set of words to the tune of the "Wearing of the Green" as the true version, his veracity was doubted. Hope said she knew it, of course, and they all went into the drawing-room, where the men grouped themselves about the piano. It was a night they remembered long afterward. Hope sat at the piano protesting and laughing, but singing the songs of which the new-comers had become so weary, but which the three men heard open-eyed, and hailed with shouts of pleasure. The others enjoyed them and their delight, as though they were people in a play expressing themselves in this extravagant manner for their enter-tainment, until they understood how poverty-stricken their lives had been and that they were not only enjoying the music for itself, but because it was characteristic of all that they had left behind them. It was pathetic to hear them boast of having read of a certain song in such a paper, and of the fact that they knew the plot of a late comic opera and the names of those who had played in it, and that it had or had not been acceptable to the New York public.

---

1 "He Never Cares to Wander From His Own Fireside" (1892), a song by
   Felix McGlennon.

"They don't even know 'Tommy Atkins'!"

"Dear me," Hope would cry, looking over her shoulder with a despairing glance at her sister and father; "they don't even know 'Tommy Atkins!'"

It was a very happy evening for them all, foreshadowing, as it did, a continuation of just such evenings. Young Langham was radiant with pleasure at the good account which Clay had given of him to his father, and Mr. Langham was gratified, and proud of the manner in which his son and heir had conducted himself; and MacWilliams, who had never before been taken so simply and sincerely by people of a class that he had always held in humorous awe, felt a sudden accession of dignity, and an unhappy fear that when they laughed at what he said, it was because its sense was so utterly different from their point of view, and not because they saw the humor of it. He did not know what the word "snob" signified, and in his roughened, easy-going nature there was no touch of false pride; but he could not help thinking how surprised his people would be if they could see him, whom they regarded as a wanderer and renegade on the face of the earth and the prodigal of the family, and for that reason the best loved, leaning over a grand piano, while one daughter of his much-revered president played comic songs for his delectation, and the other, who according to the newspapers refused princes daily, and who was the most wonderful creature he had ever seen, poured out his coffee and brought it to him with her own hands.

The evening came to an end at last, and the new arrivals accompanied their visitors to the veranda as they started to their cabin for the night. Clay was asking Mr. Langham when he wished to visit the mines, and the others were laughing over farewell speeches, when young Langham startled them all by hurrying down the length of the veranda and calling on them to follow.

"Look!" he cried, pointing down the inlet. "Here comes a man-of-war, or a yacht. Isn't she smart-looking? What can she want here at this hour of the night? They won't let them land. Can you make her out, MacWilliams?"

A long, white ship was steaming slowly up the inlet, and passed within a few hundred feet of the cliff on which they were standing.

"Why, it's the *Vesta!*" exclaimed Hope, wonderingly.[1] "I thought she wasn't coming for a week?"

"It can't be the *Vesta!*" said the elder sister; "she was not to have sailed from Havana until to-day."

"What do you mean?" asked Langham. "Is it King's boat? Do you expect him here? Oh, what fun! I say, Clay, here's the *Vesta*, Reggie King's yacht, and he's no end of a sport. We can go all over the place now, and he can land us right at the door of the mines if we want to."

"Is it the King I met at dinner that night?" asked Clay, turning to Miss Langham.

"Yes," she said. "He wanted us to come down on the yacht, but we thought the steamer would be faster; so he sailed without us and was to have touched at Havana, but he has apparently changed his course. Doesn't she look like a phantom ship in the moonlight?"

Young Langham thought he could distinguish King among the white figures on the bridge, and tossed his hat and shouted, and a man in the stern of the yacht replied with a wave of his hand.

"That must be Mr. King," said Hope. "He didn't bring any one with him, and he seems to be the only man aft."

---

1   *Vesta*, a reference to William Walker, the American filibuster; he and his "Immortals" traveled to Nicaragua aboard a ship of that name.

They stood watching the yacht as she stopped with a rattle of anchor-chains and a confusion of orders that came sharply across the water, and then the party separated and the three men walked down the hill, Langham eagerly assuring the other two that King was a very good sort, and telling them what a treasure-house his yacht was, and how he would have probably brought the latest papers, and that he would certainly give a dance on board in their honor.

The men stood for some short time together after they had reached the office, discussing the great events of the day, and then with cheerful good-nights disappeared into their separate rooms.

An hour later Clay stood without his coat, and with a pen in his hand, at MacWilliams's bedside and shook him by the shoulder.

"I'm not asleep," said MacWilliams, sitting up; "what is it? What have you been doing?" he demanded. "Not working?"

"There were some reports came in after we left," said Clay, "and I find I will have to see Kirkland to-morrow morning. Send them word to run me down on an engine at five-thirty, will you? I am sorry to have to wake you, but I couldn't remember in which shack that engineer lives."

MacWilliams jumped from his bed and began kicking about the floor for his boots. "Oh, that's all right," he said. "I wasn't asleep, I was just—" he lowered his voice that Langham might not hear him through the canvas partitions—"I was just lying awake playing duets with the President, and racing for the International Cup in my new centre-board yacht, that's all!"

MacWilliams buttoned a waterproof coat over his pajamas and stamped his bare feet into his boots. "Oh, I tell you, Clay," he said with a grim chuckle, "we're mixing right in with the four hundred, we are! I'm substitute and understudy when anybody gets ill. We're right in our own class at last! Pure amateurs with no professional record against us. Me and President Langham, I guess!" He struck a match and lit the smoky wick in a tin lantern.

"But now," he said, cheerfully, "my time being too valuable for me to sleep, I will go wake up that nigger engine-driver and set his alarm clock at five-thirty. Five-thirty, I believe you said. All right; good-night." And whistling cheerfully to himself MacWilliams disappeared up the hill, his body hidden in the darkness and his legs showing fantastically in the light of the swinging lantern.

Clay walked out upon the veranda and stood with his back to

one of the pillars. MacWilliams and his pleasantries disturbed and troubled him. Perhaps, after all, the boy was right. It seemed absurd, but it was true. They were only employees of Langham— two of the thousands of young men who were working all over the United States to please him, to make him richer, to whom he was only a name and a power, which meant an increase of salary or the loss of place.

Clay laughed and shrugged his shoulders. He knew that he was not in that class; if he did good work it was because his self-respect demanded it of him; he did not work for Langham or the Olancho Mining Company (Limited). And yet he turned with almost a feeling of resentment toward the white yacht lying calmly in magnificent repose a hundred yards from his porch.

He could see her as clearly in her circle of electric lights as though she were a picture and held in the light of a stereopticon on a screen. He could see her white decks, and the rails of polished brass, and the comfortable wicker chairs and gay cushions and flat coils of rope, and the tapering masts and intricate rigging. How easy it was made for some men! This one had come like the prince in the fairy tale on his magic carpet. If Alice Langham were to leave Valencia that next day, Clay could not follow her. He had his duties and responsibilities; he was at another man's bidding.

But this Prince Fortunatus had but to raise anchor and start in pursuit, knowing that he would be welcome wherever he found her.[1] That was the worst of it to Clay, for he knew that men did not follow women from continent to continent without some assurance of a friendly greeting. Clay's mind went back to the days when he was a boy, when his father was absent fighting for a lost cause; when his mother taught in a little schoolhouse under the shadow of Pike's Peak,[2] and when Kit Carson[3] was his hero. He thought of the poverty of those days—poverty so mean and hopeless that it was almost something to feel shame for; of the

---

1   *The New Prince Fortunatas* (1890), a novel by William Black (1841–98), a popular Scottish writer. Clay clearly envies King's "fortunate" circumstances.

2   Located near Colorado Springs, Pikes Peak is one of Colorado's highest mountains.

3   Kit Carson (1809–68), famed American hunter and scout. He played a key role in the conquest of California during the Mexican-American War (1846–48), and his adventures and exploits were widely celebrated in dime novels in the 1860s and 1870s.

days that followed when, an orphan and without a home, he had sailed away from New Orleans to the Cape. How the mind of the mathematician, which he had inherited from the Boston schoolmistress, had been swayed by the spirit of the soldier, which he had inherited from his father, and which led him from the mines of South Africa to little wars in Madagascar, Egypt, and Algiers. It had been a life as restless as the seaweed on a rock. But as he looked back to its poor beginnings and admitted to himself its later successes, he gave a sigh of content, and shaking off the mood stood up and paced the length of the veranda.

He looked up the hill to the low-roofed bungalow with the palm-leaves about it, outlined against the sky, and as motionless as patterns cut in tin. He had built that house. He had built it for her. That was her room where the light was shining out from the black bulk of the house about it like a star. And beyond the house he saw his five great mountains, the knuckles of the giant hand, with its gauntlet of iron that lay shut and clenched in the face of the sea that swept up whimpering before it. Clay felt a boyish, foolish pride rise in his breast as he looked toward the great mines he had discovered and opened, at the iron mountains that were crumbling away before his touch.

He turned his eyes again to the blazing yacht, and this time there was no trace of envy in them. He laughed instead, partly with pleasure at the thought of the struggle he scented in the air, and partly at his own braggadocio.

"I'm not afraid," he said, smiling, and shaking his head at the white ship that loomed up like a man-of-war in the black waters. "I'm not afraid to fight you for anything worth fighting for."

He bowed his bared head in good-night toward the light on the hill, as he turned and walked back into his bedroom. "And I think," he murmured, grimly, as he put out the light, "that she is worth fighting for."

IV

The work which had called Clay to the mines kept him there for some time, and it was not until the third day after the arrival of the Langhams that he returned again to the Palms. On the afternoon when he climbed the hill to the bungalow he found the Langhams as he had left them, with the difference that King now occupied a place in the family circle. Clay was made so welcome, and especially so by King, that he felt rather ashamed of his sentiments toward him, and considered his three days of absence to be well repaid by the heartiness of their greeting.

"For myself," said Mr. Langham, "I don't believe you had anything to do at the mines at all. I think you went away just to show us how necessary you are. But if you want me to make a good report of our resident director on my return, you had better devote yourself less to the mines while you are here and more to us." Clay said he was glad to find that his duties were to be of so pleasant a nature, and asked them what they had seen and what they had done.

They told him they had been nowhere, but had waited for his return in order that he might act as their guide.

"Then you should see the city at once," said Clay, "and I will have the volante brought to the door, and we can all go in this afternoon. There is room for the four of you inside, and I can sit on the box-seat with the driver."

"No," said King, "let Hope or me sit on the box-seat. Then we can practise our Spanish on the driver."

"Not very well," Clay replied, "for the driver sits on the first horse, like a postilion. It's a sort of tandem without reins. Haven't you seen it yet? We consider the volante our proudest exhibit."[1] So Clay ordered the volante to be brought out, and placed them facing each other in the open carriage, while he climbed to the box-seat, from which position of vantage he pointed out and explained the objects of interest they passed, after the manner of a professional guide. It was a warm, beautiful afternoon, and the clear mists of the atmosphere intensified the rich blue of the sky, and the brilliant colors of the houses, and the different shades of green of the trees and bushes that lined the highroad to the capital.

"To the right, as we descend," said Clay, speaking over his shoulder, "you see a tin house. It is the home of the resident director of the Olancho Mining Company (Limited), and of his able lieutenants, Mr. Theodore Langham and Mr. MacWilliams. The building on the extreme left is the round-house, in which Mr. MacWilliams stores his three locomotive engines, and in the far middle-distance is Mr. MacWilliams himself in the act of repairing a water-tank. He is the one in a suit of blue overalls, and as his language at such times is free, we will drive rapidly on and

---

1 Volante, a two-wheeled carriage; the driver rides the horse while the passengers sit behind in the carriage.

not embarrass him. Besides," added the engineer, with the happy laugh of a boy who had been treated to a holiday, "I am sure that I am not setting him the example of fixity to duty which he should expect from his chief."

They passed between high hedges of Spanish bayonet, and came to mud cabins thatched with palm-leaves, and alive with naked, little brown-bodied children, who laughed and cheered to them as they passed.

"It's a very beautiful country for the *pueblo*," was Clay's comment.[1] "Different parts of the same tree furnish them with food, shelter, and clothing, and the sun gives them fuel, and the Government changes so often that they can always dodge the tax-collector."

From the mud cabins they came to more substantial one-story houses of adobe, with the walls painted in two distinct colors, blue, pink, or yellow, with red-tiled roofs, and the names with which they had been christened in bold black letters above the entrances. Then the carriage rattled over paved streets, and they drove between houses of two stories painted more decorously in pink and light blue, with wide-open windows, guarded by heavy bars of finely wrought iron and ornamented with scrollwork in stucco. The principal streets were given up to stores and cafés, all wide open to the pavement and protected from the sun by brilliantly striped awnings, and gay with the national colors of Olancho in flags and streamers. In front of them sat officers in uniform, and the dark-skinned dandies of Valencia, in white duck suits and Panama hats, toying with tortoise-shell canes, which could be converted, if the occasion demanded, into blades of Toledo steel. In the streets were priests and bare-legged mule-drivers, and ragged ranchmen with red-caped cloaks hanging to their sandals, and negro women, with bare shoulders and long trains, vending lottery tickets and rolling huge cigars between their lips. It was an old story to Clay and King, but none of the others had seen a Spanish-American city before; they were familiar with the Far East and the Mediterranean, but not with the fierce, hot tropics of their sister continent, and so their eyes were wide open, and they kept calling continually to one another to notice some new place or figure.

They in their turn did not escape from notice or comment. The two sisters would have been conspicuous anywhere—in a

---

1 *Pueblo* here means "the people" rather than a reference to the famous communal dwellings found in the US southwest.

queen's drawing-room or on an Indian reservation. Theirs was a type that the caballeros and señoritas did not know. With them dark hair was always associated with dark complexions, the rich duskiness of which was always vulgarized by a coat of powder, and this fair blending of pink and white skin under masses of black hair was strangely new, so that each of the few women who were to be met on the street turned to look after the carriage, while the American women admired their mantillas,[1] and felt that the straw sailor-hats they wore had become heavy and unfeminine.

Clay was very happy in picking out what was most characteristic and picturesque, and every street into which he directed the driver to take them seemed to possess some building or monument that was of peculiar interest. They did not know that he had mapped out this ride many times before, and was taking them over a route which he had already travelled with them in imagination. King knew what the capital would be like before he entered it, from his experience of other South American cities, but he acted as though it were all new to him, and allowed Clay to explain, and to give the reason for those features of the place that were unusual and characteristic. Clay noticed this and appealed to him from time to time, when he was in doubt; but the other only smiled back and shook his head, as much as to say, "This is your city; they would rather hear about it from you."

Clay took them to the principal shops, where the two girls held whispered consultations over lace mantillas, which they had at once determined to adopt, and bought the gorgeous paper fans, covered with brilliant pictures of bull-fighters in suits of silver tinsel; and from these open stores he led them to a dingy little shop, where there was old silver and precious hand-painted fans of mother-of-pearl that had been pawned by families who had risked and lost all in some revolution; and then to another shop, where two old maiden ladies made a particularly good guava; and to tobacconists, where the men bought a few of the native cigars, which, as they were a monopoly of the Government, were as bad as Government monopolies always are.

Clay felt a sudden fondness for the city, so grateful was he to it for entertaining her as it did, and for putting its best front forward for her delectation. He wanted to thank some one for building the quaint old convent, with its yellow walls washed to an orange tint, and black in spots with dampness; and for the

---

1 A lace scarf worn over the head and shoulders.

fountain covered with green moss that stood before its gate, and around which were gathered the girls and women of the neighborhood with red water-jars on their shoulders, and little donkeys buried under stacks of yellow sugar-cane, and the negro drivers of the city's green water-carts, and the blue wagons that carried the manufactured ice. Toward five o'clock they decided to spend the rest of the day in the city, and to telephone for the two boys to join them at La Venus, the great restaurant on the plaza, where Clay had invited them to dine.

He suggested that they should fill out the time meanwhile by a call on the President, and after a search for cards in various pocketbooks, they drove to the Government Palace, which stood in an open square in the heart of the city.

As they arrived the President and his wife were leaving for their afternoon drive on the Alameda, the fashionable parade-ground of the city, and the state carriage and a squad of cavalry appeared from the side of the palace as the visitors drove up to the entrance. But at the sight of Clay, General Alvarez and his wife retreated to the house again and made them welcome. The President led the men into his reception-room and entertained them with champagne and cigarettes, not manufactured by his Government; and his wife, after first conducting the girls through the state drawing-room, where the late sunlight shone gloomily on strange old portraits of assassinated presidents and victorious generals, and garish yellow silk furniture, brought them to her own apartments and gave them tea after a civilized fashion, and showed them how glad she was to see some one of her own world again.

During their short visit Madame Alvarez talked a greater part of the time herself, addressing what she said to Miss Langham, but looking at Hope. It was unusual for Hope to be singled out in this way when her sister was present, and both the sisters noticed it and spoke of it afterwards. They thought Madame Alvarez very beautiful and distinguished-looking, and she impressed them, even after that short knowledge of her, as a woman of great force of character.

"She was very well dressed for a Spanish woman," was Miss Langham's comment, later in the afternoon. "But everything she had on was just a year behind the fashions, or twelve steamer days behind, as Mr. MacWilliams puts it."

"She reminded me," said Hope, "of a black panther I saw once in a circus."

"Dear me!" exclaimed the sister, "I don't see that at all. Why?"

Hope said she did not know why; she was not given to analyzing her impressions or offering reasons for them. "Because the panther looked so unhappy," she explained, doubtfully, "and restless; and he kept pacing up and down all the time, and hitting his head against the bars as he walked as though he liked the pain. Madame Alvarez seemed to me to be just like that—as though she were shut up somewhere and wanted to be free."

When Madame Alvarez and the two sisters had joined the men, they all walked together to the terrace, and the visitors waited until the President and his wife should take their departure. Hope noticed, in advance of the escort of native cavalry, an auburn-haired, fair-skinned young man who was sitting an English saddle.

The officer's eyes were blue and frank and attractive-looking, even as they then were fixed ahead of him with a military lack of expression; but he came to life very suddenly when the President called to him, and prodded his horse up to the steps and dismounted. He was introduced by Alvarez as "Captain Stuart of my household troops, late of the Gordon Highlanders. Captain Stuart," said the President, laying his hand affectionately on the younger man's epaulette, "takes care of my life and the safety of my home and family. He could have the command of the army if he wished; but no, he is fond of us, and he tells me we are in more need of protection from our friends at home than from our enemies on the frontier. Perhaps he knows best. I trust him, Mr. Langham," added the President, solemnly, "as I trust no other man in all this country."

"I am very glad to meet Captain Stuart, I am sure," said Mr. Langham, smiling, and appreciating how the shyness of the Englishman must be suffering under the praises of the Spaniard. And Stuart was indeed so embarrassed that he flushed under his tan, and assured Clay, while shaking hands with them all, that he was delighted to make his acquaintance; at which the others laughed, and Stuart came to himself sufficiently to laugh with them, and to accept Clay's invitation to dine with them later.

They found the two boys waiting in the café of the restaurant where they had arranged to meet, and they ascended the steps together to the table on the balcony that Clay had reserved for them.

The young engineer appeared at his best as host. The responsibility of seeing that a half-dozen others were amused and content sat well upon him; and as course followed course, and the wines changed, and the candles left the rest of the room in darkness and showed only the table and the faces around it, they all became rapidly more merry and the conversation intimately familiar.

Clay knew the kind of table-talk to which the Langhams were accustomed, and used the material around his table in such a way that the talk there was vastly different. From King he drew forth tales of the buried cities he had first explored and then robbed of their ugliest idols. He urged MacWilliams to tell carefully edited stories of life along the Chagres[1] before the Scandal came, and of the fastnesses of the Andes; and even Stuart grew braver and remembered "something of the same sort" he had seen at Fort Nilt, in Upper Burma.

"Of course," was Clay's comment at the conclusion of one of these narratives, "being an Englishman, Stuart left out the point of the story, which was that he blew in the gates of the fort with a charge of dynamite. He got a D.S.O. for doing it."[2]

"Being an Englishman," said Hope, smiling encouragingly on the conscious Stuart, "he naturally would leave that out."

Mr. Langham and his daughters formed an eager audience. They had never before met at one table three men who had known such experiences, and who spoke of them as though they must be as familiar in the lives of the others as in their own—men who spoiled in the telling, stories that would have furnished incidents for melodramas, and who impressed their hearers more with what they left unsaid, and what was only suggested, than what in their view was the most important point.

The dinner came to an end at last, and Mr. Langham proposed that they should go down and walk with the people in the plaza; but his two daughters preferred to remain as spectators on the balcony, and Clay and Stuart stayed with them.

"At last!" sighed Clay, under his breath, seating himself at Miss Langham's side as she sat leaning forward with her arms

---

1 A river in central Panama that supplies water for the Panama Canal. Before the US took over building the canal in 1903, the project had been overseen by a French conglomerate run by Ferdinand Marie de Lesseps (1805–94), a French diplomat and engineer. The French worked on the canal from 1881–88, but the failure of the company provoked several scandals and Lesseps and his son, Charles, were charged with mismanagement and misappropriation of funds.

2 Fort Nilt, a Hunza and Nagir stronghold in India, was attacked on 2 December 1891, by Kashmir Imperial Service troops under English command. Davis bases Stuart's D.S.O. (Distinguished Service Order) on the exploits of actual British officers.

upon the railing and looking down into the plaza below. She made no sign at first that she had heard him, but as the voices of Stuart and Hope rose from the other end of the balcony she turned her head and asked, "Why at last?"

"Oh, you couldn't understand," laughed Clay. "You have not been looking forward to just one thing and then had it come true. It is the only thing that ever did come true to me, and I thought it never would."

"You don't try to make me understand," said the girl, smiling, but without turning her eyes from the moving spectacle below her. Clay considered her challenge silently. He did not know just how much it might mean from her, and the smile robbed it of all serious intent; so he, too, turned and looked down into the great square below them, content, now that she was alone with him, to take his time.

At one end of the plaza the President's band was playing native waltzes that came throbbing through the trees and beating softly above the rustling skirts and clinking spurs of the señoritas and officers, sweeping by in two opposite circles around the edges of the tessellated pavements. Above the palms around the square arose the dim, white façade of the cathedral, with the bronze statue of Anduella, the liberator of Olancho, who answered with his upraised arm and cocked hat the cheers of an imaginary populace. Clay's had been an unobtrusive part in the evening's entertainment, but he saw that the others had been pleased, and felt a certain satisfaction in thinking that King himself could not have planned and carried out a dinner more admirable in every way. He was gratified that they should know him to be not altogether a barbarian. But what he best liked to remember was that whenever he had spoken she had listened, even when her eyes were turned away and she was pretending to listen to some one else. He tormented himself by wondering whether this was because he interested her only as a new and strange character, or whether she felt in some way how eagerly he was seeking her approbation. For the first time in his life he found himself considering what he was about to say, and he suited it for her possible liking. It was at least some satisfaction that she had, if only for the time being, singled him out as of especial interest, and he assured himself that the fault would be his if her interest failed. He no longer looked on himself as an outsider.

Stuart's voice arose from the farther end of the balcony, where the white figure of Hope showed dimly in the darkness.

"They are talking about you over there," said Miss Langham, turning toward him.

"Well, I don't mind," answered Clay, "as long as they talk about me—over there."

Miss Langham shook her head. "You are very frank and audacious," she replied, doubtfully, "but it is rather pleasant as a change."

"I don't call that audacious, to say I don't want to be interrupted when I am talking to you. Aren't the men you meet generally audacious?" he asked. "I can see why not—though," he continued, "you awe them."

"I can't think that's a nice way to affect people," protested Miss Langham, after a pause. "I don't awe you, do I?"

"Oh, you affect me in many different ways," returned Clay, cheerfully. "Sometimes I am very much afraid of you, and then again my feelings are only those of unlimited admiration."

"There, again, what did I tell you?" said Miss Langham.

"Well, I can't help doing that," said Clay. "That is one of the few privileges that is left to a man in my position—it doesn't matter what I say. That is the advantage of being of no account and hopelessly detrimental. The eligible men of the world, you see, have to be so very careful. A Prime Minister, for instance, can't talk as he wishes, and call names if he wants to, or write letters, even. Whatever he says is so important, because he says it, that he must be very discreet. I am so unimportant that no one minds what I say, and so I say it. It's the only comfort I have."

"Are you in the habit of going around the world saying whatever you choose to every woman you happen to—to—" Miss Langham hesitated.

"To admire very much," suggested Clay.

"To meet," corrected Miss Langham. "Because, if you are, it is a very dangerous and selfish practise, and I think your theory of non-responsibility is a very wicked one."

"Well, I wouldn't say it to a child," mused Clay, "but to one who must have heard it before——"

"And who, you think, would like to hear it again, perhaps," interrupted Miss Langham.

"No, not at all," said Clay. "I don't say it to give her pleasure, but because it gives me pleasure to say what I think."

"If we are to continue good friends, Mr. Clay," said Miss Langham, in decisive tones, "we must keep our relationship on more of a social and less of a personal basis. It was all very well that first night I met you," she went on, in a kindly tone. "You rushed in then and by a sort of *tour de force* made me think a great deal about myself and also about you. Your stories of cherished photographs and distant devotion and all that were very interesting; but now we are to be together a great deal, and if we are to talk about ourselves all the time, I for one shall grow very tired of it. As a matter of fact, you don't know what your feelings are concerning me, and until you do we will talk less about them and more about the things you are certain of. When are you going to take us to the mines, for instance, and who was Anduella, the Liberator of Olancho, on that pedestal over there? Now, isn't that much more instructive?"

Clay smiled grimly and made no answer, but sat with knitted brows looking out across the trees of the plaza. His face was so serious and he was apparently giving such earnest consideration to what she had said that Miss Langham felt an uneasy sense of remorse. And, moreover, the young man's profile, as he sat looking away from her, was very fine, and the head on his broad shoulders was as well-modelled as the head of an Athenian statue.

Miss Langham was not insensible to beauty of any sort, and she regarded the profile with perplexity and with a softening spirit.

"You understand," she said, gently, being quite certain that she did not understand this new order of young man herself. "You are not offended with me?" she asked.

Clay turned and frowned, and then smiled in a puzzled way and stretched out his hand toward the equestrian statue in the plaza.

"Andulla or Anduella, the Treaty-Maker, as they call him, was born in 1700," he said; "he was a most picturesque sort of a chap, and freed this country from the yoke of Spain. One of the stories they tell of him gives you a good idea of his character." And so, without any change of expression or reference to what had just passed between them, Clay continued through the remainder of their stay on the balcony to discourse in humorous, graphic phrases on the history of Olancho, its heroes, and its revolutions, the buccaneers and pirates of the old days, and the concession-hunters and filibusters of the present. It was some time before Miss Langham was able to give him her full attention, for she was considering whether he could be so foolish as to have taken offence at what she said, and whether he would speak of it again, and in wondering whether a personal basis for conversation was not, after all, more entertaining than anecdotes of the victories and heroism of dead and buried Spaniards.

"That Captain Stuart," said Hope to her sister, as they drove home together through the moonlight, "I like him very much. He seems to have such a simple idea of what is right and good. It is like a child talking. Why, I am really much older than he is in everything but years—why is that?"

"I suppose it's because we always talk before you as though you were a grown-up person," said her sister. "But I agree with you about Captain Stuart; only, why is he down here? If he is a gentleman, why is he not in his own army? Was he forced to leave it?"

"Oh, he seems to have a very good position here," said Mr. Langham. "In England, at his age, he would be only a second-lieutenant. Don't you remember what the President said, that he would trust him with the command of his army? That's certainly a responsible position, and it shows great confidence in him."

"Not so great, it seems to me," said King, carelessly, "as he is showing him in making him the guardian of his hearth and home. Did you hear what he said to-day? 'He guards my home and my family.' I don't think a man's home and family are among the things he can afford to leave to the protection of stray English subalterns. From all I hear, it would be better if President Alvarez did less plotting and protected his own house himself."

"The young man did not strike me as the sort of person," said Mr. Langham, warmly, "who would be likely to break his word to the man who is feeding him and sheltering him, and whose uniform he wears. I don't think the President's home is in any danger from within. Madame Alvarez——"

Clay turned suddenly in his place on the box-seat of the carriage, where he had been sitting, a silent, misty statue in the moonlight, and peered down on those in the carriage below him.

"Madame Alvarez needs no protection, as you were about to say, Mr. Langham," he interrupted, quickly. "Those who know her could say nothing against her, and those who do not know her would not so far forget themselves as to dare to do it. Have you noticed the effect of the moonlight on the walls of the convent?" he continued, gently. "It makes them quite white."

"No!" exclaimed Mr. Langham and King, hurriedly, as they both turned and gazed with absorbing interest at the convent on the hills above them.

Before the sisters went to sleep that night Hope came to the door of her sister's room and watched Alice admiringly as she sat before the mirror brushing out her hair.

"I think it's going to be fine down here; don't you, Alice?" she asked. "Everything is so different from what it is at home, and so beautiful, and I like the men we've met. Isn't that Mr. MacWilliams funny—and he is so tough. And Captain Stuart—it is a pity he's shy. The only thing he seems to be able to talk about is Mr. Clay. He worships Mr. Clay!"

"Yes," assented her sister, "I noticed on the balcony that you seemed to have found some way to make him speak."

"Well, that was it. He likes to talk about Mr. Clay, and I wanted to listen. Oh! he is a fine man. He has done more exciting things——"

"Who? Captain Stuart?"

"No—Mr. Clay. He's been in three real wars and about a dozen little ones, and he's built thousands of miles of railroads, I don't know how many thousands, but Captain Stuart knows; and he built the highest bridge in Peru. It swings in the air across a chasm, and it rocks when the wind blows. And the German Emperor made him a Baron."

"Why?"

"I don't know. I couldn't understand. It was something about plans for fortifications. He, Mr. Clay, put up a fort in the harbor of Rio Janeiro during a revolution, and the officers on a German man-of-war saw it and copied the plans, and the Germans built one just like it, only larger, on the Baltic, and when the Emperor found out whose design it was, he sent Mr. Clay the order of something-or-other, and made him a Baron."

"Really!" exclaimed the elder sister, "isn't he afraid that some one will marry him for his title?"

"Oh, well, you can laugh, but I think it's pretty fine, and so does Ted," added Hope, with the air of one who propounds a final argument.

"Oh, I beg your pardon," laughed Alice. "If Ted approves we must all go down and worship."

"And father, too," continued Hope. "He said he thought Mr. Clay was one of the most remarkable men for his years that he had ever met."

Miss Langham's eyes were hidden by the masses of her black hair that she had shaken over her face, and she said nothing.

"And I liked the way he shut Reggie King up too," continued Hope, stoutly, "when he and father were talking that way about Madame Alvarez."

"Yes, upon my word!" exclaimed her sister, impatiently tossing her hair back over her shoulders. "I really cannot see that Madame Alvarez is in need of any champion. I thought Mr. Clay made it very much worse by rushing in the way he did. Why should he take it upon himself to correct a man as old as my father?"

"I suppose because Madame Alvarez is a friend of his," Hope answered.

"My dear child, a beautiful woman can always find some man to take her part," said Miss Langham. "But I've no doubt," she added, rising and kissing her sister good-night, "that he is all that your Captain Stuart thinks him; but he is not going to keep us awake any longer, is he, even if he does show such gallant interest in old ladies?"

"Old ladies!" exclaimed Hope in amazement. "Why, Alice!"

But her sister only laughed and waved her out of the room, and Hope walked away frowning in much perplexity.

V

The visit to the city was imitated on the three succeeding evenings by similar excursions. On one night they returned to the plaza, and the other two were spent in drifting down the harbor and along the coast on King's yacht. The President and Madame Alvarez were King's guests on one of these moonlight excursions, and were saluted by the proper number of guns, and their native band played on the forward deck. Clay felt that King held the centre of the stage for the time being, and obliterated himself completely. He thought of his own paddle-wheel tug-boat that he had had painted and gilded in her honor, and smiled grimly.

MacWilliams approached him as he sat leaning back on the rail and looking up, with the eye of a man who had served before the mast, at the lacework of spars and rigging above him. MacWilliams came toward him on tiptoe and dropped carefully into a wicker chair. "There don't seem to be any door-mats on this boat," he said. "In every other respect she seems fitted out quite complete; all the latest magazines and enamelled bath-tubs, and Chinese waiter-boys with cock-tails up their sleeves. But there ought to be a mat at the top of each of those stairways that hang over the side, otherwise some one is sure to soil the deck. Have you been down in the engine-room yet?" he asked. "Well, don't go, then," he advised, solemnly. "It will only make you feel badly. I have asked the Admiral if I can send those half-breed engine drivers over to-morrow to show them what a clean engine-room looks like. I've just been talking to the chief. His name's MacKenzie, and I told him I was Scotch myself, and he said it 'was a greet pleesure' to find a gentleman so well acquainted with the movements of machinery. He thought I was one of King's friends, I guess, so I didn't tell him I pulled a lever for a living myself. I gave him a cigar though, and he said, 'Thankee, sir,' and touched his cap to me."

MacWilliams chuckled at the recollection, and crossed his legs comfortably. "One of King's cigars, too," he said. "Real Havana; he leaves them lying around loose in the cabin. Have you had one? Ted Langham and I took about a box between us."

Clay made no answer, and MacWilliams settled himself contentedly in the great wicker chair and puffed grandly on a huge cigar.

"It's demoralizing, isn't it?" he said at last.

"What?" asked Clay, absently.

"Oh, this associating with white people again, as we're doing now. It spoils you for tortillas and rice, doesn't it? It's going to be great fun while it lasts, but when they've all gone, and Ted's gone, too, and the yacht's vanished, and we fall back to tramping around the plaza twice a week, it won't be gay, will it? No; it won't be gay. We're having the spree of our lives now, I guess, but there's going to be a difference in the morning."

"Oh, it's worth a headache, I think," said Clay, as he shrugged his shoulders and walked away to find Miss Langham.

The day set for the visit to the mines rose bright and clear. MacWilliams had rigged out his single passenger-car with rugs and cushions, and flags flew from its canvas top that flapped and billowed in the wind of the slow-moving train. Their observation-car, as MacWilliams termed it, was placed in front of the locomotive, and they were pushed gently along the narrow rails between forests of Manaca palms, and through swamps and jungles, and at times over the limestone formation along the coast, where the waves dashed as high as the smokestack of the locomotive, covering the excursionists with a sprinkling of white spray. Thousands of land-crabs, painted red and black and yellow, scrambled with a rattle like dead men's bones across the rails to be crushed by the hundreds under the wheels of the Juggernaut; great lizards ran from sunny rocks at the sound of their approach, and a deer bounded across the tracks fifty feet in front of the cow-catcher. MacWilliams escorted Hope out into the cab of the locomotive, and taught her how to increase and slacken the speed of the engine, until she showed an unruly desire to throw the lever open altogether and shoot them off the rails into the ocean beyond.

Clay sat at the back of the car with Miss Langham, and told her and her father of the difficulties with which young MacWilliams had had to contend. Miss Langham found her chief pleasure in noting the attention which her father gave to all that Clay had to tell him. Knowing her father as she did, and being familiar with his manner toward other men, she knew that he was treating Clay with unusual consideration. And this pleased her greatly, for it justified her own interest in him. She regarded Clay as a discovery of her own, but she was glad to have her opinion of him shared by others.

Their coming was a great event in the history of the mines. Kirkland, the foreman, and Chapman, who handled the dynamite, Weimer, the Consul, and the native doctor, who cared for the fever-stricken and the casualties, were all at the station to meet them in the whitest of white duck and with a bunch of ponies to carry them on their tour of inspection, and the village of mud cabins and zinc huts that stood clear of the bare sun-baked earth on whitewashed wooden piles was as clean as Clay's hundred policemen could sweep it. Mr. Langham rode in advance of the cavalcade, and the head of each of the different departments took his turn in riding at his side, and explained what had been done, and showed him the proud result. The village was empty, except for the families of the native workmen and the ownerless dogs, the scavengers of the colony, that snarled and barked and ran leaping in front of the ponies' heads.

Rising abruptly above the zinc village, lay the first of the five great hills, with its open front cut into great terraces, on which the men clung like flies on the side of a wall, some of them in groups around an opening, or in couples pounding a steel bar that a fellow-workman turned in his bare hands, while others gathered about the panting steam-drills that shook the solid rock with fierce, short blows, and hid the men about them in a throbbing curtain of steam. Self-important little dummy-engines, dragging long trains of ore-cars, rolled and rocked on the uneven surface of the ground, and swung around corners with warning screeches of their whistles. They could see, on peaks outlined against the sky, the signal-men waving their red flags, and then plunging down the mountain-side out of danger, as the earth rumbled and shook and vomited out a shower of stones and rubbish into the calm hot air. It was a spectacle of desperate activity and puzzling to the uninitiated, for it seemed to be scattered over an unlimited extent, with no head nor direction, and with each man, or each group of men, working alone, like ragpickers on a heap of ashes.

After the first half-hour of curious interest Miss Langham admitted to herself that she was disappointed. She confessed she had hoped that Clay would explain the meaning of the mines to her, and act as her escort over the mountains which he was blowing into pieces.

But it was King, somewhat bored by the ceaseless noise and heat, and her brother, incoherently enthusiastic, who rode at her side, while Clay moved on in advance and seemed to have forgotten her existence. She watched him pointing up at the openings in the mountains and down at the ore-road, or stooping to pick up a piece of ore from the ground in cowboy fashion, without leaving his saddle, and pounding it on the pommel before he passed it to the others. And, again, he would stand for minutes at a time up to his boot-tops in the sliding waste, with his bridle rein over his arm and his thumbs in his belt, listening to what his lieutenants were saying, and glancing quickly from them to Mr. Langham to see if he were following the technicalities of their speech. All of the men who had welcomed the appearance of the women on their arrival with such obvious delight and with so much embarrassment seemed now as oblivious of their presence as Clay himself.

Miss Langham pushed her horse up into the group beside Hope, who had kept her pony close at Clay's side from the beginning; but she could not make out what it was they were saying, and no one seemed to think it necessary to explain. She caught Clay's eye at last and smiled brightly at him; but, after staring at her for fully a minute, until Kirkland had finished speaking, she heard him say, "Yes, that's it exactly; in open-face workings there is no other way," and so showed her that he had not been even conscious of her presence. But a few minutes later she saw him look up at Hope, folding his arms across his chest tightly and shaking his head. "You see it was the only thing to do," she heard him say, as though he were defending some course of action, and as though Hope were one of those who must be convinced. "If we had cut the opening on the first level, there was the danger of the whole thing sinking in, so we had to begin to clear away at the top and work down. That's why I ordered the bucket-trolley. As it turned out, we saved money by it."

Hope nodded her head slightly. "That's what I told father when Ted wrote us about it," she said; "but you haven't done it at Mount Washington."

"Oh, but it's like this, Miss—" Kirkland replied, eagerly. "It's because Washington is a solider foundation. We can cut openings all over it and they won't cave, but this hill is most all rubbish; it's the poorest stuff in the mines."

Hope nodded her head again and crowded her pony on after the moving group, but her sister and King did not follow. King looked at her and smiled. "Hope is very enthusiastic," he said. "Where did she pick it up?"

"Oh, she and father used to go over it in his study last winter after Ted came down here," Miss Langham answered, with a touch of impatience in her tone. "Isn't there some place where we can go to get out of this heat?"

Weimer, the Consul, heard her and led her back to Kirkland's bungalow, that hung like an eagle's nest from a projecting cliff. From its porch they could look down the valley over the greater part of the mines, and beyond to where the Caribbean Sea lay flashing in the heat.

"I saw very few Americans down there, Weimer," said King. "I thought Clay had imported a lot of them."

"About three hundred altogether, wild Irishmen and negroes," said the Consul; "but we use the native soldiers chiefly. They can stand the climate better, and, besides," he added, "they act as a reserve in case of trouble. They are Mendoza's men, and Clay is trying to win them away from him."

"I don't understand," said King.

Weimer looked around him and waited until Kirkland's servant had deposited a tray full of bottles and glasses on a table near them, and had departed. "The talk is," he said, "that Alvarez means to proclaim a dictatorship in his own favor before the spring elections. You've heard of that, haven't you?" King shook his head.

"Oh, tell us about it," said Miss Langham; "I should so like to be in plots and conspiracies."

"Well, they're rather common down here," continued the Consul, "but this one ought to interest you especially, Miss Langham, because it is a woman who is at the head of it. Madame Alvarez, you know, was the Countess Manueleta Hernandez before her marriage. She belongs to one of the oldest families in Spain. Alvarez married her in Madrid, when he was Minister there, and when he returned to run for President, she came with him. She's a tremendously ambitious woman, and they do say she wants to convert the republic into a monarchy, and make her husband King, or, more properly speaking, make herself Queen. Of course that's absurd, but she is supposed to be plotting to turn Olancho into a sort of dependency of Spain, as it was long ago, and that's why she is so unpopular."

"Indeed?" interrupted Miss Langham, "I did not know that she was unpopular."

"Oh, rather. Why, her party is called the Royalist Party already, and only a week before you came the Liberals plastered the city with denunciatory placards against her, calling on the people to drive her out of the country."

"What cowards—to fight a woman!" exclaimed Miss Langham. "Well, she began it first, you see," said the Consul.

"Who is the leader of the fight against her?" asked King.

"General Mendoza; he is commander-in-chief and has the greater part of the army with him, but the other candidate, old General Rojas, is the popular choice and the best of the three. He is Vice-President now, and if the people were ever given a fair chance to vote for the man they want, he would unquestionably be the next President. The mass of the people are sick of revolutions. They've had enough of them, but they will have to go through another before long, and if it turns against Dr. Alvarez, I'm afraid Mr. Langham will have hard work to hold these mines. You see, Mendoza has already threatened to seize the whole plant and turn it into a Government monopoly."

"And if the other one, General Rojas, gets into power, will he seize the mines, too?"

"No, he is honest, strange to relate," laughed Weimer, "but he won't get in. Alvarez will make himself dictator, or Mendoza will make himself President. That's why Clay treats the soldiers here so well. He thinks he may need them against Mendoza. You may be turning your saluting-gun on the city yet, Commodore," he added, smiling, "or, what is more likely, you'll need the yacht to take Miss Langham and the rest of the family out of the country."

King smiled and Miss Langham regarded Weimer with flattering interest. "I've got a quick-firing gun below decks," said King, "that I used in the Malaysian Peninsula on a junkful of Black Flags,[1] and I think I'll have it brought up. And there are about thirty of my men on the yacht who wouldn't ask for their wages

---

1 Slang for pirates.

in a year if I'd let them go on shore and mix up in a fight. When do you suppose this——"

A heavy step and the jingle of spurs on the bare floor of the bungalow startled the conspirators, and they turned and gazed guiltily out at the mountain-tops above them as Clay came hurrying out upon the porch.

"They told me you were here," he said, speaking to Miss Langham. "I'm so sorry it tired you. I should have remembered—it is a rough trip when you're not used to it," he added, remorsefully. "But I'm glad Weimer was here to take care of you."

"It was just a trifle hot and noisy," said Miss Langham, smiling sweetly. She put her hand to her forehead with an expression of patient suffering. "It made my head ache a little, but it was most interesting." She added, "You are certainly to be congratulated on your work."

Clay glanced at her doubtfully with a troubled look, and turned away his eyes to the busy scene below him. He was greatly hurt that she should have cared so little, and indignant at himself for being so unjust. Why should he expect a woman to find interest in that hive of noise and sweating energy? But even as he stood arguing with himself his eyes fell on a slight figure sitting erect and graceful on her pony's back, her white habit soiled and stained red with the ore of the mines, and green where it had crushed against the leaves. She was coming slowly up the trail with a body-guard of half a dozen men crowding closely around her, telling her the difficulties of the work, and explaining their successes, and eager for a share of her quick sympathy.

Clay's eyes fixed themselves on the picture, and he smiled at its significance. Miss Langham noticed the look, and glanced below to see what it was that had so interested him, and then back at him again. He was still watching the approaching cavalcade intently, and smiling to himself. Miss Langham drew in her breath and raised her head and shoulders quickly, like a deer that hears a footstep in the forest, and when Hope presently stepped out upon the porch, she turned quickly toward her, and regarded her steadily, as though she were a stranger to her, and as though she were trying to see her with the eyes of one who looked at her for the first time.

"Hope!" she said, "do look at your dress!"

Hope's face was glowing with the unusual exercise, and her eyes were brilliant. Her hair had slipped down beneath the visor of her helmet. "I am so tired—and so hungry." She was laughing and looking directly at Clay. "It has been a wonderful thing to have seen," she said, tugging at her heavy gauntlet, "and to have done," she added. She pulled off her glove and held out her hand to Clay, moist and scarred with the pressure of the reins.

"Thank you," she said, simply.

The master of the mines took it with a quick rush of gratitude, and looking into the girl's eyes saw something there that startled him, so that he glanced quickly past her at the circle of booted men grouped in the door behind her. They were each smiling in appreciation of the tableau; her father and Ted, MacWilliams and Kirkland, and all the others who had helped him. They seemed to envy, but not to grudge, the whole credit which the girl had given to him.

Clay thought, "Why could it not have been the other?" But he said aloud, "Thank *you*. You have given me my reward."

Miss Langham looked down impatiently into the valley below, and found that it seemed more hot and noisy, and more grimy than before.

VI

Clay believed that Alice Langham's visit to the mines had opened his eyes fully to vast differences between them. He laughed and railed at himself for having dared to imagine that he was in a position to care for her. Confident as he was at times, and sure as he was of his ability in certain directions, he was uneasy and fearful when he matched himself against a man of gentle birth and gentle breeding, and one who, like King, was part of a world of which he knew little, and to which, in his ignorance concerning it, he attributed many advantages that it did not possess. He believed that he would always lack the mysterious something which these others held by right of inheritance. He was still young and full of the illusions of youth, and so gave false values to his own qualities, and values equally false to the qualities he lacked. For the next week he avoided Miss Langham, unless there were other people present, and whenever she showed him special favor, he hastily recalled to his mind her failure to sympathize in his work, and assured himself that if she could not interest herself in the engineer, he did not care to have her interested in the man. Other women had found him attractive in himself; they had cared for his strength of will and mind, and because he was good to look at. But he determined that this one must sympathize with his work in the world, no matter how unpicturesque it might seem to her. His work was the best of him, he assured himself, and he would stand or fall with it.

It was a week after the visit to the mines that President Alvarez gave a great ball in honor of the Langhams, to which all of the important people of Olancho, and the Foreign Ministers were invited. Miss Langham met Clay on the afternoon of the day set for the ball, as she was going down the hill to join Hope and her father at dinner on the yacht.

"Are you not coming, too?" she asked.

"I wish I could," Clay answered. "King asked me, but a steamer-load of new machinery arrived to-day, and I have to see it through the Custom-House."

Miss Langham gave an impatient little laugh, and shook her head. "You might wait until we were gone before you bother with your machinery," she said.

"When you are gone I won't be in a state of mind to attend to machinery or anything else," Clay answered.

Miss Langham seemed so far encouraged by this speech that she seated herself in the boat-house at the end of the wharf. She pushed her mantilla back from her face and looked up at him, smiling brightly.

"'The time has come, the walrus said,'" she quoted, "'to talk of many things.'"[1]

Clay laughed and dropped down beside her. "Well?" he said. "You have been rather unkind to me this last week," the girl began, with her eyes fixed steadily on his. "And that day at the mines, when I counted on you so, you acted abominably."

Clay's face showed so plainly his surprise at this charge, which he thought he only had the right to make, that Miss Langham stopped.

"I don't understand," said Clay, quietly. "How did I treat you abominably?"

He had taken her so seriously that Miss Langham dropped her lighter tone and spoke in one more kindly:

"I went out there to see your work at its best. I was only interested in going because it was your work, and because it was you who had done it all, and I expected that you would try to explain it to me and help me to understand, but you didn't. You treated me as though I had no interest in the matter at all, as though I

---

1   The quote comes from Lewis Carroll's (1832–98) *Through the Looking-Glass and What Alice Found There* (1871), the sequel to his most famous work, *Alice's Adventures in Wonderland* (1865).

was not capable of understanding it. You did not seem to care whether I was interested or not. In fact, you forgot me altogether."

Clay exhibited no evidence of a reproving conscience. "I am sorry you had a stupid time," he said, gravely.

"I did not mean that, and you know I didn't mean that," the girl answered. "I wanted to hear about it from you, because you did it. I wasn't interested so much in what had been done, as I was in the man who had accomplished it."

Clay shrugged his shoulders impatiently, and looked across at Miss Langham with a troubled smile.

"But that's just what I don't want," he said. "Can't you see? These mines and other mines like them are all I have in the world. They are my only excuse for having lived in it so long. I want to feel that I've done something outside of myself, and when you say that you like me personally, it's as little satisfaction to me as it must be to a woman to be congratulated on her beauty, or on her fine voice. That is nothing she has done herself. I should like you to value what I have done, not what I happen to be."

Miss Langham turned her eyes to the harbor, and it was some short time before she answered.

"You are a very difficult person to please," she said, "and most exacting. As a rule men are satisfied to be liked for any reason. I confess frankly, since you insist upon it, that I do not rise to the point of appreciating your work as the others do. I suppose it is a fault," she continued, with an air that plainly said that she considered it, on the contrary, something of a virtue. "And if I knew more about it technically, I might see more in it to admire. But I am looking farther on for better things from you. The friends who help us the most are not always those who consider us perfect, are they?" she asked, with a kindly smile. She raised her eyes to the great ore-pier that stretched out across the water, the one ugly blot in the scene of natural beauty about them. "I think that is all very well," she said; "but I certainly expect you to do more than that. I have met many remarkable men in all parts of the world, and I know what a strong man is, and you have one of the strongest personalities I have known. But you can't mean that you are content to stop with this. You should be something bigger and more wide-reaching and more lasting. Indeed, it hurts me to see you wasting your time here over my father's interests. You should exert that same energy on a broader map. You could make yourself anything you chose. At home you would be your party's leader in politics, or you could be a great general, or a great financier. I say this because I know there are better things in you, and because I want you to make the most of your talents. I am anxious to see you put your powers to something worth while."

Miss Langham's voice carried with it such a tone of sincerity that she almost succeeded in deceiving herself. And yet she would have hardly cared to explain just why she had reproached the man before her after this fashion. For she knew that when she spoke as she had done, she was beating about to find some reason that would justify her in not caring for him, as she knew she could care—as she would not allow herself to care. The man at her side had won her interest from the first, and later had occupied her thoughts so entirely, that it troubled her peace of mind. Yet she would not let her feeling for him wax and grow stronger, but kept it down. And she was trying now to persuade herself that she did this because there was something lacking in him and not in her.

She was almost angry with him for being so much to her and for not being more acceptable in little things, like the other men she knew. So she found this fault with him in order that she might justify her own lack of feeling.

But Clay, who only heard the words and could not go back of them to find the motive, could not know this. He sat perfectly still when she had finished and looked steadily out across the harbor. His eyes fell on the ugly ore-pier, and he winced and uttered a short grim laugh.

"That's true, what you say," he began, "I haven't done much. You are quite right. Only—" he looked up at her curiously and smiled—"only you should not have been the one to tell me of it."

Miss Langham had been so far carried away by her own point of view that she had not considered Clay, and now that she saw what mischief she had done, she gave a quick gasp of regret, and leaned forward as though to add some explanation to what she had said. But Clay stopped her. "I mean by that," he said, "that the great part of the inspiration I have had to do what little I have done came from you. You were a sort of promise of something better to me. You were more of a type than an individual woman, but your picture, the one I carry in my watch, meant all that part of life that I have never known, the sweetness and the nobleness and grace of civilization,—something I hoped I would some day have time to enjoy. So you see," he added, with an uncertain laugh, "it's less pleasant to hear that I have failed to make the most of myself from you than from almost any one else."

"But, Mr. Clay," protested the girl, anxiously, "I think you have done wonderfully well. I only said that I wanted you to do more. You are so young and you have——"

Clay did not hear her. He was leaning forward looking moodily out across the water, with his folded arms clasped across his knees.

"I have not made the most of myself," he repeated; "that is what you said." He spoke the words as though she had delivered a sentence. "You don't think well of what I have done, of what I am."

He drew in his breath and shook his head with a hopeless laugh, and leaned back against the railing of the boat-house with the weariness in his attitude of a man who has given up after a long struggle.

"No," he said with a bitter flippancy in his voice, "I don't amount to much. But, my God!" he laughed, and turning his head away, "when you think what I was! This doesn't seem much to you, and it doesn't seem much to me now that I have your point of view on it, but when I remember!" Clay stopped again and pressed his lips together and shook his head. His half-closed eyes, that seemed to be looking back into his past, lighted as they fell on King's white yacht, and he raised his arm and pointed to it with a wave of the hand. "When I was sixteen I was a sailor before the mast," he said, "the sort of sailor that King's crew out there wouldn't recognize in the same profession. I was of so little account that I've been knocked the length of the main deck at the end of the mate's fist, and left to lie bleeding in the scuppers for dead. I hadn't a thing to my name then but the clothes I wore, and I've had to go aloft in a hurricane and cling to a swinging rope with my bare toes and pull at a wet sheet until my finger-nails broke and started in their sockets; and I've been a cowboy, with no companions for six months of the year but eight thousand head of cattle and men as dumb and untamed as the steers themselves. I've sat in my saddle night after night, with nothing overhead but the stars, and no sound but the noise of the steers breathing in their sleep. The women I knew were Indian squaws, and the girls of the sailors' dance-houses and the gambling-hells of Sioux City and Abilene, and Callao and Port Saïd.[1] That was what I was and those were my companions. Why!" he laughed, rising and striding across the boat-house with his hands locked

---

1 Callao, Peru's chief port city; Port Said, a city in northeastern Egypt, on the Mediterranean Sea.

behind him, "I've fought on the mud floor of a Mexican shack, with a naked knife in my hand, for my last dollar. I was as low and as desperate as that. And now—" Clay lifted his head and smiled. "Now," he said, in a lower voice and addressing Miss Langham with a return of his usual grave politeness, "I am able to sit beside you and talk to you. I have risen to that. I am quite content."

He paused and looked at Miss Langham uncertainly for a few moments as though in doubt as to whether she would understand him if he continued.

"And though it means nothing to you," he said, "and though as you say I am here as your father's employee, there are other places, perhaps, where I am better known. In Edinburgh or Berlin or Paris, if you were to ask the people of my own profession, they could tell you something of me. If I wished it, I could drop this active work to-morrow and continue as an adviser, as an expert, but I like the active part better. I like doing things myself. I don't say, 'I am a salaried servant of Mr. Langham's'; I put it differently. I say, 'There are five mountains of iron. You are to take them up and transport them from South America to North America, where they will be turned into railroads and ironclads.' That's my way of looking at it. It's better to bind a laurel to the plough than to call yourself hard names. It makes your work easier—almost noble. Cannot you see it that way, too?"

Before Miss Langham could answer, a deprecatory cough from one side of the open boat-house startled them, and turning they saw MacWilliams coming toward them. They had been so intent upon what Clay was saying that he had approached them over the soft sand of the beach without their knowing it. Miss Langham welcomed his arrival with evident pleasure.

"The launch is waiting for you at the end of the pier," MacWilliams said. Miss Langham rose and the three walked together down the length of the wharf, MacWilliams moving briskly in advance in order to enable them to continue the conversation he had interrupted, but they followed close behind him, as though neither of them were desirous of such an opportunity.

Hope and King had both come for Miss Langham, and while the latter was helping her to a place on the cushions, and repeating his regrets that the men were not coming also, Hope started the launch, with a brisk ringing of bells and a whirl of the wheel and a smile over her shoulder at the figures on the wharf.

"Why didn't you go?" said Clay; "you have no business at the Custom-House."

"Neither have you," said MacWilliams. "But I guess we both understand. There's no good pushing your luck too far."

"What do you mean by that—this time?"

"Why, what have we to do with all of this?" cried MacWilliams. "It's what I keep telling you every day. We're not in that class, and you're only making it harder for yourself when they've gone. I call it cruelty to animals myself, having women like that around. Up North, where everybody's white, you don't notice it so much, but down here—Lord!"

"That's absurd," Clay answered. "Why should you turn your back on civilization when it comes to you, just because you're not going back to civilization by the next steamer? Every person you meet either helps you or hurts you. Those girls help us, even if they do make the life here seem bare and mean."

"Bare and mean!" repeated MacWilliams, incredulously. "I think that's just what they don't do. I like it all the better because they're mixed up in it. I never took so much interest in your mines until she took to riding over them, and I didn't think great shakes of my old ore-road, either, but now that she's got to acting as engineer, it's sort of nickel-plated the whole outfit. I'm going to name the new engine after her—when it gets here—if her old man will let me."

"What do you mean? Miss Langham hasn't been to the mines but once, has she?"

"Miss Langham!" exclaimed MacWilliams. "No, I mean the other, Miss Hope. She comes out with Ted nearly every day now, and she's learning how to run a locomotive. Just for fun, you know," he added, reassuringly.

"I didn't suppose she had any intention of joining the Brotherhood," said Clay. "So she's been out every day, has she? I like that," he commented, enthusiastically. "She's a fine, sweet girl."

"Fine, sweet girl!" growled MacWilliams. "I should hope so. She's the best. They don't make them any better than that, and just think, if she's like that now, what will she be when she's grown up, when she's learned a few things? Now her sister. You can see just what her sister will be at thirty, and at fifty, and at eighty. She's thoroughbred and she's the most beautiful woman to look at I ever saw—but, my son—she is too careful. She hasn't any illusions, and no sense of humor. And a woman with no illusions and no sense of humor is going to be monotonous. You can't teach her anything. You can't imagine yourself telling her anything she doesn't know. The things we think important don't reach her at all. They're not in her line, and in everything else she knows more than we could ever guess at. But that Miss Hope! It's a privilege to show her about. She wants to see everything, and learn everything, and she goes poking her head into openings and down shafts like a little fox terrier. And she'll sit still and listen with her eyes wide open and tears in them, too, and she doesn't know it—until you can't talk yourself for just looking at her."

Clay rose and moved on to the house in silence. He was glad that MacWilliams had interrupted him when he did. He wondered whether he understood Alice Langham after all. He had seen many fine ladies before during his brief visits to London, and Berlin, and Vienna, and they had shown him favor. He had known other women not so fine. Spanish-American señoritas through Central and South America, the wives and daughters of English merchants exiled along the Pacific coast, whose fair skin and yellow hair whitened and bleached under the hot tropical suns. He had known many women, and he could have quoted

Trials and troubles amany,
Have proved me;
One or two women, God bless them!
Have loved me.

But the woman he was to marry must have all the things he lacked. She must fill out and complete him where he was wanting. This woman possessed all of these things. She appealed to every ambition and to every taste he cherished, and yet he knew that he had hesitated and mistrusted her, when he should have declared himself eagerly and vehemently, and forced her to listen with all the strength of his will.

★★★★★

Miss Langham dropped among the soft cushions of the launch with a sense of having been rescued from herself and of delight in finding refuge again in her own environment. The sight of King standing in the bow beside Hope with his cigarette hanging from his lips, and peering with half-closed eyes into the fading light, gave her a sense of restfulness and content. She did not know what she wished from that other strange young man. He was so bold, so handsome, and he looked at life and spoke of it in such a fresh, unhackneyed spirit. He might make himself anything he pleased. But here was a man who already had everything, or who could get it as easily as he could increase the speed of the launch, by pulling some wire with his finger.

She recalled one day when they were all on board of this same launch, and the machinery had broken down, and MacWilliams had gone forward to look at it. He had called Clay to help him, and she remembered how they had both gone down on their knees and asked the engineer and fireman to pass them wrenches and oil-cans, while King protested mildly, and the rest sat helplessly in the hot glare of the sea, as the boat rose and fell on the waves. She resented Clay's interest in the accident, and his pleasure when he had made the machinery right once more, and his appearance as he came back to them with oily hands and with his face glowing from the heat of the furnace, wiping his grimy fingers on a piece of packing. She had resented the equality with which he treated the engineer in asking his advice, and it rather surprised her that the crew saluted him when he stepped into the launch again that night as though he were the owner. She had expected that they would patronize him, and she imagined after this incident that she detected a shade of difference in the manner of the sailors toward Clay, as though he had cheapened himself to them—as he had to her.

VII

At ten o'clock that same evening Clay began to prepare himself for the ball at the Government palace, and MacWilliams, who was not invited, watched him dress with critical approval that showed no sign of envy.

The better to do honor to the President, Clay had brought out several foreign orders, and MacWilliams helped him to tie around his neck the collar of the Red Eagle which the German Emperor had given him, and to fasten the ribbon and cross of the Star of Olancho across his breast, and a Spanish Order and the Legion of Honor to the lapel of his coat. MacWilliams surveyed the effect of the tiny enamelled crosses with his head on one side, and with the same air of affectionate pride and concern that a mother shows over her daughter's first ball-dress.

"Got any more?" he asked, anxiously.

"I have some war medals," Clay answered, smiling doubtfully. "But I'm not in uniform."

"Oh, that's all right," declared MacWilliams. "Put 'em on, put 'em all on. Give the girls a treat. Everybody will think they were given for feats of swimming, anyway; but they will show up well from the front. Now, then, you look like a drum-major or a conjuring chap."

"I do not," said Clay. "I look like a French Ambassador, and I hardly understand how you find courage to speak to me at all."

He went up the hill in high spirits, and found the carriage at the door and King, Mr. Langham, and Miss Langham sitting waiting for him. They were ready to depart, and Miss Langham had but just seated herself in the carriage when they heard hurrying across the tiled floor a quick, light step and the rustle of silk, and turning they saw Hope standing in the doorway, radiant and smiling. She wore a white frock that reached to the ground, and that left her arms and shoulders bare. Her hair was dressed high upon her head, and she was pulling vigorously at a pair of long, tan-colored gloves. The transformation was so complete, and the girl looked so much older and so stately and beautiful, that the two young men stared at her in silent admiration and astonishment.

"Why, Hope!" exclaimed her sister. "What does this mean?"

Hope stopped in some alarm, and clasped her hair with both hands.

"What is it?" she asked; "is anything wrong?"

"Why, my dear child," said her sister, "you're not thinking of going with us, are you?"

"Not going?" echoed the younger sister, in dismay. "Why, Alice, why not? I was asked."

"But, Hope—Father," said the elder sister, stepping out of the carriage and turning to Mr. Langham, "you didn't intend that Hope should go, did you? She's not out yet."

"Oh, nonsense," said Hope, defiantly. But she drew in her breath quickly and blushed, as she saw the two young men moving away out of hearing of this family crisis. She felt that she was being made to look like a spoiled child. "It doesn't count down here," she said, "and I want to go. I thought you knew I was going all the time. Marie made this frock for me on purpose."

"I don't think Hope is old enough," the elder sister said, addressing her father, "and if she goes to dances here, there's no reason why she should not go to those at home."

"But I don't want to go to dances at home," interrupted Hope.

Mr. Langham looked exceedingly uncomfortable, and turned appealingly to his elder daughter. "What do you think, Alice?" he said, doubtfully.

"I'm sorry," Miss Langham replied, "but I know it would not be at all proper. I hate to seem horrid about it, Hope, but indeed you are too young, and the men here are not the men a young girl ought to meet."

"You meet them, Alice," said Hope, but pulling off her gloves in token of defeat.

"But, my dear child, I'm fifty years older than you are."

"Perhaps Alice knows best, Hope," Mr. Langham said. "I'm sorry if you are disappointed."

Hope held her head a little higher, and turned toward the door.

"I don't mind if you don't wish it, father," she said. "Good-night." She moved away, but apparently thought better of it, and came back and stood smiling and nodding to them as they seated themselves in the carriage. Mr. Langham leaned forward and said, in a troubled voice, "We will tell you all about it in the morning. I'm very sorry. You won't be lonely, will you? I'll stay with you if you wish."

"Nonsense!" laughed Hope. "Why, it's given to you, father; don't bother about me. I'll read something or other and go to bed."

"Good-night, Cinderella," King called out to her.

"Good-night, Prince Charming," Hope answered.

Both Clay and King felt that the girl would not mind missing the ball so much as she would the fact of having been treated like a child in their presence, so they refrained from any expression of sympathy or regret, but raised their hats and bowed a little more impressively than usual as the carriage drove away.

The picture Hope made, as she stood deserted and forlorn on the steps of the empty house in her new finery, struck Clay as unnecessarily pathetic. He felt a strong sense of resentment against her sister and her father, and thanked heaven devoutly that he was out of their class, and when Miss Langham continued to express her sorrow that she had been forced to act as she had done, he remained silent. It seemed to Clay such a simple thing to give children pleasure, and to remember that their woes were always out of all proportion to the cause. Children, dumb animals, and blind people were always grouped together in his mind as objects demanding the most tender and constant consideration. So the pleasure of the evening was spoiled for him while he remembered the hurt and disappointed look in Hope's face, and when Miss Langham asked him why he was so preoccupied, he told her bluntly that he thought she had been very unkind to Hope, and that her objections were absurd.

Miss Langham held herself a little more stiffly. "Perhaps you do not quite understand, Mr. Clay," she said. "Some of us have to conform to certain rules that the people with whom we best like to associate have laid down for themselves. If we choose to be conventional, it is probably because we find it makes life easier for the greater number. You cannot think it was a pleasant task for me. But I have given up things of much more importance than a dance for the sake of appearances, and Hope herself will see tomorrow that I acted for the best."

Clay said he trusted so, but doubted it, and by way of re-establishing himself in Miss Langham's good favor, asked her if she could give him the next dance. But Miss Langham was not to be propitiated.

"I'm sorry," she said, "but I believe I am engaged until supper-time. Come and ask me then, and I'll have one saved for you. But there is something you can do," she added. "I left my fan in the carriage—do you think you could manage to get it for me without much trouble?"

"The carriage did not wait. I believe it was sent back," said Clay, "but I can borrow a horse from one of Stuart's men, and ride back and get it for you, if you like."

"How absurd!" laughed Miss Langham, but she looked pleased, notwithstanding.

"Oh, not at all," Clay answered. He was smiling down at her in some amusement, and was apparently much entertained at his idea. "Will you consider it an act of devotion?" he asked.

There was so little of devotion, and so much more of mischief in his eyes, that Miss Langham guessed he was only laughing at her, and shook her head.

"You won't go," she said, turning away. She followed him with her eyes, however, as he crossed the room, his head and shoulders towering above the native men and women. She had never seen him so resplendent, and she noted, with an eye that considered trifles, the orders, and his well-fitting white gloves, and his manner of bowing in the Continental fashion, holding his opera-hat on his thigh, as though his hand rested on a sword. She noticed that the little Olanchoans stopped and looked after him, as he pushed his way among them, and she could see that the men were telling the women who he was. Sir Julian Pindar, the old British Minister, stopped him, and she watched them as they laughed together over the English war medals on the American's breast, which Sir Julian touched with his finger. He called the French Minister and his pretty wife to look, too, and they all laughed and talked together in great spirits, and Miss Langham wondered if Clay was speaking in French to them.

Miss Langham did not enjoy the ball; she felt injured and aggrieved, and she assured herself that she had been hardly used.

She had only done her duty, and yet all the sympathy had gone to her sister, who had placed her in a trying position. She thought it was most inconsiderate.

Hope walked slowly across the veranda when the others had gone, and watched the carriage as long as it remained in sight. Then she threw herself into a big arm-chair, and looked down upon her pretty frock and her new dancing-slippers. She, too, felt badly used.

The moonlight fell all about her, as it had on the first night of their arrival, a month before, but now it seemed cold and cheerless, and gave an added sense of loneliness to the silent house. She did not go inside to read, as she had promised to do, but sat for the next hour looking out across the harbor. She could not blame Alice. She considered that Alice always moved by rules and precedents, like a queen in a game of chess, and she wondered why. It made life so tame and uninteresting, and yet people invariably admired Alice, and some one had spoken of her as the noblest example of the modern gentlewoman. She was sure she could not grow up to be any thing like that. She was quite confident that she was going to disappoint her family. She wondered if people would like her better if she were discreet like Alice, and less like her brother Ted. If Mr. Clay, for instance, would like her better? She wondered if he disapproved of her riding on the engine with MacWilliams, and of her tearing through the mines on her pony, and spearing with a lance of sugar-cane at the mongrel curs that ran to snap at his flanks. She remembered his look of astonished amusement the day he had caught her in this impromptu pig-sticking, and she felt herself growing red at the recollection. She was sure he thought her a tomboy. Probably he never thought of her at all.

Hope leaned back in the chair and looked up at the stars above the mountains and tried to think of any of her heroes and princes in fiction who had gone through such interesting experiences as had Mr. Clay. Some of them had done so, but they were creatures in a book and this hero was alive, and she knew him, and had probably made him despise her as a silly little girl who was scolded and sent off to bed like a disobedient child. Hope felt a choking in her throat and something like a tear creep to her eyes: but she was surprised to find that the fact did not make her ashamed of herself. She owned that she was wounded and disappointed, and to make it harder she could not help picturing Alice and Clay laughing and talking together in some corner away from the ball-room, while she, who understood him so well, and who could not find the words to tell him how much she valued what he was and what he had done, was forgotten and sitting here alone, like Cinderella, by the empty fireplace.

The picture was so pathetic as Hope drew it, that for a moment she felt almost a touch of self-pity, but the next she laughed scornfully at her own foolishness, and rising with an impatient shrug, walked away in the direction of her room.

But before she had crossed the veranda she was stopped by the sound of a horse's hoofs galloping over the hard sun-baked road that led from the city, and before she had stepped forward out of the shadow in which she stood the horse had reached the steps and his rider had pulled him back on his haunches and swung himself off before the forefeet had touched the ground.

Hope had guessed that it was Clay by his riding, and she feared from his haste that some one of her people were ill. So she ran anxiously forward and asked if anything were wrong.

Clay started at her sudden appearance, and gave a short boyish laugh of pleasure.

"I'm so glad you're still up," he said. "No, nothing is wrong." He stopped in some embarrassment. He had been moved to return by the fact that the little girl he knew was in trouble, and now that he was suddenly confronted by this older and statelier young person, his action seemed particularly silly, and he was at a loss to explain it in any way that would not give offence.

"No, nothing is wrong," he repeated. "I came after something."

Clay had borrowed one of the cloaks the troopers wore at night from the same man who had lent him the horse, and as he stood bareheaded before her, with the cloak hanging from his shoulders to the floor and the star and ribbon across his breast, Hope felt very grateful to him for being able to look like a Prince or a hero in a book, and to yet remain her Mr. Clay at the same time.

"I came to get your sister's fan," Clay explained. "She forgot it."

The young girl looked at him for a moment in surprise and then straightened herself slightly. She did not know whether she was the more indignant with Alice for sending such a man on so foolish an errand, or with Clay for submitting to such a service.

"Oh, is that it?" she said at last. "I will go and find you one."
She gave him a dignified little bow and moved away toward the
door, with every appearance of disapproval.

"Oh, I don't know," she heard Clay say, doubtfully; "I don't
have to go just yet, do I? May I not stay here a little while?"

Hope stood and looked at him in some perplexity.

"Why, yes," she answered, wonderingly. "But don't you want
to go back? You came in a great hurry. And won't Alice want her
fan?"

"Oh, she has it by this time. I told Stuart to find it. She left it
in the carriage, and the carriage is waiting at the end of the
plaza."

"Then why did you come?" asked Hope, with rising suspicion.

"Oh, I don't know," said Clay, helplessly. "I thought I'd just
like a ride in the moonlight. I hate balls and dances anyway, don't
you? I think you were very wise not to go."

Hope placed her hands on the back of the big arm-chair and
looked steadily at him as he stood where she could see his face in
the moonlight. "You came back," she said, "because they thought
I was crying, and they sent you to see. Is that it? Did Alice send
you?" she demanded.

Clay gave a gasp of consternation.

"You know that no one sent me," he said. "I thought they
treated you abominably, and I wanted to come and say so. That's
all. And I wanted to tell you that I missed you very much, and
that your not coming had spoiled the evening for me, and I came
also because I preferred to talk to you than to stay where I was.
No one knows that I came to see you. I said I was going to get
the fan, and I told Stuart to find it after I'd left. I just wanted to
see you, that's all. But I will go back again at once."

While he had been speaking Hope had lowered her eyes from his
face and had turned and looked out across the harbor. There was a
strange, happy tumult in her breast, and she was breathing so
rapidly that she was afraid he would notice it. She also felt an absurd
inclination to cry, and that frightened her. So she laughed and
turned and looked up into his face again. Clay saw the same look in
her eyes that he had seen there the day when she had congratulated
him on his work at the mines. He had seen it before in the eyes of
other women and it troubled him. Hope seated herself in the big
chair, and Clay tossed his cloak on the floor at her feet and sat down
with his shoulders against one of the pillars. He glanced up at her
and found that the look that had troubled him was gone, and that
her eyes were now smiling with excitement and pleasure.

"And did you bring me something from the ball in your pocket to comfort me," she asked, mockingly.

"Yes, I did," Clay answered, unabashed. "I brought you some bonbons."

"You didn't, really!" Hope cried, with a shriek of delight. "How absurd of you! The sort you pull?"

"The sort you pull," Clay repeated, gravely. "And also a dance-card, which is a relic of barbarism still existing in this Southern capital. It has the arms of Olancho on it in gold, and I thought you might like to keep it as a souvenir." He pulled the card from his coat-pocket and said, "May I have this dance?"

"You may," Hope answered. "But you wouldn't mind if we sat it out, would you?"

"I should prefer it," Clay said, as he scrawled his name across the card. "It is so crowded inside, and the company is rather mixed." They both laughed lightly at their own foolishness, and Hope smiled down upon him affectionately and proudly. "You may smoke, if you choose; and would you like something cool to drink?" she asked, anxiously. "After your ride, you know," she suggested, with hospitable intent. Clay said that he was very comfortable without a drink, but lighted a cigar and watched her covertly through the smoke, as she sat smiling happily and quite unconsciously upon the moonlit world around them. She caught Clay's eye fixed on her, and laughed lightly.

"What is it?" he said.

"Oh, I was just thinking," Hope replied, "that it was much better to have a dance come to you, than to go to the dance."

"Does one man and a dance-card and three bonbons constitute your idea of a ball?"

"Doesn't it? You see, I am not out yet; I don't know."

"I should think it might depend a good deal upon the man," Clay suggested.

"That sounds as though you were hinting," said Hope, doubtfully. "Now what would I say to that if I were out?"

"I don't know, but don't say it," Clay answered. "It would probably be something very unflattering or very forward, and in either case I should take you back to your chaperon and leave you there."

Hope had not been listening. Her eyes were fixed on a level with his tie, and Clay raised his hand to it in some trepidation. "Mr. Clay," she began abruptly, and leaning eagerly forward, "would you think me very rude if I asked you what you did to get all those crosses? I know they mean something, and I do so want to know what. Please tell me."

"Oh, those!" said Clay. "The reason I put them on to-night is because wearing them is supposed to be a sort of compliment to your host. I got in the habit abroad——"

"I didn't ask you that," said Hope, severely. "I asked you what you did to get them. Now begin with the Legion of Honor on the left, and go right on until you come to the end, and please don't skip anything. Leave in all the bloodthirsty parts, and please don't be modest."

"Like Othello,"[1] suggested Clay.

"Yes," said Hope; "I will be Desdemona."

"Well, Desdemona, it was like this," said Clay, laughing. "I got that medal and that star for serving in the Nile campaign, under Wolseley.[2] After I left Egypt, I went up the coast to Algiers, where I took service under the French in a most disreputable organization known as the Foreign Legion——"[3]

"Don't tell me," exclaimed Hope, in delight, "that you have been a Chasseur d'Afrique! Not like the man in 'Under Two Flags?'"[4]

"No, not at all like that man," said Clay, emphatically. "I was just a plain, common, or garden, sappeur,[5] and I showed the

---

1   *Othello* (c. 1604), a tragedy by William Shakespeare (1564–1616). Othello, a Moor in the service of Venice, secretly marries Desdemona, the daughter of a Venetian senator. When Othello first woos Desdemona, she asks to hear about his military campaigns and adventures in exotic lands. Unfortunately, matters go very badly for the couple: due to the manipulations of Iago, a soldier bitter about being passed over for promotion, Othello murders his wife and kills himself. (My thanks to John Hunt for talking with me about all matters Shakespearean.)

2   Field Marshal Lord Garnet Wolseley (1833–1913), celebrated British military leader, and the Commander-in-Chief of the British army during the Nile operations of 1884–85. Wolseley is also known for his failure to rescue Charles George Gordon (1833–85) at Khartoum in the Sudan.

3   The French Foreign Legion, a notorious division of the French military comprised largely of criminals and exiles from nations around the world. The Legion was infamous not only for its brutality in battle, but for its brutal disciplinary regime.

4   A popular novel about the French Foreign Legion, written by Ouida, the pseudonym of Marie Louise de la Ramée (1839–1908), an English novelist.

5   A soldier responsible for setting or detonating mines and for building fortifications in the field.

other good-for-nothings how to dig trenches. Well, I contaminated the Foreign Legion for eight months, and then I went to Peru, where I——"

"You're skipping," said Hope. "How did you get the Legion of Honor?"

"Oh, that?" said Clay. "That was a gallery play I made once when we were chasing some Arabs. They took the French flag away from our color-bearer, and I got it back again and waved it frantically around my head until I was quite certain the Colonel had seen me doing it, and then I stopped as soon as I knew that I was sure of promotion."

"Oh, how can you?" cried Hope. "You didn't do anything of the sort. You probably saved the entire regiment."

"Well, perhaps I did," Clay returned. "Though I don't remember it, and nobody mentioned it at the time."

"Go on about the others," said Hope. "And do try to be truthful."

"Well, I got this one from Spain, because I was President of an International Congress of Engineers at Madrid. That was the ostensible reason, but the real reason was because I taught the Spanish Commissioners to play poker instead of baccarat. The German Emperor gave me this for designing a fort, and the Sultan of Zanzibar gave me this, and no one but the Sultan knows why, and he won't tell. I suppose he's ashamed. He gives them away instead of cigars. He was out of cigars the day I called."[1]

"What a lot of places you have seen," sighed Hope. "I have been in Cairo and Algiers, too, but I always had to walk about with a governess, and she wouldn't go to the mosques because she said they were full of fleas. We always go to Homburg and Paris in the summer, and to big hotels in London. I love to travel, but I don't love to travel that way, would you?"

"I travel because I have no home," said Clay. "I'm different from the chap that came home because all the other places were shut. I go to other places because there is no home open."

---

1   Zanzibar, an archipelago made up of Zanzibar and the Pemba Islands off the coast of Tanzania. In the nineteenth century, the island of Zanzibar was a bustling trade center (dealing in slaves and ivory) and the colonial powers of Germany and Britain often negotiated with—and sought to influence—the various Sultans, or Muslim leaders, of East Africa. Davis, like many Western writers of his era, here presents the Sultan as a foolish, comic figure.

"What do you mean?" said Hope, shaking her head. "Why have you no home?"

"There was a ranch in Colorado that I used to call home," said Clay, "but they've cut it up into town lots. I own a plot in the cemetery outside of the town, where my mother is buried, and I visit that whenever I am in the States, and that is the only piece of earth anywhere in the world that I have to go back to."

Hope leaned forward with her hands clasped in front of her and her eyes wide open.

"And your father?" she said, softly; "is he—is he there, too——"

Clay looked at the lighted end of his cigar as he turned it between his fingers.

"My father, Miss Hope," he said, "was a filibuster, and went out on the *Virginius* to help free Cuba, and was shot, against a stone wall. We never knew where he was buried."[1]

"Oh, forgive me; I beg your pardon," said Hope. There was such distress in her voice that Clay looked at her quickly and saw the tears in her eyes. She reached out her hand timidly, and touched for an instant his own rough, sunburned fist, as it lay clenched on his knee. "I am so sorry," she said, "so sorry." For the first time in many years the tears came to Clay's eyes and blurred the moonlight and the scene before him, and he sat unmanned and silent before the simple touch of a young girl's sympathy.

An hour later, when his pony struck the gravel from beneath his hoofs on the race back to the city, and Clay turned to wave his hand to Hope in the doorway, she seemed, as she stood with the moonlight falling about her white figure, like a spirit beckoning the way to a new paradise.

VIII

Clay reached the President's Palace during the supper-hour, and found Mr. Langham and his daughter at the President's table. Madame Alvarez pointed to a place for him beside Alice

---

1 A reference to William Walker, the American filibuster who conquered Nicaragua in 1856. After his expulsion from Central America in 1857, he attempted to return to the isthmus on a number of occasions, only to be captured and executed on a beach in Honduras in 1860. His remains were buried in an unmarked grave. Walker, here, figures as Clay's free-booting father.

Langham, who held up her hand in welcome. "You were very foolish to rush off like that," she said.

"It wasn't there," said Clay, crowding into the place beside her.

"No, it was here in the carriage all the time. Captain Stuart found it for me."

"Oh, he did, did he?" said Clay; "that's why I couldn't find it. I am hungry," he laughed, "my ride gave me an appetite." He looked over and grinned at Stuart, but that gentleman was staring fixedly at the candles on the table before him, his eyes filled with concern. Clay observed that Madame Alvarez was covertly watching the young officer, and frowning her disapproval at his preoccupation. So he stretched his leg under the table and kicked viciously at Stuart's boots. Old General Rojas, the Vice-President, who sat next to Stuart, moved suddenly and then blinked violently at the ceiling with an expression of patient suffering, but the exclamation which had escaped him brought Stuart back to the present, and he talked with the woman next him in a perfunctory manner.

Miss Langham and her father were waiting for their carriage in the great hall of the Palace as Stuart came up to Clay, and putting his hand affectionately on his shoulder, began pointing to something farther back in the hall. To the night-birds of the streets and the noisy fiacre drivers outside, and to the crowd of guests who stood on the high marble steps waiting for their turn to depart, he might have been relating an amusing anecdote of the ball just over.

"I'm in great trouble, old man," was what he said. "I must see you alone to-night. I'd ask you to my rooms, but they watch me all the time, and I don't want them to suspect you are in this until they must. Go on in the carriage, but get out as you pass the Plaza Bolivar[1] and wait for me by the statue there."

Clay smiled, apparently in great amusement. "That's very good," he said.

He crossed over to where King stood surveying the powdered beauties of Olancho and their gowns of a past fashion, with an intensity of admiration which would have been suspicious to those who knew his tastes. "When we get into the carriage," said Clay, in a low voice, "we will both call to Stuart that we will see him to-morrow morning at breakfast."

---

1 Named for Simón Bolívar (1783–1830), the Venezuelan statesman, politician, and military commander who led the struggle for South American independence from Spain.

"All right," assented King. "What's up?"

Stuart helped Miss Langham into her carriage, and as it moved away King shouted to him in English to remember that he was breakfasting with him on the morrow, and Clay called out in Spanish, "Until to-morrow at breakfast, don't forget." And Stuart answered, steadily, "Good-night until to-morrow at one."

As their carriage jolted through the dark and narrow street, empty now of all noise or movement, one of Stuart's troopers dashed by it at a gallop, with a lighted lantern swinging at his side. He raised it as he passed each street crossing, and held it high above his head so that its light fell upon the walls of the houses at the four corners. The clatter of his horse's hoofs had not ceased before another trooper galloped toward them riding more slowly, and throwing the light of his lantern over the trunks of the trees that lined the pavements. As the carriage passed him, he brought his horse to its side with a jerk of the bridle, and swung his lantern in the faces of its occupants.

"Who lives?" he challenged.

"Olancho," Clay replied.

"Who answers?"

"Free men," Clay answered again, and pointed at the star on his coat.

The soldier muttered an apology, and striking his heels into his horse's side, dashed noisily away, his lantern tossing from side to side, high in the air, as he drew rein to scan each tree and passed from one lamp-post to the next.

"What does that mean?" said Mr. Langham; "did he take us for highwaymen?"

"It is the custom," said Clay. "We are out rather late, you see."

"If I remember rightly, Clay," said King, "they gave a ball at Brussels on the eve of Waterloo."[1]

"I believe they did," said Clay, smiling. He spoke to the driver to stop the carriage, and stepped down into the street.

"I have to leave you here," he said; "drive on quickly, please; I can explain better in the morning."

The Plaza Bolivar stood in what had once been the centre of the fashionable life of Olancho, but the town had moved farther up the hill, and it was now far in the suburbs, its walks neglected and its turf overrun with weeds. The houses about it had fallen into disuse, and the few that were still occupied at the time Clay entered it showed no sign of life. Clay picked his way over the

---

1 The site of Napoleon Bonaparte's (1769–1821) final military defeat.

grass-grown paths to the statue of Bolivar, the hero of the sister republic of Venezuela, which still stood on its pedestal in a tangle of underbrush and hanging vines. The iron railing that had once surrounded it was broken down, and the branches of the trees near were black with sleeping buzzards. Two great palms reared themselves in the moonlight at either side, and beat their leaves together in the night wind, whispering and murmuring together like two living conspirators.

"This ought to be safe enough," Clay murmured to himself. "It's just the place for plotting. I hope there are no snakes." He seated himself on the steps of the pedestal, and lighting a cigar, remained smoking and peering into the shadows about him, until a shadow blacker than the darkness rose at his feet, and a voice said, sternly, "Put out that light. I saw it half a mile away."

Clay rose and crushed his cigar under his foot. "Now then, old man," he demanded, briskly, "what's up? It's nearly daylight and we must hurry."

Stuart seated himself heavily on the stone steps, like a man tired in mind and body, and unfolded a printed piece of paper. Its blank side was damp and sticky with paste.

"It is too dark for you to see this," he began, in a strained voice, "so I will translate it to you. It is an attack on Madame Alvarez and myself. They put them up during the ball, when they knew my men would be at the Palace. I have had them scouring the streets for the last two hours tearing them down, but they are all over the place, in the cafés and clubs. They have done what they were meant to do."

Clay took another cigar from his pocket and rolled it between his lips. "What does it say?" he asked.

"It goes over the old ground first. It says Alvarez has given the richest birthright of his country to aliens—that means the mines and Langham—and has put an alien in command of the army—that is meant for me. I've no more to do with the army than you have—I only wish I had! And then it says that the boundary aggressions of Ecuador and Venezuela have not been resented in consequence. It asks what can be expected of a President who is as blind to the dishonor of his country as he is to the dishonor of his own home?"

Clay muttered under his breath, "Well, go on. Is it explicit? More explicit than that?"

"Yes," said Stuart, grimly. "I can't repeat it. It is quite clear what they mean."

"Have you got any of them?" Clay asked. "Can you fix it on some one that you can fight?"

"Mendoza did it, of course," Stuart answered, "but we cannot prove it. And if we could, we are not strong enough to take him. He has the city full of his men now, and the troops are pouring in every hour."

"Well, Alvarez can stop that, can't he?"

"They are coming in for the annual review. He can't show the people that he is afraid of his own army."

"What are you going to do?"

"What am I going to do?" Stuart repeated, dully. "That is what I want you to tell me. There is nothing I can do now. I've brought trouble and insult on people who have been kinder to me than my own blood have been. Who took me in when I was naked and clothed me, when I hadn't a friend or a sixpence to my name. You remember—I came here from that row in Colombia with my wound, and I was down with the fever when they found me, and Alvarez gave me the appointment. And this is how I reward them. If I stay I do more harm. If I go away I leave them surrounded by enemies, and not enemies who fight fair, but damned thieves and scoundrels, who stab at women and who fight in the dark. I wouldn't have had it happen, old man, for my right arm! They— they have been so kind to me, and I have been so happy here— and now!" The boy bowed his face in his hands and sat breathing brokenly while Clay turned his unlit cigar between his teeth and peered at him curiously through the darkness. "Now I have made them both unhappy, and they hate me, and I hate myself, and I have brought nothing but trouble to every one. First I made my own people miserable, and now I make my best friends miserable, and I had better be dead. I wish I were dead. I wish I had never been born."

Clay laid his hand on the other's bowed shoulder and shook him gently. "Don't talk like that," he said; "it does no good. Why do you hate yourself?"

"What?" asked Stuart, wearily, without looking up. "What did you say?"

"You said you had made them hate you, and you added that you hated yourself. Well, I can see why they naturally would be angry for the time, at least. But why do you hate yourself? Have you reason to?"

"I don't understand," said Stuart.

"Well, I can't make it any plainer," Clay replied. "It isn't a question I will ask. But you say you want my advice. Well, my advice to my friend and to a man who is not my friend, differ. And in this case it depends on whether what that thing—" Clay kicked the paper which had fallen on the ground—"what that thing says is true."

The younger man looked at the paper below him and then back at Clay, and sprang to his feet.

"Why, damn you!" he cried, "what do you mean?"

He stood above Clay with both arms rigid at his side and his head bent forward. The dawn had just broken, and the two men saw each other in the ghastly gray light of the morning. "If any man," cried Stuart, thickly, "dares to say that that blackguardly lie is true I'll kill him. You or any one else. Is that what you mean, damn you? If it is, say so, and I'll break every bone of your body."

"Well, that's much better," growled Clay, sullenly. "The way you went on wishing you were dead and hating yourself made me almost lose faith in mankind. Now you go make that speech to the President, and then find the man who put up those placards, and if you can't find the right man, take any man you meet and make him eat it, paste and all, and beat him to death if he doesn't. Why, this is no time to whimper—because the world is full of liars. Go out and fight them and show them you are not afraid. Confound you, you had me so scared there that I almost thrashed you myself. Forgive me, won't you?" he begged, earnestly. He rose and held out his hand and the other took it, doubtfully. "It was your own fault, you young idiot," protested Clay. "You told your story the wrong way. Now go home and get some sleep and I'll be back in a few hours to help you. Look!" he said. He pointed through the trees to the sun that shot up like a red-hot disk of heat above the cool green of the mountains. "See," said Clay, "God has given us another day. Seven battles were fought in seven days once in my country. Let's be thankful, old man, that we're *not* dead, but alive to fight our own and other people's battles."

The younger man sighed and pressed Clay's hand again before he dropped it.

"You are very good to me," he said. "I'm not just quite myself this morning. I'm a bit nervous, I think. You'll surely come, won't you?"

"By noon," Clay promised. "And if it does come," he added, "don't forget my fifteen hundred men at the mines."

"Good! I won't," Stuart replied. "I'll call on you if I need them." He raised his fingers mechanically to his helmet in salute, and catching up his sword turned and strode away erect and soldierly through the débris and weeds of the deserted plaza.

Clay remained motionless on the steps of the pedestal and followed the younger man with his eyes. He drew a long breath and began a leisurely search through his pockets for his match-box, gazing about him as he did so, as though looking for some one to whom he could speak his feelings. He lifted his eyes to the stern, smooth-shaven face of the bronze statue above him that seemed to be watching Stuart's departing figure.

"General Bolivar," Clay said, as he lit his cigar, "observe that young man. He is a soldier and a gallant gentleman. You, sir, were a great soldier—the greatest this God-forsaken country will ever know—and you were, sir, an ardent lover. I ask you to salute that young man as I do, and to wish him well." Clay lifted his high hat to the back of the young officer as it was hidden in the hanging vines, and once again, with grave respect to the grim features of the great general above him, and then smiling at his own conceit, he ran lightly down the steps and disappeared among the trees of the plaza.

IX

Clay slept for three hours. He had left a note on the floor instructing MacWilliams and young Langham not to go to the mines, but to waken him at ten o'clock, and by eleven the three men were galloping off to the city. As they left the Palms they met Hope returning from a morning ride on the Alameda, and Clay begged her, with much concern, not to ride abroad again. There was a difference in his tone toward her. There was more anxiety in it than the occasion seemed to justify, and he put his request in the form of a favor to himself, while the day previous he would simply have told her that she must not go riding alone.

"Why?" asked Hope, eagerly. "Is there going to be trouble?"

"I hope not," Clay said, "but the soldiers are coming in from the provinces for the review, and the roads are not safe."

"I'd be safe with you, though," said Hope, smiling persuasively upon the three men. "Won't you take me with you, please?"

"Hope," said young Langham, in the tone of the elder brother's brief authority, "you must go home at once."

Hope smiled wickedly. "I don't want to," she said.

"I'll bet you a box of cigars I can beat you to the veranda by fifty yards," said MacWilliams, turning his horse's head.

Hope clasped her sailor hat in one hand and swung her whip with the other. "I think not," she cried, and disappeared with a flutter of skirts and a scurry of flying pebbles.

"You, sir, were a great soldier."

"At times," said Clay, "MacWilliams shows an unexpected knowledge of human nature."

"Yes, he did quite right," assented Langham, nodding his head mysteriously. "We've no time for girls at present, have we?"

"No, indeed," said Clay, hiding any sign of a smile.

Langham breathed deeply at the thought of the part he was to play in this coming struggle, and remained respectfully silent as they trotted toward the city. He did not wish to disturb the plots and counterplots that he was confident were forming in Clay's brain, and his devotion would have been severely tried had he known that his hero's mind was filled with a picture of a young girl in a blue shirt-waist and a whipcord riding-skirt.

Clay sent for Stuart to join them at the restaurant, and MacWilliams arriving at the same time, the four men seated themselves conspicuously in the centre of the café and sipped their chocolate as though unconscious of any imminent danger, and in apparent freedom from all responsibilities and care. While MacWilliams and Langham laughed and disputed over a game of dominoes, the older men exchanged, under cover of their chatter, the few words which they had met to speak.

The manifestoes, Stuart said, had failed of their purpose. He had already called upon the President, and had offered to resign his position and leave the country, or to stay and fight his maligners, and take up arms at once against Mendoza's party. Alvarez had treated him like a son, and bade him be patient. He held that Cæsar's wife was above suspicion because she was Cæsar's wife, and that no canards posted at midnight could affect his faith in his wife or in his friend.[1] He refused to believe that any *coup d'état* was imminent, save the one which he himself meditated when he was ready to proclaim the country in a state of revolution, and to assume a military dictatorship.

"What nonsense!" exclaimed Clay. "What is a military dictatorship without soldiers? Can't he see that the army is with Mendoza?"

"No," Stuart replied. "Rojas and I were with him all the morning. Rojas is an old trump, Clay. He's not bright and he's old-fashioned; but he is honest. And the people know it. If I had Rojas for a chief instead of Alvarez, I'd arrest Mendoza with my own hand, and I wouldn't be afraid to take him to the carcel[2]

---

1   Canard, a false, unfounded, or, especially, fabricated report or story designed to damage reputations and cause harm.

2   A local jail.

through the streets. The people wouldn't help him. But the President doesn't dare. Not that he hasn't pluck," added the young lieutenant, loyally, "for he takes his life in his hands when he goes to the review to-morrow, and he knows it. Think of it, will you, out there alone with a field of five thousand men around him! Rojas thinks he can hold half of them, as many as Mendoza can, and I have my fifty. But you can't tell what any one of them will do for a drink or a dollar. They're no more soldiers than these waiters. They're bandits in uniform, and they'll kill for the man that pays best."

"Then why doesn't Alvarez pay them?" Clay growled.

Stuart looked away and lowered his eyes to the table. "He hasn't the money, I suppose," he said, evasively. "He—he has transferred every cent of it into drafts on Rothschild. They are at the house now, representing five millions of dollars in gold—and her jewels, too—packed ready for flight."

"Then he does expect trouble?" said Clay. "You told me——"

"They're all alike; you know them," said Stuart. "They won't believe they're in danger until the explosion comes, but they always have a special train ready, and they keep the funds of the government under their pillows. He engaged apartments on the Avenue Kleber six months ago."

"Bah!" said Clay. "It's the old story. Why don't you quit him?"

Stuart raised his eyes and dropped them again, and Clay sighed. "I'm sorry," he said.

MacWilliams interrupted them in an indignant stage-whisper. "Say, how long have we got to keep up this fake game?" he asked. "I don't know anything about dominoes, and neither does Ted. Tell us what you've been saying. Is there going to be trouble? If there is, Ted and I want to be in it. We are looking for trouble."

Clay had tipped back his chair, and was surveying the restaurant and the blazing plaza beyond its open front with an expression of cheerful unconcern. Two men were reading the morning papers near the door, and two others were dragging through a game of dominoes in a far corner. The heat of midday had settled on the place, and the waiters dozed, with their chairs tipped back against the walls. Outside, the awning of the restaurant threw a broad shadow across the marble-topped tables on the sidewalk, and half a dozen fiacre drivers slept peacefully in their carriages before the door.

The town was taking its siesta, and the brisk step of a stranger who crossed the tessellated floor and rapped with his knuckles on the top of the cigar-case was the only sign of life. The new-comer turned with one hand on the glass case and swept the room carelessly with his eyes. They were hard blue eyes under straight eyebrows. Their owner was dressed unobtrusively in a suit of rough tweed, and this and his black hat, and the fact that he was smooth-shaven, distinguished him as a foreigner.

As he faced them the forelegs of Clay's chair descended slowly to the floor, and he began to smile comprehendingly and to nod his head as though the coming of the stranger had explained something of which he had been in doubt. His companions turned and followed the direction of his eyes, but saw nothing of interest in the newcomer. He looked as though he might be a concession hunter from the States, or a Manchester drummer, prepared to offer six months' credit on blankets and hardware.

Clay rose and strode across the room, circling the tables in such a way that he could keep himself between the stranger and the door. At his approach the new-comer turned his back and fumbled with his change on the counter.

"Captain Burke, I believe?" said Clay. The stranger bit the cigar he had just purchased, and shook his head. "I am very glad to see you," Clay continued. "Sit down, won't you? I want to talk with you."

"I think you've made a mistake," the stranger answered, quietly. "My name is——"

"Colonel, perhaps, then," said Clay. "I might have known it. I congratulate you, Colonel." The man looked at Clay for an instant, with the cigar clenched between his teeth and his blue eyes fixed steadily on the other's face. Clay waved his hand again invitingly toward a table, and the man shrugged his shoulders and laughed, and, pulling a chair toward him, sat down.

"Come over here, boys," Clay called. "I want you to meet an old friend of mine, Captain Burke."

The man called Burke stared at the three men as they crossed the room and seated themselves at the table, and nodded to them in silence.

"We have here," said Clay, gayly, but in a low voice, "the key to the situation. This is the gentleman who supplies Mendoza with the sinews of war. Captain Burke is a brave soldier and a citizen of my own or of any country, indeed, which happens to have the most sympathetic Consul-General."

Burke smiled grimly, with a condescending nod, and putting away the cigar, took out a brier pipe and began to fill it from his tobacco-pouch. "The Captain is a man of few words and extremely modest about himself," Clay continued, lightly; "so I must tell you who he is myself. He is a promoter of revolutions. That is his business—a professional promoter of revolutions, and that is what makes me so glad to see him again. He knows all about the present crisis here, and he is going to tell us all he knows as soon as he fills his pipe. I ought to warn you, Burke," he added, "that this is Captain Stuart, in charge of the police and the President's cavalry troop. So, you see, whatever you say, you will have one man who will listen to you."

Burke crossed one short, fat leg over the other, and crowded the tobacco in the bowl of his pipe with his thumb.

"I thought you were in Chili, Clay," he said.[1]

"No, you didn't think I was in Chili," Clay replied, kindly. "I left Chili two years ago. The Captain and I met there," he explained to the others, "when Balmaceda[2] was trying to make himself dictator. The Captain was on the side of the Congressionalists, and was furnishing arms and dynamite. The Captain is always on the winning side, at least he always has been—up to the present. He is not a creature of sentiment; are you, Burke? The Captain believes with Napoleon that God is on the side that has the heaviest artillery."

Burke lighted his pipe and drummed absent-mindedly on the table with his match-box.

"I can't afford to be sentimental," he said. "Not in my business."

"Of course not," Clay assented, cheerfully. He looked at Burke and laughed, as though the sight of him recalled pleasant memories. "I wish I could give these boys an idea of how clever you are, Captain," he said. "The Captain was the first man, for instance, to think of packing cartridges in tubs of lard, and of sending rifles in piano-cases. He represents the Welby revolver people in England, and half a dozen firms in the States, and he has his little stores in Tampa and Mobile and Jamaica, ready to ship off at a moment's notice to any revolution in Central America. When I first met the Captain," Clay continued, gleefully, and quite unmindful of the other's continued silence, "he was starting off

---

1 "Chili" is a former spelling of Chile.

2 José Manuel Balmaceda, Chilean politician and president (1886–91) who attempted a *coup d'état* following a no confidence measure in the national assembly. His bid to become dictator of Chile failed, and he committed suicide.

to rescue Arabi Pasha[1] from the island of Ceylon. You may remember, boys, that when Dufferin saved Arabi from hanging, the British shipped him to Ceylon as a political prisoner. Well, the Captain was sent by Arabi's followers in Egypt to bring him back to lead a second rebellion. Burke had everybody bribed at Ceylon, and a fine schooner fitted out and a lot of ruffians to do the fighting, and then the good, kind British Government pardoned Arabi the day before Burke arrived in port. And you never got a cent for it; did you, Burke?"

Burke shook his head and frowned.

"Six thousand pounds sterling I was to have got for that," he said, with a touch of pardonable pride in his voice, "and they set him free the day before I got there, just as Mr. Clay tells you."

"And then you headed Granville Prior's expedition for buried treasure off the island of Cocos,[2] didn't you?" said Clay. "Go on, tell them about it. Be sociable. You ought to write a book about your different business ventures, Burke, indeed you ought; but then," Clay added, smiling, "nobody would believe you." Burke rubbed his chin, thoughtfully, with his fingers, and looked modestly at the ceiling, and the two younger boys gazed at him with open-mouthed interest.

"There ain't anything in buried treasure," he said, after a pause, "except the money that's sunk in the fitting out. It sounds good, but it's all foolishness."

"All foolishness, eh?" said Clay, encouragingly. "And what did you do after Balmaceda was beaten?—after I last saw you?"

"Crespo," Burke replied, after a pause, during which he pulled gently on his pipe. "*Caroline Brewer*—cleared from Key West for Curaçao, with cargo of sewing-machines and ploughs—beached below Maracaibo—thirty-five thousand rounds and two thousand rifles—at twenty bolivars apiece."

"Of course," said Clay, in a tone of genuine appreciation. "I might have known you'd be in that. He says," he explained, "that

---

1 Arabi Pasha (1839–1911), an Egyptian politician who led a revolt in 1882 against British domination. Wolseley's men crushed the revolt, and the task fell to Lord Dufferin (1826–1902), the British High Commissioner in Egypt, to restore colonial order in the country. Pasha was sentenced to hang, but Dufferin commuted his sentence and sent him into exile in Ceylon (present-day Sri Lanka).
2 The Cocos Islands, a group of twenty-seven coral islands in the eastern Indian Ocean, a dependancy of Australia.

he assisted General Crespo in Venezuela during his revolution against Guzman Blanco's party,[1] and loaded a tramp steamer called the *Caroline Brewer* at Key West with arms, which he landed safely at a place for which he had no clearance papers, and he received forty thousand dollars in our money for the job—and very good pay, too, I should think," commented Clay.

"Well, I don't know," Burke demurred. "You take in the cost of leasing the boat and provisioning her, and the crew's wages, and the cost of the cargo; that cuts into profits. Then I had to stand off shore between Trinidad and Curaçao[2] for over three weeks before I got the signal to run in, and after that I was chased by a gun-boat for three days, and the crazy fool put a shot clean through my engine-room. Cost me about twelve hundred dollars in repairs."

There was a pause, and Clay turned his eyes to the street, and then asked, abruptly, "What are you doing now?"

"Trying to get orders for smokeless powder," Burke answered, promptly. He met Clay's look with eyes as undisturbed as his own. "But they won't touch it down here," he went on. "It doesn't appeal to 'em. It's too expensive, and they'd rather see the smoke. It makes them think——"

"How long did you expect to stay here?" Clay interrupted.

"How long?" repeated Burke, like a man in a witness-box who is trying to gain time. "Well, I was thinking of leaving by Friday, and taking a mule-train over to Bogota instead of waiting for the steamer to Colon." He blew a mouthful of smoke into the air and watched it drifting toward the door with apparent interest.

"The *Santiago* leaves here Saturday for New York. I guess you had better wait over for her," Clay said. "I'll engage your passage, and, in the meantime, Captain Stuart here will see that they treat you well in the cuartel."[3]

The men around the table started, and sat motionless looking at Clay, but Burke only took his pipe from his mouth and knocked the ashes out òn the heel of his boot. "What am I going to the cuartel for?" he asked.

"Well, the public good, I suppose," laughed Clay. "I'm sorry,

---

1 Maracaibo is a port city in Venezuela. Antonio Guzmán Blanco (1829–99), dictator of Venezuela (1870–88). Joaquín Crespo (1841–98), military dictator of Venezuela, 1892–98.

2 Trinidad and Tobago, the southernmost islands in the Caribbean; Curaçao, largest island in the Dutch Antilles, off the coast of Venezuela.

3 A barracks used as a military jail.

but it's your own fault. You shouldn't have shown yourself here at all."

"What have you got to do with it?" asked Burke, calmly, as he began to refill his pipe. He had the air of a man who saw nothing before him but an afternoon of pleasant discourse and leisurely inactivity.

"You know what I've got to do with it," Clay replied. "I've got our concession to look after."

"Well, you're not running the town, too, are you?" asked Burke.

"No, but I'm going to run you out of it," Clay answered. "Now, what are you going to do—make it unpleasant for us and force our hand, or drive down quietly with our friend MacWilliams here? He is the best one to take you, because he's not so well known."

Burke turned his head and looked over his shoulder at Stuart.

"You taking orders from Mr. Clay, to-day, Captain Stuart?" he asked.

"Yes," Stuart answered, smiling. "I agree with Mr. Clay in whatever he thinks right."

"Oh, well, in that case," said Burke, rising reluctantly, with a protesting sigh, "I guess I'd better call on the American minister."

"You can't. He's in Ecuador on his annual visit," said Clay.

"Indeed! That's bad for me," muttered Burke, as though in much concern. "Well, then, I'll ask you to let me see our consul here."

"Certainly," Clay assented, with alacrity. "Mr. Langham, this young gentleman's father, got him his appointment, so I've no doubt he'll be only too glad to do anything for a friend of ours."

Burke raised his eyes and looked inquiringly at Clay, as though to assure himself that this was true, and Clay smiled back at him.

"Oh, very well," Burke said. "Then, as I happen to be an Irishman by the name of Burke, and a British subject, I'll try Her Majesty's representative, and we'll see if he will allow me to be locked up without a reason or a warrant."

"That's no good, either," said Clay, shaking his head. "You fixed your nationality, as far as this continent is concerned, in Rio harbor, when Peixoto[1] handed you over to the British admiral, and you claimed to be an American citizen, and were sent on board the *Detroit*. If there's any doubt about that we've only got to cable to Rio Janeiro—to either legation. But what's the use?

---

1 Floriano Peixoto (1842–95), dictator of Brazil (1891–94).

They know me here, and they don't know you, and I do. You'll have to go to jail and stay there."

"Oh, well, if you put it that way, I'll go," said Burke. "But," he added, in a lower voice, "it's too late, Clay."

The expression of amusement on Clay's face, and his ease of manner, fell from him at the words, and he pulled Burke back into the chair again. "What do you mean?" he asked, anxiously.

"I mean just that, it's too late," Burke answered. "I don't mind going to jail. I won't be there long. My work's all done and paid for. I was only staying on to see the fun at the finish, to see you fellows made fools of."

"Oh, you're sure of that, are you?" asked Clay.

"My dear boy!" exclaimed the American, with a suggestion in his speech of his Irish origin, as his interest rose. "Did you ever know me to go into anything of this sort for the sentiment of it? Did you ever know me to back the losing side? No. Well, I tell you that you fellows have no more show in this than a parcel of Sunday-school children. Of course, I can't say when they mean to strike. I don't know, and I wouldn't tell you if I did. But when they do strike there'll be no striking back. It'll be all over but the cheering."

Burke's tone was calm and positive. He held the centre of the stage now, and he looked from one to the other of the serious faces around him with an expression of pitying amusement.

"Alvarez may get off, and so may Madame Alvarez," he added, lowering his voice and turning his face away from Stuart. "But not if she shows herself in the streets, and not if she tries to take those drafts and jewels with her."

"Oh, you know that, do you?" interrupted Clay.

"I know nothing," Burke replied. "At least, nothing to what the rest of them know. That's only the gossip I pick up at headquarters. It doesn't concern me. I've delivered my goods and given my receipt for the money, and that's all I care about. But if it will make an old friend feel any more comfortable to have me in jail, why, I'll go, that's all."

Clay sat with pursed lips looking at Stuart. The two boys leaned with their elbows on the tables and stared at Burke, who was searching leisurely through his pockets for his match-box. From outside came the lazy cry of a vendor of lottery tickets, and the swift, uneven patter of bare feet, as company after company of dust-covered soldiers passed on their way from the provinces, with their shoes swinging from their bayonets.

Clay slapped the table with an exclamation of impatience.

"After all, this is only a matter of business," he said, "with all of us. What do you say, Burke, to taking a ride with me to Stuart's rooms, and having a talk there with the President and Mr. Langham? Langham has three millions sunk in these mines, and Alvarez has even better reasons than that for wanting to hold his job. What do you say? That's better than going to jail. Tell us what they mean to do, and who is to do it, and I'll let you name your own figure, and I'll guarantee you that they'll meet it. As long as you've no sentiment, you might as well fight on the side that will pay best."

Burke opened his lips as though to speak, and then shut them again, closely. If the others thought that he was giving Clay's proposition a second and more serious thought, he was quick to undeceive them.

"There *are* men in the business who do that sort of thing," he said. "They sell arms to one man, and sell the fact that he's got them to the deputy-marshals, and sell the story of how smart they've been to the newspapers. And they never make any more sales after that. I'd look pretty, wouldn't I, bringing stuff into this country, and getting paid for it, and then telling you where it was hid, and everything else I knew? I've no sentiment, as you say, but I've got business instinct, and that's not business. No, I've told you enough, and if you think I'm not safe at large, why I'm quite ready to take a ride with your young friend here."

MacWilliams rose with alacrity, and beaming with pleasure at the importance of the duty thrust upon him.

Burke smiled. "The young 'un seems to like the job," he said.

"It's an honor to be associated with Captain Burke in any way," said MacWilliams, as he followed him into a cab, while Stuart galloped off before them in the direction of the cuartel.

"You wouldn't think so if you knew better," said Burke. "My friends have been watching us while we have been talking in there for the last hour. They're watching us now, and if I were to nod my head during this ride, they'd throw you out into the street and set me free, if they had to break the cab into kindling-wood while they were doing it."

MacWilliams changed his seat to the one opposite his prisoner, and peered up and down the street in some anxiety.

"I suppose you know there's an answer to that, don't you?" he asked. "Well, the answer is, that if you nod your head once, you lose the top of it."

Burke gave an exclamation of disgust, and gazed at his zealous guardian with an expression of trepidation and unconcealed disapproval. "You're not armed, are you?" he asked. MacWilliams nodded. "Why not?" he said; "these are rather heavy weather times, just at present, thanks to you and your friends. Why, you seem rather afraid of fire-arms," he added, with the intolerance of youth.

The Irish-American touched the young man on the knee, and lifted his hat. "My son," he said, "when your hair is as gray as that, and you have been through six campaigns, you'll be brave enough to own that you're afraid of fire-arms, too."

X

Clay and Langham left MacWilliams and Stuart to look after their prisoner, and returned to the Palms, where they dined in state, and made no reference, while the women were present, to the events of the day.

The moon rose late that night, and as Hope watched it, from where she sat at the dinner-table facing the open windows, she saw the figure of a man standing outlined in silhouette upon the edge of the cliff. He was dressed in the uniform of a sailor, and the moonlight played along the barrel of a rifle upon which he leaned, motionless and menacing, like a sentry on a rampart.

Hope opened her lips to speak, and then closed them again, and smiled with pleasurable excitement. A moment later King, who sat on her right, called one of the servants to his side and whispered some instructions, pointing meanwhile at the wine upon the table. And a minute after, Hope saw the white figure of the servant cross the garden and approach the sentinel. She saw the sentry fling his gun sharply to his hip, and then, after a moment's parley, toss it up to his shoulder and disappear from sight among the plants of the garden.

The men did not leave the table with the ladies, as was their custom, but remained in the dining-room, and drew their chairs closer together.

Mr. Langham would not believe that the downfall of the Government was as imminent as the others believed it to be. It was only after much argument, and with great reluctance, that he had even allowed King to arm half of his crew, and to place them on guard around the Palms. Clay warned him that in the disorder that followed every successful revolution, the homes of unpopular members of the Cabinet were often burned, and that he feared, should Mendoza succeed, and Alvarez fall, that the mob might possibly vent its victorious wrath on the Palms because it was the home of the alien, who had, as they thought, robbed the country of the iron mines. Mr. Langham said he did not think the people would tramp five miles into the country seeking vengeance.

There was an American man-of-war lying in the harbor of Truxillo, a seaport of the republic that bounded Olancho on the south, and Clay was in favor of sending to her captain by Weimer, the Consul, and asking him to anchor off Valencia, to protect American interests. The run would take but a few hours, and the sight of the vessel's white hull in the harbor would, he thought, have a salutary effect upon the revolutionists. But Mr. Langham said, firmly, that he would not ask for help until he needed it.

"Well, I'm sorry," said Clay. "I should very much like to have that man-of-war here. However, if you say no, we will try to get along without her. But, for the present, I think you had better imagine yourself back in New York, and let us have an entirely free hand. We've gone too far to drop out," he went on, laughing at the sight of Mr. Langham's gloomy countenance. "We've got to fight them now. It's against human nature not to do it."

Mr. Langham looked appealingly at his son and at King.

They both smiled back at him in unanimous disapproval of his policy of non-interference.

"Oh, very well," he said, at last. "You gentlemen can go ahead, kill, burn, and destroy if you wish. But, considering the fact that it is my property you are all fighting about, I really think I might have something to say in the matter." Mr. Langham gazed about him helplessly, and shook his head.

"My doctor sends me down here from a quiet, happy home," he protested, with humorous pathos, "that I may rest and get away from excitement, and here I am with armed men patrolling my garden-paths, with a lot of filibusters plotting at my own dinner-table, and a civil war likely to break out, entirely on my account. And Dr. Winter told me this was the only place that would cure my nervous prostration!"

Hope joined Clay as soon as the men left the dining-room, and beckoned him to the farther end of the veranda. "Well, what is it?" she said.

"What is what?" laughed Clay. He seated himself on the rail of the veranda, with his face to the avenue and the driveway leading to the house. They could hear the others from the back of the house, and the voice of young Langham, who was giving an imitation of MacWilliams, and singing with peculiar emphasis, "There is no place like Home, Sweet Home."

"Why are the men guarding the Palms, and why did you go to the Plaza Bolivar this morning at daybreak? Alice says you left them there. I want to know what it means. I am nearly as old as Ted, and he knows. The men wouldn't tell me."

"What men?"

"King's men from the *Vesta*. I saw some of them dodging around in the bushes, and I went to find out what they were doing, and I walked into fifteen of them at your office. They have hammocks swung all over the veranda, and a quick-firing gun made fast to the steps, and muskets stacked all about, just like real soldiers, but they wouldn't tell me why."

"We'll put you in the carcel," said Clay, "if you go spying on our forces. Your father doesn't wish you to know anything about it, but, since you have found it out for yourself, you might as well know what little there is to know. It's the same story. Mendoza is getting ready to start his revolution, or, rather, he has started it."

"Why don't you stop him?" asked Hope.

"You are very flattering," said Clay. "Even if I could stop him, it's not my business to do it as yet. I have to wait until he interferes with me, or my mines, or my workmen. Alvarez is the man who should stop him, but he is afraid. We cannot do anything until he makes the first move. If I were the President, I'd have Mendoza shot to-morrow morning and declare martial law. Then I'd arrest everybody I didn't like, and levy forced loans on all the merchants, and sail away to Paris and live happy ever after. That's what Mendoza would do if he caught any one plotting against him. And that's what Alvarez should do, too, according to his lights, if he had the courage of his convictions, and of his education. I like to see a man play his part properly, don't you? If you are an emperor, you ought to conduct yourself like one, as our German friend does. Or if you are a prize-fighter, you ought to be a human bull-dog. There's no such thing as a gentlemanly pugilist, any more than there can be a virtuous burglar. And if you're a South American Dictator, you can't afford to be squeamish about throwing your enemies into jail or shooting them for treason. The way to dictate is to dictate—not to hide indoors all day while your wife plots for you."

"Does she do that?" asked Hope. "And do you think she will be in danger—any personal danger, if the revolution comes?"

"Well, she is very unpopular," Clay answered, "and unjustly

so, I think. But it would be better, perhaps, for her if she went as quietly as possible, when she does go."

"Is our Captain Stuart in danger, too?" the girl continued, anxiously. "Alice says they put up placards about him all over the city last night. She saw his men tearing them down as she was coming home. What has he done?"

"Nothing," Clay answered, shortly. "He happens to be in a false position, that's all. They think he is here because he is not wanted in his own country; that is not so. That is not the reason he remains here. When he was even younger than he is now, he was wild and foolish, and spent more money than he could afford, and lent more money to his brother-officers, I have no doubt, than they ever paid back. He had to leave the regiment because his father wouldn't pay his debts, and he has been selling his sword for the last three years to one or another king or sultan or party all over the world, in China and Madagascar, and later in Siam.[1] I hope you will be very kind to Stuart and believe well of him, and that you will listen to no evil against him. Somewhere in England Stuart has a sister like you—about your age, I mean, that loves him very dearly, and a father whose heart aches for him, and there is a certain royal regiment that still drinks his health with pride. He is a lonely little chap, and he has no sense of humor to help him out of his difficulties, but he is a very brave gentleman. And he is here fighting for men who are not worthy to hold his horse's bridle, because of a woman. And I tell you this because you will hear many lies about him—and about her. He serves her with the same sort of chivalric devotion that his ancestors felt for the woman whose ribbons they tied to their lances, and for whom they fought in the lists."

"I understand," Hope said, softly. "I am glad you told me. I shall not forget." She sighed and shook her head. "I wish they'd let you manage it for them," she said.

Clay laughed. "I fear my executive ability is not of so high an order; besides, as I haven't been born to it, my conscience might trouble me if I had to shoot my enemies and rob the worthy merchants. I had better stick to digging holes in the ground. That is all I seem to be good for."

Hope looked up at him, quickly, in surprise.

"What do you mean by that?" she demanded. There was a

---

1 Present-day Thailand.

tone of such sharp reproach in her voice that Clay felt himself put on the defensive.

"I mean nothing by it," he said. "Your sister and I had a talk the other day about a man's making the best of himself, and it opened my eyes to—to many things. It was a very healthy lesson."

"It could not have been a very healthy lesson," Hope replied, severely, "if it makes you speak of your work slightingly, as you did then. That didn't sound at all natural, or like you. It sounded like Alice. Tell me, did Alice say that?"

The pleasure of hearing Hope take his part against himself was so comforting to Clay that he hesitated in answering in order to enjoy it the longer. Her enthusiasm touched him deeply, and he wondered if she were enthusiastic because she was young, or because she was sure she was right, and that he was in the wrong.

"It started this way," Clay began, carefully. He was anxious to be quite fair to Miss Langham, but he found it difficult to give her point of view correctly, while he was hungering for a word that would re-establish him in his own good opinion. "Your sister said she did not think very much of what I had done, but she explained kindly that she hoped for better things from me. But what troubles me is, that I will never do anything much better or very different in kind from the work I have done lately, and so I am a bit discouraged about it in consequence. You see," said Clay, "when I come to die, and they ask me what I have done with my ten fingers, I suppose I will have to say, 'Well, I built such and such railroads, and I dug up so many tons of ore, and opened new countries, and helped make other men rich.' I can't urge in my behalf that I happen to have been so fortunate as to have gained the good-will of yourself or your sister. That is quite reason enough to me, perhaps, for having lived, but it might not appeal to them. I want to feel that I have accomplished something outside of myself—something that will remain after I go. Even if it is only a breakwater or a patent coupling. When I am dead it will not matter to any one what I personally was, whether I was a bore or a most charming companion, or whether I had red hair or blue. It is the work that will tell. And when your sister, whose judgment is the judgment of the outside world, more or less, says that the work is not worth while, I naturally feel a bit discouraged. It meant so much to me, and it hurt me to find it meant so little to others."

Hope remained silent for some time, but the rigidity of her attitude, and the tightness with which she pressed her lips together, showed that her mind was deeply occupied. They both sat silent for some few moments, looking down toward the distant lights of the city. At the farther end of the double row of bushes that lined the avenue they could see one of King's sentries passing to and fro across the roadway, a long black shadow on the moonlit road.

"You are very unfair to yourself," the girl said at last, "and Alice does not represent the opinion of the world, only of a very small part of it—her own little world. She does not know how little it is. And you are wrong as to what they will ask you at the end. What will they care whether you built railroads or painted impressionist pictures? They will ask you 'What have you made of yourself? Have you been fine, and strong, and sincere?' That is what they will ask. And we like you because you are all of these things, and because you look at life so cheerfully, and are unafraid. We do not like men because they build railroads, or because they are prime ministers. We like them for what they are themselves. And as to your work!" Hope added, and then paused in eloquent silence. "I think it is a grand work, and a noble work, full of hardships and self-sacrifices. I do not know of any man who has done more with his life than you have done with yours." She stopped and controlled her voice before she spoke again. "You should be very proud," she said.

Clay lowered his eyes and sat silent, looking down the roadway. The thought that the girl felt what she said so deeply, and that the fact that she had said it meant more to him than anything else in the world could mean, left him thrilled and trembling. He wanted to reach out his hand and seize both of hers, and tell her how much she was to him, but it seemed like taking advantage of the truths of a confessional, or of a child's innocent confidences.

"No, Miss Hope," he answered, with an effort to speak lightly, "I wish I could believe you, but I know myself better than any one else can, and I know that while my bridges may stand examination—*I* can't."

Hope turned and looked at him with eyes full of such sweet meaning that he was forced to turn his own away.

"I could trust both, I think," the girl said.

Clay drew a quick, deep breath, and started to his feet, as though he had thrown off the restraint under which he had held himself.

It was not a girl, but a woman who had spoken then, but, though he turned eagerly toward her, he stood with his head bowed, and did not dare to read the verdict in her eyes.

The clatter of horses' hoofs coming toward them at a gallop broke in rudely upon the tense stillness of the moment, but neither noticed it. "How far," Clay began, in a strained voice, "how far," he asked, more steadily, "could you trust me?"

Hope's eyes had closed for an instant, and opened again, and she smiled upon him with a look of perfect confidence and content. The beat of the horses' hoofs came now from the end of the driveway, and they could hear the men at the rear of the house pushing back their chairs and hurrying toward them. Hope raised her head, and Clay moved toward her eagerly. The horses were within a hundred yards. Before Hope could speak, the sentry's voice rang out in a hoarse, sharp challenge, like an alarm of fire on the silent night. "Halt!" they heard him cry. And as the horses tore past him, and their riders did not turn to look, he shouted again, "Halt, damn you!" and fired. The flash showed a splash of red and yellow in the moonlight, and the report started into life hundreds of echoes which carried it far out over the waters of the harbor, and tossed it into sharp angles, and distant corners, and in an instant a myriad of sounds answered it; the frightened cry of night-birds, the barking of dogs in the village below, and the footsteps of men running.

Clay glanced angrily down the avenue, and turned beseechingly to Hope.

"Go," she said. "See what is wrong," and moved away as though she already felt that he could act more freely when she was not near him.

The two horses fell back on their haunches before the steps, and MacWilliams and Stuart tumbled out of their saddles, and started, running back on foot in the direction from which the shot had come, tugging at their revolvers.

"Come back," Clay shouted to them. "That's all right. He was only obeying orders. That's one of King's sentries."

"Oh, is that it?" said Stuart, in matter-of-fact tones, as he turned again to the house. "Good idea. Tell him to fire lower next time. And, I say," he went on, as he bowed curtly to the assembled company on the veranda, "since you have got a picket out, you had better double it. And, Clay, see that no one leaves here without permission—no one. That's more important, even, than keeping them out."

"King, will you—" Clay began.

"All right, General," laughed King, and walked away to meet his sailors, who came running up the hill in great anxiety.

MacWilliams had not opened his lips, but he was bristling

with importance, and his effort to appear calm and soldierly, like Stuart, told more plainly than speech that he was the bearer of some invaluable secret. The sight filled young Langham with a disquieting fear that he had missed something.

Stuart looked about him, and pulled briskly at his gauntlets. King and his sailors were grouped together on the grass before the house. Mr. Langham and his daughters, and Clay, were standing on the steps, and the servants were peering around the corners of the house.

Stuart saluted Mr. Langham, as though to attract his especial attention, and then addressed himself in a low tone to Clay.

"It's come," he said. "We've been in it since dinner-time, and we've got a whole night's work cut out for you." He was laughing with excitement, and paused for a moment to gain breath. "I'll tell you the worst of it first. Mendoza has sent word to Alvarez that he wants the men at the mines to be present at the review to-morrow. He says they must take part. He wrote a most insolent letter. Alvarez got out of it by saying that the men were under contract to you, and that you must give your permission first. Mendoza sent me word that if you would not let the men come, he would go out and fetch them in himself."

"Indeed!" growled Clay. "Kirkland needs those men to-morrow to load ore-cars for Thursday's steamer. He can't spare them. That is our answer, and it happens to be a true one, but if it weren't true, if to-morrow was All Saints' Day, and the men had nothing to do but to lie in the sun and sleep, Mendoza couldn't get them. And if he comes to take them to-morrow, he'll have to bring his army with him to do it. And he couldn't do it then, Mr. Langham!" Clay cried, turning to that gentleman, "if I had better weapons. The five thousand dollars I wanted you to spend on rifles, sir, two months ago, might have saved you several millions to-morrow."

Clay's words seemed to bear some special significance to Stuart and MacWilliams, for they both laughed, and Stuart pushed Clay up the steps before him.

"Come inside," he said. "That is why we are here. MacWilliams has found out where Burke hid his shipment of arms. We are going to try and get them to-night." He hurried into the dining-room, and the others grouped themselves about the table. "Tell them about it, MacWilliams," Stuart commanded. "I will see that no one overhears you."

MacWilliams was pushed into Mr. Langham's place at the head of the long table, and the others dragged their chairs up close around him. King put the candles at the opposite end of the table, and set some decanters and glasses in the centre. "To look as though we were just enjoying ourselves," he explained, pleasantly.

Mr. Langham, with his fine, delicate fingers beating nervously on the table, observed the scene as an on-looker, rather than as the person chiefly interested. He smiled as he appreciated the incongruity of the tableau, and the contrast which the actors presented to the situation. He imagined how much it would amuse his contemporaries of the Union Club, at home, if they could see him then, with the still, tropical night outside, the candles reflected on the polished table and on the angles of the decanters, and showing the intent faces of the young girls and the men leaning eagerly forward around MacWilliams, who sat conscious and embarrassed, his hair dishevelled, and his face covered with dust, while Stuart paced up and down in the shadow, his sabre clanking as he walked.

"Well, it happened like this," MacWilliams began, nervously, and addressing himself to Clay. "Stuart and I put Burke safely in a cell by himself. It was one of the old ones that face the street. There was a narrow window in it, about eight feet above the floor, and no means of his reaching it, even if he stood on a chair. We stationed two troopers before the door, and sent out to a café across the street for our dinners. I finished mine about nine o'clock, and said 'Good-night' to Stuart, and started to come out here. I went across the street first, however, to give the restaurant man some orders about Burke's breakfast. It is a narrow street, you know, with a long garden-wall and a row of little shops on one side, and with the jail-wall taking up all of the other side. The street was empty when I left the jail, except for the sentry on guard in front of it, but just as I was leaving the restaurant I saw one of Stuart's police come out and peer up and down the street and over at the shops. He looked frightened and anxious, and as I wasn't taking chances on anything, I stepped back into the restaurant and watched him through the window. He waited until the sentry had turned his back, and started away from him on his post, and then I saw him drop his sabre so that it rang on the sidewalk. He was standing, I noticed then, directly under the third window from the door of the jail. That was the window of Burke's cell. When I grasped that fact I got out my gun and walked to the door of the restaurant. Just as I reached it a piece of paper shot out through the bars of Burke's cell and fell at the policeman's feet, and he stamped his boot down on it and looked all around again to see if any one had noticed him. I thought that was my cue, and I ran across the street with my gun pointed, and shouted to him to give me the paper. He jumped about a foot when he first saw me, but he was game, for he grabbed up the paper and stuck it in his mouth and began to chew on it. I was right up on him then, and I hit him on the chin with my left fist and knocked him down against the wall, and dropped on him with both knees and choked him till I made him spit out the paper—and two teeth," MacWilliams added, with a conscientious regard for details. "The sentry turned just then and came at me with his bayonet, but I put my finger to my lips, and that surprised him, so that he didn't know just what to do, and hesitated. You see, I didn't want Burke to hear the row outside, so I grabbed my policeman by the collar and pointed to the jail-door, and the sentry ran back and brought out Stuart and the guard. Stuart was pretty mad when he saw his policeman all bloody. He thought it would prejudice his other men against us, but I explained out loud that the man had been insolent, and I asked Stuart to take us both to his private room for a hearing, and, of course, when I told him what had happened, he wanted to punch the chap, too. We put him ourselves into a cell where he could not communicate with any one, and then we read the paper. Stuart has it," said MacWilliams, pushing back his chair, "and he'll tell you the rest." There was a pause, in which every one seemed to take time to breathe, and then a chorus of questions and explanations. King lifted his glass to MacWilliams, and nodded.

"'Well done, Condor,'" he quoted, smiling.[1]

"Yes," said Clay, tapping the younger man on the shoulder as he passed him. "That's good work. Now show us the paper, Stuart."

Stuart pulled the candles toward him, and spread a slip of paper on the table.

"Burke did this up in one of those paper boxes for wax matches," he explained, "and weighted it with a twenty-dollar gold piece. MacWilliams kept the gold piece, I believe."

"Going to use it for a scarf-pin," explained MacWilliams, in parenthesis. "Sort of war-medal, like the Chief's," he added, smiling.

---

1 During the British campaign against the Egyptian revolt lead by Arabi Pasha, Lord Charles Beresford (1846–1919), commander of the gunship *Condor*, attacked Fort Marabout at close range for over an hour. The close action prompted Admiral Frederick Beauchamp Seymour (1821–95) to signal, "Well done, Condor."

"This is in Spanish," Stuart explained. "I will translate it. It is not addressed to any one, and it is not signed, but it was evidently written to Mendoza, and we know it is in Burke's handwriting, for we compared it with some notes of his that we took from him before he was locked up. He says, 'I cannot keep the appointment, as I have been arrested.' The line that follows here," Stuart explained, raising his head, "has been scratched out, but we spent some time over it, and we made out that it read: 'It was Mr. Clay who recognized me, and ordered my arrest. He is the best man the others have. Watch him.' We think he rubbed that out through good feeling toward Clay. There seems to be no other reason. He's a very good sort, this old Burke, I think."

"Well, never mind him; it was very decent of him, anyway," said Clay. "Go on. Get to Hecuba."[1]

"'I cannot keep the appointment, as I have been arrested,'" repeated Stuart. "'I landed the goods last night in safety. I could not come in when first signalled, as the wind and tide were both off shore. But we got all the stuff stored away by morning. Your agent paid me in full and got my receipt. Please consider this as the same thing—as the equivalent'—it is difficult to translate it exactly," commented Stuart—"'as the equivalent of the receipt I was to have given when I made my report to-night. I sent three of your guards away on my own responsibility, for I think more than that number might attract attention to the spot, and they might be seen from the ore-trains.' That is the point of the note for us, of course," Stuart interrupted himself to say. "Burke adds," he went on, "'that they are to make no effort to rescue him, as he is quite comfortable, and is willing to remain in the carcel until they are established in power.'"

"Within sight of the ore-trains!" exclaimed Clay. "There are no ore-trains but ours. It must be along the line of the road."

"MacWilliams says he knows every foot of land along the railroad," said Stuart, "and he is sure the place Burke means is the

---

1   Hecuba, in Greek mythology, the wife of King Priam of Troy. In saying, "Go on. Get to Hecuba," Davis plays upon William Shakespeare's *Hamlet* (1600–01), Act 2, Scene 2, where Hamlet asks one of the visiting players to perform an impassioned monologue on the death of King Priam. As he listens to the monologue, Hamlet, hearing Polonius complain that the speech goes on too long, urges the player to speed along, remarking, "Say on; come to Hecuba." He means for the player to get to the dramatic climax of the monologue; here, Clay means for Stuart to get to the key point of his report. (My thanks to James McKusick for directing my attention to this scene in *Hamlet*.)

old fortress on the Platta inlet, because——"

"It is the only place," interrupted MacWilliams, "where there is no surf. They could run small boats up the inlet and unload in smooth water within twenty feet of the ramparts; and another thing, that is the only point on the line with a wagon road running direct from it to the Capital. It's an old road, and hasn't been travelled over for years, but it could be used. No," he added, as though answering the doubt in Clay's mind, "there is no other place. If I had a map here I could show you in a minute; where the beach is level there is a jungle between it and the road, and wherever there is open country, there is a limestone formation and rocks between it and the sea, where no boat could touch."

"But the fortress is so conspicuous," Clay demurred; "the nearest rampart is within twenty feet of the road. Don't you remember we measured it when we thought of laying the double track?"

"That is just what Burke says," urged Stuart. "That is the reason he gives for leaving only three men on guard—'I think more than that number might attract attention to the spot, as they might be seen from the ore-trains.'"

"Have you told any one of this?" Clay asked. "What have you done so far?"

"We've done nothing," said Stuart. "We lost our nerve when we found out how much we knew, and we decided we'd better leave it to you."

"Whatever we do must be done at once," said Clay. "They will come for the arms to-night, most likely, and we must be there first. I agree with you entirely about the place. It is only a question now of our being on time. There are two things to do. The first thing is, to keep them from getting the arms, and the second is, if we are lucky, to secure them for ourselves. If we can pull it off properly, we ought to have those rifles in the mines before midnight. If we are hurried or surprised, we must dump them off the fort into the sea." Clay laughed and looked about him at the men. "We are only following out General Bolivar's saying, 'When you want arms take them from the enemy.' Now, there are three places we must cover. This house, first of all," he went on, inclining his head quickly toward the two sisters, "then the city, and the mines. Stuart's place, of course, is at the Palace. King must take care of this house and those in it, and MacWilliams and Langham and I must look after the arms. We must organize two parties, and they had better approach the fort from here and from the mines at the same time. I will need you to do some telegraphing for me, Mac; and, King, I must ask you for some more men from the yacht. How many have you?"

King answered that there were fifteen men still on board, ten of whom would be of service. He added that they were all well equipped for fighting.

"I believe King's a pirate in business hours," Clay said, smiling. "All right, that's good. Now go tell ten of them to meet me at the round-house in half an hour. I will get MacWilliams to telegraph Kirkland to run an engine and flat cars to within a half mile of the fort on the north, and we will come up on it with the sailors and Ted, here, from the south. You must run the engine yourself, MacWilliams, and perhaps it would be better, King, if your men joined us at the foot of the grounds here and not at the round-house. None of the workmen must see our party start. Do you agree with me?" he asked, turning to those in the group about him. "Has anybody any criticism to make?"

Stuart and King looked at one another ruefully and laughed. "I don't see what good I am doing in town," protested Stuart. "Yes, and I don't see where I come in, either," growled King, in aggrieved tones. "These youngsters can't do it all; besides I ought to have charge of my own men."

"Mutiny," said Clay, in some perplexity, "rank mutiny. Why, it's only a picnic. There are but three men there. We don't need sixteen white men to frighten off three Olanchoans."

"I'll tell you what to do," cried Hope, with the air of having discovered a plan which would be acceptable to every one, "let's all go."

"Well, I certainly mean to go," said Mr. Langham, decidedly. "So some one else must stay here. Ted, you will have to look after your sisters."

The son and heir smiled upon his parent with a look of affectionate wonder, and shook his head at him in fond and pitying disapproval.

"I'll stay," said King. "I have never seen such ungallant conduct. Ladies," he said, "I will protect your lives and property, and we'll invent something exciting to do ourselves, even if we have to bombard the Capital."

The men bade the women good-night, and left them with King and Mr. Langham, who had been persuaded to remain overnight, while Stuart rode off to acquaint Alvarez and General Rojas with what was going on.

XI

There was no chance for Clay to speak to Hope again, though he felt the cruelty of having to leave her with everything between them in this interrupted state. But their friends stood about her, interested and excited over this expedition of smuggled arms, unconscious of the great miracle that had come into his life and of his need to speak to and to touch the woman who had wrought it. Clay felt how much more binding than the laws of life are the little social conventions that must be observed at times, even though the heart is leaping with joy or racked with sorrow. He stood within a few feet of the woman he loved, wanting to cry out at her and to tell her all the wonderful things which he had learned were true for the first time that night, but he was forced instead to keep his eyes away from her face and to laugh and answer questions, and at the last to go away content with having held her hand for an instant, and to have heard her say "good-luck."

MacWilliams called Kirkland to the office at the other end of the Company's wire, and explained the situation to him. He was instructed to run an engine and freight-cars to a point a quarter of a mile north of the fort, and to wait there until he heard a loco-motive whistle or pistol shots, when he was to run on to the fort as quickly and as noiselessly as possible. He was also directed to bring with him as many of the American workmen as he could trust to keep silent concerning the events of the evening. At ten o'clock MacWilliams had the steam up in a locomotive, and with his only passenger-car in the rear, ran it out of the yard and stopped the train at the point nearest the cars where ten of the *Vesta*'s crew were waiting. The sailors had no idea as to where they were going, or what they were to do, but the fact that they had all been given arms filled them with satisfaction, and they huddled together at the bottom of the car smoking and whisper-ing, and radiant with excitement and satisfaction.

The train progressed cautiously until it was within a half mile below the fort, when Clay stopped it, and, leaving two men on guard, stepped off the remaining distance on the ties, his little band following noiselessly behind him like a procession of ghosts in the moonlight. They halted and listened from time to time as they drew near the ruins, but there was no sound except the beating of the waves on the rocks and the rustling of the sea-breeze through the vines and creepers about them.

Clay motioned to the men to sit down, and, beckoning to MacWilliams, directed him to go on ahead and reconnoitre.

"If you fire we will come up," he said. "Get back here as soon as you can."

"Aren't you going to make sure first that Kirkland is on the other side of the fort?" MacWilliams whispered.

Clay replied that he was certain Kirkland had already arrived. "He had a shorter run than ours, and he wired you he was ready to start when we were, didn't he?" MacWilliams nodded.

"Well, then, he is there. I can count on Kirk."

MacWilliams pulled at his heavy boots and hid them in the bushes, with his helmet over them to mark the spot. "I feel as though I was going to rob a bank," he chuckled, as he waved his hand and crept off into the underbrush.

For the first few moments the men who were left behind sat silent, but as the minutes wore on, and MacWilliams made no sign, they grew restless, and shifted their positions, and began to whisper together, until Clay shook his head at them, and there was silence again until one of them, in trying not to cough, almost strangled, and the others tittered and those nearest pummelled him on the back.

Clay pulled out his revolver, and after spinning the cylinder under his finger-nail, put it back in its holder again, and the men, taking this as an encouraging promise of immediate action, began to examine their weapons again for the twentieth time, and there was a chorus of short, muffled clicks as triggers were drawn back and cautiously lowered and levers shot into place and caught again.

One of the men farthest down the track raised his arm, and all turned and half rose as they saw MacWilliams coming toward them on a run, leaping noiselessly in his stocking feet from tie to tie. He dropped on his knees between Clay and Langham.

"The guns are there all right," he whispered, panting, "and there are only three men guarding them. They are all sitting on the beach smoking. I hustled around the fort and came across the whole outfit in the second gallery. It looks like a row of coffins, ten coffins and about twenty little boxes and kegs. I'm sure that means they are coming for them to-night. They've not tried to hide them nor to cover them up. All we've got to do is to walk down on the guards and tell them to throw up their hands. It's too easy."

Clay jumped to his feet. "Come on," he said.

"Wait till I get my boots on first," begged MacWilliams. "I

wouldn't go over those cinders again in my bare feet for all the buried treasure in the Spanish Main.[1] You can make all the noise you want; the waves will drown it."

With MacWilliams to show them the way, the men scrambled up the outer wall of the fort and crossed the moss-covered ramparts at the run. Below them, on the sandy beach, were three men sitting around a driftwood fire that had sunk to a few hot ashes. Clay nodded to MacWilliams. "You and Ted can have them," he said. "Go with him, Langham."

The sailors levelled their rifles at the three lonely figures on the beach as the two boys slipped down the wall and fell on their hands and feet in the sand below, and then crawled up to within a few feet of where the men were sitting.

As MacWilliams raised his revolver one of the three, who was cooking something over the fire, raised his head and with a yell of warning flung himself toward his rifle.

"Up with your hands!" MacWilliams shouted in Spanish, and Langham, running in, seized the nearest sentry by the neck and shoved his face down between his knees into the sand.

There was a great rattle of falling stones and of breaking vines as the sailors tumbled down the side of the fort, and in a half minute's time the three sentries were looking with angry, frightened eyes at the circle of armed men around them.

"Now gag them," said Clay. "Does anybody here know how to gag a man?" he asked. "I don't."

"Better make him tell what he knows first," suggested Langham.

But the Spaniards were too terrified at what they had done, or at what they had failed to do, to further commit themselves.

"Tie us and gag us," one of them begged. "Let them find us so. It is the kindest thing you can do for us."

"Thank you, sir," said Clay. "That is what I wanted to know. They are coming to-night, then. We must hurry."

The three sentries were bound and hidden at the base of the wall, with a sailor to watch them. He was a young man with a high sense of the importance of his duties, and he enlivened the prisoners by poking them in the ribs whenever they moved.

---

1 A term first used to designate Spanish territory in South America, particularly from the Orinoco River to Panama; later expanded to include Spanish possessions in the Caribbean. The Spanish Main remains a popular setting for pirate tales.

Langham ... shoved his face down between his knees into the sand.

Clay deemed it impossible to signal Kirkland as they had arranged to do, as they could not know now how near those who were coming for the arms might be. So MacWilliams was sent back for his engine, and a few minutes later they heard it rumble heavily past the fort on its way to bring up Kirkland and the flat cars. Clay explored the lower chambers of the fort and found the boxes as MacWilliams had described them. Ten men, with some effort, could lift and carry the larger coffin-shaped boxes, and Clay guessed that, granting their contents to be rifles, there must be a hundred pieces in each box, and that there were a thousand rifles in all.

They had moved half of the boxes to the side of the track when the train of flat cars and the two engines came crawling and twisting toward them, between the walls of the jungle, like a great serpent, with no light about it but the glow from the hot ashes as they fell between the rails. Thirty men, equally divided between Irish and negroes, fell off the flat cars before the wheels had ceased to revolve, and, without a word of direction, began loading the heavy boxes on the train and passing the kegs of cartridges from hand to hand and shoulder to shoulder. The sailors spread out up the road that led to the Capital to give warning in case the enemy approached, but they were recalled before they had reason to give an alarm, and in a half hour Burke's entire shipment of arms was on the ore-cars, the men who were to have guarded them were prisoners in the cab of the engine, and both trains were rushing at full speed toward the mines. On arriving there Kirkland's train was switched to the siding that led to the magazine in which was stored the rackarock[1] and dynamite used in the blasting. By midnight all of the boxes were safely under lock in the zinc building, and the number of the men who always guarded the place for fear of fire or accident was doubled, while a reserve, composed of Kirkland's thirty picked men, were hidden in the surrounding houses and engine-sheds.

Before Clay left he had one of the boxes broken open, and found that it held a hundred Mannlicher rifles.[2]

"Good!" he said. "I'd give a thousand dollars in gold if I could bring Mendoza out here and show him his own men armed with his own Mannlichers and dying for a shot at him. How old Burke will enjoy this when he hears of it!"

The party from the Palms returned to their engine after many promises of reward to the men for their work "overtime," and were soon flying back with their hearts as light as the smoke above them.

MacWilliams slackened speed as they neared the fort, and moved up cautiously on the scene of their recent victory, but a warning cry from Clay made him bring his engine to a sharp stop. Many lights were flashing over the ruins and they could see

---

1 An explosive used in mining.
2 Mannlicher, a very reliable, very accurate Austrian-made rifle; for military action, one of the best weapons then in existence.

in their reflection the figures of men running over the same walls on which the lizards had basked in undisturbed peace for years.

"They look like a swarm of hornets after some one has chucked a stone through their nest," laughed MacWilliams. "What shall we do now? Go back, or wait here, or run the blockade?"

"Oh, ride them out," said Langham; "the family's anxious, and I want to tell them what's happened. Go ahead."

Clay turned to the sailors in the car behind them. "Lie down, men," he said. "And don't any of you fire unless I tell you to. Let them do all the shooting. This isn't our fight yet, and, besides, they can't hit a locomotive standing still, certainly not when it's going at full speed."

"Suppose they've torn the track up?" said MacWilliams, grinning. "We'd look sort of silly flying through the air."

"Oh, they've not sense enough to think of that," said Clay. "Besides, they don't know it was we who took their arms away, yet."

MacWilliams opened the throttle gently, and the train moved slowly forward, gaining speed at each revolution of the wheels.

As the noise of its approach beat louder and louder on the air, a yell of disappointed rage and execration rose into the night from the fort, and a mass of soldiers swarmed upon the track, leaping up and down and shaking the rifles in their hands.

"That sounds a little as though they thought we had something to do with it," said MacWilliams, grimly. "If they don't look out someone will get hurt."

There was a flash of fire from where the mass of men stood, followed by a dozen more flashes, and the bullets rattled on the smokestack and upon the boiler of the engine.

"Low bridge," cried MacWilliams, with a fierce chuckle. "Now, watch her!"

He threw open the throttle as far as it would go, and the engine answered to his touch like a race-horse to the whip. It seemed to spring from the track into the air. It quivered and shook like a live thing, and as it shot in between the soldiers they fell back on either side, and MacWilliams leaned far out of his cab-window shaking his fist at them.

"You got left, didn't you?" he shouted. "Thank you for the Mannlichers."

As the locomotive rushed out of the jungle, and passed the point on the road nearest to the Palms, MacWilliams loosened three long triumphant shrieks from his whistle and the sailors stood up and cheered.

"Let them shout," cried Clay. "Everybody will have to know now. It's begun at last," he said, with a laugh of relief.

"And we took the first trick," said MacWilliams, as he ran his engine slowly into the railroad yard.

The whistles of the engine and the shouts of the sailors had carried far through the silence of the night, and as the men came hurrying across the lawn to the Palms, they saw all of those who had been left behind grouped on the veranda awaiting them.

"Do the conquering heroes come?" shouted King.

"They do," young Langham cried, joyously. "We've got all their arms, and they shot at us. We've been under fire!"

"Are any of you hurt?" asked Miss Langham, anxiously, as she and the others hurried down the steps to welcome them, while those of the *Vesta*'s crew who had been left behind looked at their comrades with envy.

"We have been so frightened and anxious about you," said Miss Langham.

Hope held out her hand to Clay and greeted him with a quiet, happy smile, that was in contrast to the excitement and confusion that reigned about them.

"I knew you would come back safely," she said. And the pressure of her hand seemed to add "to me."

XII

The day of the review rose clear and warm, tempered by a light breeze from the sea. As it was a fête day, the harbor wore an air of unwonted inactivity; no lighters passed heavily from the levees to the merchantmen at anchor, and the warehouses along the wharves were closed and deserted. A thin line of smoke from the funnels of the *Vesta* showed that her fires were burning, and the fact that she rode on a single anchor chain seemed to promise that at any moment she might slip away to sea.

As Clay was finishing his coffee two notes were brought to him from messengers who had ridden out that morning, and who sat in their saddles looking at the armed force around the office with amused intelligence.

One note was from Mendoza, and said he had decided not to call out the regiment at the mines, as he feared their long absence from drill would make them compare unfavorably with their comrades, and do him more harm than credit. "He is afraid of them since last night," was Clay's comment, as he passed the note on to MacWilliams. "He's quite right, they might do him harm."

The second note was from Stuart. He said the city was already wide awake and restless, but whether this was due to the fact that it was a fête day, or to some other cause which would disclose itself later, he could not tell. Madame Alvarez, the afternoon before, while riding in the Alameda, had been insulted by a group of men around a café, who had risen and shouted after her, one of them throwing a wine-glass into her lap as she rode past. His troopers had charged the sidewalk and carried off six of the men to the carcel. He and Rojas had urged the President to make every preparation for immediate flight, to have the horses put to his travelling carriage, and had warned him when at the review to take up his position at the point nearest to his own body-guard, and as far as possible from the troops led by Mendoza. Stuart added that he had absolute confidence in the former. The policeman who had attempted to carry Burke's note to Mendoza had confessed that he was the only traitor in the camp, and that he had tried to work on his comrades without success. Stuart begged Clay to join him as quickly as possible. Clay went up the hill to the Palms, and after consulting with Mr. Langham, dictated an order to Kirkland, instructing him to call the men together and to point out to them how much better their condition had been since they had entered the mines, and to promise them an increase of wages if they remained faithful to Mr. Langham's interests, and a small pension to any one who might be injured "from any cause whatsoever" while serving him.

"Tell them, if they are loyal, they can live in their shacks rent free hereafter," wrote Clay. "They are always asking for that. It's a cheap generosity," he added aloud to Mr. Langham, "because we've never been able to collect rent from any of them yet."

At noon young Langham ordered the best three horses in the stables to be brought to the door of the Palms for Clay, MacWilliams, and himself. Clay's last words to King were to have the yacht in readiness to put to sea when he telephoned him to do so, and he advised the women to have their dresses and more valuable possessions packed ready to be taken on board.

"Don't you think I might see the review if I went on horseback?" Hope asked. "I could get away then, if there should be any trouble."

Clay answered with a look of such alarm and surprise that Hope laughed.

"See the review! I should say not," he exclaimed. "I don't even want Ted to be there."

"Oh, that's always the way," said Hope, "I miss everything. I think I'll come, however, anyhow. The servants are all going, and I'll go with them disguised in a turban."

As the men neared Valencia, Clay turned in his saddle, and asked Langham if he thought his sister would really venture into the town.

"She'd better not let me catch her, if she does," the fond brother replied.

The reviewing party left the Government Palace for the Alameda at three o'clock, President Alvarez riding on horseback in advance, and Madame Alvarez sitting in the State carriage with one of her attendants, and with Stuart's troopers gathered so closely about her that the men's boots scraped against the wheels, and their numbers hid her almost entirely from sight.

The great square in which the evolutions were to take place was lined on its four sides by the carriages of the wealthy Olanchoans, except at the two gates, where there was a wide space left open to admit the soldiers. The branches of the trees on the edges of the bare parade ground were black with men and boys, and the balconies and roofs of the houses that faced it were gay with streamers and flags, and alive with women wrapped for the occasion in their colored shawls. Seated on the grass between the carriages, or surging up and down behind them, were thousands of people, each hurrying to gain a better place of vantage, or striving to hold the one he had, and forming a restless, turbulent audience in which all individual cries were lost in a great murmur of laughter, and calls, and cheers. The mass knit together, and pressed forward as the President's band swung jauntily into the square and halted in one corner, and a shout of expectancy went up from the trees and housetops as the President's body-guard entered at the lower gate, and the broken place in its ranks showed that it was escorting the State carriage. The troopers fell back on two sides, and the carriage, with the President riding at its head, passed on, and took up a position in front of the other carriages, and close to one of the sides of the hollow square. At Stuart's orders Clay, MacWilliams, and Langham had pushed their horses into the rear rank of cavalry, and remained wedged between the troopers within twenty feet of where Madame Alvarez was sitting. She was very white, and the powder on her face gave her an added and unnatural pallor. As the people cheered her husband and herself she raised her head slightly and seemed to be trying to catch any sound of dissent in their greeting, or some possible undercurrent of disfavor, but the welcome appeared to be both genuine and hearty, until a second shout smothered it completely as the figure of old General Rojas, the Vice-President, and the most dearly loved by the common people, came through the gate at the head of his regiment. There was such greeting for him that the welcome to the President seemed mean in comparison, and it was with an embarrassment which both felt that the two men drew near together, and each leaned from his saddle to grasp the other's hand. Madame Alvarez sank back rigidly on her cushions, and her eyes flashed with anticipation and excitement. She drew her mantilla a little closer about her shoulders, with a nervous shudder as though she were cold. Suddenly the look of anxiety in her eyes changed to one of annoyance, and she beckoned Clay imperiously to the side of the carriage.

"Look," she said, pointing across the square. "If I am not mistaken that is Miss Langham, Miss Hope. The one on the black horse—it must be she, for none of the native ladies ride. It is not safe for her to be here alone. Go," she commanded, "bring her here to me. Put her next to the carriage, or perhaps she will be safer with you among the troopers."

Clay had recognized Hope before Madame Alvarez had finished speaking, and dashed off at a gallop, skirting the line of carriages. Hope had stopped her horse beside a victoria,[1] and was talking to the native women who occupied it, and who were scandalized at her appearance in a public place with no one but a groom to attend her.

"Why, it's the same thing as a polo match," protested Hope, as Clay pulled up angrily beside the victoria. "I always ride over to polo alone at Newport, at least with James," she added, nodding her head toward the servant.

The man approached Clay and touched his hat apologetically, "Miss Hope would come, sir," he said, "and I thought I'd better be with her than to go off and tell Mr. Langham, sir. I knew she wouldn't wait for me."

"I asked you not to come," Clay said to Hope, in a low voice.

"I wanted to know the worst at once," she answered. "I was anxious about Ted—and you."

"Well, it can't be helped now," he said. "Come, we must hurry, here is our friend, the enemy." He bowed to their acquaintances

---

1 Victoria, a Victorian era, horse-drawn carriage for the upper-classes.

in the victoria and they trotted briskly off to the side of the President's carriage, just as a yell arose from the crowd that made all the other shouts which had preceded it sound like the cheers of children at recess.

"It reminds me of a football match," whispered young Langham, excitedly, "when the teams run on the field. Look at Alvarez and Rojas watching Mendoza."

Mendoza advanced at the front of his three troops of cavalry, looking neither to the left nor right, and by no sign acknowledging the fierce uproarious greeting of the people. Close behind him came his chosen band of cowboys and ruffians.

They were the best equipped and least disciplined soldiers in the army, and were, to the great relief of the people, seldom seen in the city, but were kept moving in the mountain passes and along the coast line, on the lookout for smugglers with whom they were on the most friendly terms. They were a picturesque body of blackguards, in their high-topped boots and silver-tipped sombreros and heavy, gaudy saddles, but the shout that had gone up at their advance was due as much to the fear they inspired as to any great love for them or their chief.

"Now all the chessmen are on the board, and the game can begin," said Clay. "It's like the scene in the play, where each man has his sword at another man's throat and no one dares make the first move." He smiled as he noted, with the eye of one who had seen Continental troops in action, the shuffling steps and slovenly carriage of the half-grown soldiers that followed Mendoza's cavalry at a quick step. Stuart's picked men, over whom he had spent many hot and weary hours, looked like a troop of Life Guardsmen[1] in comparison. Clay noted their superiority, but he also saw that in numbers they were most woefully at a disadvantage.

It was a brilliant scene for so modest a capital. The sun flashed on the trappings of the soldiers, on the lacquer and polished metal work of the carriages; and the Parisian gowns of their occupants and the fluttering flags and banners filled the air with color and movement, while back of all, framing the parade ground with a band of black, was the restless mob of people applauding the evolutions, and cheering for their favorites, Alvarez, Mendoza, and Rojas, moved by an excitement that was in disturbing contrast to the easy good-nature of their usual manner.

---

1   The senior regiment in the British army, charged with providing the monarch with armed, mounted escort. The Life Guard are famous for their red tunics and the white plumes on their helmets.

The marching and countermarching of the troops had continued with spirit for some time, and there was a halt in the evolutions which left the field vacant, except for the presence of Mendoza's cavalrymen, who were moving at a walk along one side of the quadrangle. Alvarez and Vice-President Rojas, with Stuart, as an adjutant at their side, were sitting their horses within some fifty yards of the State carriage and the body-guard. Alvarez made a conspicuous contrast in his black coat and high hat to the brilliant greens and reds of his generals' uniforms, but he sat his saddle as well as either of the others, and his white hair, white imperial and mustache, and the dignity of his bearing distinguished him above them both.[1] Little Stuart, sitting at his side, with his blue eyes glaring from under his white helmet and his face burned to almost as red a tint as his curly hair, looked like a fierce little bull-dog in comparison. None of the three men spoke as they sat motionless and quite alone waiting for the next movement of the troops.

It proved to be one of moment. Even before Mendoza had ridden toward them with his sword at salute, Clay gave an exclamation of enlightenment and concern. He saw that the men who were believed to be devoted to Rojas, had been halted and left standing at the farthest corner of the plaza, nearly two hundred yards from where the President had taken his place, that Mendoza's infantry surrounded them on every side, and that Mendoza's cowboys, who had been walking their horses, had wheeled and were coming up with an increasing momentum, a flying mass of horses and men directed straight at the President himself.

Mendoza galloped up to Alvarez with his sword still in salute. His eyes were burning with excitement and with the light of success. No one but Stuart and Rojas heard his words; to the spectators and to the army he appeared as though he was, in his capacity of Commander-in-Chief, delivering some brief report, or asking for instructions.

"Dr. Alvarez," he said, "as the head of the army I arrest you for high treason; you have plotted to place yourself in office without popular election. You are also accused of large thefts of public

---

1 An imperial, a grown-out goatee or small, tufted beard; an imperial mustache, one grown full and long and curled up at the ends almost into a circle. Emperor Napoleon III of France and other early nineteenth-century royals and politicians of Europe favored the imperial mustache and beard.

funds. I must ask you to ride with me to the military prison. General Rojas, I regret that as an accomplice of the President's, you must come with us also. I will explain my action to the people when you are safe in prison, and I will proclaim martial law. If your troops attempt to interfere, my men have orders to fire on them and you."

Stuart did not wait for his sentence. He had heard the heavy beat of the cavalry coming up on them at a trot. He saw the ranks open and two men catch at each bridle rein of both Alvarez and Rojas and drag them on with them, buried in the crush of horses about them, and swept forward by the weight and impetus of the moving mass behind. Stuart dashed off to the State carriage and seized the nearest of the horses by the bridle. "To the Palace!" he shouted to his men. "Shoot any one who tries to stop you. Forward, at a gallop," he commanded.

The populace had not discovered what had occurred until it was finished. The *coup d'état* had been long considered and the manner in which it was to be carried out carefully planned. The cavalry had swept across the parade ground and up the street before the people saw that they carried Rojas and Alvarez with them. The regiment commanded by Rojas found itself hemmed in before and behind by Mendoza's two regiments. They were greatly outnumbered, but they fired a scattering shot, and following their captured leader, broke through the line around them and pursued the cavalry toward the military prison.

It was impossible to tell in the uproar which followed how many or how few had been parties to the plot. The mob, shrieking and shouting and leaping in the air, swarmed across the parade ground, and from a dozen different points men rose above the heads of the people and harangued them in violent speeches. And while some of the soldiers and the citizens gathered anxiously about these orators, others ran through the city calling for the rescue of the President, for an attack on the palace, and shrieking "Long live the Government!" and "Long live the Revolution!" The State carriage raced through the narrow streets with its body-guard galloping around it, sweeping down in its rush stray pedestrians, and scattering the chairs and tables in front of the cafés. As it dashed up the long avenue of the Palace, Stuart called his men back and ordered them to shut and barricade the great iron gates and to guard them against the coming of the mob, while MacWilliams and young Langham pulled open the carriage door and assisted the President's wife and her terrified companion to alight. Madame Alvarez was trembling with excitement as she leaned on Langham's arm, but she showed no signs of fear in her face or in her manner.

"Mr. Clay has gone to bring your travelling carriage to the rear door," Langham said. "Stuart tells us it is harnessed and ready. You will hurry, please, and get whatever you need to carry with you. We will see you safely to the coast."

As they entered the hall, and were ascending the great marble stairway, Hope and her groom, who had followed in the rear of the cavalry, came running to meet them. "I got in by the back way," Hope explained. "The streets there are all deserted. How can I help you?" she asked, eagerly.

"By leaving me," cried the older woman. "Good God, child, have I not enough to answer for without dragging you into this? Go home at once through the botanical garden, and then by way of the wharves. That part of the city is still empty."

"Where are your servants; why are they not here?" Hope demanded without heeding her. The Palace was strangely empty; no footsteps came running to greet them, no doors opened or shut as they hurried to Madame Alvarez's apartments. The servants of the household had fled at the first sound of the uproar in the city, and the dresses and ornaments scattered on the floor told that they had not gone empty-handed. The woman who had accompanied Madame Alvarez to the review sank weeping on the bed, and then, as the shouts grew suddenly louder and more near, ran to hide herself in the upper stories of the house. Hope crossed to the window and saw a great mob of soldiers and citizens sweep around the corner and throw themselves against the iron fence of the Palace. "You will have to hurry," she said. "Remember, you are risking the lives of those boys by your delay."

There was a large bed in the room, and Madame Alvarez had pulled it forward and was bending over a safe that had opened in the wall, and which had been hidden by the head-board of the bed. She held up a bundle of papers in her hand, wrapped in a leather portfolio. "Do you see these?" she cried, "they are drafts for five millions of dollars." She tossed them back into the safe and swung the door shut.

"You are a witness. I do not take them," she said.

"I don't understand," Hope answered, "but hurry. Have you everything you want—have you your jewels?"

"Yes," the woman answered, as she rose to her feet, "they are mine."

A yell more loud and terrible than any that had gone before

rose from the garden below, and there was the sound of iron beating against iron, and cries of rage and execration from a great multitude.

"I will not go!" the Spanish woman cried, suddenly. "I will not leave Alvarez to that mob. If they want to kill me, let them kill me." She threw the bag that held her jewels on the bed, and pushing open the window stepped out upon the balcony. She was conspicuous in her black dress against the yellow stucco of the wall, and in an instant the mob saw her and a mad shout of exultation and anger rose from the mass that beat and crushed itself against the high iron railings of the garden. Hope caught the woman by the skirt and dragged her back. "You are mad," she said. "What good can you do your husband here? Save yourself and he will come to you when he can. There is nothing you can do for him now; you cannot give your life for him. You are wasting it, and you are risking the lives of the men who are waiting for us below. Come, I tell you."

MacWilliams left Clay waiting beside the diligence and ran from the stable through the empty house and down the marble stairs to the garden without meeting any one on his way. He saw Stuart helping and directing his men to barricade the gates with iron urns and garden benches and sentry-boxes. Outside the mob were firing at him with their revolvers, and calling him foul names, but Stuart did not seem to hear them. He greeted MacWilliams with a cheerful little laugh. "Well," he asked, "is she ready?"

"No, but we are. Clay and I've been waiting there for five minutes. We found Miss Hope's groom and sent him back to the Palms with a message to King. We told him to run the yacht to Los Bocos and lie off shore until we came. He is to take her on down the coast to Truxillo, where our man-of-war is lying, and they will give her shelter as a political refugee."

"Why don't you drive her to the Palms at once?" demanded Stuart, anxiously, "and take her on board the yacht there? It is ten miles to Bocos and the roads are very bad."

"Clay says we could never get her through the city," MacWilliams answered. "We should have to fight all the way. But the city to the south is deserted, and by going out by the back roads, we can make Bocos by ten o'clock to-night. The yacht should reach there by seven."

"You are right; go back. I will call off some of my men. The rest must hold this mob back until you start; then I will follow with the others. Where is Miss Hope?"

"We don't know. Clay is frantic. Her groom says she is somewhere in the Palace."

"Hurry," Stuart commanded. "If Mendoza gets here before Madame Alvarez leaves, it will be too late."

MacWilliams sprang up the steps of the Palace, and Stuart, calling to the men nearest him to follow, started after him on a run.

As Stuart entered the palace with his men at his heels, Clay was hurrying from its rear entrance along the upper hall, and Hope and Madame Alvarez were leaving the apartments of the latter at its front. They met at the top of the main stairway just as Stuart put his foot on its lower step. The young Englishman heard the clatter of his men following close behind him and leaped eagerly forward. Half way to the top the noise behind him ceased, and turning his head quickly he looked back over his shoulder and saw that the men had halted at the foot of the stairs and stood huddled together in disorder looking up at him. Stuart glanced over their heads and down the hallway to the garden beyond to see if they were followed, but the mob still fought from the outer side of the barricade. He waved his sword impatiently and started forward again. "Come on!" he shouted. But the men below him did not move. Stuart halted once more and this time turned about and looked down upon them with surprise and anger. There was not one of them he could not have called by name. He knew all their little troubles, their love-affairs, even. They came to him for comfort and advice, and to beg for money. He had regarded them as his children, and he was proud of them as soldiers because they were the work of his hands.

So, instead of a sharp command, he asked, "What is it?" in surprise, and stared at them wondering. He could not or would not comprehend, even though he saw that those in the front rank were pushing back and those behind were urging them forward. The muzzles of their carbines were directed at every point, and on their faces fear and hate and cowardice were written in varying likenesses.

"What does this mean?" Stuart demanded, sharply. "What are you waiting for?"

Clay had just reached the top of the stairs. He saw Madame Alvarez and Hope coming toward him, and at the sight of Hope he gave an exclamation of relief.

Then his eyes turned and fell on the tableau below, on Stuart's back, as he stood confronting the men, and on their scowling upturned faces and half-lifted carbines. Clay had lived for a longer time among Spanish-Americans than had the English subaltern, or else he was the quicker of the two to believe in evil and ingratitude, for he gave a cry of warning, and motioned the women away.

"Stuart!" he cried. "Come away; for God's sake, what are you doing? Come back!"

The Englishman started at the sound of his friend's voice, but he did not turn his head. He began to descend the stairs slowly, a step at a time, staring at the mob so fiercely that they shrank back before the look of wounded pride and anger in his eyes. Those in the rear raised and levelled their rifles. Without taking his eyes from theirs, Stuart drew his revolver, and with his sword swinging from its wrist-strap, pointed his weapon at the mass below him.

"What does this mean?" he demanded. "Is this mutiny?"

A voice from the rear of the crowd of men shrieked: "Death to the Spanish woman. Death to all traitors. Long live Mendoza," and the others echoed the cry in chorus.

Clay sprang down the broad stairs calling, "Come to me"; but before he could reach Stuart, a woman's voice rang out, in a long terrible cry of terror, a cry that was neither a prayer nor an imprecation, but which held the agony of both. Stuart started, and looked up to where Madame Alvarez had thrown herself toward him across the broad balustrade of the stairway. She was silent with fear, and her hand clutched at the air, as she beckoned wildly to him. Stuart stared at her with a troubled smile and waved his empty hand to reassure her. The movement was final, for the men below, freed from the reproach of his eyes, flung up their carbines and fired, some wildly, without placing their guns at rest, and others steadily and aiming straight at his heart.

As the volley rang out and the smoke drifted up the great staircase, the subaltern's hands tossed high above his head, his body sank into itself and toppled backward, and, like a tired child falling to sleep, the defeated soldier of fortune dropped back into the outstretched arms of his friend.

Clay lifted him upon his knee, and crushed him closer against his breast with one arm, while he tore with his free hand at the stock about the throat and pushed his fingers in between the buttons of the tunic. They came forth again wet and colored crimson.

"Stuart!" Clay gasped. "Stuart, speak to me, look at me!" He shook the body in his arms with fierce roughness, peering into the face that rested on his shoulder, as though he could command the eyes back again to light and life. "Don't leave me!" he said. "For God's sake, old man, don't leave me!"

But the head on his shoulder only sank the closer and the body stiffened in his arms. Clay raised his eyes and saw the soldiers still standing, irresolute and appalled at what they had done, and awe-struck at the sight of the grief before them.

Clay gave a cry as terrible as the cry of a woman who has seen her child mangled before her eyes, and lowering the body quickly to the steps, he ran at the scattering mass below him. As he came they fled down the corridor, shrieking and calling to their friends to throw open the gates and begging them to admit the mob. When they reached the outer porch they turned, encouraged by the touch of numbers, and halted to fire at the man who still fol-lowed them.

Clay stopped, with a look in his eyes which no one who knew them had ever seen there, and smiled with pleasure in knowing himself a master in what he had to do. And at each report of his revolver one of Stuart's assassins stumbled and pitched heavily forward on his face. Then he turned and walked slowly back up the hall to the stairway like a man moving in his sleep. He neither saw nor heard the bullets that bit spitefully at the walls about him and rattled among the glass pendants of the great chandeliers above his head. When he came to the step on which the body lay he stooped and picked it up gently, and holding it across his breast, strode on up the stairs. MacWilliams and Langham were coming toward him, and saw the helpless figure in his arms.

"What is it?" they cried; "is he wounded, is he hurt?"

"He is dead," Clay answered, passing on with his burden. "Get Hope away."

Madame Alvarez stood with the girl's arms about her, her eyes closed and her figure trembling.

"Let me be!" she moaned. "Don't touch me; let me die. My God, what have I to live for now?" She shook off Hope's sup-porting arm, and stood before them, all her former courage gone, trembling and shivering in agony. "I do not care what they do to me!" she cried. She tore her lace mantilla from her shoulders and threw it on the floor. "I shall not leave this place. He is dead. Why should I go? He is dead. They have murdered him; he is dead."

"She is fainting," said Hope. Her voice was strained and hard.

To her brother she seemed to have grown suddenly much older, and he looked to her to tell him what to do.

"Take hold of her," she said. "She will fall." The woman sank back into the arms of the men, trembling and moaning feebly.

He strode on up the stairs.

"Now carry her to the carriage," said Hope. "She has fainted; it is better; she does not know what has happened."

Clay, still bearing the body in his arms, pushed open the first door that stood ajar before him with his foot. It opened into the great banqueting hall of the palace, but he could not choose.

He had to consider now the safety of the living, whose lives were still in jeopardy.

The long table in the centre of the hall was laid with places for many people, for it had been prepared for the President and the President's guests, who were to have joined with him in celebrating the successful conclusion of the review. From outside the light of the sun, which was just sinking behind the mountains, shone dimly upon the silver on the board, on the glass and napery, and the massive gilt centre-pieces filled with great clusters of fresh flowers. It looked as though the servants had but just left the room. Even the candles had been lit in readiness, and as their flames wavered and smoked in the evening breeze they cast uncertain shadows on the walls and showed the stern faces of the soldier presidents frowning down on the crowded table from their gilded frames.

There was a great leather lounge stretching along one side of the hall, and Clay moved toward this quickly and laid his burden down. He was conscious that Hope was still following him. He straightened the limbs of the body and folded the arms across the breast and pressed his hand for an instant on the cold hands of his friend, and then whispering something between his lips, turned and walked hurriedly away.

Hope confronted him in the doorway. She was sobbing silently. "Must we leave him," she pleaded, "must we leave him—like this?"

From the garden there came the sound of hammers ringing on the iron hinges, and a great crash of noises as the gate fell back from its fastenings, and the mob rushed over the obstacles upon which it had fallen. It seemed as if their yells of exultation and anger must reach even the ears of the dead man.

"They are calling Mendoza," Clay whispered, "he must be with them. Come, we will have to run for our lives now."

But before he could guess what Hope was about to do, or could prevent her, she had slipped past him and picked up Stuart's sword that had fallen from his wrist to the floor, and laid it on the soldier's body, and closed his hands upon its hilt. She glanced quickly about her as though looking for something, and then with a sob of relief ran to the table, and sweeping it of armful of its flowers, stepped swiftly back again to the lounge and heaped them upon it.

"Come, for God's sake, come!" Clay called to her in a whisper from the door.

Hope stood for an instant staring at the young Englishman as the candle-light flickered over his white face, and then, dropping on her knees, she pushed back the curly hair from about the boy's forehead and kissed him. Then, without turning to look again, she placed her hand in Clay's and he ran with her, dragging her behind him down the length of the hall, just as the mob entered it on the floor below them and filled the palace with their shouts of triumph.

As the sun sank lower its light fell more dimly on the lonely figure in the vast dining-hall, and as the gloom deepened there, the candles burned with greater brilliancy, and the faces of the portraits shone more clearly.

They seemed to be staring down less sternly now upon the white mortal face of the brother-in-arms who had just joined them.

One who had known him among his own people would have seen in the attitude and in the profile of the English soldier a likeness to his ancestors of the Crusades who lay carved in stone in the village church, with their faces turned to the sky, their faithful hounds waiting at their feet, and their hands pressed upward in prayer.

And when, a moment later, the half-crazed mob of men and boys swept into the great room, with Mendoza at their head, something of the pathos of the young Englishman's death in his foreign place of exile must have touched them, for they stopped appalled and startled, and pressed back upon their fellows, with eager whispers. The Spanish-American General strode boldly forward, but his eyes lowered before the calm, white face, and either because the lighted candles and the flowers awoke in him some memory of the great Church that had nursed him, or because the jagged holes in the soldier's tunic appealed to what was bravest in him, he crossed himself quickly, and then raising his hands slowly to his visor, lifted his hat and pointed with it to the door. And the mob, without once looking back at the rich treasure of silver on the table, pushed out before him, stepping softly, as though they had intruded on a shrine.

XIII

The President's travelling carriage was a double-seated diligence covered with heavy hoods and with places on the box for two men. Only one of the coachmen, the same man who had driven the State carriage from the review, had remained at the stables.

As he knew the roads to Los Bocos, Clay ordered him up to the driver's seat, and MacWilliams climbed into the place beside him after first storing three rifles under the lap-robe.

Hope pulled open the leather curtains of the carriage and found Madame Alvarez where the men had laid her upon the cushions, weak and hysterical. The girl crept in beside her, and lifting her in her arms, rested the older woman's head against her shoulder, and soothed and comforted her with tenderness and sympathy.

Clay stopped with his foot in the stirrup and looked up anxiously at Langham who was already in the saddle.

"Is there no possible way of getting Hope out of this and back to the Palms?" he asked.

"No, it's too late. This is the only way now." Hope opened the leather curtains and looking out shook her head impatiently at Clay. "I wouldn't go now if there were another way," she said. "I couldn't leave her like this."

"You're delaying the game, Clay," cried Langham, warningly, as he stuck his spurs into his pony's side.

The people in the diligence lurched forward as the horses felt the lash of the whip and strained against the harness, and then plunged ahead at a gallop on their long race to the sea. As they sped through the gardens, the stables and the trees hid them from the sight of those in the palace, and the turf, upon which the driver had turned the horses for greater safety, deadened the sound of their flight.

They found the gates of the botanical gardens already opened, and Clay, in the street outside, beckoning them on. Without waiting for the others the two outriders galloped ahead to the first cross street, looked up and down its length, and then, in evident concern at what they saw in the distance, motioned the driver to greater speed, and crossing the street signalled him to follow them. At the next corner Clay flung himself off his pony, and throwing the bridle to Langham, ran ahead into the cross street on foot, and after a quick glance pointed down its length away from the heart of the city to the mountains.

The driver turned as Clay directed him, and when the man found that his face was fairly set toward the goal he lashed his horses recklessly through the narrow street, so that the murmur of the mob behind them grew perceptibly fainter at each leap forward.

The noise of the galloping hoofs brought women and children to the barred windows of the houses, but no men stepped into the road to stop their progress, and those few they met running in the direction of the palace hastened to get out of their way, and stood with their backs pressed against the walls of the narrow thoroughfare looking after them with wonder.

Even those who suspected their errand were helpless to detain them, for sooner than they could raise the hue and cry or formulate a plan of action, the carriage had passed and was disappearing in the distance, rocking from wheel to wheel like a ship in a gale. Two men who were so bold as to start to follow, stopped abruptly when they saw the outriders draw rein and turn in their saddles as though to await their coming.

Clay's mind was torn with doubts, and his nerves were drawn taut like the strings of a violin. Personal danger exhilarated him, but this chance of harm to others who were helpless, except for him, depressed his spirit with anxiety. He experienced in his own mind all the nervous fears of a thief who sees an officer in every passing citizen, and at one moment he warned the driver to move more circumspectly, and so avert suspicion, and the next urged him into more desperate bursts of speed. In his fancy every cross street threatened an ambush, and as he cantered now before and now behind the carriage, he wished that he was a multitude of men who could encompass it entirely and hide it.

But the solid streets soon gave way to open places, and low mud cabins, where the horses' hoofs beat on a sun-baked road, and where the inhabitants sat lazily before the door in the fading light, with no knowledge of the changes that the day had wrought in the city, and with only a moment's curious interest in the hooded carriage, and the grim, white-faced foreigners who guarded it.

Clay turned his pony into a trot at Langham's side. His face was pale and drawn.

As the danger of immediate pursuit and capture grew less, the carriage had slackened its pace, and for some minutes the outriders galloped on together side by side in silence. But the same thought was in the mind of each, and when Langham spoke it was as though he were continuing where he had but just been interrupted.

He laid his hand gently on Clay's arm. He did not turn his face toward him, and his eyes were still peering into the shadows before them. "Tell me?" he asked.

"He was coming up the stairs," Clay answered. He spoke in so low a voice that Langham had to lean from his saddle to hear him. "They were close behind; but when they saw her they stopped and refused to go farther. I called to him to come away, but he would not understand. They killed him before he really understood what they meant to do. He was dead almost before I reached him. He died in my arms." There was a long pause. "I wonder if he knows that?" Clay said.

Langham sat erect in the saddle again and drew a short breath. "I wish he could have known how he helped me," he whispered, "how much just knowing him helped me."

Clay bowed his head to the boy as though he were thanking him. "His was the gentlest soul I ever knew," he said.

"That's what I wanted to say," Langham answered. "We will let that be his epitaph," and touching his spur to his horse he galloped on ahead and left Clay riding alone.

Langham had proceeded for nearly a mile when he saw the forest opening before them, and at the sight he gave a shout of relief, but almost at the same instant he pulled his pony back on his haunches and whirling him about, sprang back to the carriage with a cry of warning.

"There are soldiers ahead of us," he cried. "Did you know it?" he demanded of the driver. "Did you lie to me? Turn back."

"He can't turn back," MacWilliams answered. "They have seen us. They are only the custom officers at the city limits. They know nothing. Go on." He reached forward and catching the reins dragged the horses down into a walk. Then he handed the reins back to the driver with a shake of the head.

"If you know these roads as well as you say you do, you want to keep us out of the way of soldiers," he said. "If we fall into a trap you'll be the first man shot on either side."

A sentry strolled lazily out into the road dragging his gun after him by the bayonet, and raised his hand for them to halt. His captain followed him from the post-house throwing away a cigarette as he came, and saluted MacWilliams on the box and bowed to the two riders in the background. In his right hand he held one of the long iron rods with which the collectors of the city's taxes were wont to pierce the bundles and packs, and even the carriage cushions of those who entered the city limits from the coast, and who might be suspected of smuggling.

"Whose carriage is this, and where is it going?" he asked.

As the speed of the diligence slackened, Hope put her head out of the curtains, and as she surveyed the soldier with apparent surprise, she turned to her brother.

"What does this mean?" she asked. "What are we waiting for?"

"We are going to the Hacienda of Señor Palácio,"

MacWilliams said, in answer to the officer. "The driver thinks that this is the road, but I say we should have taken the one to the right."

"No, this is the road to Señor Palácio's plantation," the officer answered, "but you cannot leave the city without a pass signed by General Mendoza. That is the order we received this morning. Have you such a pass?"

"Certainly not," Clay answered, warmly. "This is the carriage of an American, the president of the mines. His daughters are inside and on their way to visit the residence of Señor Palácio. They are foreigners—Americans. We are all foreigners, and we have a perfect right to leave the city when we choose. You can only stop us when we enter it."

The officer looked uncertainly from Clay to Hope and up at the driver on the box. His eyes fell upon the heavy brass mountings of the harness. They bore the arms of Olancho. He wheeled sharply and called to his men inside the post-house, and they stepped out from the veranda and spread themselves leisurely across the road.

"Ride him down, Clay," Langham muttered, in a whisper. The officer did not understand the words, but he saw Clay gather the reins tighter in his hands and he stepped back quickly to the safety of the porch, and from that ground of vantage smiled pleasantly.

"Pardon," he said, "there is no need for blows when one is rich enough to pay. A little something for myself and a drink for my brave fellows, and you can go where you please."

"Damned brigands," growled Langham, savagely.

"Not at all," Clay answered. "He is an officer and a gentleman. I have no money with me," he said, in Spanish, addressing the officer, "but between caballeros a word of honor is sufficient. I shall be returning this way to-morrow morning, and I will bring a few hundred sols from Señor Palácio for you and your men; but if we are followed you will get nothing, and you must have forgotten in the mean time that you have seen us pass."

There was a murmur inside the carriage, and Hope's face disappeared from between the curtains to reappear again almost immediately. She beckoned to the officer with her hand, and the men saw that she held between her thumb and little finger a diamond ring of size and brilliancy. She moved it so that it flashed in the light of the guard lantern above the post-house.

"My sister tells me you shall be given this to-morrow morning," Hope said, "if we are not followed."

The man's eyes laughed with pleasure. He swept his sombrero to the ground.

"I am your servant, Señorita," he said. "Gentlemen," he cried, gayly, turning to Clay, "if you wish it, I will accompany you with my men. Yes, I will leave word that I have gone in the sudden pursuit of smugglers; or I will remain here as you wish, and send those who may follow back again."

"You are most gracious, sir," said Clay. "It is always a pleasure to meet with a gentleman and a philosopher. We prefer to travel without an escort, and remember, you have seen nothing and heard nothing." He leaned from the saddle, and touched the officer on the breast. "That ring is worth a king's ransom."

"Or a president's," muttered the man, smiling. "Let the American ladies pass," he commanded.

The soldiers scattered as the whip fell, and the horses once more leaped forward, and as the carriage entered the forest, Clay looked back and saw the officer exhaling the smoke of a fresh cigarette, with the satisfaction of one who enjoys a clean conscience and a sense of duty well performed.

The road through the forest was narrow and uneven, and as the horses fell into a trot the men on horseback closed up together behind the carriage.

"Do you think that road-agent will keep his word?" Langham asked.

"Yes; he has nothing to win by telling the truth," Clay answered. "He can say he saw a party of foreigners, Americans, driving in the direction of Palácio's coffee plantation. That lets him out, and in the morning he knows he can levy on us for the gate money. I am not so much afraid of being overtaken as I am that King may make a mistake and not get to Bocos on time. We ought to reach there, if the carriage holds together, by eleven. King should be there by eight o'clock, and the yacht ought to make the run to Truxillo in three hours. But we shall not be able to get back to the city before five to-morrow morning. I suppose your family will be wild about Hope. We didn't know where she was when we sent the groom back to King."

"Do you think that driver is taking us the right way?" Langham asked, after a pause.

"He'd better. He knows it well enough. He was through the last revolution, and carried messages from Los Bocos to the city on foot for two months. He has covered every trail on the way, and if he goes wrong he knows what will happen to him."

"And Los Bocos—it is a village, isn't it, and the landing must be in sight of the Custom-House?"

"The village lies some distance back from the shore, and the only house on the beach is the Custom-House itself; but every one will be asleep by the time we get there, and it will take us only a minute to hand her into the launch. If there should be a guard there, King will have fixed them one way or another by the time we arrive. Anyhow, there is no need of looking for trouble that far ahead. There is enough to worry about in between. We haven't got there yet."

The moon rose grandly a few minutes later, and flooded the forest with light so that the open places were as clear as day. It threw strange shadows across the trail, and turned the rocks and fallen trees into figures of men crouching or standing upright with uplifted arms. They were so like to them that Clay and Langham flung their carbines to their shoulders again and again, and pointed them at some black object that turned as they advanced into wood or stone. From the forest they came to little streams and broad shallow rivers where the rocks in the fording places churned the water into white masses of foam, and the horses kicked up showers of spray as they made their way, slipping and stumbling, against the current. It was a silent pilgrimage, and never for a moment did the strain slacken or the men draw rein. Sometimes, as they hurried across a broad tableland, or skirted the edge of a precipice and looked down hundreds of feet below at the shining waters they had just forded, or up at the rocky points of the mountains before them, the beauty of the night overcame them and made them forget the significance of their journey.

They were not always alone, for they passed at intervals through sleeping villages of mud huts with thatched roofs, where the dogs ran yelping out to bark at them, and where the pine-knots, blazing on the clay ovens, burned cheerily in the moonlight. In the low lands where the fever lay, the mist rose above the level of their heads and enshrouded them in a curtain of fog, and the dew fell heavily, penetrating their clothing and chilling their heated bodies so that the sweating horses moved in a lather of steam.

They had settled down into a steady gallop now, and ten or fifteen miles had been left behind them.

"We are making excellent time," said Clay. "The village of San Lorenzo should lie beyond that ridge." He drove up beside the driver and pointed with his whip. "Is not that San Lorenzo?" he asked.

"Yes, señor," the man answered, "but I mean to drive around it by the old wagon trail. It is a large town, and people may be awake. You will be able to see it from the top of the next hill."

The cavalcade stopped at the summit of the ridge and the men looked down into the silent village. It was like the others they had passed, with a few houses built round a square of grass that could hardly be recognized as a plaza, except for the church on its one side, and the huge wooden cross planted in its centre. From the top of the hill they could see that the greater number of the houses were in darkness, but in a large building of two stories lights were shining from every window.

"That is the comandáncia," said the driver, shaking his head. "They are still awake. It is a telegraph station."

"Great Scott!" exclaimed MacWilliams. "We forgot the telegraph. They may have sent word to head us off already."

"Nine o'clock is not so very late," said Clay. "It may mean nothing."

"We had better make sure, though," MacWilliams answered, jumping to the ground. "Lend me your pony, Ted, and take my place. I'll run in there and dust around and see what's up. I'll join you on the other side of the town after you get back to the main road."

"Wait a minute," said Clay. "What do you mean to do?"

"I can't tell till I get there, but I'll try to find out how much they know. Don't you be afraid. I'll run fast enough if there's any sign of trouble. And if you come across a telegraph wire, cut it. The message may not have gone over yet."

The two women in the carriage had parted the flaps of the hoods and were trying to hear what was being said, but could not understand, and Langham explained to them that they were about to make a slight detour to avoid San Lorenzo while MacWilliams was going into it to reconnoitre. He asked if they were comfortable, and assured them that the greater part of the ride was over, and that there was a good road from San Lorenzo to the sea.

MacWilliams rode down into the village along the main trail, and threw his reins over a post in front of the comandáncia. He mounted boldly to the second floor of the building and stopped at the head of the stairs, in front of an open door. There were three men in the room before him, one an elderly man, whom he rightly guessed was the comandánte, and two younger men who were standing behind a railing and bending over a telegraph instrument on a table. As he stamped into the room, they looked up and stared at him in surprise; their faces showed that he had interrupted them at a moment of unusual interest.

MacWilliams saluted the three men civilly, and, according to the native custom, apologized for appearing before them in his spurs.

He had been riding from Los Bocos to the capital, he said, and his horse had gone lame. Could they tell him if there was any one in the village from whom he could hire a mule, as he must push on to the capital that night?

The comandánte surveyed him for a moment, as though still disturbed by the interruption, and then shook his head impatiently. "You can hire a mule from one Pulido Paul, at the corner of the plaza," he said. And as MacWilliams still stood uncertainly, he added, "You say you have come from Los Bocos. Did you meet any one on your way?"

The two younger men looked up at him anxiously, but before he could answer, the instrument began to tick out the signal, and they turned their eyes to it again, and one of them began to take its message down on paper.

The instrument spoke to MacWilliams also, for he was used to sending telegrams daily from the office to the mines, and could make it talk for him in either English or Spanish. So, in his effort to hear what it might say, he stammered and glanced at it involuntarily, and the comandánte, without suspecting his reason for doing so, turned also and peered over the shoulder of the man who was receiving the message. Except for the clicking of the instrument, the room was absolutely still; the three men bent silently over the table, while MacWilliams stood gazing at the ceiling and turning his hat in his hands. The message MacWilliams read from the instrument was this: "They are reported to have left the city by the south, so they are going to Para, or San Pedro, or to Los Bocos. She must be stopped—take an armed force and guard the roads. If necessary, kill her. She has in the carriage or hidden on her person, drafts for five million sols. You will be held responsible for every one of them. Repeat this message to show you understand, and relay it to Los Bocos. If you fail——"

MacWilliams could not wait to hear more; he gave a curt nod to the men and started toward the stairs. "Wait," the comandánte called after him.

MacWilliams paused with one hand on top of the banisters balancing himself in readiness for instant flight.

"You have not answered me. Did you meet with any one on your ride here from Los Bocos?"

"I met several men on foot, and the mail carrier passed me a league out from the coast, and oh, yes, I met a carriage at the cross roads, and the driver asked me the way of San Pedro Sula."

"A carriage?—yes—and what did you tell him?"

"I told him he was on the road to Los Bocos, and he turned back and——"

"You are sure he turned back?"

"Certainly, sir. I rode behind him for some distance. He turned finally to the right into the trail to San Pedro Sula."

The man flung himself across the railing.

"Quick," he commanded, "telegraph to Morales, Comandánte San Pedro Sula——"

He had turned his back on MacWilliams, and as the younger man bent over the instrument, MacWilliams stepped softly down the stairs, and mounting his pony rode slowly off in the direction of the capital. As soon as he had reached the outskirts of the town, he turned and galloped round it and then rode fast with his head in air, glancing up at the telegraph wire that sagged from tree-trunk to tree-trunk along the trail. At a point where he thought he could dismount in safety and tear down the wire, he came across it dangling from the branches and he gave a shout of relief. He caught the loose end and dragged it free from its support, and then laying it across a rock pounded the blade of his knife upon it with a stone, until he had hacked off a piece some fifty feet in length. Taking this in his hand he mounted again and rode off with it, dragging the wire in the road behind him. He held it up as he rejoined Clay, and laughed triumphantly. "They'll have some trouble splicing that circuit," he said, "you only half did the work. What wouldn't we give to know all this little piece of copper knows, eh?"

"Do you mean you think they have telegraphed to Los Bocos already?"

"I know that they were telegraphing to San Pedro Sula as I left and to all the coast towns. But whether you cut this down before or after is what I should like to know."

"We shall probably learn that later," said Clay, grimly.

The last three miles of the journey lay over a hard, smooth road, wide enough to allow the carriage and its escort to ride abreast.

It was in such contrast to the tortuous paths they had just followed, that the horses gained a fresh impetus and galloped forward as freely as though the race had but just begun.

Madame Alvarez stopped the carriage at one place and asked

the men to lower the hood at the back that she might feel the fresh air and see about her, and when this had been done, the women seated themselves with their backs to the horses where they could look out at the moonlit road as it unrolled behind them.

Hope felt selfishly and wickedly happy. The excitement had kept her spirits at the highest point, and the knowledge that Clay was guarding and protecting her was in itself a pleasure. She leaned back on the cushions and put her arm around the older woman's waist, and listened to the light beat of his pony's hoofs outside, now running ahead, now scrambling and slipping up some steep place, and again coming to a halt as Langham or MacWilliams called, "Look to the right, behind those trees," or "Ahead there! Don't you see what I mean, something crouching?"

She did not know when the false alarms would turn into a genuine attack, but she was confident that when the time came he would take care of her, and she welcomed the danger because it brought that solace with it.

Madame Alvarez sat at her side, rigid, silent, and beyond the help of comfort. She tortured herself with thoughts of the ambitions she had held, and which had been so cruelly mocked that very morning; of the chivalric love that had been hers, of the life even that had been hers, and which had been given up for her so tragically. When she spoke at all, it was to murmur her sorrow that Hope had exposed herself to danger on her poor account, and that her life, as far as she loved it, was at an end. Only once after the men had parted the curtains and asked concerning her comfort with grave solicitude did she give way to tears.

"Why are they so good to me?" she moaned. "Why are you so good to me? I am a wicked, vain woman, I have brought a nation to war and I have killed the only man I ever trusted."

Hope touched her gently with her hand and felt guiltily how selfish she herself must be not to feel the woman's grief, but she could not. She only saw in it a contrast to her own happiness, a black background before which the figure of Clay and his solicitude for her shone out, the only fact in the world that was of value.

Her thoughts were interrupted by the carriage coming to a halt, and a significant movement upon the part of the men. MacWilliams had descended from the box-seat and stepping into the carriage took the place the women had just left.

He had a carbine in his hand, and after he was seated Langham handed him another which he laid across his knees.

"They thought I was too conspicuous on the box to do any good there," he explained in a confidential whisper. "In case there is any firing now, you ladies want to get down on your knees here at my feet, and hide your heads in the cushions. We are entering Los Bocos."

Langham and Clay were riding far in advance, scouting to the right and left, and the carriage moved noiselessly behind them through the empty streets. There was no light in any of the windows, and not even a dog barked, or a cock crowed. The women sat erect, listening for the first signal of an attack, each holding the other's hand and looking at MacWilliams, who sat with his thumb on the trigger of his carbine, glancing to the right and left and breathing quickly. His eyes twinkled, like those of a little fox terrier. The men dropped back, and drew up on a level with the carriage.

"We are all right, so far," Clay whispered. "The beach slopes down from the other side of that line of trees. What is the matter with you?" he demanded, suddenly, looking up at the driver, "are you afraid?"

"No," the man answered, hurriedly, his voice shaking; "it's the cold."

Langham had galloped on ahead and as he passed through the trees and came out upon the beach, he saw a broad stretch of moonlit water and the lights from the yacht shining from a point a quarter of a mile off shore. Among the rocks on the edge of the beach was the *Vesta*'s long-boat and her crew seated in it or standing about on the beach. The carriage had stopped under the protecting shadow of the trees, and he raced back toward it.

"The yacht is here," he cried. "The long-boat is waiting and there is not a sign of light about the Custom-House. Come on," he cried. "We have beaten them after all."

A sailor, who had been acting as lookout on the rocks, sprang to his full height, and shouted to the group around the long-boat, and King came up the beach toward them running heavily through the deep sand.

Madame Alvarez stepped down from the carriage, and as Hope handed her her jewel case in silence, the men draped her cloak about her shoulders. She put out her hand to them, and as Clay took it in his, she bent her head quickly and kissed his hand. "You were his friend," she murmured.

She held Hope in her arms for an instant, and kissed her, and then gave her hand in turn to Langham and to MacWilliams.

"I do not know whether I shall ever see you again," she said, looking slowly from one to the other, "but I will pray for you every day, and God will reward you for saving a worthless life." As she finished speaking King came up to the group, followed by three of his men.

"Is Hope with you, is she safe?" he asked.

"Yes, she is with me," Madame Alvarez answered.

"Thank God," King exclaimed, breathlessly. "Then we will start at once, Madame. Where is she? She must come with us!"

"Of course," Clay assented, eagerly, "she will be much safer on the yacht."

But Hope protested. "I must get back to father," she said. "The yacht will not arrive until late to-morrow, and the carriage can take me to him five hours earlier. The family have worried too long about me as it is, and, besides, I will not leave Ted. I am going back as I came."

"It is most unsafe," King urged.

"On the contrary, it is perfectly safe now," Hope answered. "It was not one of us they wanted."

"You may be right," King said. "They don't know what has happened to you, and perhaps after all it would be better if you went back the quicker way." He gave his arm to Madame Alvarez and walked with her toward the shore. As the men surrounded her on every side and moved away, Clay glanced back at Hope and saw her standing upright in the carriage looking after them.

"We will be with you in a minute," he called, as though in apology for leaving her for even that brief space. And then the shadow of the trees shut her and the carriage from his sight. His footsteps made no sound in the soft sand, and except for the whispering of the palms and the sleepy wash of the waves as they ran up the pebbly beach and sank again, the place was as peaceful and silent as a deserted island, though the moon made it as light as day.

The long-boat had been drawn up with her stern to the shore, and the men were already in their places, some standing waiting for the order to shove off, and others seated balancing their oars.

King had arranged to fire a rocket when the launch left the shore, in order that the captain of the yacht might run in closer to pick them up. As he hurried down the beach, he called to his boatswain to give the signal, and the man answered that he understood and stooped to light a match. King had jumped into the stern and lifted Madame Alvarez after him, leaving her late escort standing with uncovered heads on the beach behind her, when the rocket shot up into the calm white air, with a roar and a rush and a sudden flash of color. At the same instant, as though in answer to its challenge, the woods back of them burst into an irregular line of flame, a volley of rifle shots shattered the silence, and a score of bullets splashed in the water and on the rocks about them.

The boatswain in the bow of the long-boat tossed up his arms and pitched forward between the thwarts.

"Give way," he shouted as he fell.

"Pull," Clay yelled, "pull, all of you."

He threw himself against the stern of the boat, and Langham and MacWilliams clutched its sides, and with their shoulders against it and their bodies half sunk in the water, shoved it off, free of the shore.

The shots continued fiercely, and two of the crew cried out and fell back upon the oars of the men behind them.

Madame Alvarez sprang to her feet and stood swaying unsteadily as the boat leaped forward.

"Take me back. Stop, I command you," she cried, "I will not leave those men. Do you hear?"

King caught her by the waist and dragged her down, but she struggled to free herself. "I will not leave them to be murdered," she cried. "You cowards, put me back."

"Hold her, King," Clay shouted. "We're all right. They're not firing at us."

His voice was drowned in the noise of the oars beating in the rowlocks, and the reports of the rifles. The boat disappeared in a mist of spray and moonlight, and Clay turned and faced about him. Langham and MacWilliams were crouching behind a rock and firing at the flashes in the woods.

"You can't stay there," Clay cried. "We must get back to Hope."

He ran forward, dodging from side to side and firing as he ran. He heard shots from the water, and looking back saw that the men in the long-boat had ceased rowing, and were returning the fire from the shore.

"Come back, Hope is all right," her brother called to him. "I haven't seen a shot within a hundred yards of her yet, they're firing from the Custom-House and below. I think Mac's hit."

"I'm not," MacWilliams's voice answered from behind a rock, "but I'd like to see something to shoot at."

A hot tremor of rage swept over Clay at the thought of a possibly fatal termination to the night's adventure. He groaned at the mockery of having found his life only to lose it now, when it was more precious to him than it had ever been, and to lose it in a silly brawl with semi-savages. He cursed himself impotently and rebelliously for a senseless fool.

"Keep back, can't you?" he heard Langham calling to him from the shore. "You're only drawing the fire toward Hope. She's got away by now. She had both the horses."

Langham and MacWilliams started forward to Clay's side, but the instant they left the shadow of the rock, the bullets threw up the sand at their feet and they stopped irresolutely. The moon showed the three men outlined against the white sand of the beach as clearly as though a search-light had been turned upon them, even while its shadows sheltered and protected their assailants. At their backs the open sea cut off retreat, and the line of fire in front held them in check. They were as helpless as chessmen upon a board.

"I'm not going to stand still to be shot at," cried MacWilliams. "Let's hide or let's run. This isn't doing anybody any good." But no one moved. They could hear the singing of the bullets as they passed them whining in the air like a banjo-string that is being tightened, and they knew they were in equal danger from those who were firing from the boat.

"They're shooting better," said MacWilliams. "They'll reach us in a minute."

"They've reached me already, I think," Langham answered, with suppressed satisfaction, "in the shoulder. It's nothing." His unconcern was quite sincere; to a young man who had galloped through two long halves of a football match on a strained tendon, a scratched shoulder was not important, except as an unsought honor.

But it was of the most importance to MacWilliams. He raised his voice against the men in the woods in impotent fury. "Come out, you cowards, where we can see you," he cried. "Come out where I can shoot your black heads off."

Clay had fired the last cartridge in his rifle, and throwing it away drew his revolver.

"We must either swim or hide," he said. "Put your heads down and run."

But as he spoke, they saw the carriage plunging out of the shadow of the woods and the horses galloping toward them down the beach. MacWilliams gave a cheer of welcome. "Hurrah!" he shouted, "it's José coming for us. He's a good man. Well done, José!" he called.

"That's not José," Langham cried, doubtfully, peering through the moonlight. "Good God! It's Hope," he exclaimed. He waved his hands frantically above his head. "Go back, Hope," he cried, "go back!"

But the carriage did not swerve on its way toward them. They all saw her now distinctly. She was on the driver's box and alone, leaning forward and lashing the horses' backs with the whip and reins, and bending over to avoid the bullets that passed above her head. As she came down upon them, she stood up, her woman's figure outlined clearly in the riding habit she still wore. "Jump in when I turn," she cried. "I'm going to turn slowly, run and jump in."

She bent forward again and pulled the horses to the right, and as they obeyed her, plunging and tugging at their bits, as though they knew the danger they were in, the men threw themselves at the carriage. Clay caught the hood at the back, swung himself up, and scrambled over the cushions and up to the box seat. He dropped down behind Hope, and reaching his arms around her took the reins in one hand, and with the other forced her down to her knees upon the footboard, so that, as she knelt, his arms and body protected her from the bullets sent after them. Langham followed Clay, and tumbled into the carriage over the hood at the back, but MacWilliams endeavored to vault in from the step, and missing his footing fell under the hind wheel, so that the weight of the carriage passed over him, and his head was buried for an instant in the sand. But he was on his feet again before they had noticed that he was down, and as he jumped for the hood, Langham caught him by the collar of his coat and dragged him into the seat, panting and gasping, and rubbing the sand from his mouth and nostrils. Clay turned the carriage at a right angle through the heavy sand, and still standing with Hope crouched at his knees, he raced back to the woods into the face of the firing, with the boys behind him answering it from each side of the carriage, so that the horses leaped forward in a frenzy of terror, and dashing through the woods, passed into the first road that opened before them.

The road into which they had turned was narrow, but level, and ran through a forest of banana palms that bent and swayed above them. Langham and MacWilliams still knelt in the rear seat of the carriage, watching the road on the chance of possible pursuit.

"Give me some cartridges," said Langham. "My belt is empty. What road is this?"

"It is a private road, I should say, through somebody's banana plantation. But it must cross the main road somewhere. It doesn't matter, we're all right now. I mean to take it easy." MacWilliams turned on his back and stretched out his legs on the seat opposite.

"Where do you suppose those men sprang from? Were they following us all the time?"

"Perhaps, or else that message got over the wire before we cut it, and they've been lying in wait for us. They were probably watching King and his sailors for the last hour or so, but they didn't want him. They wanted her and the money. It was pretty exciting, wasn't it? How's your shoulder?"

"It's a little stiff, thank you," said Langham. He stood up and by peering over the hood could just see the top of Clay's sombrero rising above it where he sat on the back seat.

"You and Hope all right up there, Clay?" he asked.

The top of the sombrero moved slightly, and Langham took it as a sign that all was well. He dropped back into his seat beside MacWilliams, and they both breathed a long sigh of relief and content. Langham's wounded arm was the one nearest MacWilliams, and the latter parted the torn sleeve and examined the furrow across the shoulder with unconcealed envy.

"I am afraid it won't leave a scar," he said, sympathetically.

"Won't it?" asked Langham, in some concern.

The horses had dropped into a walk, and the beauty of the moonlit night put its spell upon the two boys, and the rustling of the great leaves above their heads stilled and quieted them so that they unconsciously spoke in whispers.

Clay had not moved since the horses turned of their own accord into the valley of the palms. He no longer feared pursuit nor any interruption to their further progress. His only sensation was one of utter thankfulness that they were all well out of it, and that Hope had been the one who had helped them in their trouble, and his dearest thought was that, whether she wished or not, he owed his safety, and possibly his life, to her.

She still crouched between his knees upon the broad footboard, with her hands clasped in front of her, and looking ahead into the vista of soft mysterious lights and dark shadows that the moon cast upon the road. Neither of them spoke, and as the silence continued unbroken, it took a weightier significance, and at each added second of time became more full of meaning.

The horses had dropped into a tired walk, and drew them smoothly over the white road; from behind the hood came broken snatches of the boys' talk, and above their heads the heavy leaves of the palms bent and bowed as though in benediction. A warm breeze from the land filled the air with the odor of ripening fruit and pungent smells, and the silence seemed to envelop them and mark them as the only living creatures awake in the brilliant tropical night.

Hope sank slowly back, and as she did so, her shoulder touched for an instant against Clay's knee; she straightened herself and made a movement as though to rise. Her nearness to him and something in her attitude at his feet held Clay in a spell. He bent forward and laid his hand fearfully upon her shoulder, and the touch seemed to stop the blood in his veins and hushed the words upon his lips. Hope raised her head slowly as though with a great effort, and looked into his eyes. It seemed to him that he had been looking into those same eyes for centuries, as though he had always known them, and the soul that looked out of them into his. He bent his head lower, and stretching out his arms drew her to him, and the eyes did not waver. He raised her and held her close against his breast. Her eyes faltered and closed.

"Hope," he whispered, "Hope." He stooped lower and kissed her, and his lips told her what they could not speak—and they were quite alone.

XIV

An hour later Langham rose with a protesting sigh and shook the hood violently.

"I say!" he called. "Are you asleep up there? We'll never get home at this rate. Doesn't Hope want to come back here and go to sleep?"

The carriage stopped, and the boys tumbled out and walked around in front of it. Hope sat smiling on the box-seat. She was apparently far from sleepy, and she was quite contented where she was, she told him.

"Do you know we haven't had anything to eat since yesterday at breakfast?" asked Langham. "MacWilliams and I are fainting. We move that we stop at the next shack we come to, and waken the people up and make them give us some supper."

Hope looked aside at Clay and laughed softly. "Supper?" she said. "They want supper!"

Their suffering did not seem to impress Clay deeply. He sat snapping his whip at the palm-trees above him, and smiled happily in an inconsequent and irritating manner at nothing.

"See here! Do you know that we are lost?" demanded Langham, indignantly, "and starving? Have you any idea at all where you are?"

"I have not," said Clay, cheerfully. "All I know is that a long time ago there was a revolution and a woman with jewels, who escaped in an open boat, and I recollect playing that I was a target and standing up to be shot at in a bright light. After that I woke up to the really important things of life—among which supper is not one."

Langham and MacWilliams looked at each other doubtfully, and Langham shook his head.

"Get down off that box," he commanded. "If you and Hope think this is merely a pleasant moonlight drive, we don't. You two can sit in the carriage now, and we'll take a turn at driving, and we'll guarantee to get you to some place soon."

Clay and Hope descended meekly and seated themselves under the hood, where they could look out upon the moonlit road as it unrolled behind them. But they were no longer to enjoy their former leisurely progress. The new whip lashed his horses into a gallop, and the trees flew past them on either hand.

"Do you remember that chap in the 'Last Ride Together?'" said Clay.

I and my mistress, side by side,
Shall be together—forever ride,
And so one more day am I deified.
Who knows—the world may end to-night.[1]

Hope laughed triumphantly, and threw out her arms as though she would embrace the whole beautiful world that stretched around them.

"Oh, no," she laughed. "To-night the world has just begun."

The carriage stopped, and there was a confusion of voices on the box-seat, and then a great barking of dogs, and they beheld MacWilliams beating and kicking at the door of a hut. The door opened for an inch, and there was a long debate in Spanish, and finally the door was closed again, and a light appeared through the windows. A few minutes later a man and woman came out of the hut, shivering and yawning, and made a fire in the sun-baked oven at the side of the house. Hope and Clay remained seated in the carriage, and watched the flames springing up from the oily

1 From "The Last Ride Together" (1845), a poem by Robert Browning.

fagots, and the boys moving about with flaring torches of pine, pulling down bundles of fodder for the horses from the roof of the kitchen, while two sleepy girls disappeared toward a mountain stream, one carrying a jar on her shoulder, and the other lighting the way with a torch. Hope sat with her chin on her hand, watching the black figures passing between them and the fire, and standing above it with its light on their faces, shading their eyes from the heat with one hand, and stirring something in a smoking caldron with the other. Hope felt an overflowing sense of gratitude to these simple strangers for the trouble they were taking. She felt how good every one was, and how wonderfully kind and generous was the world that she lived in.

Her brother came over to the carriage and bowed with mock courtesy.

"I trust, now that we have done all the work," he said, "that your excellencies will condescend to share our frugal fare, or must we bring it to you here?"

The clay oven stood in the middle of a hut of laced twigs, through which the smoke drifted freely. There was a row of wooden benches around it, and they all seated themselves and ate ravenously of rice and fried plantains, while the woman patted and tossed tortillas between her hands, eyeing her guests curiously. Her glance fell upon Langham's shoulder, and rested there for so long that Hope followed the direction of her eyes. She leaped to her feet with a cry of fear and reproach, and ran toward her brother.

"Ted!" she cried, "you are hurt! you are wounded, and you never told me! What is it? Is it very bad?" Clay crossed the floor in a stride, his face full of concern.

"Leave me alone!" cried the stern brother, backing away and warding them off with the coffee-pot. "It's only scratched. You'll spill the coffee."

But at the sight of the blood Hope had turned very white, and throwing her arms around her brother's neck, hid her eyes on his other shoulder and began to cry.

"I am so selfish," she sobbed. "I have been so happy and you were suffering all the time."

Her brother stared at the others in dismay. "What nonsense," he said, patting her on the shoulder. "You're a bit tired, and you need rest. That's what you need. The idea of my sister going off in hysterics after behaving like such a sport—and before these young ladies, too. Aren't you ashamed?"

"I should think they'd be ashamed," said MacWilliams,

severely, as he continued placidly with his supper. "They haven't got enough clothes on."

Langham looked over Hope's shoulder at Clay and nodded significantly. "She's been on a good deal of a strain," he explained apologetically, "and no wonder; it's been rather an unusual night for her."

Hope raised her head and smiled at him through her tears. Then she turned and moved toward Clay. She brushed her eyes with the back of her hand and laughed. "It has been an unusual night," she said. "Shall I tell him?" she asked.

Clay straightened himself unconsciously, and stepped beside her and took her hand; MacWilliams quickly lowered to the bench the dish from which he was eating, and stood up, too. The people of the house stared at the group in the firelight with puzzled interest, at the beautiful young girl, and at the tall, sun-burned young man at her side. Langham looked from his sister to Clay and back again, and laughed uneasily.

"Langham, I have been very bold," said Clay. "I have asked your sister to marry me—and she has said that she would."

Langham flushed as red as his sister. He felt himself at a dis-advantage in the presence of a love as great and strong as he knew this must be. It made him seem strangely young and inadequate. He crossed over to his sister awkwardly and kissed her, and then took Clay's hand, and the three stood together and looked at one another, and there was no sign of doubt or question in the face of any one of them. They stood so for some little time, smiling and exclaiming together, and utterly unconscious of anything but their own delight and happiness. MacWilliams watched them, his face puckered into odd wrinkles and his eyes half-closed. Hope suddenly broke away from the others and turned toward him with her hands held out.

"Have you nothing to say to me, Mr. MacWilliams?" she asked.

MacWilliams looked doubtfully at Clay, as though from force of habit he must ask advice from his chief first, and then took the hands that she held out to him and shook them up and down. His usual confidence seemed to have forsaken him, and he stood, shifting from one foot to the other, smiling and abashed.

"Well, I always said they didn't make them any better than you," he gasped at last. "I was always telling him that, wasn't I?" He nodded energetically at Clay. "And that's so; they don't make 'em any better than you."

He dropped her hands and crossed over to Clay, and stood surveying him with a smile of wonder and admiration.

"How'd you do it?" he demanded. "How did you do it? I suppose you know," he asked sternly, "that you're not good enough for Miss Hope? You know that, don't you?"

"Of course I know that," said Clay.

MacWilliams walked toward the door and stood in it for a second, looking back at them over his shoulder. "They don't make them any better than that," he reiterated gravely, and disappeared in the direction of the horses, shaking his head and muttering his astonishment and delight.

"Please give me some money," Hope said to Clay. "All the money you have," she added, smiling at her presumption of authority over him, "and you, too, Ted." The men emptied their pockets, and Hope poured the mass of silver into the hands of the women, who gazed at it uncomprehendingly.

"Thank you for your trouble and your good supper," Hope said in Spanish, "and may no evil come to your house."

The woman and her daughters followed her to the carriage, bowing and uttering good wishes in the extravagant metaphor of their country; and as they drove away, Hope waved her hand to them as she sank closer against Clay's shoulder.

"The world is full of such kind and gentle souls," she said.

In an hour they had regained the main road, and a little later the stars grew dim and the moonlight faded, and trees and bushes and rocks began to take substance and to grow into form and outline. They saw by the cool, gray light of the morning the familiar hills around the capital, and at a cry from the boys on the box-seat, they looked ahead and beheld the harbor of Valencia at their feet, lying as placid and undisturbed as the water in a bathtub. As they turned up the hill into the road that led to the Palms, they saw the sleeping capital like a city of the dead below them, its white buildings reddened with the light of the rising sun. From three places in different parts of the city, thick columns of smoke rose lazily to the sky.

"I had forgotten!" said Clay; "they have been having a revolution here. It seems so long ago."

By five o'clock they had reached the gate of the Palms, and their appearance startled the sentry on post into a state of undisciplined joy. A riderless pony, the one upon which José had made his escape when the firing began, had crept into the stable an hour previous, stiff and bruised and weary, and had led the people at the Palms to fear the worst.

Mr. Langham and his daughter were standing on the veranda as the horses came galloping up the avenue. They had been awake all the night, and the face of each was white and drawn with anxiety and loss of sleep. Mr. Langham caught Hope in his arms and held her face close to his in silence.

"Where have you been?" he said at last. "Why did you treat me like this? You knew how I would suffer."

"I could not help it," Hope cried. "I had to go with Madame Alvarez."

Her sister had suffered as acutely as had Mr. Langham himself, as long as she was in ignorance of Hope's whereabouts. But now that she saw Hope in the flesh again, she felt a reaction against her for the anxiety and distress she had caused them.

"My dear Hope," she said, "is every one to be sacrificed for Madame Alvarez? What possible use could you be to her at such a time? It was not the time nor the place for a young girl. You were only another responsibility for the men."

"Clay seemed willing to accept the responsibility," said Langham, without a smile. "And, besides," he added, "if Hope had not been with us we might never have reached home alive."

But it was only after much earnest protest and many explanations that Mr. Langham was pacified, and felt assured that his son's wound was not dangerous, and that his daughter was quite safe.

Miss Langham and himself, he said, had passed a trying night. There had been much firing in the city, and continual uproar. The houses of several of the friends of Alvarez had been burned and sacked. Alvarez himself had been shot as soon as he had entered the yard of the military prison. It was then given out that he had committed suicide. Mendoza had not dared to kill Rojas, because of the feeling of the people toward him, and had even shown him to the mob from behind the bars of one of the windows in order to satisfy them that he was still living. The British Minister had sent to the Palace for the body of Captain Stuart, and had had it escorted to the Legation, from whence it would be sent to England. This, as far as Mr. Langham had heard, was the news of the night just over.

"Two native officers called here for you about midnight, Clay," he continued, "and they are still waiting for you below at your office. They came from Rojas's troops, who are encamped on the hills at the other side of the city. They wanted you to join them with the men from the mines. I told them I did not know when you would return, and they said they would wait. If you could have been here last night, it is possible that we might have done something, but now that it is all over, I am glad that you saved that woman instead. I should have liked, though, to have struck one blow at them. But we cannot hope to win against assassins. The death of young Stuart has hurt me terribly, and the murder of Alvarez, coming on top of it, has made me wish I had never heard of nor seen Olancho. I have decided to go away at once, on the next steamer, and I will take my daughters with me, and Ted, too. The State Department at Washington can fight with Mendoza for the mines. You made a good stand, but they made a better one, and they have beaten us. Mendoza's *coup d'état* has passed into history, and the revolution is at an end."

On his arrival Clay had at once asked for a cigar, and while Mr. Langham was speaking he had been biting it between his teeth, with the serious satisfaction of a man who had been twelve hours without one. He knocked the ashes from it and considered the burning end thoughtfully. Then he glanced at Hope as she stood among the group on the veranda. She was waiting for his reply and watching him intently. He seemed to be confident that she would approve of the only course he saw open to him.

"The revolution is not at an end by any means, Mr. Langham," he said at last, simply. "It has just begun." He turned abruptly and walked away in the direction of the office, and MacWilliams and Langham stepped off the veranda and followed him as a matter of course.

The soldiers in the army who were known to be faithful to General Rojas belonged to the Third and Fourth regiments, and numbered four thousand on paper, and two thousand by count of heads. When they had seen their leader taken prisoner, and swept off the parade-ground by Mendoza's cavalry, they had first attempted to follow in pursuit and recapture him, but the men on horseback had at once shaken off the men on foot and left them, panting and breathless, in the dust behind them. So they halted uncertainly in the road, and their young officers held counsel together. They first considered the advisability of attacking the military prison, but decided against doing so, as it would lead, they feared, whether it proved successful or not, to the murder of Rojas. It was impossible to return to the city, where Mendoza's First and Second regiments greatly outnumbered them. Having no leader and no headquarters, the officers marched the men to the hills above the city and went into camp to await further developments.

Throughout the night they watched the illumination of the city and of the boats in the harbor below them; they saw the flames bursting from the homes of the members of Alvarez's

Cabinet, and when the morning broke they beheld the grounds of the Palace swarming with Mendoza's troops, and the red and white barred flag of the revolution floating over it. The news of the assassination of Alvarez and the fact that Rojas had been spared for fear of the people, had been carried to them early in the evening, and with this knowledge of their General's safety hope returned and fresh plans were discussed. By midnight they had definitely decided that should Mendoza attempt to dislodge them the next morning, they would make a stand, but that if the fight went against them, they would fall back along the mountain roads to the Valencia mines, where they hoped to persuade the fifteen hundred soldiers there installed to join forces with them against the new Dictator.

In order to assure themselves of this help, a messenger was despatched by a circuitous route to the Palms, to ask the aid of the resident director, and another was sent to the mines to work upon the feelings of the soldiers themselves. The officer who had been sent to the Palms to petition Clay for the loan of his soldier-workmen, had decided to remain until Clay returned, and another messenger had been sent after him from the camp on the same errand.

These two lieutenants greeted Clay with enthusiasm, but he at once interrupted them, and began plying them with questions as to where their camp was situated and what roads led from it to the Palms.

"Bring your men at once to this end of our railroad," he said. "It is still early, and the revolutionists will sleep late. They are drugged with liquor and worn out with excitement, and whatever may have been their intentions toward you last night, they will be late in putting them into practise this morning. I will telegraph Kirkland to come up at once with all of his soldiers and with his three hundred Irishmen. Allowing him a half-hour to collect them and to get his flat cars together, and another half-hour in which to make the run, he should be here by half-past six—and that's quick mobilization. You ride back now and march your men here at a double-quick. With your two thousand we shall have in all three thousand and eight hundred men. I must have absolute control over my own troops. Otherwise I shall act independently of you and go into the city alone with my workmen."

"That is unnecessary," said one of the lieutenants. "We have no officers. If you do not command us, there is no one else to do it. We promise that our men will follow you and give you every obedience. They have been led by foreigners before, by young

Captain Stuart and Major Fergurson and Colonel Shrevington. They know how highly General Rojas thinks of you, and they know that you have led Continental armies in Europe."

"Well, don't tell them I haven't until this is over," said Clay. "Now, ride hard, gentlemen, and bring your men here as quickly as possible."

The lieutenants thanked him effusively and galloped away, radiant at the success of their mission, and Clay entered the office where MacWilliams was telegraphing his orders to Kirkland. He seated himself beside the instrument, and from time to time answered the questions Kirkland sent back to him over the wire, and in the intervals of silence thought of Hope. It was the first time he had gone into action feeling the touch of a woman's hand upon his sleeve, and he was fearful lest she might think he had considered her too lightly.

He took a piece of paper from the table and wrote a few lines upon it, and then rewrote them several times. The message he finally sent to her was this: "I am sure you understand, and that you would not have me give up beaten now, when what we do to-day may set us right again. I know better than any one else in the world can know, what I run the risk of losing, but you would not have that fear stop me from going on with what we have been struggling for so long. I cannot come back to see you before we start, but I know your heart is with me. With great love, Robert Clay."

He gave the note to his servant, and the answer was brought to him almost immediately. Hope had not rewritten her message: "I love you because you are the sort of man you are, and had you given up as father wished you to do, or on my account, you would have been some one else, and I would have had to begin over again to learn to love you for some different reasons. I know that you will come back to me bringing your sheaves with you. Nothing can happen to you now. Hope."

He had never received a line from her before, and he read and reread this with a sense of such pride and happiness in his face that MacWilliams smiled covertly and bent his eyes upon his instrument. Clay went back into his room and kissed the page of paper gently, flushing like a boy as he did so, and then folding it carefully, he put it away beneath his jacket. He glanced about him guiltily, although he was quite alone, and taking out his watch, pried it open and looked down into the face of the photograph that had smiled up at him from it for so many years. He thought how unlike it was to Alice Langham as he knew her. He judged that it must have been taken when she was very young, at the age Hope was then, before the little world she lived in had crippled and narrowed her and marked her for its own. He remembered what she had said to him the first night he had seen her. "That is the picture of the girl who ceased to exist four years ago, and whom you have never met." He wondered if she had ever existed.

"It looks more like Hope than her sister," he mused. "It looks very much like Hope." He decided that he would let it remain where it was until Hope gave him a better one; and smiling slightly he snapped the lid fast, as though he were closing a door on the face of Alice Langham and locking it forever.

Kirkland was in the cab of the locomotive that brought the soldiers from the mine. He stopped the first car in front of the freight station until the workmen had filed out and formed into a double line on the platform. Then he moved the train forward the length of that car, and those in the one following were mustered out in a similar manner. As the cars continued to come in, the men at the head of the double line passed on through the freight station and on up the road to the city in an unbroken column. There was no confusion, no crowding, and no haste.

When the last car had been emptied, Clay rode down the line and appointed a foreman to take charge of each company, stationing his engineers and the Irish-Americans in the van. It looked more like a mob than a regiment. None of the men were in uniform, and the native soldiers were barefoot. But they showed a winning spirit, and stood in as orderly an array as though they were drawn up in line to receive their month's wages. The Americans in front of the column were humorously disposed, and inclined to consider the whole affair as a pleasant outing. They had been placed in front, not because they were better shots than the natives, but because every South American thinks that every citizen of the United States is a master either of the rifle or the revolver, and Clay was counting on this superstition. His assistant engineers and foremen hailed him as he rode on up and down the line with good-natured cheers, and asked him when they were to get their commissions, and if it were true that they were all captains, or only colonels, as they were at home.

They had been waiting for a half-hour, when there was the sound of horses' hoofs on the road, and the even beat of men's feet, and the advance guard of the Third and Fourth regiments came toward them at a quickstep. The men were still in the full-dress uniforms they had worn at the review the day before, and in comparison with the soldier-workmen and the Americans in flannel shirts, they presented so martial a showing that they were welcomed with tumultuous cheers. Clay threw them into a double line on one side of the road, down the length of which his own marched until they had reached the end of it nearest to the city, when they took up their position in a close formation, and the native regiments fell in behind them. Clay selected twenty of the best shots from among the engineers and sent them on ahead as a skirmish line. They were ordered to fall back at once if they saw any sign of the enemy. In this order the column of four thousand men started for the city.

It was a little after seven when they advanced, and the air was mild and peaceful. Men and women came crowding to the doors and windows of the huts as they passed, and stood watching them in silence, not knowing to which party the small army might belong. In order to enlighten them, Clay shouted, "Viva Rojas." And his men took it up, and the people answered gladly.

They had reached the closely built portion of the city when the skirmish line came running back to say that it had been met by a detachment of Mendoza's cavalry, who had galloped away as soon as they saw them. There was then no longer any doubt that the fact of their coming was known at the Palace, and Clay halted his men in a bare plaza and divided them into three columns. Three streets ran parallel with one another from this plaza to the heart of the city, and opened directly upon the garden of the Palace where Mendoza had fortified himself. Clay directed the columns to advance up these streets, keeping the head of each column in touch with the other two. At the word they were to pour down the side streets and rally to each others' assistance.

As they stood, drawn up on the three sides of the plaza, he rode out before them and held up his hat for silence. They were there with arms in their hands, he said, for two reasons: the greater one, and the one which he knew actuated the native soldiers, was their desire to preserve the Constitution of the Republic. According to their own laws, the Vice-President must succeed when the President's term of office had expired, or in the event of his death. President Alvarez had been assassinated, and the Vice-President, General Rojas, was, in consequence, his legal successor. It was their duty, as soldiers of the Republic, to rescue him from prison, to drive the man who had usurped his place into exile, and by so doing uphold the laws which they had themselves laid down. The second motive, he went on, was a less worthy and more selfish one. The Olancho mines, which now gave work to thousands and brought millions of dollars into the country, were coveted by Mendoza, who would, if he could, convert them into a monopoly of his government. If he remained in power all foreigners would be driven out of the country, and the soldiers would be forced to work in the mines without payment. Their condition would be little better than that of the slaves in the salt mines of Siberia. Not only would they no longer be paid for their labor, but the people as a whole would cease to receive that share of the earnings of the mines which had hitherto been theirs.

"Under President Rojas you will have liberty, justice, and prosperity," Clay cried. "Under Mendoza you will be ruled by martial law. He will rob and overtax you, and you will live through a reign of terror. Between them—which will you choose?"

The native soldiers answered by cries of "Rojas," and breaking ranks rushed across the plaza toward him, crowding around his horse and shouting, "Long live Rojas," "Long live the Constitution," "Death to Mendoza." The Americans stood as they were and gave three cheers for the Government.

They were still cheering and shouting as they advanced upon the Palace, and the noise of their coming drove the people indoors, so that they marched through deserted streets and between closed doors and sightless windows. No one opposed them, and no one encouraged them. But they could now see the façade of the Palace and the flag of the Revolutionists hanging from the mast in front of it.

Three blocks distant from the Palace they came upon the buildings of the United States and English Legations, where the flags of the two countries had been hung out over the narrow thoroughfare.

The windows and the roofs of each legation were crowded with women and children who had sought refuge there, and the column halted as Weimer, the Consul, and Sir Julian Pindar, the English Minister, came out, bare-headed, into the street and beckoned to Clay to stop.

"As our Minister was not here," Weimer said, "I telegraphed to Truxillo for the man-of-war there. She started some time ago, and we have just heard that she is entering the lower harbor. She should have her blue-jackets on shore in twenty minutes. Sir Julian and I think you ought to wait for them."

The English Minister put a detaining hand on Clay's bridle. "If you attack Mendoza at the Palace with this mob," he remonstrated, "rioting and lawlessness generally will break out all over the city. I ask you to keep them back until we get your sailors to police the streets and protect property."

Clay glanced over his shoulder at the engineers and the Irish workmen standing in solemn array behind him. "Oh, you can hardly call this a mob," he said. "They look a little rough and ready, but I will answer for them. The two other columns that are coming up the streets parallel to this are Government troops and properly engaged in driving a usurper out of the Government building. The best thing you can do is to get down to the wharf and send the marines and blue-jackets where you think they will do the most good. I can't wait for them. And they can't come too soon."

The grounds of the Palace occupied two entire blocks; the Botanical Gardens were in the rear, and in front a series of low terraces ran down from its veranda to the high iron fence which separated the grounds from the chief thoroughfare of the city.

Clay sent word to the left and right wing of his little army to make a detour one street distant from the Palace grounds and form in the street in the rear of the Botanical Gardens. When they heard the firing of his men from the front they were to force their way through the gates at the back and attack the Palace in the rear.

"Mendoza has the place completely barricaded," Weimer warned him, "and he has three field pieces covering each of these streets. You and your men are directly in line of one of them now. He is only waiting for you to get a little nearer before he lets loose."

From where he sat Clay could count the bars of the iron fence in front of the grounds. But the boards that backed them prevented his forming any idea of the strength or the distribution of Mendoza's forces. He drew his staff of amateur officers to one side and explained the situation to them.

"The Theatre National and the Club Union," he said, "face the Palace from the opposite corners of this street. You must get into them and barricade the windows and throw up some sort of shelter for yourselves along the edge of the roofs and drive the men behind that fence back to the Palace. Clear them away from the cannon first, and keep them away from it. I will be waiting in the street below. When you have driven them back, we will charge the gates and have it out with them in the gardens. The Third and Fourth regiments ought to take them in the rear about the same time. You will continue to pick them off from the roof."

The two supporting columns had already started on their

roundabout way to the rear of the Palace. Clay gathered up his reins, and telling his men to keep close to the walls, started forward, his soldiers following on the sidewalks and leaving the middle of the street clear. As they reached a point a hundred yards below the Palace, a part of the wooden shield behind the fence was thrown down, there was a puff of white smoke and a report, and a cannon-ball struck the roof of a house which they were passing and sent the tiles clattering about their heads. But the men in the lead had already reached the stage-door of the theatre and were opposite one of the doors to the club. They drove these in with the butts of their rifles, and raced up the stairs of each of the deserted buildings until they reached the roof. Langham was swept by a weight of men across a stage, and jumped among the music racks in the orchestra. He caught a glimpse of the early morning sun shining on the tawdry hangings of the boxes and the exaggerated perspective of the scenery. He ran through corridors between two great statues of Comedy and Tragedy, and up a marble stair case to a lobby in which he saw the white faces about him multiplied in long mirrors, and so out to an iron balcony from which he looked down, panting and breathless, upon the Palace Gardens, swarming with soldiers and white with smoke. Men poured through the windows of the club opposite, dragging sofas and chairs out to the balcony and upon the flat roof. The men near him were tearing down the yellow silk curtains in the lobby and draping them along the railing of the balcony to better conceal their movements from the enemy below. Bullets spattered the stucco about their heads, and panes of glass broke suddenly and fell in glittering particles upon their shoulders. The firing had already begun from the roofs near them. Beyond the club and the theatre and far along the street on each side of the Palace the merchants were slamming the iron shutters of their shops, and men and women were running for refuge up the high steps of the church of Santa Maria. Others were gathered in black masses on the balconies and roofs of the more distant houses, where they stood outlined against the soft blue sky in gigantic silhouette. Their shouts of encouragement and anger carried clearly in the morning air, and spurred on the gladiators below to greater effort. In the Palace Gardens a line of Mendoza's men fought from behind the first barricade, while others dragged tables and bedding and chairs across the green terraces and tumbled them down to those below, who seized them and formed them into a second line of defense.

Two of the assistant engineers were kneeling at Langham's feet with the barrels of their rifles resting on the railing of the balcony. Their eyes had been trained for years to judge distances and to measure space, and they glanced along the sights of their rifles as though they were looking through the lens of a transit, and at each report their faces grew more earnest and their lips pressed tighter together. One of them lowered his gun to light a cigarette, and Langham handed him his match-box, with a certain feeling of repugnance.

"Better get under cover, Mr. Langham," the man said, kindly. "There's no use our keeping your mines for you if you're not alive to enjoy them. Take a shot at that crew around the gun."

"I don't like this long range business," Langham answered. "I am going down to join Clay. I don't like the idea of hitting a man when he isn't looking at you."

The engineer gave an incredulous laugh.

"If he isn't looking at you, he's aiming at the man next to you. 'Live and let Live' doesn't apply at present."

As Langham reached Clay's side triumphant shouts arose from the roof-tops, and the men posted there stood up and showed themselves above the barricades and called to Clay that the cannon were deserted.

Kirkland had come prepared for the barricade, and, running across the street, fastened a dynamite cartridge to each gate post and lit the fuses. The soldiers scattered before him as he came leaping back, and in an instant later there was a racking roar, and the gates were pitched out of their sockets and thrown forward, and those in the street swept across them and surrounded the cannon.

Langham caught it by the throat as though it were human, and did not feel the hot metal burning the palms of his hands as he choked it and pointed its muzzle toward the Palace, while the others dragged at the spokes of the wheel. It was fighting at close range now, close enough to suit even Langham. He found himself in the front rank of it without knowing exactly how he got there. Every man on both sides was playing his own hand, and seemed to know exactly what to do. He felt neglected and very much alone, and was somewhat anxious lest his valor might be wasted through his not knowing how to put it to account. He saw the enemy in changing groups of scowling men, who seemed to eye him for an instant down the length of a gun-barrel and then disappear behind a puff of smoke. He kept thinking that war made men take strange liberties with their fellow-men, and it struck him as being most absurd that strangers should stand up and try to kill one another, men who had so little in common that they did not even know one another's names. The soldiers who were fighting on his own side were equally unknown to him, and he looked in vain for Clay. He saw MacWilliams for a moment through the smoke, jabbing at a jammed cartridge with his penknife, and hacking the lead away to make it slip. He was remonstrating with the gun and swearing at it exactly as though it were human, and as Langham ran toward him he threw it away and caught up another from the ground. Kneeling beside the wounded man who had dropped it and picking the cartridges from his belt, he assured him cheerfully that he was not so badly hurt as he thought.

"You all right?" Langham asked.

"I'm all right. I'm trying to get a little laddie hiding behind that blue silk sofa over there. He's taken an unnatural dislike to me, and he's nearly got me three times. I'm knocking horse-hair out of his rampart, though."

The men of Stuart's body-guard were fighting outside of the breastworks and mattresses. They were using their swords as though they were machetes, and the Irishmen were swinging their guns around their shoulders like sledge-hammers, and beating their foes over the head and breast. The guns at his own side sounded close at Langham's ear, and deafened him, and those of the enemy exploded so near to his face that he was kept continually winking and dodging, as though he were being taken by a flash-light photograph. When he fired he aimed where the mass was thickest, so that he might not see what his bullet did, but he remembered afterward that he always reloaded with the most anxious swiftness in order that he might not be killed before he had had another shot, and that the idea of being killed was of no concern to him except on that account. Then the scene before him changed, and apparently hundreds of Mendoza's soldiers poured out from the Palace and swept down upon him, cheering as they came, and he felt himself falling back naturally and as a matter of course, as he would have stepped out of the way of a locomotive, or a runaway horse, or any other unreasoning thing. His shoulders pushed against a mass of shouting, sweating men, who in turn pressed back upon others, until the mass reached the iron fence and could move no farther. He heard Clay's voice shouting to them, and saw him run forward, shooting rapidly as he ran, and he followed him, even though his reason told him it was a useless thing to do, and then there came a great shout from the rear of the Palace, and more soldiers, dressed exactly like the others, rushed through the great doors and swarmed around the two wings of the building, and he recognized them as Rojas's men and knew that the fight was over.

He saw a tall man with a negro's face spring out of the first mass of soldiers and shout to them to follow him. Clay gave a yell of welcome and ran at him, calling upon him in Spanish to surrender. The negro stopped and stood at bay, glaring at Clay and at the circle of soldiers closing in around him. He raised his revolver and pointed it steadily. It was as though the man knew he had only a moment to live, and meant to do that one thing well in the short time left him.

Clay sprang to one side and ran toward him, dodging to the right and left, but Mendoza followed his movements carefully with his revolver.

It lasted but an instant. Then the Spaniard threw his arm suddenly across his face, drove the heel of his boot into the turf, and spinning about on it fell forward.

"If he was shot where his sash crosses his heart, I know the man who did it," Langham heard a voice say at his elbow, and turning saw MacWilliams wetting his fingers at his lips and touching them gingerly to the heated barrel of his Winchester.

The death of Mendoza left his followers without a leader and without a cause. They threw their muskets on the ground and held their hands above their heads, shrieking for mercy. Clay and his officers answered them instantly by running from one group to another, knocking up the barrels of the rifles and calling hoarsely to the men on the roofs to cease firing, and as they were obeyed the noise of the last few random shots was drowned in tumultuous cheering and shouts of exultation, that, starting in the gardens, were caught up by those in the streets and passed on quickly as a line of flame along the swaying housetops.

The native officers sprang upon Clay and embraced him after their fashion, hailing him as the Liberator of Olancho, as the Preserver of the Constitution, and their brother patriot. Then one of them climbed to the top of a gilt and marble table and proclaimed him military President.

"You'll proclaim yourself an idiot, if you don't get down from there," Clay said, laughing. "I thank you for permitting me to serve with you, gentlemen. I shall have great pleasure in telling our President how well you acquitted yourself in this row—battle, I mean. And now I would suggest that you store the prisoners' weapons in the Palace and put a guard over them, and then conduct the men themselves to the military prison, where you can release General Rojas and escort him back to the city in a triumphal procession. You'd like that, wouldn't you?"

But the natives protested that that honor was for him alone. Clay declined it, pleading that he must look after his wounded.

"I can hardly believe there are any dead," he said to Kirkland. "For, if it takes two thousand bullets to kill a man in European warfare, it must require about two hundred thousand to kill a man in South America."

He told Kirkland to march his men back to the mines and to see that there were no stragglers. "If they want to celebrate, let them celebrate when they get to the mines, but not here. They have made a good record to-day and I won't have it spoiled by rioting. They shall have their reward later. Between Rojas and Mr. Langham they should all be rich men."

The cheering from the housetops since the firing ceased had changed suddenly into hand-clappings, and the cries, though still undistinguishable, were of a different sound. Clay saw that the Americans on the balconies of the club and of the theatre had thrown themselves far over the railings and were all looking in the same direction and waving their hats and cheering loudly, and he heard above the shouts of the people the regular tramp of men's feet marching in step, and the rattle of a machine gun as it bumped and shook over the rough stones. He gave a shout of pleasure, and Kirkland and the two boys ran with him up the slope, crowding each other to get a better view. The mob parted at the Palace gates, and they saw two lines of blue-jackets, spread out like the sticks of a fan, dragging the gun between them, the middies in their tight-buttoned tunics and gaiters, and behind them more blue-jackets with bare, bronzed throats, and with the swagger and roll of the sea in their legs and shoulders. An American flag floated above the white helmets of the marines. Its presence and the sense of pride which the sight of these men from home awoke in them made the fight just over seem mean and petty, and they took off their hats and cheered with the others.

A first lieutenant, who felt his importance and also a sense of disappointment at having arrived too late to see the fighting, left his men at the gate of the Palace, and advanced up the terrace; stopping to ask for information as he came. Each group to which he addressed himself pointed to Clay. The sight of his own flag had reminded Clay that the banner of Mendoza still hung from the mast beside which he was standing, and as the officer approached he was busily engaged in untwisting its halyards and pulling it down.

The lieutenant saluted him doubtfully.

"Can you tell me who is in command here?" he asked. He spoke somewhat sharply, for Clay was not a military looking personage, covered as he was with dust and perspiration, and with his sombrero on the back of his head.

"Our Consul here told us at the landing-place," continued the lieutenant in an aggrieved tone, "that a General Mendoza was in power, and that I had better report to him, and then ten minutes later I hear that he is dead and that a General Rojas is President, but that a man named Clay has made himself Dictator. My instructions are to recognize no belligerents, but to report to the Government party. Now, who is the Government party?"

Clay brought the red-barred flag down with a jerk, and ripped it free from the halyards. Kirkland and the two boys were watching him with amused smiles.

"I appreciate your difficulty," he said. "President Alvarez is dead, and General Mendoza, who tried to make himself Dictator, is also dead, and the real President, General Rojas, is still in jail. So at present I suppose that I represent the Government party, at least I am the man named Clay. It hadn't occurred to me before, but, until Rojas is free, I guess I am the Dictator of Olancho. Is Madame Alvarez on board your ship?"

"Yes, she is with us," the officer replied, in some confusion. "Excuse me—are you the three gentlemen who took her to the yacht? I am afraid I spoke rather hastily just now, but you are not in uniform, and the Government seems to change so quickly down here that a stranger finds it hard to keep up with it."

Six of the native officers had approached as the lieutenant was speaking and saluted Clay gravely. "We have followed your instructions," one of them said, "and the regiments are ready to march with the prisoners. Have you any further orders for us— can we deliver any messages to General Rojas?"

"Present my congratulations to General Rojas, and best wishes," said Clay. "And tell him for me, that it would please me greatly if he would liberate an American citizen named Burke, who is at present in the cuartel. And that I wish him to promote all of you gentlemen one grade and give each of you the Star of Olancho. Tell him that in my opinion you have deserved even higher reward and honor at his hands."

The boy-lieutenants broke out into a chorus of delighted thanks. They assured Clay that he was most gracious; that he overwhelmed them, and that it was honor enough for them that they had served under him. But Clay laughed, and drove them off with a paternal wave of the hand.

The officer from the man-of-war listened with an uncomfortable sense of having blundered in his manner toward this powder-splashed young man who set American citizens at liberty, and created captains by the half-dozen at a time.

"Are you from the States?" he asked as they moved toward the man-of-war's men.

"I am, thank God. Why not?"

"I thought you were, but you saluted like an Englishman."

"I was an officer in the English army once in the Soudan,[1] when they were short of officers." Clay shook his head and looked wistfully at the ranks of the blue-jackets drawn up on either side of them. The horses had been brought out and Langham and MacWilliams were waiting for him to mount. "I have worn several uniforms since I was a boy," said Clay. "But never that of my own country."

The people were cheering him from every part of the square. Women waved their hands from balconies and housetops, and men climbed to awnings and lampposts and shouted his name. The officers and men of the landing party took note of him and of this reception out of the corner of their eyes, and wondered.

"And what had I better do?" asked the commanding officer.

"Oh, I would police the Palace grounds, if I were you, and picket that street at the right, where there are so many wine shops, and preserve order generally until Rojas gets here. He won't be more than an hour; now. We shall be coming over to pay our respects to your captain to-morrow. Glad to have met you."

"Well, I'm glad to have met you," answered the officer, heartily. "Hold on a minute. Even if you haven't worn our uniform, you're as good, and better, than some I've seen that have, and you're a sort of a commander-in-chief, anyway, and I'm damned if I don't give you a sort of salute."

Clay laughed like a boy as he swung himself into the saddle. The officer stepped back and gave the command; the middies raised their swords and Clay passed between massed rows of his countrymen with their muskets held rigidly toward him. The housetops rocked again at the sight, and as he rode out into the brilliant sunshine, his eyes were wet and winking.

The two boys had drawn up at his side, but MacWilliams had

---

1   Present day Sudan.

turned in the saddle and was still looking toward the Palace, with his hand resting on the hindquarters of his pony.

"Look back, Clay," he said. "Take a last look at it, you'll never see it after to-day. Turn again, turn again, Dictator of Olancho."

The men laughed and drew rein as he bade them, and looked back up the narrow street. They saw the green and white flag of Olancho creeping to the top of the mast before the Palace, the blue-jackets driving back the crowd, the gashes in the walls of the houses, where Mendoza's cannon-balls had dug their way through the stucco, and the silk curtains, riddled with bullets, flapping from the balconies of the opera-house.

"You had it all your own way an hour ago," MacWilliams said, mockingly. "You could have sent Rojas into exile, and made us all Cabinet Ministers—and you gave it up for a girl. Now, you're Dictator of Olancho. What will you be to-morrow? To-morrow you will be Andrew Langham's son-in-law—Benedict, the married man. Andrew Langham's son-in-law cannot ask his wife to live in such a hole as this, so—Good-bye, Mr. Clay. We have been long together."

Clay and Langham looked curiously at the boy to see if he were in earnest, but MacWilliams would not meet their eyes.

"There were three of us," he said, "and one got shot, and one got married, and the third—? You will grow fat, Clay, and live on Fifth Avenue and wear a high silk hat, and some day when you're sitting in your club you'll read a paragraph in a newspaper with a queer Spanish date-line to it, and this will all come back to you—this heat, and the palms, and the fever, and the days when you lived on plantains and we watched our trestles grow out across the canyons, and you'll be willing to give your hand to sleep in a hammock again, and to feel the sweat running down your back, and you'll want to chuck your gun up against your chin and shoot into a line of men, and the policemen won't let you, and your wife won't let you. That's what you're giving up. There it is. Take a good look at it. You'll never see it again."

XV

The steamer *Santiago*, carrying "passengers, bullion, and coffee," was headed to pass Porto Rico by midnight, when she would be free of land until she anchored at the quarantine station of the green hills of Staten Island. She had not yet shaken off the contamination of the earth; a soft inland breeze still tantalized her with odors of tree and soil, the smell of the fresh coat of paint that had followed her coaling rose from her sides, and the odor of spilt coffee-grains that hung around the hatches had yet to be blown away by a jealous ocean breeze, or washed by a welcoming cross sea.

The captain stopped at the open entrance of the Social Hall. "If any of you ladies want to take your last look at Olancho you've got to come now," he said. "We'll lose the Valencia light in the next quarter hour."

Miss Langham and King looked up from their novels and smiled, and Miss Langham shook her head. "I've taken three final farewells of Olancho already," she said: "before we went down to dinner, and when the sun set, and when the moon rose. I have no more sentiment left to draw on. Do you want to go?" she asked.

"I'm very comfortable, thank you," King said, and returned to the consideration of his novel.

But Clay and Hope arose at the captain's suggestion with suspicious alacrity, and stepped out upon the empty deck, and into the encompassing darkness, with a little sigh of relief.

Alice Langham looked after them somewhat wistfully and bit the edges of her book. She sat for some time with her brows knitted, glancing occasionally and critically toward King and up with unseeing eyes at the swinging lamps of the saloon. He caught her looking at him once when he raised his eyes as he turned a page, and smiled back at her, and she nodded pleasantly and bent her head over her reading. She assured herself that after all King understood her and she him, and that if they never rose to certain heights, they never sank below a high level of mutual esteem, and that perhaps was the best in the end.

King had placed his yacht at the disposal of Madame Alvarez, and she had sailed to Colon, where she could change to the steamers for Lisbon, while he accompanied the Langhams and the wedding party to New York.

Clay recognized that the time had now arrived in his life when he could graduate from the position of manager-director and become the engineering expert, and that his services in Olancho were no longer needed.

With Rojas in power Mr. Langham had nothing further to fear from the Government, and with Kirkland in charge and young Langham returning after a few months' absence to resume his work, he felt himself free to enjoy his holiday.

They had taken the first steamer out, and the combined efforts of all had been necessary to prevail upon MacWilliams to accompany them; and even now the fact that he was to act as Clay's best man and, as Langham assured him cheerfully, was to wear a frock coat and see his name in all the papers, brought on such sudden panics of fear that the fast-fading coast line filled his soul with regret, and a wilful desire to jump overboard and swim back.

Clay and Hope stopped at the door of the chief engineer's cabin and said they had come to pay him a visit. The chief had but just come from the depths where the contamination of the earth was most evident in the condition of his stokers; but his chin was now cleanly shaven, and his pipe was drawing as well as his engine fires, and he had wrapped himself in an old P. & O. white duck jacket to show what he had been before he sank to the level of a coasting steamer. They admired the clerk-like neatness of the report he had just finished, and in return he promised them the fastest run on record, and showed them the portrait of his wife, and of their tiny cottage on the Isle of Wight, and his jade idols from Corea, and carved cocoanut gourds from Brazil, and a picture from the *Graphic* of Lord Salisbury, tacked to the partition and looking delightedly down between two highly colored lithographs of Miss Ellen Terry and the Princess May.[1]

Then they called upon the captain, and Clay asked him why captains always hung so much lace about their beds when they invariably slept on a red velvet sofa with their boots on, and the captain ordered his Chinese steward to mix them a queer drink and offered them the choice of a six months' accumulation of paper novels, and free admittance to his bridge at all hours. And then they passed on to the door of the smoking-room and beckoned MacWilliams to come out and join them. His manner as he did so bristled with importance, and he drew them eagerly to the rail.

"I've just been having a chat with Captain Burke," he said, in an undertone. "He's been telling Langham and me about a new game that's better than running railroads. He says there's a country called Macedonia that's got a native prince who wants to

---

1 Corea, the nineteenth-century spelling of Korea. The *Graphic*, a British journal of political illustrations founded in 1869. Robert Arthur Talbot Gascoyne-Cecil, Lord Salisbury (1830–1903), British diplomat and prime minister (1885–86, 1886–92, and 1895–1902). Ellen Terry (1848–1928), British stage actress. Princess Victoria Mary of Teck (1867–1953), popularly known as Princess May, wife of King George V and mother of Edward VIII and George VI.

be free from Turkey, and the Turks won't let him, and Burke says if we'll each put up a thousand dollars, he'll guarantee to get the prince free in six months. He's made an estimate of the cost and submitted it to the Russian Embassy at Washington, and he says they will help him secretly, and he knows a man who has just patented a new rifle, and who will supply him with a thousand of them for the sake of the advertisement. He says it's a mountainous country, and all you have to do is to stand on the passes and roll rocks down on the Turks as they come in. It sounds easy, doesn't it?"

"Then you're thinking of turning professional filibuster yourself?" said Clay.

"Well, I don't know. It sounds more interesting than engineering. Burke says I beat him on his last fight, and he'd like to have me with him in the next one—sort of young-blood-in-the-firm idea—and he calculates that we can go about setting people free and upsetting governments for some time to come. He says there is always something to fight about if you look for it. And I must say the condition of those poor Macedonians does appeal to me. Think of them all alone down there bullied by that Sultan of Turkey, and wanting to be free and independent.[1] That's not right. You, as an American citizen, ought to be the last person in the world to throw cold water on an undertaking like that. In the name of Liberty now?"

"I don't object; set them free, of course," laughed Clay. "But how long have you entertained this feeling for the enslaved Macedonians, Mac?"

"Well, I never heard of them until a quarter of an hour ago, but they oughtn't to suffer through my ignorance."

"Certainly not. Let me know when you're going to do it, and Hope and I will run over and look on. I should like to see you and Burke and the Prince of Macedonia rolling rocks down on the Turkish Empire."

Hope and Clay passed on up the deck laughing, and MacWilliams looked after them with a fond and paternal smile. The lamp in the wheelhouse threw a broad belt of light across the forward deck as they passed through it into the darkness of the

---

1 In the late nineteenth century, Macedonians attempted to free themselves from the rule of the Ottoman Turks. Self-rule, however, was not
   easily obtained, and the Macedonians were subsequently ruled by the
   Greeks and have been involved in several Balkan wars and struggles for
   independence.

bow, where the lonely lookout turned and stared at them suspiciously, and then resumed his stern watch over the great waters.

They leaned upon the rail and breathed the soft air which the rush of the steamer threw in their faces, and studied in silence the stars that lay so low upon the horizon line that they looked like the harbor lights of a great city.

"Do you see that long line of lamps off our port bow?" asked Clay.

Hope nodded.

"Those are the electric lights along the ocean drive at Long Branch and up the Rumson Road, and those two stars a little higher up are fixed to the mast-heads of the Scotland Lightship. And that mass of light that you think is the Milky Way, is the glare of the New York street lamps thrown up against the sky."

"Are we so near as that?" said Hope, smiling. "And what lies over there?" she asked, pointing to the east.

"Over there is the coast of Africa. Don't you see the lighthouse on Cape Bon? If it wasn't for Gibraltar being in the way, I could show you the harbor lights of Bizerta, and the terraces of Algiers shining like a *café chantant* in the night."[1]

"Algiers," sighed Hope, "where you were a soldier of Africa, and rode across the deserts. Will you take me there?"

"There, of course, but to Gibraltar first, where we will drive along the Alameda by moonlight.[2] I drove there once coming home from a mess dinner with the Colonel. The drive lies between broad white balustrades, and the moon shone down on us between the leaves of the Spanish bayonet. It was like an Italian garden. But he did not see it, and he would talk to me about the Watkins range finder on the lower ramparts, and he puffed on a huge cigar.[3] I tried to imagine I was there on my honeymoon, but the end of his cigar would light up and I would see his white mustache and the glow on his red jacket, so I vowed I would go over that drive again with the proper person. And we won't talk of range finders, will we?"

---

1 Cape Bon is on the Mediterranean in Tunisia, northeast of the capital, Tunis. Bizerta is a seaport of Tunisia. *Café chantant*, a precursor of cabarets, or clubs and restaurants that featured performers and singers while the patrons dine.

2 Alameda, famous botanical gardens in the city of Gibraltar, a British outpost on the Western edge of the Mediterranean Sea.

3 Watkins and Hill, a British company that manufactured a variety of scientific and mathematical instruments. A range finder was used to measure distances by means of triangulation.

"Over there is the coast of Africa."

"There to the North is Paris; your Paris, and my Paris, with London only eight hours away. If you look very closely, you can see the thousands of hansom cab lamps flashing across the asphalt, and the open theatres, and the fairy lamps in the gardens back of the houses in Mayfair, where they are giving dances in your honor, in honor of the beautiful American bride, whom every one wants to meet. And you will wear the finest tiara we can get on Bond Street, but no one will look at it; they will only look at you. And I will feel very miserable and tease you to come home."

Hope put her hand in his, and he held her finger-tips to his lips for an instant and closed his other hand upon hers.

"And after that?" asked Hope.

"After that we will go to work again, and take long journeys to Mexico and Peru or wherever they want me, and I will sit in judgment on the work other chaps have done. And when we get back to our car at night, or to the section house, for it will be very rough sometimes,"—Hope pressed his hand gently in answer—"I will tell you privately how very differently your husband would have done it, and you, knowing all about it, will say that had it been left to me, I would certainly have accomplished it in a vastly superior manner."

"Well, so you would," said Hope, calmly.

"That's what I said you'd say," laughed Clay. "Dearest," he begged, "promise me something. Promise me that you are going to be very happy."

Hope raised her eyes and looked up at him in silence, and had the man in the wheelhouse been watching the stars, as he should have been, no one but the two foolish young people on the bow of the boat would have known her answer.

The ship's bell sounded eight times, and Hope moved slightly.

"So late as that," she sighed. "Come. We must be going back."

A great wave struck the ship's side a friendly slap, and the wind caught up the spray and tossed it in their eyes, and blew a strand of her hair loose so that it fell across Clay's face, and they laughed happily together as she drew it back and he took her hand again to steady her progress across the slanting deck.

As they passed hand in hand out of the shadow into the light from the wheelhouse, the lookout in the bow counted the strokes of the bell to himself, and then turned and shouted back his measured cry to the bridge above them. His voice seemed to be a part of the murmuring sea and the welcoming winds.

"Listen," said Clay.

"Eight bells," the voice sang from the darkness. "The for'ard light's shining bright—and all's well."

Appendix A: Images of Davis

1. Davis as he looked when he first came to New York in 1890

Source: Charles Belmont Davis, *Adventures and Letters of Richard Harding Davis* (New York: Charles Scribner's Sons, 1917), between pages 46 and 47.

2. The Three Gringos

Source: Richard Harding Davis, *Three Gringos in Venezuela and Central America* (New York: Harper and Brothers, 1896), 64. For fun, the three gringos arranged to sit on the cow catcher of this train in Honduras, taking over (from two boys) the job of periodically pouring sand on the rails if the train were descending too quickly. The three pictured are Somers Somerset (left), Davis, and Lloyd C. Griscom.

3. Davis in his Spanish-American War kit

Source: *The Critic*, No. 844 (23 April 1898), 283. Upon publication of this photograph, a number of Davis' detractors jeered at his costume. Lubow records a prime example: "'If he were cut up into small pieces' jeered the Springfield *Republic*, 'he would furnish the insurgents with arms and equipments for a whole winter'; without doubt 'there will be a terrific inkshed when he reaches the front.'"[1]

---

1   Quoted in Lubow, *The Reporter Who Would Be King*, 156.

4. Davis and Theodore Roosevelt at the beginning of the Spanish-American War

Source: Fairfax Downey, *Richard Harding Davis: His Day* (New York: Charles Scribner's Sons, 1933), between pages 154 and 155. Most biographers suggest that this photograph was taken in Cuba, but Downey's caption reads: "Lieut.-Colonel Roosevelt and R.H.D. at Tampa, Fla., at the beginning of the Spanish War."

Appendix B: How Others Saw Davis

1. Booth Tarkington, "Richard Harding Davis," 1916[1]

[In this memorial essay, Tarkington (1869–1946), an American novelist and Pulitzer Prize-winning author of *The Magnificent Ambersons* (1918), captures, in rather purple munificence, Davis at the height of his popularity.]

To the college boy of the early nineties Richard Harding Davis was the "beau ideal of *jeunesse dorée*," a sophisticated heart of gold. He was of that college boy's own age, but already an editor—already publishing books! His stalwart good looks were as familiar to us as were those of our own football captain; we knew his face as we knew the face of the President of the United States, but we infinitely preferred Davis's. When the Waldorf was wondrously completed, and we cut an exam in Cuneiform Inscriptions for an excursion to see the world at lunch in its new magnificence, and Richard Harding Davis came into the Palm Room—then, oh, then, our day was radiant! That was the top of our fortune: we could never have hoped for so much. Of all the great people of every continent, this was the one we most desired to see.

The boys of those days left college to work, to raise families, to grow grizzled; but the glamour remained about Davis; *he* never grew grizzled. Youth was his great quality.

All his writing has the liveliness of springtime; it stirs with an unsuppressible gayety, and it has the attraction which companionship with him had: there is never enough. He could be sharp; he could write angrily and witheringly; but even when he was fiercest he was buoyant, and when his words were hot they were not scalding but rather of a dry, clean indignation with things which he believed could, if they would, be better. He never saw evil but as temporary.

Following him through his books, whether he wrote of home or carried his kind, stout heart far, far afield, we can see an American writing to Americans. He often told us about things abroad

---

1 Source: Richard Harding Davis, *Van Bibber and Others* (New York: Charles Scribner's Sons, 1918), ix–xi. Tarkington's essay was included in the "Crossroads Edition" of Davis' fiction, published after Davis' death.

in terms of New York; and we have all been to New York, so he made for us the pictures he wished us to see. And when he did not thus use New York for his colors he found other means as familiar to us and as suggestive; he always made us *see*. What claims our thanks in equal measure, he knew our kind of curiosity so well that he never failed to make us see what we were most anxious to see. He knew where our dark spots were, cleared up the field of vision, and left us unconfused. This discernment of our needs, and this power of enlightening and pleasuring the reader, sprang from seeds native in him. They were, as we say, gifts; for he always had them but did not make them. He was a national figure at twenty-three. He *knew how*, before he began.

Youth called to youth: all ages read him, but the young men and young women have turned to him ever since his precocious fame made him their idol. They got many things from him, but above all they live with a happier bravery because of him. Reading the man beneath the print, they found their prophet and gladly perceived that a prophet is not always cowed and bearded, but may be a gallant young gentleman. This one called merrily to them in his manly voice; and they followed him. He bade them see that pain is negligible, that fear is a joke, and that the world is poignantly interesting, joyously lovable.

They will always follow him.

2. From Theodore Roosevelt, letter to James Brander Matthews, 6 December 1892[1]

[In December 1892, Roosevelt published "A Colonial Survival," an article condemning what he saw as the habit, among those he called the American "vulgar rich," to mimic the manners and style of the British aristocracy. Davis, ever an admirer of the upper classes and a mimic-man himself, objected to the article and told Roosevelt so at a dinner party. Here, we see what Roosevelt thought about the exchange—and we also learn that Roosevelt thought Rudyard Kipling rather coarse and uncouth.]

[...] Richard Harding Davis was here yesterday and I met him at a dinner given by two of the British Legation. He was of course stirred up to much wrath by my *Cosmopolitan* article, and was so entirely unintelligent that it was a little difficult to argue with

---

1   Source: Elting E. Morison, ed., *The Letters of Theodore Roosevelt* 1 (Cambridge: Harvard UP, 1951), 298.

him, as he apparently considered it a triumphant answer to my position to inquire if I believed in the American custom of chewing tobacco and spitting all over the floor. To this I deemed it wisest to respond that I did; and in that consequence the British Minister, who otherwise liked me, felt very badly about having me at the house, especially because I sat with my legs on the table during dinner. The man has the gift of narration; but when it comes to breeding, upon my word it is hardly too much to say that even Kipling could give him points. [...]

3. From Theodore Roosevelt, letter to James Brander Matthews, 30 January 1894[1]

[After some further consideration, Roosevelt clarified his position on Davis.]

What an everlasting cad R.H. Davis is!

4. From Stephen Crane, letter to Nellie Crouse, 26 January 1896[2]

[In the process of explaining his awkwardness in social settings, Crane contrasts his discomfort with Davis' ready ease.]

[Lucius L.] Button, good a soul as he is, only dragged me forth on that call because he was exhibiting his literary friend. You know what I mean. It seems that to some men there is a mild glamor about their literary friends and they like to gently exhibit them. I was used to it and usually submitted as decently as possible. It is awfully nice to be exhibited like a stuffed parrot. They say Davis enjoys it. I should think he would. He has, I believe, the intelligence of the average saw-log and he can no doubt enjoy anything.

5. From Frank Norris, "Van Bubbles' Story," 1897[3]

[While on the staff of *Wave*, a magazine published in San Francisco, Norris (1870–1902), an American novelist, wrote a series

---

1 Ibid., 1, 358.
2 Source: R.W. Stallmen and Lillian Gilkes, eds., *Stephen Crane: Letters* (New York: New York UP, 1960), 104.
3 Source: Frank Norris, "Perverted Tales," *Wave* 16 (18 December 1897), 5–7.

of parodies of contemporary writers. In "Van Bubbles' Story," he mocks both Davis' short fiction, particularly "Van Bibber," and the journalist's penchant for adopting a pseudo-military kit, complete with medals and ribbons. At a dinner party, where "Young Charding-Davis" whacks a skye-terrier across the room with a "golf-stick," one of the guests remarks, "I say, Davis, tell us how you came by some of your decorations and orders."]

[...] "Really, they are mere trifles," [Charding-Davis] replied, easily. "I would not have worn them only my serving man insists it is good form. The Cham of Tartary gave me this," he continued, lightly touching a nickel-plated apple-pie that was pinned to his sweater, "for leaving the country in twenty-four hours, and this chest protector was presented me by the French Legation in Kamschatka for protecting a chest—but we'll let that pass," he said, enveloping himself with a smile of charming ingenuousness. "*This* is the badge of the Band of Hope to which I belong. I got this pie-plate from the Grand Mufti for conspicuous egoism in the absence of the enemy, and this Grand Army badge from a pawnbroker for four dollars. Then I have a few swimming medals for swimming across Whirlpool Rapids and a five-cent piece given me by Mr. Sage. I have several showcases full of other medals in my rooms. I'm thinking of giving an exhibition and reception, if I could get some pretty girls to receive me. I've knocked about a bit, you know, and I pick them up here and there. I've crossed Africa two or three times, and I got up the late Greek war in order to make news for the New York papers, and I'm organizing an insurrection in South America for the benefit of a bankrupt rifle manufacturer who wants to dispose of some arms." [...]

6. Theodore Roosevelt, "Davis and the Rough Riders," 1916[1]

[When Davis died, Roosevelt offered a considerably more sympathetic view than in his letters to Matthews.]

I knew Richard Harding Davis for many years, and I was among the number who were immediately drawn to him by the power

---

1   Source: Theodore Roosevelt, "Davis and the Rough Riders," in Richard Harding Davis, *Captain Macklin* (New York: Charles Scribner's Sons, 1916), vii–viii.

and originality of "Gallegher," the story which first made his reputation.

My intimate association with him, however, was while he was with my regiment in Cuba. He joined us immediately after landing, and was not merely present at but took part in the fighting. For example, at the Guasimas fight it was he, I think, with his field-glasses, who first placed the trench from which the Spaniards were firing at the right wing of the regiment, which right wing I, at that time, commanded. We were then able to make out the trench, opened fire on it, and drove out the Spaniards.

He was indomitably cheerful under hardships and difficulties and entirely indifferent to his own personal safety or comfort. He so won the esteem and regard of the regiment that he was one of the three men we made honorary members of the regiment's association. We gave him the same medal worn by our own members.

He was as good an American as ever lived and his heart flamed against cruelty and injustice. His writings form a text-book of Americanism which all our people would do well to read at the present time.

Appendix C: Reviews of Soldiers of Fortune

1. *New York Times Saturday Review of Books and Art* (5 June 1897), 10

Mr. Davis's new story, and the longest he has yet written, can be cheerfully and honestly commended. It is a good book to tell your friends about. It will be generally liked, even though few enthusiasts are likely to rave over it. It does not place Mr. Davis in the front rank of American novelists, and it shows he has not yet either caught the knack of "sustaining the interest," unflaggingly through many chapters, and welding together in a perfectly harmonious whole the various elements that go to make a good work of this kind—a novel of incident—or developed the power and sympathy to make a veritable picture of life of these proportions. But that does not matter. One who picks up "Soldiers of Fortune" will finish it, even if the story might have been more "real," (without being a bit less "improbable,") and the "love interest" stronger. But we all remember how well Mr. Davis showed he can do the sentimental in "Princess Aline."

The recent book, "Soldiers of Fortune," most reminds one of Anthony Hope's "Man of Mark."[1] Comparison of them is inevitable. But in his delightful yarn of a South American republic, Anthony Hope is both romancer and satirist. There is not a hint of satire in Davis's story. Indeed, there are few indications in it of the author's well-attested sense of humor, and these are nearly all concerned with the denotement of minor traits of character—particularly with the peculiarities of the "cub" in his relation to polite or artificial society.

Three types of the "cub" are conspicuous in "Soldiers of Fortune." They are the three soldiers, the Athos, Porthos, and Aramis[2] of this romance of invested capital and modern engineering. The best of the three is Mac Williams [sic], whose self-consciousness would doubtlessly be disagreeable in real life, but is amusing in fiction, and who is the most direct and potent of them. Young Langham, who is fresh from Yale, ranks next, and is

---

1 Hope's first novel, published in 1890.
2 The title characters of Alexandre Dumas' (1802–70) perennially popular adventure novel, *The Three Musketeers* (1844).

probably the most life-like of any one of them. He is lively and decent. Clay is very fine, to be sure, big, handsome, strong, all-controlling, and a successful lover. But, unfortunately, he is something of a prig, more of a sentimentalist, and a bit of a Bounderby.[1] And, in spite of his supposed maturity, he is as surely an undeveloped cub as either of the others; and for this reason only his faults are pardonable.

Hope Langham is a nice, smart girl, but Alice and Mme. Alvarez are not really interesting. Some of the episodic personages, however, are very good, especially Burke, the American promoter of revolutions, who is, perhaps, the most striking figure in the whole book. In this fellow, too, Mr. Davis's sense of humor again asserts itself, and he is most naturally and effectively managed in his comings and goings. There is just enough of him.

The ride across country is spirited description, and the account of the revolution is fairly good stuff. One has moods to which such incidents as the killing of Mendoza irresistibly appeal. But one is generally the worse for having such moods, and perhaps no book is better for containing such incidents. Still it is all in jest—"murder is jest."

2. *The Critic* 798 (5 June 1897), 385

So much extravagant praise has been lavished upon Mr. Davis's first novel; so much has been said about its place in contemporary literature, and all the rest of it, by amiable but not too critical reviewers, that it is a pleasant duty to state the plain facts in the case. Mr. Davis has not written a "great" novel, nor a book that will live for generations; nor has he created characters that will be all but immortal. He has simply produced a rousing tale of adventure, with several fine fellows in it, and one woman whom we are glad to know, and who has gone straight to our hearts and made there for herself a corner that we will keep warm and to which we will turn with pleasure time and again to love her for all her fine traits—most of all, perhaps, for her genius for

---

1 · Josiah Bounderby, a character in *Hard Times* (1854), a novel by British author Charles Dickens (1812–70). Bounderby, a banker and factory owner, professes to be a self-made man who has risen from poverty to become wealthy and influential. As the narrative progresses, however, we learn that he comes from a stable and caring family; through Bounderby, Dickens skewers the myth of the self-made man and critiques claims of social mobility from the lower to the upper classes.

camaraderie, which found so graceful a climax in the kiss she imprinted on the forehead of the young Englishman who had been murdered by his own treacherous troopers.

The hero is almost worthy of her—not quite. But then, it would be hard to match such a girl even at the Table Round.[1] It is only her propinquity that makes him seem less heroic than he really is. He is an American to the backbone, this young man who started the struggle for life at fourteen, and drifted from Kimberley to the Sudan, and all the world over until he became the manager of her father's iron mines in Central America [sic]. A born leader he was, and a leader he became, in the troublous days of revolution that led to happiness at last. The men that are grouped with him in the foreground are all endowed with life and individuality—Mr. Langham, the mine-owner, and his son; Reggie King, the millionaire; MacWilliams, the engineer; the young English commander of the President's bodyguard, the President himself, all stand before us not merely as foils for the hero, but as people who have their own lives to live, their own ambitions, cares and joys.

It is not necessary to commend this story. It has won its way already. But to those who have not yet read it, we can say, "Do so at once." Its interest is unflagging, and its prevalent tone is one of healthful manliness—of strong muscles and clean minds. Of Mr. Davis's workmanship nothing can be said but words of praise. Those who have visited the regions where the plot is laid, will recognize the marvellous fidelity of his crisp, short descriptions; and his whole story is constructed with a firm purpose from first to last. We cannot refrain, in closing, from quoting the following graphic description of the way in which an expert shot handles his weapon:—"Then he raised his revolver. He did not apparently hold it away from him by the butt, as other men do, but let it lie in the palm of his hand, into which it seemed to fit like the hand of a friend."

3. *The Atlantic Monthly* 80:482 (December 1897), 859–60

The cause for the success of Mr. Richard Harding Davis's Soldiers of Fortune is not far to seek. It is a story of brave action,

---

1 A reference to King Arthur and the Knights of the Round Table. Not all the knights, of course, were perfectly gallant or perfectly chaste and responsible. For more, see Sir Thomas Malory's *Works* (first published as *Le Morte Darthur* in 1485).

performed by persons at once beautiful and young. To prove that they are beautiful, we have Mr. Davis's word and our own opinion, but chiefly Mr. Gibson's most suitable illustrations. That they are young, there can be no doubt upon any ground. It were pitiful if these two qualities of youth and beauty did not touch at least forty thousand of the great public. To all this it must be added that Mr. Davis has an excellent gift of narrative, and speaks a language which is especially grateful to many ears, whether by custom or through curiosity, for it is the language of the world of which Mr. Davis's own Van Bibber is the recognized type.

How strong this appeal must be one realizes when the book's elements of weakness, through unreality and a failure to convince, are considered even for a moment. It is needful only to look at the central figure, a hero such as "never was on sea or land." He is defined as "a tall broad-shouldered youth," and surely he cannot be far beyond thirty at the utmost. At sixteen he embarked at New Orleans as a sailor before the mast. From the diamond fields of South Africa, where he landed from his first voyage, he went on to Madagascar, Egypt, and Algiers. It must have been in this period of his life that he was an officer in the English army, "when they were short of officers" in the Soudan, received a medal from the Sultan of Zanzibar, since "he was out of cigars the day I called," and won the Legion of Honor while fighting as a Chasseur d'Afrique against the Arabs. It was presumably later that he built a harbor fort at Rio, and, because it was successfully reproduced on the Baltic, was created a German baron. In a later year, possibly, he was president of an International Congress of Engineers at Madrid; but in his casual accounts of himself it is a little difficult to keep track of the years, and to know just where he had time for his visits to Chili and Peru, and incidentally for his experiences as a cowboy on our own plains, and as the builder of the Jalisco and Mexican Railroad. When a youth has done all these things, there is no reason why he should not take the further steps, in which we follow him, as the head of an enormous mining enterprise in South America, the temporary, and of course successful, commander in a revolution at Olancho, and the perfectly "turned out" man of the world, who soon discovers the superiority of his employer's younger daughter, and wins her hand without having to ask for it.

It should be said in justice to this Admirable Crichton that he defines some of his own actions as "gallery plays."[1] In like manner, when the cloud of the revolution is about to burst, the heroine appears on the scene, protesting, "I always ride over to polo alone at Newport, at least with James"; her brother says, "It reminds me of a football match, when the teams run on the field"; and the hero himself likens it to a scene in a play. When a revolution begins on this wise, with such participants, one is well prepared to see it go forward somewhat like a performance of amateur theatricals, in which the players enjoy themselves exceedingly, but make very timid and incipient approaches to reality. Indeed, for all of Mr. Davis's brave and familiar habit of speech, as if from the very core of things, the real scene of the revolution seems to be the author's study-table, and the merit of the book grows sensibly less as the fight proceeds.

The inherent elements of its structure, already mentioned, go far to redeem the book. But not only by their means has Mr. Davis shown his strength. In the sisters, Alice and Hope Langham, he has made two excellent types of the girl spoiled and unspoiled by the world. In MacWilliams, with his "barber-shop chords" and his good vulgarity, he has drawn a picture admirably true to life. In the vivid reproduction of scenes, in none more notably than that of the killing of Stuart and the leaving of his dead body in the empty room, he has sometimes shown the hand almost of a master in description.

It is no disheartening sign of the times that such a book is read, for youth and beauty and prowess march across its pages, and behind them one feels that creator's honest sympathy with these things.

4. *The Nation* 66: 1699 (20 January 1898), 54

It is almost a relief to have Mr. Richard Harding Davis's hero misplace his "wills" and "shalls," because in every other respect he is such an incomparable conqueror that the ordinary human

---

1   James Crichton (1560–82), a Scots adventurer, scholar, and poet, known as "The Admirable," a sobriquet bestowed on him in *Heroes Scotici* ("Scottish Heroes," 1603) by Scots poet John Johnston. He served in the French army during the wars of Henry III against the Huguenots, traveled in Italy, and died in a street fight in Mantua. His good looks, wit, and exploits are celebrated in Sir Thomas Urquhart's (1611–60) compendium, *Ekskubalauron* (1651).

eye falls, dazzled, before his radiance. However, with practice a cat may look at a king, and we poor mortals, when used to the light, find this sovereign gentleman a pleasant one to gaze upon. If there are in real life few such paragons, more's the pity. There is a deal of entertaining engineering and geography in this book, culminating in a brisk account of a South American revolution, in which all the characters in the story figure, having arrived from Fifth Avenue just in time, in their yachts and by train, like the second act of a society drama. The hero's attitudes toward the two heroines are visibly affected by the atmosphere of revolution, and his hypersensitiveness as to whether he is loved as a man or as engineer is harder to follow than even his military exploits from the Nile to Peru via Zanzibar. Some men are satisfied if their Dulcineas smile upon them without subjecting the smiles to an X-ray.[1] But Robert Clay was different, and, wishing to be beloved as an engineer, he told a charming woman that it was as little satisfaction to him to have her like him personally as to a woman to be congratulated on her beauty. No wonder that it was "some short time" before the beauty replied. There is, notwithstanding, no morbid strain in the book. Horses, hoydens, and boys impart wholesome cheer, and South America contributes a bright landscape. For clean stories of adventure and love, with no dull word, readers must ever be thankful.

---

1 Dulcinea, a character referred to (yet who does not actually appear) in Miguel de Cervantes' *Don Quixote de la Mancha* (1605, 1615). Quixote, a would-be knight errant, imagines the rather plain Dulcinea as the most beautiful woman in the world, and dedicates his adventures to her. In this context, the reviewer mocks Davis and his characterizations, suggesting they are as overdone and silly as the don's imaginings of his ideal woman.

Appendix D: Social Darwinism, Survival of the Richest, and Other Notions of Anglo-American Superiority[1]

1. From Herbert Spencer, *Social Statics* (New York: D. Appleton and Company, 1897), 238–40

[Spencer (1820–1903), a British sociologist, began working with notions of natural selection *before* Darwin published *The Origin of Species* in 1859. Spencer applied these ideas to the social world, coining the phrase "survival of the fittest" in 1850 (Darwin later took up the phrase and acknowledged his debt to Spencer). Spencer argued that human affairs develop in a similar pattern to organisms, moving from the homogeneous to the heterogeneous; in other words, they evolve from the lower and simpler to the higher and more complex. His writings were more popular in the US than in England, and found many admirers among capitalists and imperialists.]

[...] The forces at work exterminate such sections of mankind as stand in the way, with the same sternness that they exterminate beasts of prey and herds of useless ruminants. Just as the savage has taken the place of the lower creatures, so must he, if he have remained too long a savage, give place to his superior. And observe, it is necessarily to his superior that, in the majority of cases, he does give place. For what are the pre-requisites to a conquering race? Numerical strength, or more powerful nature, or an improved system of warfare; all of them indications of advancement. Numerical strength implies certain civilizing antecedents. Deficiency of game may have necessitated agricultural pursuits, and so made the existence of a larger population possible; or distance from other tribes may have rendered war less frequent, and so have prevented its perpetual decimations; or accidental superiority over neighbouring tribes, may have led to the final subjugation and enslaving of these: in any of which cases the comparatively peaceful condition resulting must have allowed progress to

---

1 I have borrowed the phrase, "Survival of the Richest," from Edward Caudill's *Darwinian Myths: The Legends and Misuses of a Theory* (Knoxville: U of Tennessee P, 1997), 83.

commence. Evidently, therefore, the conquest of one people over another has been, in the main, the conquest of the social man over the anti-social man; or, strictly speaking, of the more adapted over the less adapted.

In another mode, too, the continuance of the unsympathetic character has indirectly aided civilization while it has directly hindered it; namely, by giving rise to slavery. It has been truly observed that only by such stringent coercion as is exercised over men held in bondage, could the needful power of continuous application have been developed. Devoid of this, as from his habits of life the aboriginal man necessarily was (and as, indeed, existing specimens show), probably the severest discipline continued for many generations, was required to make him submit contentedly to the necessities of his new state. And if so, the barbarous selfishness which maintained that discipline, must be considered as having worked a collateral benefit, though in itself so radically bad.

Let not the reader be alarmed. Let him not fear that these admissions will excuse new invasions and new oppressions. Nor let any one who fancies himself called upon to take Nature's part in this matter, by providing discipline for idle negroes or others, suppose that these dealings of the past will serve for precedents. Rightly understood, they will do no such thing. That phase of civilization during which forcible supplantings of the weak by the strong, and systems of savage coercion, are on the whole advantageous, is a phase which spontaneously and necessarily gives birth to these things. It is not in pursuance of any calmly-reasoned conclusions respecting Nature's intentions that men conquer and enslave their fellows—it is not that they smother their kindly feelings to subserve civilization; but it is that, as yet constituted, they care little what suffering they inflict in the pursuit of gratification, and even think the achievement and exercise of mastery honourable. As soon, however, as there arises a perception that these subjugations and tyrannies are not right— as soon as the sentiment to which they are repugnant becomes sufficiently powerful to suppress them, it is time for them to cease. The question altogether depends upon the amount of moral feeling possessed by men, or, in other words, on the degree of adaptation to the social state they have undergone. Unconsciousness that there is anything wrong in exterminating inferior races, or in reducing them to bondage, presupposes an almost rudimentary state of men's sympathies and their sense of human rights. The oppressions they then inflict and submit to, are not, therefore, detrimental to their characters—do not retard in them the growth of the social sentiments; for these have not yet reached a development great enough to be offended by such doings. And hence the aids given to civilization by clearing the Earth of its least advanced inhabitants, and by forcibly compelling the rest to acquire industrial habits, are given without moral adaptation receiving any corresponding check [...].

2. From Charles Darwin, *The Descent of Man and Selection in Relation to Sex* (1874)[1]

[Although not a "social Darwinist," Darwin read Spencer's works and comes close, in this passage, to describing a model of the survival of the fittest among different races and cultures.]

Extinction follows chiefly from the competition of tribe with tribe, and race with race. Various checks are always in action, serving to keep down the numbers of each savage tribe,—such as periodic famines, nomadic habits and the consequent deaths of infants, prolonged suckling, wars, accidents, sickness, licentiousness, the stealing of women, infanticide, and especially lessened fertility. If any one of these checks increases in power, even slightly, the tribe thus affected tends to decrease; and when of two adjoining tribes one becomes less numerous and less powerful than the other, the contest is soon settled by war, slaughter, cannibalism, slavery, and absorption. Even when a weaker tribe is not thus abruptly swept away, if it once begins to decrease, it generally goes on decreasing until it becomes extinct.

When civilised nations come into contact with barbarians the struggle is short, except where a deadly climate gives its aid to the native race. Of the causes which lead to the victory of civilised nations, some are plain and simple, others complex and obscure. We can see that the cultivation of the land will be fatal in many ways to savages, for they cannot, or will not, change their habits. New diseases and vices have in some cases proved highly destructive; and it appears that a new disease causes much death, until those who are most susceptible to its destructive influence are gradually weeded out; and so it may be with the evil affects from

---

1 Source: Charles Darwin, *The Descent of Man and Selection in Relation to Sex*, 2nd ed., Revised and Augmented (New York: D. Appleton and Company, 1904), 186. My thanks to John Glendening for drawing this passage in Darwin to my attention.

spirituous liquors, as well as with the unconquerably strong taste for them shewn by so many savages.

3. From Rebecca Harding Davis, "Life in the Iron-Mills" (1861)[1]

[As outlined in the Introduction, Davis' mother offers a critique of industrial capitalism in her recovered novella. When Kirby, the mill-owner's son, and his two friends, Dr. May and Mitchell, come across Hugh and his powerful korl statue, they begin to debate whether they, as members of the upperclass, have any responsibility for the plight of the workers or whether they have any obligation to help out someone like Hugh, who has considerable artistic talent. Kirby, the voice of social Darwinism, denies that big business has any obligations to the workers other than paying them, asserting that American democracy is "a ladder which any man can scale."]

They looked a moment [at the statue]; then May turned to the mill-owner:—

"Have you many such hands as this? What are you going to do with them? Keep them at puddling iron?

Kirby shrugged his shoulders. Mitchell's look irritated him.

"*Ce n'est pas mon affaire.* I have no fancy for nursing infant geniuses. I suppose there are some stray gleams of mind and soul among these wretches. The Lord will take care of his own; or else they can work out their own salvation. I have heard you call our American system a ladder which any man can scale. Do you doubt it? Or perhaps you want to banish all social ladders, and put us all on a flat table-land,—eh, May?"

The Doctor looked vexed, puzzled. Some terrible problem lay hid in [the statue's] face, and troubled these men. Kirby waited for an answer, and, receiving none, went on, warming with his subject.

"I tell you, there's something wrong that no talk of '*Liberté*' or '*Egalité*' will do away. If I had the making of men, these men who do the lowest part of the world's work should be machines,— nothing more,—hands. It would be kindness. God help them! What are taste, reason, to creatures who must live such lives as that?" He pointed to Deborah [Hugh's cousin, who has brought

---

1   Source: Rebecca Harding Davis, *Life in the Iron-Mills, Atlantic Monthly*, Vol. VII (April, 1861), 438-39.

him food], sleeping on the ash-heap. "So many nerves to sting them to pain. What if God had put your brain, with all its agony of touch, into your fingers, and bid you work and strike with that?"

"You think you could govern the world better?" laughed the Doctor.

"I do not think at all."

"That is true philosophy. Drift with the stream, because you cannot dive deep enough to find bottom, eh?"

"Exactly," rejoined Kirby. "I do not think. I wash my hands of all social problems,—slavery, caste, white or black. My duty to my operatives has a narrow limit,—the pay-hour on Saturday night. Outside of that, if they cut korl, or cut each other's throats, (the more popular amusement of the two,) I am not responsible."

4. From Andrew Carnegie, *The Gospel of Wealth* (1900)[1]

[Carnegie (1835-1919), a steel magnate, philanthropist, and avid reader and admirer of Spencer, applies notions of the survival of the fittest to economics, and argues in favor of the generation of great individual wealth on the part of those who are most able to succeed. Over time, he believes, everyone will benefit from the creation of wealth.]

The problem of our age is the proper administration of wealth, that the ties of brotherhood may still bind together the rich and poor in harmonious relationship. The conditions of human life have not only been changed, but revolutionized, within the past few hundred years. In former days there was little difference between the dwelling, dress, food, and environment of the chief and those of his retainers. The Indians are to-day where civilized man then was. When visiting the Sioux, I was led to the wigwam of the chief. It was like the others in external appearance, and even within the difference was trifling between it and those of the poorest of the braves. The contrast between the palace of the millionaire and the cottage of the laborer with us to-day measures the change which has come with civilization. This change, however, is not to be deplored, but welcomed as highly beneficial. It is well, nay, essential, for the progress of the race that the

---

1   Source: Andrew Carnegie, *The Gospel of Wealth and Other Timely Essays* (New York: The Century Co., 1900), 1-5.

houses of some should be homes for all that is highest and best in literature and the arts, and for all the refinements of civilization, rather than that none should be so. Much better this great irregularity than universal squalor. Without wealth there can be no Mæcenas.[1] The "good old times" were not good old times. Neither master nor servant was as well situated then as to-day. A relapse to old conditions would be disastrous to both—not the least so to him who serves—and would sweep away civilization with it. But whether the change be for good or ill, it is upon us, beyond our power to alter, and, therefore, to be accepted and made the best of. It is a waste of time to criticize the inevitable.

It is easy to see how the change has come. One illustration will serve for almost every phase of the cause. In the manufacture of products we have the whole story. It applies to all combinations of human industry, as stimulated and enlarged by the inventions of this scientific age. Formerly, articles were manufactured at the domestic hearth, or in small shops which formed part of the household. The master and his apprentices worked side by side, the latter living with the master, and therefore subject to the same conditions. When these apprentices rose to be masters, there was little or no change in the mode of life, and they, in turn, educated succeeding apprentices in the same routine. There was, substantially, social equality, and even political equality, for those engaged in industrial pursuits had then little or no voice in the State.

The inevitable result of such a mode of manufacture was crude articles at high prices. To-day the world obtains commodities of excellent quality at prices which even the preceding generation would have deemed incredible. In the commercial world similar causes have produced similar results, and the race is benefitted thereby. What were luxuries have become the necessaries of life. The laborer now has more comforts than the farmer had a few generations ago. The farmer has more luxuries than the landlord had, and is more richly clad and better housed. The landlord has books and pictures rarer and appointments more artistic than the king could then obtain.

The price we pay for this salutary change is, no doubt, great. We assemble thousands of operatives in the factory, and in the mine, of whom the employer can know little or nothing, and to

---

1 Mæcenas (c. 74-4 BCE), Roman statesman and noted patron of
   the arts. He helped support a number of important poets of his era,
   including Horace and Virgil.

whom he is little better than a myth. All intercourse between them is at an end. Rigid castes are formed, and, as usual, mutual ignorance breeds mutual distrust. Each caste is without sympathy with the other, and ready to credit anything disparaging in regard to it. Under the law of competition, the employer of thousands is forced into the strictest economies, among which the rates paid to labor figure prominently, and often there is friction between the employer and the employed, between capital and labor, between rich and poor. Human society loses homogeneity.

The price which society pays for the law of competition, like the price it pays for cheap comforts and luxuries, is also great; but the advantages of this law are also greater still than its cost—for it is to this law that we owe our wonderful material development, which brings improved conditions in its train. But, whether the law be benign or not, we must say of it, as we say of the change in the conditions of men to which we have referred: It is here; we cannot evade it; no substitutes for it have been found; and while the law may be sometimes hard for the individual, it is best for the race, because it insures the survival of the fittest in every department. We accept and welcome, therefore, as conditions to which we must accommodate ourselves, great inequality of environment; the concentration of business, industrial and commercial, in the hands of a few; and the law of competition between these, as being not only beneficial, but essential to the future progress of the race. Having accepted these, it follows that there must be great scope for the exercise of special ability in the merchant and in the manufacturer who has to conduct affairs upon a great scale. That this talent for organization and management is rare among men is proved by the fact that it invariably secures enormous rewards for its possessor, no matter where or under what laws or conditions. The experienced in affairs always rate the MAN whose services can be obtained as a partner as not only the first consideration, but such as render the question of his capital scarcely worth consideration: for able men soon create capital; in the hands of those without the special talent required, capital soon takes wings. Such men become interested in firms or corporations using millions; and, estimating only simple interest to be made upon the capital invested, it is inevitable that their income must exceed their expenditure and that they must, therefore, accumulate wealth [...].

5. From Theodore Roosevelt, "The Expansion of the White Races," An Address Given at the Methodist Episcopal Church, Washington, D.C., 18 January 1909[1]

[Although not always sympathetic toward the social Darwinists, Roosevelt admired Darwin, believed in the social evolution of the races, and argued for the superiority of "the white races."[2] One need not, of course, be a follower of Spencer to believe in hierarchies or to hold others in low regard; Roosevelt often displays plenty of old-fashioned racism.]

[...] On the whole, and speaking generally, one extraordinary fact of this expansion of the European races is that with it has gone an increase in population and well-being among the natives of the countries where the expansion has taken place. As a result of this expansion there now live outside of Europe over a hundred million of people wholly of European blood and many millions more partly of European blood; and as another result there are now on the whole more people of native blood in the regions where these hundred million intruders dwell than there were when the intruders went thither. In America the Indians of the West Indies were well-nigh exterminated, wantonly and cruelly. The merely savage tribes, both in North and South America, who were very few in number, have much decreased or have vanished, and grave wrongs have often been committed against them as well as by them. But all of the Indians who had attained to an even low grade of industrial and social efficiency have remained in the land, and have for the most part simply been assimilated with the intruders, the assimilation marking on the whole a very considerable rise in their conditions. Taking into account the Indians of pure blood, and the mixed bloods in which the Indian element is large, it is undoubtedly true that the Indian population of America is larger to-day than it was when Columbus discovered the continent, and stands on a far higher plane of happiness and efficiency. In Australia the few savages tend to die out simply because their grade of culture is so low that nothing can be

---

1   Source: *The Works of Theodore Roosevelt* National Edition 16 (New York: Charles Scriber's Sons, 1925), 259–61.

2   For more on Roosevelt's views on race and Darwinism, see, for example, Edmund Morris, *Theodore Rex* (New York: Modern Library, 2001), 52–54.

done with them; doubtless occasional brutalities have been committed by white settlers but these brutalities were not an appreciable factor in the dying out of the natives. In India and Java there has been a great increase in well-being and population under the English and the Dutch, and the advance made has been in striking contrast to what has occurred during the same period in the near-by lands which have remained under native rule. In Egypt, in the Philippines, in Algiers, the native people have thriven under the rule of the foreigner, advancing as under no circumstances could they possibly have advanced if left to themselves, the increase in population going hand in hand with the increase in general well-being. In the Soudan, Mahdism during the ten years of its unchecked control was responsible for the death of half the population and meant physical and moral ruin, a fact which should be taken into account by the perverted pseudophilanthropy which fails to recognize the enormous advantages conferred by the English occupation of the Soudan, if not on the English themselves, certainly on the natives and on the humanity at large.[1] In the same way the Russian advance into Turkestan has meant the real advance in the well-being of the people, as well as the spread of civilization.[2] In Natal the English found an empty desert; because of the peace they established it has filled up so densely with natives as to create very serious and totally new problems.[3] There have been very dark spots in the European conquest and control of Africa; but on the whole the African regions which during the past century have seen the greatest cruelty, degradation, and suffering, the greatest diminution of population, are those where native control has been unchecked. The advance has been made in the regions· that have been under European control or influence; that have been profoundly influenced by European administrators, and by European and American missionaries. Of course the best that can happen to any people that has not already a high civilization of its own is to assimilate and profit by American or European ideas, the ideas of civilization

---

1   Mahdism, messianic movements in nineteenth-century Islam; an effort to restore Islam, at least in the eyes of the Mahdic leaders, to a pure state (a state reminiscent, in other words, of Islam during the era of the Prophet Muhammad).
2   Turkestan, a region in Central Asia.
3   Natal, a region of South Africa; now known as KwaZulu-Natal Province.

and Christianity, without submitting to alien control; but such control, in spite of all its defects, is in a very large number of cases the prerequisite condition to the moral and material advance of the peoples who dwell in the darker corners of the earth.

Appendix E: Davis and Others on American Masculinity

1. From Richard Harding Davis, *Captain Macklin* (1902)[1]

[In *Macklin*, Davis criticizes the part the US plays in the political instability of Latin American countries; but although he offers a less flattering portrait of American capital, he does not doubt for a minute what it means to be a "real man,"—a man of action, a man unfettered by women, children, or a home. Here, Macklin shares his epiphany about the ideal life.]

[…] I was no longer to be deceived; the one and only thing I understood and craved, was the free, homeless, untrammelled [sic] life of the soldier of fortune. I wanted to see the shells splash up the earth again, I wanted to throw my leg across a saddle, I wanted to sleep on a blanket by a camp-fire, I wanted the kiss and caress of danger, the joy which comes when the sword wins honor and victory together, and I wanted the clear, clean view of right and wrong, that is given only to those who hourly walk with death. […]

2. From Richard Harding Davis, "William Walker, The King of the Filibusters" (1906)[2]

[Davis had great admiration for men of action, particularly soldiers and mercenaries. In William Walker, the American soldier of fortune who conquered Nicaragua in 1856, Davis found a model of martial-masculine fearlessness and imperial desire: real men, he believed, should invade foreign countries, driven by dreams of regenerating their civilizations and economies. In this biographical sketch, he explores Walker's life and wonders what the freebooter might have accomplished if he had not been executed on a beach in Honduras in 1860.]

---

1   Source: Richard Harding Davis, *Captain Macklin* (New York: Charles Scriber's Sons, 1916), 325–26.
2   Source: Richard Harding Davis, "William Walker, The King of Filibusters," *Real Soldiers of Fortune* (New York: Charles Scribner's Sons, 1906), 147, 187–88.

[...] It is safe to say that to members of the younger generation the name of William Walker conveys absolutely nothing. To them, as a name, "William Walker" awakens no pride of race or country. It certainly does not suggest poetry and adventure. To obtain a place in even this group of Soldiers of Fortune, William Walker, the most distinguished of all American Soldiers of Fortune, the one who but for his countrymen would have single-handed attained the most far-reaching results, had to wait his turn behind adventurers of other lands and boy officers of his own. And had this man with the plain name, the name that to-day means nothing, accomplished what he adventured, he would on this continent have solved the problem of slavery, have established an empire in Mexico and in Central America, and, incidentally, have brought us into war with all of Europe. That is all he would have accomplished [...].

★★★★★

Had Walker lived four years longer to exhibit upon the great board of the Civil War his ability as a general, he would, I believe, to-day be ranked as one of America's greatest fighting men.

And because the people of his own day destroyed him is no reason that we should withhold from this American, the greatest of all filibusters, the recognition of his genius. [...]

3. From Theodore Roosevelt, "The Strenuous Life," A Speech Given before the Hamilton Club, Chicago, 10 April 1899[1]

[This is perhaps the most important essay in the canon of the American empire. Roosevelt passionately defines "the strenuous life" and explains how one must think and act to be a real man, a man's man, a man able to do what he sees as the great work of the world.]

[...] In speaking to you, men of the greatest city of the West, men of the State which gave to the country Lincoln and Grant,[2] men

---

1   Source: Theodore Roosevelt, "The Strenuous Life," *The Works of Theodore Roosevelt*, National Edition 13 (New York: Charles Scribner's Sons, 1925), 319–23.

2   Abraham Lincoln (1805–69), sixteenth President of the United States. Ulysses S. Grant (1822–85), eighteenth President of the United States.

who preëminently and distinctly embody all that is most American in the American character, I wish to preach, not the doctrine of ignoble ease, but the doctrine of the strenuous life, the life of toil and effort, of labor and strife; to preach that highest form of success which comes, not to the man who desires mere easy peace, but to the man who does not shrink from danger, from hardship, or from bitter toil, and who out of these wins the splendid ultimate triumph.

A life of slothful ease, a life of that peace which springs merely from lack either of desire or of power to strive after great things, is as little worthy of a nation as of an individual. I ask only that what every self-respecting American demands from himself and from his sons shall be demanded of the American nation as a whole. Who among you would teach your boys that ease, that peace, is to be the first consideration in their eyes—to be the ultimate goal after which they strive? You men of Chicago have made this city great, you men of Illinois have done your share, and more than your share, in making America great, because you neither preach nor practise such a doctrine. You work yourselves, and you bring up your sons to work. If you are rich and are worth your salt, you will teach your sons that though they may have leisure, it is not to be spent in idleness; for wisely used leisure merely means that those who possess it, being free from the necessity of working for their livelihood, are all the more bound to carry on some kind of non-remunerative work in science, in letters, in art, in exploration, in historical research—work of the type we most need in this country, the successful carrying out of which reflects most honor upon the nation. We do not admire the timid man of peace. We admire the man who embodies victorious effort; the man who never wrongs his neighbor, who is prompt to help a friend, but who has those virile qualities necessary to win in the stern strife of actual life. It is hard to fail, but it is worse never to have tried to succeed. In this life we get nothing save by effort. Freedom from effort in the present merely means that there has been stored up effort in the past. A man can be freed from the necessity of work only by the fact that he or his fathers before him have worked to good purpose. If the freedom thus purchased is used aright, and the man still does actual work, though of a different kind, whether as a writer or a general, whether in the field of politics or in the field of exploration and adventure, he shows he deserves his good fortune [...].

In the last analysis a healthy state can exist only when the men and women who make it up lead clean, vigorous, healthy lives;

when the children are so trained that they shall endeavor, not to shirk difficulties, but to overcome them; not to seek ease, but to know how to wrest triumph from toil and risk. The man must be glad to do a man's work, to dare and endure and to labor; to keep himself, and to keep those dependent upon him. The woman must be housewife, the helpmeet of the homemaker, the wise and fearless mother of many healthy children [...].

We of this generation do not have to face a task such as that our fathers faced [i.e., the Civil War], but we have our tasks, and woe to us if we fail to perform them! We cannot, if we would, play the part of China, and be content to rot by inches in ignoble ease within our borders, taking no interest in what goes on beyond them, sunk in a scrambling commercialism; heedless of the higher life, the life of aspiration, of toil and risk, busying ourselves only with the wants of our bodies for the day, until suddenly we should find, beyond a shadow of question, what China had already found, that in this world the nation that has trained itself to a career of unwarlike and isolated ease is bound, in the end, to go down before other nations which have not lost the manly and adventurous qualities. If we are to be a really great people, we must strive in good faith to play a great part in the world. We cannot avoid meeting great issues. All that we can determine for ourselves is whether we shall meet them well or ill. In 1898 we could not help being brought face to face with the problem of war with Spain. All we could decide was whether we should shrink like cowards from the contest, or enter into it as beseemed a brave and high-spirited people; and, once in, whether failure or success should crown our banners. So it is now. We cannot avoid the responsibilities that confront us in Hawaii, Cuba, Porto Rico, and the Philippines.[1] All we can decide is whether we shall meet them in a way that will redound to the national credit, or whether we shall make of our dealings with these new problems a dark and shameful page in our history. To refuse to deal with them at all merely amounts to dealing with them badly. We have a given problem to solve. If we undertake the solution, there is, of course, always danger that we may not solve it aright; but to refuse to undertake the solution simply renders it certain that we cannot possibly solve it aright. The timid man, the lazy man, the man who distrusts his country, the over-civilized man, who has lost the great fighting, masterful virtues, the ignorant man, and the man of dull mind, whose soul

---

1 Porto Rico, a past spelling of Puerto Rico.

is incapable of feeling the mighty life that thrills "stern men with empires in their brains"—all these, of course, shrink from seeing the nation undertake its new duties; shrink from seeing us build a navy and an army adequate to our needs; shrink from seeing us do our share of the world's work, by bringing order out of chaos in the great, fair tropic islands from which the valor of our soldiers and sailors has driven the Spanish flag. These are men who fear the strenuous life, who fear the only national life which is really worth leading. They believe in that cloistered life which saps the hardy virtues in a nation, as it saps them in the individual; or else they are wedded to that base spirit of gain and greed which recognizes in commercialism the be-all and end-all of national life, instead of realizing that, though an indispensable element, it is, after all, but one of many elements that go to make up true national greatness. No country can long endure if its foundations are not laid deep in the material prosperity which comes from thrift, from business energy and enterprise, from hard, unsparing effort in the fields of industrial activity; but neither was any nation ever yet truly great if it relied upon material prosperity alone. All honor must be paid to the architects of our material prosperity, to the great captains of industry who have built our factories and our railroads, to the strong men who toil for wealth with brain or hand; for great is the debt of the nation to these and their kind. But our debt is yet greater to the men whose highest type is to be found in a statesman like Lincoln, a soldier like Grant. They showed by their lives that they recognized the law of work, the law of strife; they toiled to win a competence for themselves and those dependent upon them; but they recognized that there were yet other and even loftier duties—duties to the nation and duties to the race. [...]

4. From William James, "Letter on Governor Roosevelt's Oration," *Boston Evening Transcript*, 15 April 1899

[In this critique of Roosevelt and his views on masculinity, war, and imperialism, James (1842–1910), a noted philosopher, psychologist, and fierce anti-imperialist—and brother to novelist Henry James—attacks his former student (at Harvard University) for what he saw as the politician's irresponsible and dangerous calls to action.]

[...] Although in middle life, as the years age, and in a situation of responsibility concrete enough, [Roosevelt] is still mentally in the Sturm and Drang[1] period of early adolescence, treats human affairs, when he makes speeches about them, from the sole point of view of the organic excitement and difficulty they may bring, gushes over war as the ideal condition of human society, for the manly strenuousness which it involves, and treats peace as a condition of blubberlike and swollen ignobility, fit only for huckstering weaklings, dwelling in gray twilight and heedless of the higher life. Not a word of the cause—one foe is as good as another, for aught he tells us; not a word of the conditions of success. [...]

---

1   Sturm und Drang, German for Storm and Stress; the phrase, taken from the title of a play, *Wirrwarr; oder, Sturm and Drang* (1776), by F.M. von Klinger, became the sobriquet for a German literary movement (c. 1770-85) that emphasized both youthful genius in rebellion against the strictures of society and a passion for nature and the natural world. Johann Wolfgang von Goethe's *The Sorrows of Young Werther* (1774) remains perhaps the most celebrated novel of the movement. Here, James clearly uses the phrase in a pejorative sense.

Appendix F: Davis and Others on American Imperialism

1. From John L. O'Sullivan, "Annexation," *United States Magazine and Democratic Review* 17 (July 1845), 5

[The infamous article in which O'Sullivan (1813–95), the editor of *United States Magazine and Democratic Review* and a vociferous expansionist, coins the phrase "manifest destiny" and argues in favor of the annexation of Texas.]

[...] Texas is now ours. Already, before these words are written, her Convention has undoubtedly ratified the acceptance, by her Congress, of our proffered invitation into the Union; and made the requisite changes in her already republican form of constitution to adapt it to its future federal relations. Her star and her stripe may already be said to have taken their place in the glorious blazon of our common nationality; and the sweep of our eagle's wings already includes within its circuit the wide extend of her fair and fertile land. She is not to us a mere geographical space—a certain combination of coast, plain, mountain, valley, forest and stream. She is no longer to us a mere country on the map. She comes within the dear and sacred designation of Our Country; no longer a "*pays*," she is a part of "*la patrie*;" and that which is at once a sentiment and a virtue, Patriotism, already begins to thrill for her too within the national heart.[1] It is time then that all should cease to treat her as alien, and even adverse—cease to denounce and vilify all and everything connected with her accession—cease to thwart and oppose the remaining steps for its consummation; or where such efforts are felt to be unavailing, at least to embitter the hour of reception by all the most ungracious frowns of aversion and words of unwelcome. There has been enough of all this. It has had its fitting day during the period when, in common with every other possible question of practical policy that can arise, it unfortunately became one of the leading topics of party division, of presidential electioneering. But that period has passed, and with it let its prejudices and its passions, its discords and it denunciations, pass away too. The next session of Congress will see the representatives of the new

---

1   *Pays*, French for country; la patrie, French for homeland.

young State in their places in both our halls of national legislation, side by side with those of the old Thirteen. Let their reception into "the family" be frank, kindly, and cheerful, as befits such an occasion, as comports not less with our own self-respect than patriotic duty towards them. Ill betide those foul birds that delight to defile their own nest, and disgust the ear with perpetual discord of ill-omened croak.

Why, were other reasoning wanting, in favor of now elevating this question of the reception of Texas into the Union, out of the lower region of our past part dissensions, up to its proper level of a high and broad nationality, it surely is to be found, found abundantly, in the manner in which other nations have undertaken to intrude themselves into it, between us and the proper parties to the case, in a spirit of hostile interference against us, for the avowed object of thwarting our policy and hampering our power, limiting our greatness and checking the fulfillment of our manifest destiny to overspread the continent allotted by Providence for the free development of our yearly multiplying millions. This we have seen done by England, our old rival and enemy; and by France, strangely coupled with her against us, under the influence of the Anglicism strongly tinging the policy of her present prime minister, [François Pierre Guillaume] Guizot. [...][1]

2. From José Martí, "Cuba and the United States" (1889)[2]

[Martí (1853–95), a Cuban writer and patriot, strongly opposed American annexation of Cuba, an idea circulating in the US in the late 1880s. A group of Republicans had posed the question "Do We Want Cuba?" in an article published on 16 March 1889 in the Philadelphia *Manufacturer*. Providing his own answer, Martí argues that the Cubans, weary of Spanish exploitation, are not looking for another country to assert control over the island. Cuba, he insists, should be for Cubans.]

This is not the occasion to discuss the question of the annexation of Cuba. It is probable that no self-respecting Cuban would like

---

1 François Pierre Guillaume Guizot (1787-1874), French historian and statesman.
2 Source: José Martí, *Our America: Writings on Latin America and the Struggle for Cuban Independence*, ed. Philip S. Foner, trans. Elinor Randall et al. (New York: Monthly Review Press, 1977), 234–35.

to see his country annexed to a nation where the leaders of opinion share towards him the prejudices excusable only to vulgar jingoism or rampant ignorance. No honest Cuban will stoop to be received as a moral pest for the sake of the usefulness of his land in a community where his ability is denied, his morality insulted, and his character despised. There are some Cubans who, from honorable motives, from an ardent admiration for progress and liberty, from a prescience of their own powers under better political conditions, from an unhappy ignorance of the history and tendency of annexation, would like to see the island annexed to the United States. But those who have fought in war and learned in exile, who have built, by the work of hands and mind, a virtuous home in the heart of an unfriendly community; who by their successful efforts as scientists and merchants, as railroad builders and engineers, as teachers, artists, lawyers, journalists, orators, and poets, as men of alert intelligence and uncommon activity, are honored where their powers have been called into action and the people are just enough to understand them; those who have raised, with their less prepared elements, a town of workingmen where the United States had previously a few huts in a barren cliff; those, more numerous than the others, do not desire the annexation of Cuba to the United States. They do not need it. They admire this nation, the greatest ever built by liberty, but they dislike the evil conditions that, like worms in the heart, have begun in this mighty republic their work of destruction. They have made of the heroes of this country their own heroes, and look to the success of the American commonwealth as the crowning glory of mankind; but they cannot honestly believe that excessive individualism, reverence for wealth, and the protracted exultation of a terrible victory are preparing the United States to be the typical nation of liberty, where no opinion is to be based in greed, and no triumph or acquisition reached against charity and justice. We love the country of Lincoln as much as we fear the country of [Francis] Cutting.[1]

We are not the people of destitute vagrants or immoral pigmies that the *Manufacturer* is pleased to picture; nor the country of petty talkers, incapable of action, hostile to hard work, that, in a mass with the other countries of Spanish America, we are by arrogant travelers and writers represented to be [...]

---

1 Francis Cutting (1828–92), one of the founders of the American Annexation League, an organization formed to promote US overseas expansion.

3. From Richard Harding Davis, *Three Gringos in Venezuela and Central America* (1896)[1]

[...] In the capital of Costa Rica there is a statue of the Republic in the form of a young woman standing with her foot on the neck of General [William] Walker, the American filibuster. We had planned to go to the capital for the express purpose of tearing that statue down some night, or blowing it up; so it is perhaps just as well for us that we could not get there; but it would have been a very good thing for Costa Rica if Walker, or any other man of force, had put his foot on the neck of every republic in Central America and turned it to some account.

Away from the coasts, where there is fever, Central America is a wonderful country, rich and beautiful, and burdened with plenty, but its people make it a nuisance and an affront to other nations, and its parcel of independent little states, with the pomp of power and none of its dignity, are and will continue to be a constant danger to the peace which should exist between two great powers.

There is no more interesting question of the present day than that of what is to be done with the world's land which is lying unimproved; whether it shall go to the great power that is willing to turn it to account, or remain with its original owner, who fails to understand its value. The Central-Americans are like a gang of semi-barbarians in a beautifully furnished house, of which they can understand neither its possibilities of comfort nor its use. They are the dogs in the manger among nations. Nature has given to their country great pasture-lands, wonderful forests of rare woods and fruits, treasures of silver and gold and iron, and soil rich enough to supply the world with coffee, and it only waits for an honest effort to make it the natural highway of traffic from every portion of the globe. The lakes of Nicaragua are ready to furnish a passageway which should save two months of sailing around the Horn, and only forty-eight miles of swamp-land at Panama separate the two greatest bodies of water on the earth's surface. Nature has done so much that there is little left for man to do, but it will have to be some other man than a native-born Central-American who is to do it. [...]

---

1 Source: From Richard Harding Davis, *Three Gringos in Venezuela and Central America* (New York: Harper and Brothers, 1896), 146–48.

4. From Mark Twain, "To the Person Sitting in Darkness" (1901)[1]

[In contrast to Davis and Roosevelt, Twain was a staunch member of the Anti-Imperialist League, and he vehemently opposed American domination of the Philippines. In this Swiftian assault on President McKinley, Twain argues that the problem with the war in the Philippines rests not in seeking an empire—he means, of course, that that is exactly the problem— but that the US has been too obvious in its pursuit of extra-continental territory. Men like McKinley and Roosevelt, he mocks, have done too little to dress up their desires for power in the fancy wrappings of "Civilization" and "Uplift."]

[...] Extending the Blessings of Civilization to our Brother who Sits in Darkness has been a good trade and has paid well, on the whole; and there is money in it yet, if carefully worked—but not enough, in my judgement, to make any considerable risk advisable. The People that Sit in Darkness are getting to be too scarce—too scare and too shy. And such darkness as is now left is really of but an indifferent quality, and not dark enough for the game. The most of those People that Sit in Darkness have been furnished with more light than was good for them or profitable for us. We have been injudicious.

The Blessings-of-Civilization Trust, wisely and cautiously administered, is a Daisy. There is more money in it, more territory, more sovereignty, and other kinds of emolument, that there is in any other game that is played. But Christendom has been playing it badly of late years, and must certainly suffer by it, in my opinion. She has been so eager to get every stake that appeared on the green cloth, that the People who Sit in Darkness have noticed it—they have noticed it, and have begun to show alarm. They have become suspicious of the Blessings of Civilization. More—they have begun to examine them. This is not well. The Blessings of Civilization are all right, and a good commercial property; there could not be a better, in a dim light. In the right kind of light, and at a proper distance, with the goods a little out of focus, they furnish this desirable exhibit to the Gentlemen who Sit in Darkness:

---

1 From Mark Twain, "To the Person Sitting in Darkness," *North American Review* 531 (February 1901), 165–66.

LOVE,	LAW AND ORDER,
JUSTICE,	LIBERTY,
GENTLENESS,	EQUALITY,
CHRISTIANITY,	HONORABLE DEALING,
PROTECTION TO THE WEAK,	MERCY,
TEMPERANCE,	EDUCATION,

—and so on.

There. Is it good? Sir, it is pie. It will bring into camp any idiot that sits in darkness anywhere. But not if we adulterate it. It is proper to be emphatic upon that point. This brand is strictly for Export—apparently. *Apparently.* Privately and confidentially, it is nothing of the kind. Privately and confidentially, it is merely an outside cover, gay and pretty and attractive, displaying the special patterns of our Civilization which we reserve for Home Consumption, while *inside* the bale is the Actual Thing that the Customer Sitting in Darkness buys with his blood and tears and land and liberty. [...]

5. From Theodore Roosevelt, "The Administration of the Island Possessions." An Address Given at the Coliseum, Hartford, Connecticut, 22 August 1902[1]

[Some readers may find echoes of the debate surrounding the wars in Vietnam and Iraq in Roosevelt's defense of his policies in the Philippines following the Spanish-American War.]

[...] It is rare indeed that a great work, a work supremely worth doing, can be done save at the cost not only of labor and toil, but of much puzzling worry during the time of the performance. Normally, the nation that achieves greatness, like the individual who achieves greatness, can do so only at the cost of anxiety and bewilderment and heart-wearing effort. Timid people, people of scant faith and hope, and good people who are not accustomed to the roughness of the life of effort—are almost sure to be disheartened and dismayed by the work and the worry, and overmuch cast down by the shortcomings, actual or seeming, which in real life always accompany the first stages even of what eventually turn out to be the most brilliant victories.

---

1 Source: *The Works of Theodore Roosevelt*, National Edition 16 (New York: Charles Scribner's Sons, 1925), 274–75.

All this is true of what has happened during the last four years in the Philippine Islands. The Spanish War itself was an easy task, but it left us certain other tasks which were much more difficult. One of those tasks was that of dealing with the Philippines. The easy thing to do—the thing which appealed not only to lazy and selfish men, but to very many good men whose thought did not drive down to the root of things—was to leave the islands. Had we done this, a period of wild chaos would have supervened, and then some stronger power would have stepped in and seized the islands and have taken up the task which we in such a case would have flinched from performing. A less easy, but infinitely more absurd course, would have been to leave the islands ourselves, and at the same time to assert that we would not permit any one else to interfere with them. This particular course would have combined all the possible disadvantages of every other course which was advocated. It would have placed us in a humiliating position, because when the actual test came it would have been quite out of the question for us, after some striking deed of savagery had occurred in the islands, to stand by and prevent the re-entry of civilization into them, while the mere fact of our having threatened thus to guarantee the local tyrants and wrong-doers against outside interference by ourselves or others, would have put a premium upon every species of tyranny and anarchy within the islands.

Finally, there was the course which we adopted—not any easy course, and one fraught with danger and difficulty, as is generally the case in this world when some great feat is to be accomplished as an incident to working out national destiny. We made up our minds to stay in the islands—to put down violence—to establish peace and order—and then to introduce a just and wise civil rule accompanied by a measure of self-government which should increase as rapidly as the islanders showed themselves fit for it. It was certainly a formidable task; but think of the marvellously [sic] successful way in which it has been accomplished! The first and vitally important feat was the establishment of the supremacy of the American flag; and this had to be done by the effort of those gallant fellow Americans of ours to whom so great a debt is due—the officers and enlisted men of the United States regular and volunteer forces. In a succession of campaigns, carried on in unknown tropic jungles against an elusive and treacherous foe vastly outnumbering them, under the most adverse conditions of climate, weather, and country, our troops completely broke the power of the insurgents, smashed their armies, and harried the broken robber bands into submission. In its last stages, the war against our rule sank down into mere brigandage; and what our troops had to do was to hunt down the parties of ladrones. It was not an easy task which it was humanly possible to accomplish in a month or a year; and therefore after the first year had elapsed, some excellent people said that it couldn't be done; but it was done. [...]

Select Bibliography

Primary Texts

Davis, Richard Harding. *Captain Macklin*. Charles Scribner's
   Sons, 1902.
——. *Cuba in War Time*. New York: Charles Scribner's Sons,
   1897.
——. *The Cuban and Porto Rican Campaigns*. New York: Charles
   Scribner's Sons, 1898.
——. *Gallegher and Other Stories*. New York: Charles Scribner's
   Sons, 1891.
——. *Three Gringos in Venezuela and Central America*. New York:
   Harper and Brothers, 1896.
——. *Van Bibber and Others*. *The Novels and Stories of Richard
   Harding Davis*. New York: Charles Scribner's Sons, 1916.
——. "William Walker, The King of the Filibusters." *Real Sol-
   diers of Fortune*. New York: Charles Scribner's Sons, 1906.
——. *A Year from a Reporter's Notebook*. New York: Harper and
   Brothers, 1898.

Biography and Letters

Davis, Charles Belmont, ed. *Adventure and Letters of Richard
   Harding Davis*. New York: Charles Scribner's Sons, 1917.
Downey, Fairfax. *Richard Harding Davis: His Day*. New York:
   Charles Scribner's Sons, 1933.
Langford, Gerald. *The Richard Harding Davis Years*. New York:
   Holt, Rinehart and Winston, 1961.
Lubow, Arthur. *The Reporter Who Would be King*. New York:
   Charles Scribner's Sons, 1992.

Checklists and Bibliographies

Barrett Library, The. *Richard Harding Davis: A Checklist of
   Printed and Manuscript Works*. Fannie Mae Elliot, Lucy Clark,
   and Marjorie D. Carver, comps. Charlottesville: U of Vir-
   ginia P, 1963.
Eichelberger, Clayton L. and Ann M. McDonald. "Richard
   Harding Davis (1864-1916): A Checklist of Secondary

Comment." *American Literary Realism* 4 (Fall 1971): 313-89.

Quinby, Henry Cole. *Richard Harding Davis: A Bibliography.* New York: E.P. Dutton, 1924.

Journal Articles, Critical Studies, Histories of Davis' Era

Brown, Charles H. *The Correspondents' War: Journalists in the Spanish-American War.* New York: Charles Scribner's Sons, 1967.

Burgess, Douglas K. "Norris's 'Van Bubbles' Story': Bursting the Bubble of the Davis Mystique." *Frank Norris Studies* 15 (Spring 1993): 10-3.

Dudley, John. "'The Manly Art of Self-Defense': Spectator Sports, American Imperialism, and the Spanish American War." *Convergencias Hispanicas: Selected Proceedings and Other Essays on Spanish and Latin American Literature, Film, and Linguistics.* Eds., Elizabeth Scarlett and Howard B. Wescott. Newark, DE: Cuesta, 2001: 119-29.

Harrison, Brady. *Agent of Empire: William Walker and the Imperial Self in American Literature.* Athens: U of Georgia P, 2004.

Hoganson, Kristin L. *Fighting for American Manhood: How Gender Politics Provoked the Spanish-American and Philippine-American Wars.* New Haven: Yale UP, 1998.

Kaplan, Amy. "Romancing the Empire: The Embodiment of American Masculinity in the Popular Historical Novel of the 1890s." *American Literary History* 2, No. 4 (Winter 1990): 659-90.

Kramer, David. "Infirm Soldiers in the Cuban War of Theodore Roosevelt and Richard Harding Davis." *War, Literature and the Arts* 14, Nos. 1-2 (2002): 28-44.

Murphy, Gretchen. "Democracy, Development and the Monroe Doctrine in Richard Harding Davis's *Soldiers of Fortune.*" *American Studies* 42, No. 2 (Summer 2001): 45-66.

Seelye, John. *War Games: Richard Harding Davis and the New Imperialism.* Amherst and Boston: U of Massachusetts P, 2003.

Solensten, John M. "The Gibson Boy: A Reassessment." *American Literary Realism* 4 (1971): 303-12.

Urraca, Beatriz. "A Textbook of Americanism: Richard Harding Davis's *Soldiers of Fortune.*" *Tropicalizations: Transcultural Rep-*

resentations of Latinidad. Eds., Francis R. Aparicio and Susana Chavez-Silverman. Hanover, NH: UP of New England, 1997: 21-50.

Wesley, Marilyn C. "'The Hero of the Hour': Ideology and Violence in the Works of Richard Harding Davis." *American Literary Realism.* 32, No. 2 (Winter 2000): 109-24.